♥Fab
Confessions
of Georgia
Nicolson
Vol. 4

Further Confessions of Georgia Nicolson:

Angus, Thongs and Full-Frontal Snogging

'It's OK, I'm Wearing Really Big Knickers!'

'Knocked Out by my Nunga-Nungas'

'Dancing in my Nuddy-Pants'

'...and that's when it fell off in my hand.'

'...then he ate my boy entrancers.'

'...startled by his furry shorts!'

'Luuurve is a many trousered thing...'

'Stop in the name of pants!'

'Are these my basoomas I see before me?'

Also available on CD:

'...and that's when it fell off in my hand.'

'...then he ate my boy entrancers.'

'...startled by his furry shorts!'

'Luuurve is a many trousered thing...'

'Stop in the name of pants!'

'Are these my basoomas I see before me?'

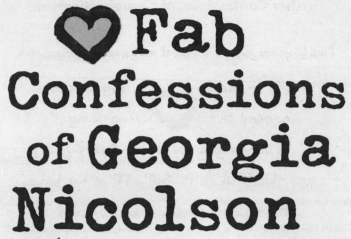

Fab Confessions of Georgia Nicolson

Vol. 4

'...startled by his furry shorts!'

and

'Luuurve is a many trousered thing...'

Louise Rennison ♥

HarperCollins *Children's Books*

Find out more about Georgia at www.georgianicolson.com

'... *startled by his furry shorts!*' was first published in Great Britain in hardback
by HarperCollins *Children's Books* in 2006
'...*startled by his furry shorts!*' was first published in paperback in 2007
'*Luuurve is a many trousered thing...*' was first published in Great Britain in hardback
by HarperCollins *Children's Books* in 2007
'*Luuurve is a many trousered thing...*' was first published in paperback in 2008
Published in this two-in-one edition by HarperCollins *Children's Books* in 2011
HarperCollins *Children's Books* is a division of HarperCollins*Publishers* Ltd,
77–85 Fulham Palace Road, Hammersmith, London, W6 8JB

1

ISBN 978-0-00-741203-7

Louise Rennison asserts the moral right to be identified as the author of the work.

Printed and bound in England by Clays Ltd, St Ives plc

Mixed Sources
Product group from well-managed
forests and other controlled sources
www.fsc.org Cert no. SW-COC-001806
© 1996 Forest Stewardship Council

FSC is a non-profit international organisation established to promote the
responsible management of the world's forests. Products carrying the FSC
label are independently certified to assure consumers that they come
from forests that are managed to meet the social, economic and
ecological needs of present and future generations.

Find out more about HarperCollins and the environment at
www.harpercollins.co.uk/green

'...startled by his furry shorts!'

A Note from Georgia

Dear worldwide Chums and Chumettes,

(Hang on a minute, when I say "worldwide" I don't mean "enormously fat", I merely mean internationalwise.) Where was I before you got the wrong end of the stick? Oh yes, do you know how much I love you all? A LOT. That is how much. I do, it is *le* fact. Why else would I spend so much time rifling through my creative drawers (oo-er) writing another diary?

Actually, as I say to anyone who will listen (i.e., no one), I am practically a saint in human form. But there's very little thanks in it. For instance, the other day I helped a little old lady across the road. I didn't have to. In fact, I was in a tearing dash on my way to get new lip gloss. But I did, and do you know what she did? She hit me with her umbrella! She said she didn't want to cross the road, she was waiting for her friend to pick her up to go pole dancing!!!

That is the kind of world we live in.

The elderly insane, like Elvis Attwood, parents, etc., say that young people only care about lipstick and snogging. I say hahahaha. If they would take the trouble to read works of geniosity like mine, they would soon realise that we do many useful and creative things. Who invented the terms "piddly-diddly department" and "poo-parlour division" that are used in schools all over the world? Before I bothered to invent "nunga-nungas", what fools we felt calling our breasty substances, er... breasts.

Do you see?

I think you do.

Goodbye and God bless you all.

And also S'laters.

Georgia

p.s. And I invented nervy b. and f.t. and so on.

p.p.s. And the Viking disco inferno dance.

p.p.p.s. I could go on but I feel slightly tired with creativitosity and I may... zzzzzzzzzzzzzzzzzzzzzzz.

In memory and love of Dezza the Vicar.

Big luuurve to my family and friends, old and new. (Look, I'm not saying some of you are old, I'm just saying that some of you are newer than others… er… but not in a less old way. Oh, look, I just love you, right?)

Enormous panty-splitting thanks to my editors and publicists and designers and sales people at HarperCollins in Billy Shakespeare land and Hamburger-a-gogo land.

Thanks as always to the Empress.

But mostly thank you to my lovely, lovely readers (which now even include some vatis, which is a bit alarming).

Living in Fiasco land

Saturday June 18th
9:00 p.m.

I can't believe I am once more on the rack of romance.

And also in the oven of luuurve.

And possibly on my way to the bakery of pain.

And maybe even going to stop along the way to get a little cake at the cake shop of agony.

Shut up, brain. Shut up.

Looking out of my bedroom window at the stars
9:01 p.m.

It says in my *Meditation for the Very Backward* book that it is soothing looking at the universe and stars and everything.

Ommmm.

9:03 p.m.

The meditation book is wrong. God, stars are annoying. Winking and blinking like twinkly idiots. Why are they so cheerful?

9:03 p.m. and a half

I'll tell you why they are so cheerful: because they are not me. They know nothing of the call of the Horn and snogging. Has a Luuurve God ever said to one of them, "I will let you know in a week's time if I want to go out with you or not"? No.

Anyway, what are stars for actually? You can't even read by them. They just hang about. Like dim torches.

9:04 p.m.

Hanging about is not exactly a job, is it?

9:05 p.m.

I am not as such feeling any calmer.

9:10 p.m.

Being in the bakery of pain is vair vair boring. Ten past nine on a Saturday night and I am in my bedroom. Alone. I am in the prime of my – er – hornosity and *joie de vivre* and nothing is going on. Nothing.

It's like a grave in this house. I...

Oh good, my darling little sister has kicked open my door and flung my cat Angus at me.

"HEGGGGOOO, Gingey!!! We is back. Heggo!!! Watch my panties dance. Sex bum, sex bum, am a sex bum!!!"

Oh dear *Gott* in *Himmel*. Angus was livid at being thrown, and once he'd stopped doing that cat sneezing and shaking thing he dug his claws into my ankle. Owwwwwww. Now I'm on the way to the cake shop of aggers with a gammy leg. Hurray!

Libby put her frock over her head and waggled her botty around like a pole dancer. Where does she see people doing these things?

They've just come back from the lunatic asylum, i.e., Grandad's sheltered housing, so it will be something she has seen there. I've seen the residents in their so-called communal lounge. They pretend to play dominoes, but secretly they practise being mad. And probably prance around in their incontinence knickers.

Then Mum came mumming in and scooped up Bibbs. "Time for Boboland, young lady."

Libby carried on singing and wiggling around in Mum's arms, and then Mum noticed me. Being in my bedroom.

"What are you up to, Georgia? Why are you in here?"

I said, "Not that anyone notices, but this is actually my room. You know, for me to be in. I was in bed, as it happens."

Mum said as she went out, "Oh, you must be sooo tired, all that lip gloss and mascara to carry round all day."

Vair vair amusing. Not.

9:25 p.m.
I've been in my bedroom for more or less twenty-four hours, give or take snack and loo breaks. Oh, and a quick visit to the shops for essentials. Mascara and a new nunga-nunga holder. And a copy of *Cosmo*. It is more than twenty-four hours since Masimo left me at my door saying he would let me know if he wanted me to be his girlfriend or not. Why did I admit I wanted him to be like my proper boyfriend? Why why?

9:26 p.m.

And also thrice why? Why why why? Why couldn't I have just been a callous sophisticate? I could for once have just shut up and been all full of casualosity and *savoir* whatsit.

9:30 p.m.

If I'd played my cards right I could have had loads of boyfriends. All at the same time. Masimo the Italian Stallion for a weekendy boyfriend, with a touch of Dave the Laugh (oo-er) for a rainy weekday. And also maybe even the former Sex God (whose name I'm not going to mention even beyond the grave) as a sort of Kiwi-a-gogo airmail boyfriend. But, oh no, I had to moan on about wanting to be Masimo's one and only.

9:40 p.m.

I was so happy snogging Masimo under the stars on our date. Stars didn't get on my nerves then. Nothing did.

9:42 p.m.

How come I am living in Fiasco land again? One minute he was snogging me under the twinkly twits, and then the next he is off to Late and Live with Wet Lindsay, stick insect and drip.

I am haunted by old Droopy Drawers. First she enticed you know who, whose name I will never mention even beyond the grave, but as a clue his name starts with "R" and ends in "obbie". Now she has slimed her way around Masimo. I hate her, I hate her.

But that is life in a nutshell, isn't it? Well, mine anyway – all fabby and marvy and then all pooey and *merde*.

9:45 p.m.
What was it Charlie Dickens said in his famous book *Oliver Twit*? Ah, yes, "Forsooth and lack a day all ye worlde is-eth a stage and verily we-eth are players in-eth it. Gadzooks." Or was that Billy Shakespeare?

Who knows? Who cares? What does it mean, anyway? And why do none of those beardy Elizabethan types know how to speak proper English?

What does anything mean?

Midnight
Oh, I can't bear this. How many hours will it be until

Masimo tells me his answer? Perhaps I should phone him and tell him that I didn't mean what I said about him being my one and only one. I could say that he can go out with Wet Lindsay as well, as long as he likes me too.

12:10 a.m.
But then I might snog him after she has snogged him, and that would mean I have practically snogged her. No one could live with that.

12:20 a.m.
I would rather snog Angus.

12:26 a.m.
I bet Angus is a much better snogger than her.
    Much better.

12:30 a.m.
He has certainly got nicer legs.

12:31 a.m.
Well, more of them, anyway.

12:36 a.m.

Everyone has gone to bed. And the kittykats are out. I can hear them yowling and spitting in the garden somewhere. Cross-eyed Gordy is practically a teenager in cat years now. I'll bet he is doing keepie-uppie like Oscar, the so-called son of Mr and Mrs Across the Road, otherwise known as Perv Boy. No, what I mean is, he will be pretending to do keepie-uppie but really keeping his eyes out for female-type kittykats.

12:39 a.m.

Actually, Gordy would be much better at keepie-uppie and girl spotting than Oscar because he could quite literally do them at the same time – keep one eye on the ball and use the other one for spotting girly kittykats. His spaggy eye would be a blessing in disguise.

12:41 a.m.

Oooh, I can't sleep. I must read a book of wisdomosity.

12:42 a.m.

It says in my (well, officially Mum's) book *How to Make Any*

Twit Fall in Love with You that if you pretend to feel how you feel, then you will feel like you feel.

Pardon?

12:45 a.m.

For instance, it says, "If you go to a party and you feel shy, enter the room with a wide smile. Put your shoulders back, hold your head high, let your arms hang loosely by your side. Then, even if you don't feel confident, no one will ever know!"

Okey dokey, I'll try that in the mirror.

Wide smile, arms loosey loose and swing. Big smile, shoulders back, head high, swing swing. Loosey loose arms and swing swing.

12:52 a.m.

Yep, I definitely look confident. There is one tiny drawback, though: hanging my arms loosely and swinging them makes me look like an orang-utan. An orang-utan called Ralf, probably. And who wants a confident orang-utan as a girlfriend? That is what I ask myself.

12:54 a.m.

Ralf the confident orang-utan wearing Teletubbies pyjamas. Which I only wore for comfortnosity. I had no idea I was going to have to go out to a party in them looking confident.

Shut up, brain.

Sunday June 19th
My bedroom
10:00 a.m.

Same rack of love.

Same oven of pain.

Same bakery of... shutup shutup.

I would usually consult with Dave the Laugh about the Luuurve God scenario. He is after all the official Hornmeister and Pants King. It still makes me laugh like a drain when I think of him singing, "The hills are alive with the sound of pants!" I would ask him to give me the benefit of his wisdomosity about boys and so on, but he's gone a bit weird with all that "What if we should have really been together?" fandango, so I feel a bit funny about seeing him again.

11:00 a.m.

Mutti popped her head round my door. "We're going to Waterworld. Do you want to come?"

I said, "Are you mad?"

I said it in a polite and inquiring way, but she still went ballisticisimus. "You are so bloody rude."

I very nearly said that swearing shows a lack of vocabulary, but I didn't because I am so vair vair tired.

11:30 a.m.

The Swiss Family Mad have "roared" off in the clown car – otherwise known as Dad's ludicrous three-wheeled Robin Reliant – leaving me alone at Château Sheer Desperadoes.

11:35 a.m.

I'm going mad. I am going to have to phone The Big Knickered One, and hope she doesn't ramble on about bat droppings.

Phoned Jas.

Jas was so much in Jas 'n' Tom land that she didn't even notice I was in the bakery of pain. She just went on rambling for Europe. "Oooh, it's so groovy that Tom's back!

I only saw him briefly yesterday. He is going to bring around his flora collection from Kiwi-a-gogo land in a bit and that will be soo... oh..."

I said, "Indescribably dull?"

She said, "I have to go now."

"Jazzy Wazzy, can I come and see you? I need your help."

"No."

Jas's bedroom
Lunchtime

I am lying amongst Jas's sad collection of stuffed toys, mostly owls, while she ponces around in front of a mirror. What is she doing?

I said, "Jas it's very distracting trying to tell you stuff, important stuff full of tragicosity about me your very bestest pally, when you keep pouting like a goldfish. What are you doing?"

"I'm practising puckering."

"What?"

"Puckering. I had, well, a bit of a problem vis-à-vis snogging with Tom last night."

Despite my world coming apart at the seams, I am always

interested in snogging tales. "Tell me."

"Well, I was quite nervy at first when I was waiting for him."

"Were you doing your annoying flicky-fringe thing?"

"I don't know; anyway, when he came in, I was sort of jelloid. But then it was all right because he got his whatsits out."

"Pardon?"

"His, you know, snapshots from Kiwi-a-gogo land, so we looked at them for a bit. Until I felt calmed down. Actually there was a really cool one of Robbie..."

Oh brilliant. On top of everything else I was now talking about someone I had vowed I would never talk about this side of the grave.

I said, "Was Robbie playing the guitar and dancing with marsupials?"

Jas wasn't even listening. "Anyway, as we were looking at them Tom got closer to me and put his arm around me. Then we, well... we, you know, started snogging and so on."

"And so on? Where is 'and so on' on the snogging scale? What number did you get to?"

"Er... five and a bit of six. It was really groovy. I felt like I was all melting in to him and then... well... then I had sort of a lip spasm."

"A LIP SPASM?"

Ten minutes later

Apparently she had been snogging away when she had suddenly had the lip spaz.

She said, "I got cramp in my lips and they sort of seized up."

"What does that look like?"

And she showed me. Blimey. You know when you put food in a baby's mouth and it doesn't like it, and its eyes go all goggly and then its whole face goes into a spasm and the food comes shooting out of its mouth? Well, even if you don't know, believe me, I do. Libby could make rice pudding reach the other side of the room.

While Jas was showing me her spazzy face, I said, "If you don't mind me saying, Jas, that is not very attractive."

She said, "I expect it was snogging withdrawal. I hadn't puckered up for ages, so... you know, being out of practice... but it won't happen again."

"Good."

22

"Because I have an exercise regime now. Shall I show you?

"No."

"OK. It goes pucker, relax, pucker, relax, pucker, relax. Do you see?"

I didn't say anything, just lay there staring at her with big starey eyes like the rest of the owls as she pouted her lips and then relaxed them. She looked like a mixture of Mick Jagger and an idiot. Not necessarily in that order.

She was in full ramble mode now. "And then for the *pièce de résistance* it's darty tongue, darty tongue."

God, it was horrible sitting there while her little tongue went in and out like a mad vole. Fortunately I was able to shove a Midget Gem in her gob so that I could tell her the sad tale of my Italian Stallion.

Ten minutes later

She said (chewy chew), "So you said that he had to be your one and only boyfriend scenario or else that was it? *Arrivederci*, Masimo?"

I said, "Yes, but..."

"Well, what in the name of Slim's outsize pyjamas were

♡ 23

you thinking of? Are you mad?"

"No, I'm not mad, Jas. I just happen to have a friend who looks a lot like you who said, 'Just be yourself.'"

"What?"

"You said being yourself and genuine was like having a generous nose. Like I have got. The exact words used were: 'Just because you have a generous nose, don't go to the nose-disguiser shop; let your own nose run free and wild.'"

"What complete fool said that?"

"YOU did, Jas."

"Did I? Well, yeah, but I didn't mean it, did I? Clearly. That was in the sanctity of our own brains, wasn't it? I mean, we were going to the PRETEND nose-disguiser shop. I didn't actually mean you should BE yourself. That is just stupid."

I really really could kill her. In fact, if I attacked her stupid fringe suddenly, she might choke on her stupid Midget Gem, and that would be good.

Sadly, Jas had got interested now. She said, "So let me get this right – he's choosing between you and Wet Lindsay? Blimey, does she know that? Because if she does, you are dead as a doughnut. Deader."

Cheers.

The doorbell rang downstairs, and a minute later Tom bounded into the room. He said, "Hey, Georgia... gidday, as our Kiwi pals say! Bonzer to see you!" And he gave me a big, proper boy hug. It felt really nice. Especially as I may never feel another boy's jumper next to my head in this lifetime, the way things are going.

He sat down on the bed and looked at both of us and said, "OK, what have you two been talking about? Lipstick?"

We both looked offended. Tom went on, "Erm... world peace, the Manchester United attacking four? Snogging?"

I said with dignitosity at all times, "I've got a lot more on my mind than boys, Tom. There are other things in the world, you know."

He said, "So it's all over with you and the Italian Stallion then?"

"No, well, er maybe... oh, I don't know." And I blurted out the whole story because it was so nice to have a boy type to talk to. And, for a boy, Tom is very nearly not quite completely insane.

At the end he lay back on Jas's stuffed owl family and said, "Wow."

I looked at him.

He looked at me. "Wowzee wow and wow."

Jas said, "I know, that's what I thought."

What are they, the idiot telepathic twins?

I said to Tom, "What do you think?"

He said, "Well, you know he's just come out of a big relationship and, well, he's a fit-looking guy, isn't he? Not that I'm on the turn or anything. But he is. He could pretty much have any chick he wanted."

Jas was nodding away like Tom was Dr Ruth, psychiatrist to the Hollywood set, or something. And she shuffled up really close to him. It's pathetic.

Tom went on talking, "Georgia, you don't think he's, you know, well, a bit worried that you might be a bit... well, unusual?"

I said, "Unusual? Like how?"

Tom said, "Well, when he first asked you if you wanted a drink, you went off disco dancing to Rolf Harris's 'Two Little Boys'."

Oh goddygodgod, am I never to be free from my own bonkerosity?

I said, "What else is a person supposed to do when their

boy entrancers get stuck together?"

Jas was still doing her nodding along wisely fiasco. She said to Tom, "Yes, yes, I see what you mean. He may be afraid to go out with her, and really who can blame him?"

I was just about to lunge for her throat when her mum knocked on the door and said, "May I come in for a moment, Jas? Dad and I are off to the allotment and then we may pop into the club for a quick game of cards, so I've left snacks in the kitchen. I know how you young people eat! Bye."

Her mutti and vati were going to their allotment. Jas's mum was wearing welligogs and a proper mum-sized pair of trousers and a cardi. Her vati probably doesn't even know what leather trousers are. My vati has a clown car and my mum came in last night with her T-shirt on inside out. How am I supposed to know how to behave? Why would any Luuurve God want to have anything to do with me? Oh nooo, please don't let me blub.

Tom looked at me and then he put his arm around me. "Listen, Georgia, if he doesn't get you then its his loss. You're fab; we all know that."

Jas even had a go at being nice. "Yes, you are, er... fab,

♡

and you are so, you know... you. I mean, you wouldn't be you if you weren't you, would you?"

What was she rambling on about?

Tom was fishing about in his rucky. "I've got something to show you, Gee."

Oh blimey, now he was going to get his newts out or something, at a time like this. He handed me a pile of photos. Oh good, they were of his trip to Kiwi-a-gogo land. How interesting. Not.

I flicked through them. Trees, trees, sheep, trees, Kiwi-a-gogo people in big boots and shorts and funny beards. And the men were just as bad!!! Hahahahahaha. Oh, shutup, brain. More sheep, wombat droppings, rogue bores, more beards, sheep, trees, sheep and... then I saw the photo of you know who. The Original Sex God Heartbreaker. Smiling into the camera. With dreamy dark blue eyes. Suntanned. Standing in a river wearing shorts. Thank goodness I had eschewed him with a firm hand and felt nothing.

One minute later
Corrrrrr. And also phwoar.

Back in my bedroom of pain
7:00 p.m.

I felt like a goosegog extraordinaire round at Jazzy Spazzy's. All that hand holding and giggling, it's pathetic. I may as well have been the wife of the Invisible Man. Mrs Invisible Man. It was all kissy kiss kiss, "Ooooooohhh, Tom, do you like my new shoes? Oooohhh, Tom, I've got a new owl." Pathetic. I would never do that in front of anyone. I needn't worry, though, because if Masimo chooses Wet Lindsay, I am going to be living in a lesbian monastery for the rest of my life.

Five minutes later

Life really has gone *merde* when I can't even speak to my besty pally because she is so BUSY with her boyfriend.

Well, so be it: if she chooses Tom above me, that is her lookout.

I will be eschewing her with a firm hand.

A LOT.

Like I am eschewing Robbie.

I will not have him in my brain. There is no room for anyone else in the cake shop of agony; it's crowded enough in there already.

And, anyway, Masimo is my one and only one.

Maybe.

Ten minutes later

I hate Jas. My so-called friend and bestie.

But I tell you this for free: she will never know how much she has hurt me. I might be in pain, but at least I have my dignitosity.

That I will never give up for anyone.

One minute later

Phoned Jas.

"Jas, what do you think Masimo will say? Do you think he wants to go out with me? Would you go out with me if you were him?"

"Oy, don't start that lezzie business again."

"Jas, I am just asking you to imagine being him and what you would think about me if you were him. I mean, you wouldn't pick Wet Lindsay over me, would you?"

"She's got quite nice arms."

"Jas, that is the wrong answer. The correct answer is, 'Of course I would choose you every time, Georgia, you gorgey creature.'"

"Well, if you already know the answer, what is the point of asking me the question?"

"And, by the way, what do you mean she has got nice arms? She's a stick insect, therefore she's got sticky thin stupid arms. And unusually enough for a stick insect, it doesn't stop there – she's got a stupid forehead and stupid feet and—"

"I've not seen her feet unclothed. Have you? When did you see her feet?"

"Jas, I don't know that I have seen her feet, but I know that they are sad. Anyway, stop going on and on about her feet. I'm not interested in her bloody feet."

"Well, I didn't start the feet business. I was only being polite."

I slammed down the phone. I may be having a nervy spaz.

I'd better eat something sweet.

In the Kitchen

Nothing to eat, of course.

I must and shall have sugar.

Five minutes later

Never have sugar on bread. It is disgusting.

7:30 p.m.

I had better plan what I'm going to wear the day he comes round to see me. It may be the deciding factor between happinosity and sadnosity.

I must make sure he doesn't see me in my school uniform. It will only remind him that I go to school.

I think I'll practise smiling in the mirror.

7:40 p.m.

Oh, what larks, I'm developing a lurker on my chin. Perfect. It should just be nicely ripening into a massive red pus-filled second chin by Friday.

Five minutes later

Typico, I have run out of spot cream. I could squirt some perfume on it; that sometimes works. What does it say in *CosmoGIRL!* vis-à-vis lurker alerts?

Five minutes later

Apparently you are supposed to lure out the lurker by encouraging it to come to a head. You should steam the area. With a steaming thing.

Ten minutes later

I've had my face over a boiling saucepan for the last year and a half, and although my face is bright red and dripping with water, the lurker is still lurking there happily.

In *Cosmo*'s beauty hints it says you can use a poultice to draw it out. What can I use as a poulticey-type thing? It says a muslin bag with herbs and stuff in it.

In the bathroom

I have just looked in the "medical chest" and it has got some mouldy old oranges, a leg from Libby's Pantalitzer doll, and some dried cat poo in it. How disgusting.

In Mutti and Vati's bedroom

I've found some corn plasters in a drawer. Maybe they would do as a poultice. I'll stick one over the lurker.

One minute later
Well, that is attractive. Not.

But who said that love was painless?

One minute later
And who said it involved corn plasters?

8:10 p.m.
God, the lurker is throbbing. I hope the corn plaster poulticey thing isn't drawing anything else out. I don't want to wake up with no chin.

Wandering lonely as a clud round the house
8:15 p.m.
I may as well be an orphan, for all the notice my family takes of me. They went out gaily laughing and singing years ago, leaving me with a measly fiver for a whole day. Just out scaring people for hours and hours.

I hate them.

It's a bit spooky in the house by myself. Even the kittykats are nowhere around. What if an escaped prisoner came in out of the night and broke into the house to get food and so on?

34

He wouldn't stay long, I can tell you that.

Ten minutes later

I never thought the day would come when I would be glad to hear the whine of Vati's half-horsepower clown car, but it has.

I scampered up to my bedroom.

Loony alert
one minute later

Bang bang, crash. Why can no one in my family open a door normally? Crashing around when starving people with two chins are trying to sleep.

Mum came upstairs into my room. I don't know why she bothers having her own room.

She sat on the bed and looked at me. What am I? A looking at person?

She said, "Could you tell me why you've got a corn plaster on your chin?"

I said, "Oh, leave me alone, will you?"

"Georgia, what is the matter with you? Seriously, you seem all worried and upset – what is it?"

And then, I don't know what happened, but I told her. "I said to the Italian Stallion that I wanted him to be like my proper boyfriend, and he said, 'Oh, this is a serious thing', you know, in that really groovy accent-type thing, and then Dave the Laugh said, 'What if you really liked someone and then you lost them', and Jas said, 'Wet Lindsay has got nice feet and he might like that'... maybe they do, the Italians, they are an ancient race and maybe they like feet... and then a lurking lurker situation occurred, so I got out the corn plaster... and he's going to choose on Friday, that's five days away... and the *coup de* whatsit is that the Original Sex God, whose name I will never mention this side of the grave, had his shorts on, in a river, probably showing off to his wombat friends... Oh, what is the point?"

Actually, for a complete fool and someone who tosses her nunga-nungas around with gay abandon, Mum was quite nice. And she seemed to understand.

Which I am surprised at, as I don't know what I'm saying myself most of the time.

And I'm in my head. Sadly.

10:00 p.m.

Mum gave me a kiss, and I even let her cuddle me. A bit. She said the corn plaster wouldn't work, but she would get me some cream tomorrow that will dry the lurker up.

She said I should keep myself busy with a list of things to do until Friday so that I don't have time to go mad.

Good idea. I will start on the list now.

Two minutes later

This is my list:

Practise not being mad.

10:35 p.m.

Mum brought Bibbs into bed with me. She was asleep, still clutching her swimming goggles and snorkel. She was also clutching the statue of Our Lord Jesus, or Sandra, as he is now called in his Barbie frock and make-up. He is Libby's new best "fwend". I looked at Bibbs in the half-light in my bedroom. She is so sweet when she is asleep. Her little eyelashes are long and curly and her mouth all pouty and pink. I cuddled up to her, and she turned over in her sleep and put her little arms round me. Ooooohhhhh. I said

♡

softly, "Night-night, my little sister. I love you."

And she said sleepily, "Night-night, Ginger. I lobe you."

Ooohhh. At least she loves me.

Then she whispered, "Ginger, I poo my jimjams, oh dear."

Midnight

After emergency removal of my pooey sister, I eventually snuggled down into my bed of pain alone. Not entirely alone because there is a bit of a residual pong and Sandra/Jesus is still in bed with me.

2:00 a.m.

Woke up from a dream.

I dreamt that I had a conversation with Jesus. He had the hump because he didn't like his frock and he said his lipstick didn't suit his complexion. It brought out the orange in it.

I wonder if it is a message from my subconscious that I must be more religious?

Monday June 20th
8:00 a.m.

The Portly One (Vati) yelled up, "Georgia, up NOW! You've got five minutes to get your bum down here."

Oh, he is so crude. And how dare he take my bum's name in vain?

My delightful little sister unexpectedly burst into my room to collect Sandra. She was wearing a see-through plastic Pacamac and some tiny tiny pants that she must have had when she was a baby. Or, more likely, she has nicked them from a poor unfortunate child at playschool. I must tell Mutti to remind the mothers not to leave their toddlers unattended when Libby's around. She came over, quite slowly because the tiny pants were making her walk with small steps, got into bed with me and grabbed Our Lord and started to cuddle him.

I said, "I'm getting up for school now, Bibbs."

She said, "Snuggle buggle."

We had a bit of a cuddle and I kissed the top of her head. Is it normal to be able to snack on Rice Krispies from your little sister's head?

Mutti came bustling in wearing a costume designed for a

teenage prostitute. "Georgia, GET UP! It's ten past eight. You'll be late."

I said, "Late for what? Six hours of misery at Stalag 14 being tortured by the Hitler Youth, followed by twelve hours of extreme boredom and starvation at home?"

She didn't even listen. She said, "Don't be so silly. You are such a drama queen."

Is everyone's life like this?

Cleaning my tushy pegs
Ten minutes later

I wish it was Friday and I could just get it all over with. Masimo comes round and says, "I am sorry, Georgia, I cannot be your one and only one. How do you say in English language? Ah, yes... so long, loser. Loser, loser, double loser, snap snap get the picture?"

Then I could just go back to being ordinarily bored and depressed.

One minute later

I grabbed a piece of toast from the kitchen to ward off death. Angus was happily chewing on something in his basket. He is better fed than me.

On the way out of the front door I heard Mum screeching like a banshee. "Bob, Bob, that horrible furry thing is eating my tights. Stop him, stop him!!! Trap him with that chair!"

Then I heard some crashing and Dad shouting and cursing. Mum hadn't finished: "Of course you haven't broken your leg, Bob. Anyway, never mind about that, get him... Oh bugger, now he's in the laundry room. Oh dear God, he's doing a poo in the ironing. That is it! They are going, they are going!!!"

8:40 a.m.

Jas was on her wall with Tom when I puffed up the hill. They were looking at something in a brown paper parcel. Jas was talking in a really silly girly voice that she uses when Hunky is around. I swear to God she will be developing a lisp soon. Pathetic. She went, "Oooooooohhh, Hunky, that is soooooo interesting. Look at this, Georgia." And she held out the brown paper bag.

There was a newt in the bag. How beyond the Valley of the Really Quite Mad and entering the World of the

Certifiably Bonkers is that?

Jas said, "It's got very unusual markings. I'm taking it into Biology to show Miss Baldwin."

I said, "Yeah, good idea. Crawler."

But she didn't even notice that I'd called her a teacher's botty-kisser because she was so busy being an idiot around her boyfriend.

Tom left us at the corner to go off to college. As he kissed her on her cheek, Jas was fiddling with her fringe so much that I thought she'd had sudden onset of rampant disco inferno dancing. At last they parted. But only after she had blown kisses at him and then he had to pretend to catch them and blow them back for about two trillion years.

She was completely lost in Jasland. "Oh, it is so so so so nice to have him back."

I said, "Is it nice to have him back then?"

But she didn't get it. She just started again. "Oh yes, it is so so so so nice to have him back. I could never not have a boyfriend; it would be so sad. Imagine not having a boyfriend. Oh, actually, I suppose you can imagine not having a boyfriend."

What a cow she can be. I didn't hit her because I think

violence is wrong, and also she was walking too quickly for me to kick. I just said, "You are a very caring person, Jas. It's almost uncanny how empathetic you are."

"I know – do you know what? Sometimes it's like I can actually read Tom's thoughts."

"Really, you mean when he's looking at you and not saying anything, and yet you know what he is thinking?"

"Yeah, like that."

"Yes, I could read his thoughts today too when he was looking at you."

"Really?"

"Yes, it was quite clear he was thinking, *Hey, I've accidentally got a prat for a girlfriend.*"

Hobbling into Stalag 14

I'm not speaking to Jas. She is vair violent. I may have to go to a support group for victims of friends' violence. UNPAL (United Kingdom's Network for Protection Against Loonies).

Assembly

I am at the far end of the Ace Gang lineup next to Rosie. Not

♡ 43

in my usual position next to Mad Dog Jas. She has given Ellen, Jools, Mabs and Ro Ro Midget Gems from her secret stash, but I don't care because I am giving her my cold shoulders. She's only got a boyfriend in the first place because of my excellent stalking skills. If it wasn't for me, she would still be Mrs Sad on the shelf of life.

One minute later
Like me.

Oh God.

Even Rosie doing her shoulder disco dancing during "Jerusalem" failed to work its usual magic. Although when she sang, "And was Jerusalem builded here amongst these dark satanic pants", I did snap and join in with the laughing attack the Ace Gang had. We had to be shuussshed by the Hitler Youth.

Slim, our beloved elephantine headmistress, was in full jelloid mode. She was wearing an unusually attractive jumper in canary yellow. It must have taken at least ten sheep to make it. When she loses her rag she trembles all over. But each bit trembles independently. Chins, jowls, basoomas. If there was such a thing as jelly wrestling, she would be top at it.

one minute later

Oh, drone on. Yawn yawn. What was she talking about?

"...No loitering without intent in the loos... In my day you were lucky to get a shoe to live in... Only nineteen more days to go till our production of *Macbeth* – I hope you're all telling your parents about it..." Blah blah blah. As if.

Then through the dark mists of boredom like a hearing-eye dog I heard my name mentioned. As I drifted back into consciousness I heard her say, "Georgia Nicolson and Rosie Mees to see me in my office immediately after assembly."

Oh dear God, what fresh hell?

I looked at Rosie and she looked back. I shrugged my shoulders, she shrugged back. I looked at the Ace Gang and shrugged my shoulders and they shrugged back. (The Ace Gang, I mean, not my shoulders. I don't mean my shoulders have a shrugging life of their own.)

What have we done?

As we were walking out in a Winter Wonderland of shrugging, Hawkeye appeared from nowhere like the Bride of Dracula and barked out, "Stop that shrugging!"

I said to Rosie, "Now shrugging is a capital offence, apparently. Don't accidentally shake your head, for God's sake."

Outside Slim's office
Ten minutes later

In the waiting room of fear there are Rosie and I and a couple of scaredy first formers playing with their pigtails. Oo-er. Ro Ro said, "Do you remember when the Bummer twins had a pigtail-cutting extravaganza?"

Ah, the Bummers. Jackie and Alison. They had taken bullying to new heights before they were expelled for shoplifting. There was for instance their famous using of first formers as armchairs. And in a particularly inspired moment they had actually superglued one of the little titches to a bench. In their pigtail campaign they used to snip off bits of first formers' pigtails as they passed by and then hang them on their havvies like scalps.

Rosie said, "I wonder what has happened to the Bummers?"

I said, "Prison with a bit of luck."

Two minutes later

Slim had the scaredy little ones in first. They came out about five minutes later all red and crying and hiccupping. I gave one of them a snot rag and asked, "What did you do?"

Ginger titch said, "We... we... drew a picture of a vole with a... a... bra on... on the blackboard in... in... blodge."

I said, "Well done, girls, keep up the good work; we are relying on you."

Rosie slapped them both on their backs, a bit hard actually. I thought their lungs might shoot out. She said, "Goodus workus, smallus idiotus." And they went off looking really pleased.

I said, "I like to think they look up to us as examples of womanhood."

And Rosie said, "Yes, but what you have to keep in mind is that you are bonkers."

Then we heard our beloved leader shout out, "Come."

Here we go. A duffing up for something that we quite clearly have not done. Whatever it is.

Slim was scribbling away at her desk. The chair she must have been sitting on (unless she was levitating) was completely hidden from view by her jelloidness. I wonder if she has a specially reinforced chair? There is probably a specialist circus furniture shop where she gets her requirements. Imagine the size of her bath! Oh nooooo, now I've got a nuddy-pants Slim in my head!

Slim finally looked up.

What had we done?

"I am returning these to you."

Wow, this was a turn up for the book! And she handed me a bag. It was the bison horns!!! The return of the bison horns! Yesss! The horns brought back especially from Hamburger-a-gogo land for the Ace Gang. I fondled the horns and thought back to when I had first worn them riding a bucking-bronco bar stool in Gaylords while *Rawhide* played. Let no one say that the Hamburgese have given us no culture besides Elvis. In fact, as I have said many times to those who will listen (i.e., no one), we have a lot to thank our tiny American chums for – mostly things beginning with "h": hamburgers, hillbillies, howdy doody, er... horns and so on.

Slim was still rambling on. "Now I like a joke as much as the next person, but there is a time and a place, and wearing bison horns during German is not the place. Ironically, you two are quite bright girls, but you waste your talents on silliness. You won't get a job as a silly person, you know."

I didn't say "Miss Wilson has" because, as Slim says, there is a time and a place for everything and time waits for nomads, etc.

I was pleased to have the horns back and it made me think quite kindly about Slim. She isn't such a bad old huge elephantine thing, really. When we got to her door to go, I did think about pretending to be a hilarious alien like in *Doctor Who* and saying, "I offer you my mandible in peace." But then I thought, er, no.

German

Herr Kamyer seems to have accidentally come to work dressed as a twit. His trousers are so short they are bordering on the Bermuda shorts area of legwear. And there is never an excuse for wearing a sleeveless jerkin with diamond patterns all over it. Even if you have been brought up on a diet of *spangleferkel*.

I stared at him. He was quite literally a sight for sore eyes. If you looked at him, he gave you sore eyes. He can always be relied on to come up trumps in the twit arena. He blinked back at me. *"Guten morgen*, Georgia and Rosie."

We clicked our heels together and said, *"Jawohl Kommandant."*

I sat next to Rosie in our comfy seats on the back row. In some of our lessons we are not allowed to sit together for some mad reason that escapes me. Something to do with attention deficit disorder. I got out my chuddie and settled down on my arms to have a little zizz. But I could feel mad beadies looking at me. I opened my eyes. It was Jas. Just looking at me. Look all you want, Miss Looking at Me Person. She soooo wanted to know why we had been to Duffing Up Headquarters and come back looking so pleased. But she will be the last to know anything about me now.

Fifteen minutes later

It is impossible to get a decent sleep in German – you just drift off and the shouting begins. It's all *Achtung!* or *Schnell!* and *Raus raus!* and more *Spangleferkel!* Cor blimey. I was awake now, so I might as well do something. I got the horns out. I nudged Rosie awake and said, "Look at my lap."

She said, "As I've said before, Georgia, you are an attractive girl and everything but I'm just not interested."

I said, "No, really look. Take a good look. Drink in the sight. The bison horns are back!" I made up a little dance with the horns on either hand.

Rosie said, "Sound out the bells of England – the fun days are back!"

Break

Yes indeedy, even though I am on the rack of luuurve I have the bison horns to comfort me. As we ambled off to Ace Gang Headquarters behind the fives court I said, "Do you know I can feel it in my waters, the bison horns are a symbol of hope. The fact that Slim gave them back is a sign from Baby Jesus, it is the dawn of a new era."

Ellen said, "What, er, do you... er, do you mean that people will be more spiritual and get back to nature and looking after the earth and..."

Is she mad? I said, "No, what it means is that Masimo will be mine, mine all miney mine mine."

I said it to the gang, apart from Jas, who I was *ignorez-vous*ing like billio. She was doing reverse *ignorez-vous*ing by pretending to be interested in what Ellen was saying. I said to the others, "In some ways I am looking forward to the autumn term because of course it means the return of the beret. Imagine the scene: a cold morning at Stalag 14, the grey day stretches ahead filled with lesbian perverts and sadistic 'teachers'; but then up the hill, past the Foxwood lads setting fire to their farts and generally being prats, comes a sight to lift the spirits. Could it be? Is it true?

♥ 51

Silhouetted against the sky is an awesome sight. It's the return of the Ace Gang in winter uniform. Berets proudly worn with bison-horn attachments. Yesssss!"

The gang broke into spontaneous Klingon saluting. Maybe everything is going to be all right.

Two minutes later

When we got to our headquarters, Rosie donned her horns. She strolled up and down just enjoying the magnificence of her own horns. Once we all had them on, I said, "Perhaps this is a good time to repeat the Ace Gang manifesto, because some people who shall remain nameless to save them shame – and that means you, Jas – seem to forget about the Ace Gang when boys turn up."

Jas didn't say anything, she just straightened her horns and smoothed down her fringe. In case she was going to have a violent spaz like this morning, I went behind Rosie because my ankle still hurt.

Rosie said, "Yes, one for all and all for one and one for the road and so on."

Jas was still fiddling about with her fringe, so Rosie put her arms round me and Jas and said, "Let bygones be bygones, shake hands and let the rule of Horn reign."

Mabs, Jools and Ellen were all looking at us. Mabs said, "One for all and one for the road and all for one."

I put my hand out first to Jas, which is vair vair nice of me seeing as it was me who was kicked. But that is me all over. Always the first to offer the hand of friendiness.

After a little minute Jas held out her hand. Rosie raised her eyebrows, and the Ace Gang started doing wise(ish) nodding. Rosie said, "Now hug."

Jas gave me a little hug, and I sort of hugged her back. There was a bit of nunga-nunga contact so I leaped back quickly and said, "Er... group hug, group hug."

This culminated in a group hug that nearly made my eyes pop out. Jools was so hyped up, she yelled, "One for all and all for one and all in a one for... anyway, hip hip hooray for Merrie England and the Ace Gang!!!"

We finished up with a sailor's hornpipe (which I have to say was a spontaneous idea of mine, because England is after all a seafaring nation and renowned for its hornpipes).

Then Wet Lindsay and Astonishingly Dim Monica came round the corner, wearing their prefect badges. How uncool is that? Vair vair uncool is the answer. They are always following us about – haven't they got lives? Lindsay has done something alarming to her head. Her hair has somehow grown a foot over the weekend. (I mean twelve inches; I don't mean that there was a foot coming out of her head, although there might as well be.) She's had extensions. What a mistake. They are spectacularly chav and naff. She said, "Aaaah, are you little girls practising games for one of your pyjama parties? Will there be lemonade and biscuits?"

How could Masimo even think of snogging her? Erlack a pongoes. I drew myself up with great dignitosity and adjusted my horns, which had slightly fallen over one eye in the excitement of the hornpipe. "Your hair is looking unusually, er, unusual, Lindsay, if you don't mind me saying?"

"I mind you saying anything. In fact I mind you breathing."

The bell rang then for end of break. And she went on: "Get back inside, because if one of you is a minute late, it's a bad conduct mark for you all."

Oooooh, fear factor ten. Not. But we all went grumbling and moaning off towards the science block. Lindsay yelled after us. "And take those horns off, you stupid idiots."

I said, "Charming, what a charming charming person she is. In every single way charming."

4:15 p.m.

Walking home with Jas and Ro Ro. Jas has even done linky-upsies with me. She can't stand being unfriends with me, really. Especially as something vair *merde* and *odure* has happened.

Ro Ro said, "I can't believe our horns have been confiscated AGAIN. How crap is life in Stalag 14? Vair vair crap, is the answer. We should write to the newspapers about it. We are almost bound to be drug addicts by the time we are seventeen because of all the trauma."

I said, "We'd only had them back for two hours. It is so so crap. Once again we are hornless."

Jas said, "Not only that but we've got detention for two nights."

I said to her, "Have you thought about going to hospitals and cheering people up, Jas? Because if you have, don't – that's all I'm saying."

Rosie said, "When we started the bison dance in blodge,

I thought Miss Baldwin was busy looking at Jas's newt."

Jas said, "She was. She was very interested in its peculiar markings. Tom said that actually it was the only one of its kind that—"

I said, "Jas, can you shut up now?"

She of course got the immediate hump and said, "It was the stools crashing over that attracted her attention."

Merde.

Jas went on raving on to me, "And even then I think she might have let us off. But you just had to cheek her."

What? What? Why was it my fault? I said that to Mrs Prissypants, "Why does the finger of shame always point towards me?"

Jas went rambling on, "Because when she asked you what you were doing, you said that it was a Viking day of celebration. That was when she snapped."

Booo.

After Jas went home, Rosie and I did a bit of skipping to raise our spirits. I think our skipping days are numbered, though, my nungas are vair heavy. We had to sit down on a bench near the park.

Home

All quiet on the Loon front. I slumped down on the sofa.

Oh God – Tues, Weds, Thurs and all of Friday to go before I know my luuurve fate. Why does he need a week to think about it? Why didn't he just say, "Of course I want to be your one and only. You are a Sex Kitty of the first water."

Dave the Laugh would have said that.

One minute later

I miss seeing Dave the Laugh, actually, but I don't feel I can call him. I still don't know what he meant about me not getting it about me and him. Get what?

I thought he said we were only young once and we must blow our horns.

Does he mean he only wants to blow my horn?

Oo-er.

No he can't mean that.

Can he?

Ten minutes later

When Masimo said he would let me know in a week, I wonder if that's a week boy time or week girl time? If a girl says a week, that's what she means, but a boy's week could mean anything. It's like when I say "s'later" to the Ace Gang, that's what I mean – see you later. But when a boy says "s'later" it could mean "you're dumped".

Twenty minutes later

Oh, this is sooooo boring. I'm going out to the park to practise my pretend confident walking where I have got room to really swing my arms. I'll see if it works and anyone thinks I'm confident.

Park

Here we are. So, shoulders back, swingy arms, walking, walking and swing, swing. Feet directly in front of me in a straight line. Make my hips go from side to side. This is a well known boy-entrancing movement. Swing, swing, hip, hip. Aaah yes, this is working, I am feeling very confident. Hello, tree, I am vair vair confident. Head up.

And that's when I saw Dave the Laugh ambling along with his mates. I hadn't seen him since the "what if we should have really been together" incident. Oh, please let him be normal and not *ignorez-vous* me. He saw me and looked across the road, just looking, not smiling. Oh no. This was awful. He didn't want to be my mate any more. I felt a bit like crying.

But then he shouted across, "*Ciao*, Georgia. *Ho due gatti e un maialino!*"

I said, "What?"

He shouted, "I thought you luuurved the Pizza-a-gogo language. I thought you loved Italian blokes. You know, all that handbags at dawn, 'Ooh, have you seen my lovely trousers?' sort of thing. 'Ooo, don't let the rain spoil my hair.'"

Oh dear, he was going to be mean to me and hold a grudge and so on. He was going to be Dave the Unlaugh. But then he smiled at me. He has ever such a nice smiley smile. I was so relieved. I smiled back, and I didn't even rein in my nostrils, I was so pleased we were friends. He didn't come over or anything, though, he just went walking on with his mates. Then he called back, "Oy, missus, you don't know what I said to you in Pizza-a-gogo-ese, do you?"

I said, "Er, yeah."

And he said, "You don't."

"I might."

"Yeah, you might, but you don't. I said, 'I have two cats and a small pig.'"

"That's a lie."

He said, "Is it, though?"

What is he on about?

Then he tapped his nose. "See you Friday at the *MacUseless* rehearsal. Get your pants ready for action!"

Cheeky cat.

Still, he was sort of friendly, so maybe he still likes me. I hope he still likes me.

Two minutes later

I still don't know what he meant about what if you liked someone and let them go.

Does he really mean me and him?

Is he saying he would like to go out with me as my proper boyfriend?

One minute later

Why would he say he has two cats and a small pig?

Boys are without doubt a complete and utter mystery.

And that is *le* fact.

Without doubtosity.

Walking up my road

Oscar was outside his house. He was doing keepie-uppie, listening to his personal stereo and casually eating a Mars bar at the same time. He said, "All right?" in what he fondly imagines is a cool way.

But he took his eye off the ball and it went over the wall. He pretended he had meant to do it by falling to his knees and going, "Yesssss!" like he had scored a goal.

What is the matter with boys?

8:00 p.m.

How disgusting is this? Mum said Angus has eaten her tights and that if I see them poking out of his bum-oley, I must pull them out!

I said to her, "Mum, are you so short of tights that you will wear some that have been in Angus's bum-oley?"

And she said, "No, I just want to strangle him with them."

She is a vair violent and unreasonable person.

In bed
11:00 p.m.
I am using positive thinking and swinging my arms around a lot as I make up an acceptance speech for when the Luuurve God says he wants to go out with me.

OK, this is my acceptance speech: "Aah, Masimo, what a lovely surprise to see you— Owwww, you furry freak!!!"

That isn't the speech. Gordy just leaped off the wardrobe and used my head as a landing pad so he didn't have to hurt his feet leaping straight on to the floor.

Anyway, on with my acceptance speech: "Aah, Masimo, *che bella sorpresa*! What a nice surprise to see you this..." Hang on, what is Italian for "this evening"? This nightio? That can't be right – he'll think I am talking about my jimjams for some reason. I'll look it up later in my *Italian for Complete Fools* book. Anyway, on with the acceptance speechio: "Oh, you would like me to be your girlfriend? Well, that would be *mucho bello*. Grassy arse."

Short and to the point; I think that is the key.

Tuesday June 21st
7:30 a.m.

Had a dream about Masimo last night, only he wasn't speaking in a nice Pizza-a-gogo land accent; he was saying things like, "That is well good" and "Shut it, my son". And most alarmingly he was in a band called the Blunder Boys. I was at the gig and he came over to me and said, "Get your tracksuit top, you've pulled." And as we rode off on his scooter, he started singing, "The Funky Moped" by Jasper Carrot. I've woken up in a cold sweat. What can it mean?

Wednesday June 22nd
6:00 p.m.

How long can this torture go on? On one hand the days seem very very long, like creeping along snaily days; on the other hand it's only a matter of hours until Friday. How many hours exactly? Well, it's 6:00 p.m. now, so that means plus six tonight and then plus twenty-four for tomorrow, and then... er, well, what time will he phone on Friday? Will he count from the hour he told me he would tell me in a week's time? I would. It was 5:45 p.m. last Friday when he told me, so a week would be 5:45 p.m. this Friday. But you never know with boys. What if he counts it from when he got home? Would that be 6:15 p.m? Or maybe he didn't go straight home; maybe he went to the shops and got a few nibbly things, then bumped into someone, so he didn't actually get home until 8:00 p.m. Oh God.

6:30 p.m.

Phoned Jas in sheer desperadoes.

"Jas, do you think he will phone me or come round?"

"Erm, I dunno."

"Yeah, but what do you think? What would you do if you were going to tell me whether you wanted to go out with me?"

"Er... but I don't want to go out with you. I would just tell you. In fact, I am just telling you now."

"Jas, you are being what is technically known as a fool."

She of course, classically, immediately for no reason, got the megahump. But I was in no mood for her humps. I said, "What does Tom think?"

She said, "Hang on, I'll ask him."

Good grief, are they joined at the hip?

She came back a few mins later and said, "Tom says he

will do a bit of detective work and see if he can find out anything."

I said thanks, but in my heart of hearts I don't know if letting Radio Jas find out things is the best foot forward. Too late now.

8:30 p.m.
Tom is going to the snooker club tonight and the Stiff Dylans are playing in a tournament there. Ohgoddygodgod.

Midnight
Jas says she will tell me anything she finds out tomorrow because Tom is going to call her first thing. How am I supposed to sleep under these conditions?

Thursday June 23rd
Banging on Jas's door
7:50 a.m.
Jas's mum answered the door all washed and dressed normally. And smiling. Crikey. It's so relaxing and normal round here; no wonder Jas has got a boyfriend and is not on the rack of love all the time. She has been brought up

properly, not dragged up by fools like I have.

Jas's mum said, "Would you like a piece of toast, dear, or maybe a boiled egg?"

A boiled egg!! Wow it was like being in a *Famous Five* book – the next thing you knew, Jas's dad would come bounding in with a cheery smile and a newspaper.

One minute later
Jas's dad came bounding in with a cheery smile and a newspaper. What is even more amazing is that although he smiled at me, he didn't say anything. Nothing. How cool is that? He didn't ask me anything or tell me a crap joke, he just went off to read his paper. Like a proper dad. He has probably got a pipe.

One minute later
He HAS got a pipe!!!

And he doesn't even light it. He just sucks on it in a pleasant way and doesn't annoy people with smoke, etc.

Amazing.

Waiting for Jas to tell me about the snooker-hall thing. I'm not going to ask her; I have too much pridenosity. She was doing tuneless humming. Very annoying. Then she started talking about *MacUseless* and her part as Lady Macbeth. Who cares about her? She said, "Have you practised your crying for the bit when Macduff finds out his wife and children have been killed?"

I just looked at her. If she thinks it is *me* that should practise crying, she's wrong; it's *her* – if she carries on rambling about rubbish for a bit longer.

But she is as sensitive as a brick. She just went on, "You know when I do the spot thing, well... do you think it should be 'OUT, damned spot'? Or 'Out, DAMNED spot'? Or 'Out, damned SPOT'?"

Finally I snapped. If she thinks I can talk about spots at a time like this, she is madder than I thought. Which doesn't seem possible. I said, "It's irrelevant how you say spot, Jas."

She got all huffy. "No, I think it carries the whole production."

"I'm not talking about the production. I'm just saying it's

irrelevant how you say spot because you won't be alive for *MacUseless* unless you tell me what happened last night at snooker. What did Tom say?"

She looked a bit shifty and began fiddling with her fringe. I resisted slapping her hand. Then she said, "Do you want a bit of chuddie?"

"No."

"What about a black Midget Gem? They are your fave and—"

"Jas."

"Well, remember, don't shoot the messenger."

"What?"

"I'm just telling you because you asked me to; it's not my fault as such."

Assembly

Apparently Lindsay had turned up at the snooker hall and stayed for about twenty minutes talking to Masimo, and then slimed off. I tried asking Jas if they looked like they were having snoggy talk, but she said that Tom had gone back to playing snooker. Typical of boys. They think about such rubbish. Tom can't even tell me what Lindsay was wearing, but apparently he told Jas every single score of each game he played and how long each game lasted.

Who cares about that?

My life is double *merde*. And a half. And that is a fact.

Break

The Ace Gang did their best to keep my spirits up. But even Rosie tucking her skirt into her knickers and walking into class as if she looked perfectly normal couldn't cheer me up.

And I'm sure Wet Lindsay was deliberately shaking her ludicrous extensions about like a ninny to show me that she had spoken to Masimo. With a bit of luck she will catch them in a locker and her head will come off.

In bed
7:30 p.m.

Under the covers. With the lights out.

Mum bustled in. She said, "What are you doing in bed?"

I said from under the covers, "Oh, you know, the shot put, that sort of thing." What does she think I am doing in bed with the light off?

She immediately got the hump, obviously: "You are so

rude, Georgia. It's not my fault you've got obsessed with some boy. And I'm not your servant, either. You just come in and drop your things anywhere. I'm a person, you know, not just here to tidy up after you and cook and clean."

That perked me up, despite my tragicosity. I sat up and removed my cucumber eye patches. "Cook and clean? Clean?? Cook?? I had a cheese sandwich for my dinner, and that is after double maths. AND I made the sandwich. AND Gordy ate half of it when I was scrabbling in the fridge hoping there might be something green in there to save me from rickets. There was something green in there as it happens, but I don't like MOSS."

Mum shouted, "Oh, here's an idea – why don't YOU clean the fridge sometime? And, anyway, don't I have any right to be myself? You know I've got aerobics on Thursdays. It keeps me in shape."

I said, "Wrong."

She stormed out then in a huff and a tizz and a strop: "You are HORRIBLE!!!"

And she slammed the door. How childish.

7:45 p.m.

I'm not horrible. She's horrible.

8:00 p.m.

What time is it now?

Only eight o'clock. Oh dear God.

9:00 p.m.

I can't sleep. I may even have to do my French homework to take my mind off Masimo and Lindsay. What were they talking about for twenty minutes?

9:10 p.m.

Here we go. Chapter fourteen in my French textbook. Jools and Jim and their fantastic excursion to the Bois de Boulogne. Why are they so excited about going to some woods? It's like reading the froggy version of Jas and Tom. I could write a book called *Jas and Tom and Their Fantastic Excursion to the Bois de Boulogne.*

Clearly no one would buy it because it would be so boring.

Samedi

Jas a dit avec sa bouche stupide, "Ooooohhh, c'est magnifique, c'est la bonne newt!!!"

Tom a dit, "Oh lalalala."

Les idiots chantent, "Non, je ne regrette rien!!!!"

And so on. What larks!!! I wonder what happens next? I can't wait! Perhaps they find some *escargots* and...

zzzzzzzzzzzzzzzz.

on the brink of madnosity

Friday June 24th

Dawn

Birds singing, clouds cludding, heart thudding. What if he comes to meet me after Stalag 14? What if he just decides spontaneously to come to school and pick me up? That's what boys do. They don't think about the preparation that has to be done – make-up and mood planning and so on.

Oh Blimey O'Reilly's trousers.

Also, if he was thinking the age gap was a bad thing, the last thing he needs to see is me in my stupid school shirt and tie. I must take a change of clothes just in case. I'll have to dash off to the tarts' wardrobe after the *MacUseless* rehearsal.

73

one minute later

But what if he doesn't know about the *MacUseless* rehearsal and comes at the normal time they open the prison gates?

Even if I keep things to the minimum – lip gloss, foundation, mascara – it is still going to take me ten minutes, and the changing as well. Oh, this is so stressful. Why do we have to go to school? I've been going for the last ten years and where has it got me? Still at school, that's where it has got me.

7:40 a.m.

Packing my rucky. I've put in my clothes and essential make-up. So clearly there is no room for my books and homework. *C'est la vie.* Anyway, I am only going to school in the first place to fill in time and to stop my mutti and vati going to jail. I don't know why I bother, though. Mum is still *ignore*zing me. She is so vair vair immature.

8:10 a.m.

Mum didn't even say good morning or look at me when I rustled around in the kitchen. She is still having the hump and strop because of what I said about her shape. You know, not having one. Maybe that was going just that tiny bit too far.

8:15 a.m.
Maybe not, though. When Mum bent over to hand Libby a spoon for her eggy and soldiers, she knocked over a cup of tea with her nunga-nungas.

8:20 a.m.
I said, "S'laters" as I went, but Mrs Giant Basoomas didn't say anything.

My lovely sister didn't ignore me though, unfortunately. She snogged me and said, "Here is your runch, Ginger, yum." And gave me a bit of soldier with egg on it. It is not as such unchewed.

8:30 a.m
Jas is being "cool". It is vair vair vair annoying and driving me to the brink of madnosity.

I wanted to know what she thought the Luuurve God would decide. She knows this is the big decision day. She is trying to be philosophical about my situation, like she is some beardy monk or something. She said, "*Que sera, sera,*

♡ 75

whatever will be, will be, the future's not ours to see, *que sera, sera.*"

I said, "Don't say *que sera* again, Jas, unless you want a duffing incident."

She just raised her eyebrows, but I know that she is deliberately saying *que sera* in her brain.

Assembly

We shuffled into the main hall past Droopy Drawers Lindsay and her astonishingly dim mate Monica. No sign of Hawkeye, seeing-eye dog and *Oberführer*. Oh dear, I hope she hasn't been accidentally kidnapped by squids.

Slim is dressed entirely in brown today, which makes her look like a giant onion bhaji. As usual, she had something depressing to say: "Settle, girls." We resisted doing our cooing-like-pigeons thing because she was on a rampage extraordinaribus. She said, "It has come to my attention that some of you girls are rolling your school skirts over at the waistband to make them shorter. Madame Slack said that she saw a group of girls this morning, and at first from a distance she thought they had forgotten to put their skirts on at all. This is a ridiculous practice and gives the school a bad name. It will cease forthwith."

Oh, ramble on, why don't you? Has she really not got anything else to think about? What is so vair vair wrong with showing a bit of knee to cheer up the nation?

Slim had finished with knees and was now on to something even more boring. "And now to fire precautions – a most important and serious subject. Mr Attwood has something to say to you."

I said to Ro Ro, "Let's hope it's 'goodbye'."

Ro Ro said, "I thought he was supposed to be retiring. Why is he still alive? Why hasn't he gone to that big caretakers' home in the sky?"

Elvis shuffled his way up on to the stage and adjusted his glasses. "Thank you, Headmistress. I am sorry to say that during last week's play rehearsal in the main hall, various incidents involved the unlawful use of fire extinguishers. They have been used in what some idiots like to call 'foam fights'. I was caught in one of these so-called 'foam fights' and have only just recovered proper hearing in my left ear. But even more serious is the fact that I came across one of my fire blankets being put over the vaulting horse in the gym by a Foxwood lad. When I asked the culprit why he had removed an important part of firefighting equipment, he said (and Elvis looked at his sad snitching diary), 'I thought the horse might be chilly, because even though it's June the nights can turn quite nippy noodles.'"

The Ace Gang had a laughing spaz, but we had to change it into coughing in case of a bad-conduct-mark-all-round fandango. I had forgotten about the gym horse and Dave the Laugh incident. I might have known Elvis would have snitched.

Elvis was still going on. "Would that lad have found it funny if he had caught fire and the blanket I would have normally used to extinguish him was missing? Do any of you see the joke now?"

I half put my hand up, but Madame Slack was on substitute glaring duty in Hawkeye's absence, so I had to turn it into scratchy ear.

Happy happy days! Apparently Hawkeye is off today, brushing up her girl hating skills at some convention (the cruelty convention probably). She'll come back with a whip and an Alsation next week. But on the plus side, I can put as much make-up on as I like this aftie! We only have Miss Wilson and Herr Kamyer. Hooorah!!!

78

Behind the fives court
Break time

I said to the Ace Gang, "I am soooooo nervous. I feel an f.t. coming on, quickly followed by a nervy b. If I smoked, you wouldn't be able to see my head for smoke. I would be smoking ten at a time. And I would have a pipe as well. Say something to calm me down."

Ellen said, "What time... what time will he call... I mean, did he say he would call or did he say see you later... because if he did, I mean if he did the s'later thing, well, that would mean... well, I don't know what that would mean."

I said, "Thanks very much for that, Ellen."

Jools said, "What exactly is the point of boys?"

Mabs said, "Pardon?"

Jools said, "I mean really, what is the point of having them around?"

Rosie said, "Snogging."

Jools said, "Yeah, fair point, but besides that? I mean, take Rollo. I like him and everything, but he turns up and we go to the pictures and snog. Or we go for a walk and we snog. Or we just snog. Which is nice. But the fact is, mostly I don't know what on earth he is going on about. He says stuff like, 'I've got the entire collection of first-edition *Beano* comics.' What am I supposed to think about that?"

We did supportive shrugging.

Rosie said, "I think your mistake is thinking you should talk to him. It's so much more soothing to have a foreign boyfriend who is also mad."

Jas got up on to her high horsey knickers and said, "Well, I think you are wrong, Rosie. Tom and I do all sorts of things together. We go beyond just snogging."

I went, "Ooooo-er."

But she was off into Jasland. "I mean, I think the important thing is to choose someone that you have things in common with."

Oh, please don't let her go on about molluscs.

Rosie was stuffing a Jammy Dodger into her gob, but she still managed to drop *le* bombshell: "Oh yes, I so agree. That is why Sven and I are going to get married."

What?

We all looked at her.

She looked back.

I said, "No, you're not."

Rosie opened her mouth and showed me her half-eaten

Jammy Dodger. Good grief. Has the strain of going out with Sven finally driven her to unusual levels of bonkerosity?

Two minutes later

Even though I tried to make Rosie admit she was joshing, she insists she is a bride to be. I said, "Oh yes, and when did you become a bride to be? Was it a minute ago, when you got bored with Jas talking about her and Hunky?"

Rosie said, "You have a very suspicious mind, Georgia. Sven proposed to me many weeks ago."

I said, "How did you know what he was asking you? Normally no one can understand a word he says."

Rosie said, "His eyes spoke for him."

"Now he's got talking eyes?"

She was talking absolute poppycock and balderdash and woopsie.

However, Ellen had got really carried away with the excitement of Rosie's forthcoming imaginary wedding. She said, "Oh, I love weddings. Can I be a bridesmaid?"

Rosie said, "Yep, you can all be bridesmaids. I am thinking of asking Herr Kamyer to be matron of honour. He's got the legs for it."

As the bell rang I said to the blushing bride to be, "What do your parents think about it? Are they, you know, over the moon that you are getting married at fifteen and a half to a madman?"

She said, "Oh yes."

Maths

Even though I know she is talking absolute pants, Rosie has managed to take my mind off my own life. Sometimes for moments at a time I can forget I am on the rack of luuurve.

One minute later

Which reminds me – only four hours to countdown. I'd better start applying my base coat of foundation. I'll do base coat, highlights and first coat of mascara in maths, and then I can continue with the second coat and first coat of eye shadow in physics. Miss Wilson won't tell me off. And even if she did try, I would convince her that I was just getting into my character. Because as everyone knows, Scottish lairds used to wear woad and so on.

Five minutes later

It's quite hard putting on mascara when you have to practically lie down on your desk to not be spotted. Honestly, school is soooo annoying. And pointless. Miss Stamp is going on about pi again. Which reminds me, I'm a bit peckish. I wonder if Jazzy Spazzy has any Wotsits secreted about her person.

Rosie has started sending notes:

> Dear all,
>
> Sven and I have decided on a Viking wedding in honour of Sven's roots. This will involve a lot of heavy lifting as the bride and bridegroom are traditionally carried around town on a replica longboat. I suggest you all start a regime of fitness. And I am thinking particularly of Ellen. I do not want the festivities spoiled by any suggestion of lardiness.
>
> Yours sincerely,

the Bride to Be

P.S. I will be compiling a wedding
gift list shortly.

P.P.S. In the meantime any spare
chuddie would be appreciated.

I wrote back:

Dear Bride to Be,
Hopefully we will have the bison horns
back in time for the wedding. By the way,
when is it?
Yours sincerely,
a friend and well-wisher

Afternoon break

It turns out that the wedding is planned for Rosie's twenty-first birthday.

I said, "Forgive me if I'm right, but that is in more than five years' time."

Rosie said, "Yes, but you can't rush a Viking wedding. There are vats to be found."

"Vats?"

"Oh yes, for the mead and so on. Shall I show you a Viking version of 'Let's go down the disco' that we could do at the reception?"

I said, "No, my base coat might run."

"Come on, you'll like it A LOT!"

She made us all trudge across to the fives court and showed us the new Viking disco inferno dance. Before I knew it, we were all doing it. We sang along to "Jingle bells, jingle bells" because although Rosie is allegedly the world expert on Viking-a-gogo land, she doesn't know any Viking songs.

I said, "What's wrong with 'Edelweiss' from *The Sound of Pants* musical?"

But as usual Mrs Prissy Knickers Jas said, "That is an Austrian song. About Austria. Which is not Svenland."

Here we go. She is absolutely obsessed with countries and where they are.

I said, "Look, Jas, it's a practice Viking dance, and number one, Rosie isn't getting married for five years and probably not even then, and number two, we don't know where Sven comes from anyway. And number three, you are annoying me and forgetting to remember that I am on the rack of luuurve."

That made her shut up. She should think of others more than herself.

I do.

I don't know why, though, because it is really boring and pointless.

Ten minutes later

We have perfected the Viking disco inferno dance. Even though I say it myself, it is a triumph. And once the horns are returned, the whole thing will have *je ne sais quoi* and harummph and possibly Good Lordnosity.

Just before we went in for an afternoon of sheer unadulterated *merde* (physics), Rosie yelled, "OK. One last time, let's hit it, lads! Jingle bells, jingle bells, jingle all the way. Oh, what fun it is to ride on a one-horse open sleigh-ay!!!"

And then all together we did the dance. Stamp, stamp to the left, left leg kick, kick. Arm up, stab, stab to the left (that's the pillaging bit). Then stamp, stamp to the right, right leg kick, kick. Arm up, stab, stab to the right. Quick twirl round with both hands raised to Thor (whatever). Then raise your (pretend) drinking horn to the left, drinking horn to the right, raise your horn to the sky, all over body shake, huddly duddly and fall to knees with a triumphant shout of "HORRRRNNNNN!!!!"

Yesss!

MacUseless rehearsals
4:10 p.m.

I have completed my make-up pre-make-up preparations. On the way down to the hall I saw Wet Lindsay laying into the first formers who had done the picture of a vole with a bra on. She had them pinned up against the wall. They were looking really scared. They had probably seen her knees. Wet Lindsay was saying to the titches, "Why were you outside the school gates at lunchtime? Well?"

They didn't say anything. They were just staring at her and blinking like she was a sort of octopus who had just leaped out and was asking them questions. It is an easy mistake to make with her no forehead and hair extensions. I wonder if Masimo has seen her head lately? Oh yes, he must have, I have just remembered the snooker fiasco.

Merde. And also how pathetic is she, trailing around after Masimo? Anyway, Octopus Head was still raving on: "Well, I'm waiting! What were you doing outside the school gates?"

The titch sisters started blubbing even more, and one said, "I... dddddon't knnnnow."

Lindsay said, "Ah, you don't know. Well, I tell you what I'll do – I'll let you have a long think about it. Until you do know. And while you are thinking, you can clear out the sports cupboard after school on Monday."

One of them said, "But, but I've got... blub blub... violin practice on Mondays."

Wet Lindsay said, "You *did* have violin practice. Clear off."

The two blubsters went blubbing off down the corridor. As I went by Octopussy I gave her my worst look. But I didn't say anything. Then I just let my eyes fix on a place where her forehead should have been if she'd had one. She put her hand up like she thought she had an antenna growing there or something. Hahahahah yesss! Result! The no-forehead staring campaign continues.

She said, "Are you wearing make-up?"

"It's for the play."

As she was about to go into the common room she said, "A bit of advice, lady – you are making yourself look like a ridiculous tart trailing around after Masimo. It makes you look like what you are: a silly cheap pathetic baby. I think you're ridiculous and he thinks you're ridiculous. He's too nice to say, but he told me he feels really sorry for you. Do yourself and all of us a favour and stop making a fool of yourself. He's out of your league."

Even though I hate her a million and a half and know she's a liar, I did feel my face going all red.

Five minutes later

The Ace Gang were in the tarts' wardrobe getting ready for the Foxwood boys' extravaganza. The whole school was on high-hysteria alert. I even saw a couple of first formers with a bit of lippy on. It's insane, really, because it's not like we're shut up in a convent. Some people really have no self-controlnosity when it comes to boys. I couldn't get near the mirror to check my final make-up, but I like to think I achieved a natural look. Unlike Ellen. Her lip gloss was so thick, she looked like she had plunged her gob into a pot of treacle. Even Jas was using eyelash curlers. Why? Tom wasn't even in *MacUseless*. I said, "Why are you curling your eyelashes when your so-called beloved is not even going to be here?"

She spluttered on about Lady Macbeth, saying that the curly eyelashes were all part of the historical detail, that she would be wearing authentic drawstring pants under her dress, and so on, rambling on. I wish I had never mentioned it.

I told the gang what Lindsay had said.

Jools said, "What a prize bitch."

And Ro Ro said, "Octopussy talks WUBBISH!!"

Mabs said, "Let's kill her. No one would notice."

It's nice that they care and offer sensible advice, but all the same I am still, as Elvis (he dared to rock) Presley said, "all shook up, ah huh."

I said to Jas as we trolled off to the main hall, "She practically said I was stalking Masimo. How could she say that?"

Jas said, "Well, she's got a point. It's just that she doesn't know she has."

"What are you rambling on about now?"

"Well, you tried to find him in Hamburger-a-gogo land, didn't you?"

"Well, yeah, but—"

"You remember, when you rang everyone in New York New York called Scarlotti—"

"Well, yeah—"

"And you ended up ordering a Chinese takeaway – from New York. And we were in Memphis."

Oh God, bang on about history, why don't you?

I said, "Jas, that was before I got maturiosity."

Jas laughed.

Which makes her look stupid.

Five minutes later

What if Masimo is at the gates? I will just sneak out in a casualosity at all times way to see if he's there.

Two minutes later

I walked across the side of the playground towards the school gates. No sign of the Luuurve God. Just in case he was hidden from view I did my hip hip, flick flick thing. As I got to the gate Mr Attwood leaped out from the herbaceous border in full madman outfit – overalls and a cap and his fire extinguisher. What is the matter with him?

He said, "What are you doing out here, young lady? You should be in the main hall. If I am not informed of where all personnel are, there might be casualties unaccounted for in the event of major conflagration."

Has the human race come to this?

Back in the tarts' wardrobe for a final make-up check
Ten minutes later

God, I can hardly move my eyes, I've got so much mascara on. I'm so on the edge of having a complete tiz and to do. And on top of everything else I feet a bit nervy and excited about seeing Dave the Laugh.

As we approached the main hall doors I said, "Shall we do a quick burst of the Viking disco inferno backstage to let Dave and his mates know that the *MacUseless* party has begun?"

Jas said, "I don't think Dave the Laugh will want to see anything you have to show him, if you know what I mean."

I glared at her in a meaningful way, but she didn't know what I meant. However, as she had said something about Dave the Laugh, Ellen went off in a dithercab. "Did you say, er, Dave the, er, Laugh wouldn't want to see anything that...

to see anything that Georgia shows him... I mean, what does that mean?"

Fortunately at that moment we entered the hall and her ditherosity was drowned out by the lads cheering and yelling, "Nunga-nungas!!!"

Dave the Laugh was at the front of the mob of lads, pretending to keep them back and saying to us, "Move along, ladeeez, there is nothing to see here. Nothing to see." Like a policeman at a road accident.

6:00 p.m.
After the usual hour and a half of chaos that Miss Wilson calls "rehearsal", we were set loose from Stalag 14. I nipped off to the tarts' wardrobe to roll my skirt up and put my black lacy top on. The Ace Gang were still in *MacUseless* mood. Rosie was doing her "eye of newt" bit but improvising by adding "yum yum". She will probably do it on performance night and then we will all be executed.

But actually that would be a blessing in disguise. I am on the rack of love and feel like going to the piddly-diddly department every five seconds. What if he is there? What should I do? Should I display glacial glaciosity or have just a hint of Eastern promise lurking across my face? I made the Ace Gang walk in front of me so I could reveal myself to him at my best angle when I saw him.

As we walked across the playground I could see that Masimo wasn't waiting outside the school gates to meet me. I felt quite relieved in a way. I don't know why. At least I didn't have to put up with all the ogling oglers looking at me making a prat of myself in front of him. Or fainting, which I probably would have done. Or having a sudden poo-parlour-division episode.

Still, he did say he would let me know in a week, and the week didn't start at the school gates, did it? It started at my house. So I needn't worry until I get to my house.

Two minutes later

I wonder if Masimo would think walking home as a gang was a hoot and a half, or if he would think it was a bit childish? But we don't *always* limp and pretend to be the Hunchbacks of Notre Dame. We only do it when it's appropriate. You know, on boring bits of walking or in lessons. I can be as full of maturiosity as the next person. Ish.

Ten minutes later

Dave and his gang leaped out from behind some bushes and nearly gave us a heart attack. Ellen's head was so red I thought it would explode. I felt funny, sort of pleased that he was with us. Even though it had literally been about ten minutes since I last saw him.

Two minutes later

Dave was doing a really bad backwards moon walk, with his bottom sticking out and his collar up. He was shouting at us, "You are my bitches!!!"

Rollo said, "Leave it out, mate, I'm not that kind of bloke."

Dave said, "No, just the bitches are my bitches!!!"

Ellen, who had turned into a walking beetroot because of Dave, said to me, "Er, do you... er, like, is it OK to call us bitches? Isn't it, like, erm... disrespectful to women?"

I said, "Yes, but he's talking to us."

She said, "Oh yeah, right, I see."

But she clearly doesn't. She soooo luuurves Dave that she would probably wear a false beard if he told her to.

Which incidentally, he might.

Also, it's going to be midnight before she gets home, because she lives in the opposite direction.

Dave was still going on doing the moon walking. He said, "OK, ma bitches, WHO'S THE DADDY?"

I said, "We don't say 'daddy' – we think it's naff. We say 'vati'."

Dave said, "OK, cool, WHO'S THE VATI?"

We just looked at him going backwards, so he shouted again, "WHO'S THE VATI?"

And Jas, Rosie, Ellen, Jools, Mabs and me had to say, "You're the vati."

At which point Dave, otherwise known as The Vati, walked backwards into the low wall of the park and fell over it.

Vair *amusant*.

6:15 p.m.

Just me and Dave now. Ambling along. The others have all gone home. Even Ellen realised that she couldn't go on being hypnotised by Dave like a... er... hypnotised beetroot, and then a bus came along going her way. I think she was half-hoping I would say why didn't she come home with me and my vati would give her a lift home later. But I just couldn't, not with the Masimo fandango.

As she was going, Ellen said to Dave, "See you next week, then."

And Dave said, "Missing you already."

And Ellen reached new heights of beetrootosity. Oh God, I wonder how long it will be before she is on the blower saying, "You know when he said he was like... er... missing me... well, does that mean... he's, like, missing me, or...?"

After she had gone I looked at Dave with raised eyebrows. He raised his eyebrows back. I raised mine even higher and did the nodding knowledgeably thing. He nodded back.

He knows what I mean, though. He knows that Ellen luuurves him. Even if he didn't, he pretty much seems to think that everyone luuurves him. In fact, he's not wrong. All the girls in the play act in a ludicrous way with him, even when he is vair vair rude. I was glad that we were matey mates and that I didn't feel awkward with him any more. Well, not much. I am still avoiding the topic of the Italian Stallion in front of him.

When Jazzy Spazzy got to her house, she unexpectedly

gave me a little hug and said, "I hope it all goes all right. Ring me later." Which was quite touching. But it did imply that there was something to "go all right" about. To cover up any questions Dave might ask me about what the thing "going all right" was and so on, I said, "Did you see how she hugged me for just that little bit too long. She is definitely on the turn. I must be on lezzie alert. She was looking at my tights when I was gallivanting around as Macduff."

Dave said, "Who *wasn't*?"

I said, "Actually, you weren't. You were being hypnotised by Melanie Griffiths' basoomas."

"You have a very suspicious mind, Kittykat. As you know, I am very safety conscious and I was making sure that Melanie did not topple over and injure herself during the juggling scene."

"Safety conscious?"

"Yep."

"You're mad."

"No, you're mad."

"Er, I think you'll find YOU'RE mad."

Then he got hold of me and started tickling me. Oh no, tickly bears!!! The next stage after tickly bears was usually number four on the snogging scale! My lips even started puckering up like Pavlov's dog's lips.

Then he stopped tickling me. He had both his arms on mine, sort of holding them against my sides. His face was very close, and he looked at me. He had very dreamy eyes. They had that soft, pre-snogging look about them. My brain was trying to have a stiff word with me: "Calling all parts, calling all parts, and that means you, lips! Stop that puckering. We are on pucker alert!!! Remember, remember, you're a Womble! Er, I mean remember you are the nearly-girlfriend of a Luuurve God."

Then, just as my lips developed their own brain and thought, *Oh, sod it, give us a snog!* Dave let me go and said, "Bad bad Sex Kitty. Bye bye."

And he went off.

Blimey, I nearly fell on to the ground when he let me go.

What was the matter with me?

6:25 p.m.

I did hip hip, loosey arms and flicky hair all the way up my street just in case Masimo was waiting for me. But he wasn't.

In my bedroom
6:45 p.m.
In the nuddy-pants in front of the full-length mirror. I have put my dressing table in front of the door so that no one can burst in and surprise me in the rudey dudeys.

If I jump up and down, my nunga-nungas practically slap me in the face.

So I must be sure not to leap up and down in front of Masimo.

Now then. Check list:

Whole body a lurker-free zone? Check.

Orang-utan gene plucked to within an inch of its life? Check.

Four layers of natural foundation? Check.

Shading applied to draw the eye away from less good features, i.e., huge conkerositiness? Well, I've done my best.

Hair not looking like bombhead? Yes, sir.

Lippy and lip gloss applied for that hint of sophisticosity beyond my years and a touch of Eastern promise? Turkish delight-flavoured lip gloss. Mmmm tasty.

Over-the-shoulder-boulder-holder and knick-knacks next. Good. All safely harnessed in.

Now then, clothes, hmmm... Tight jeans, but not so tight that I can't get my leg over... his Vespa. Or should I wear my skirt with the fringey bit on? Yes, yes, that's better.

Is it?

7:00 p.m.
I think I'll put the jeans back on. They seem more casual.

7:15 p.m.
Not as full of SexKittynosity, though. I'll put the skirt back on.

7:30 p.m.
What if it's a bit nippy noodles? Jeans, I think.

7:45 p.m.
Skirt back on.

7:55 p.m.
Jeans, now that is it. I am not changing again.

7:58 p.m.
Skirt!

7:59 p.m.
This is absolutely it. The jeans are on and that is it.

8:00 p.m.
He's still not called. The only slight silver lining is that Swiss Family Mad are out again and I have some privacy.

8:05 p.m.
Phone rang. Oh gadzooks!!! I leaped down the stairs. With Angus and Gordy attached to each leg. I thought they had been suspiciously quiet; they must have been lurking outside my door just waiting for me to come out. They clung on all the way down, even though their heads were bumping against each step. Don't they feel pain?

Sadly not. Got to the phone with my cat-legs and did a lot of calmy calm breathing. Ommmmm.

I picked up the phone.

"Georgia?"

"Jas! Why are you calling me now?"

"Because I wanted to know if you were on the phone to Masimo. I didn't know you were going to answer it."

"Why wouldn't I answer the phone if it rang?"

"Because, as I have explained, it wouldn't have rung if you had been on the phone and—"

"Look, Jas, I have to go."

"He hasn't rung, has he? I can tell. You sound really really bad. Are you feeling awful? I would. Have you been blubbing?"

"No, I—"

"It must be awful being dumped. Especially when you had never really, you know, been—"

"Jas."

"What?"

"Shut up."

"I was just being a chum."

"Well, don't."

"Well, I won't."

"Good."

I slammed the phone down so that she couldn't go off in a strop. I had out-stropped her for once. Ha ha and double ha.

8:10 p.m.

Managed to eventually get the kittys off by spraying them with the shower attachment. I had to be careful to just focus the water on to their heads and not get any on my jeans. They hate the idea of being clean and they leaped off, sneezing and shaking like loonies, and charged outside to roll in some fox poo or something.

8:30 p.m.

Perhaps he's got a Stiff Dylans gig.

9:02 p.m.

Or perhaps Wet Lindsay was telling the truth and he does think I am pathetic. And he feels sorry for me. So that's why he's being nice.

9:03 p.m.

Perhaps he's held up because he is telling Wet Lindsay that she looks like an octopus.

I wish.

9:08 p.m.

Perhaps he is seeing her on a date? Oh noooooo.

Still, girdey loins, girdey loins.

9:10 p.m.

I must consult with my boy manual *How to Make Any Twit Fall in Love with You.*

9:20 p.m.

Oh God goddy God, I have done the wrong thing! It says you shouldn't let boys know that you want something because then they feel under pressure. Ohhhh noooo.

9:30 p.m.

It's true, isn't it? The rule with boys is glaciosity at all times. I remember when Dave the Laugh told me I had inadvertently displayed glaciosity to Masimo when I ran off when he asked for my phone number.

Oh, I wish I could phone up the Hornmeister now. I miss him.

Only in a matey way.

He hasn't said anything nice to me lately.

Although he did say "bad Sex Kitty".

9:32 p.m.
He used to say that despite being certifiably insane I was a lovely, funny person. And that is nice. Just what a proper boy mate would say.

9:33 p.m.
But if he is just a boy mate, how come we got to number six?

9:34 p.m.
But my ad-hoc and red-bottomosity days are over. I will never feel Dave the Laugh's nip-libbling technique again. Which is a shame. Shut up shut up, voice of the Horn.

9:35 p.m.
I don't know why I'm bothering giving up the Horn in my head when in fact no one is asking me to be their one and only girlfriend anyway.
   I may as well take off my make-up.

9:40 p.m.

No, why should I bother cleansing and toning? What's the point of having toned skin if there's no one there to say, "Blimey, your skin is toned. Will you be mine?"

Downstairs
9:45 p.m.

I looked out of the front-room window at the dark street. I may as well go to bed. For ever. I looked up at the dark sky. Surely there is some beardy bloke up there somewhere who cares about me? Maybe I should go to church more. My last visit was not what you would call an all-round success – vis-à-vis the accidental pensioner inferno. Which I have to say was a lot of fuss about nothing. The elderly can be vair hysterical. My votive candle merely set fire to the pensioner's headscarf. She shouldn't have worn acrylic material as it clearly is a fire hazard. Even before that, I was having an unlaugh. In his sermon Call-me-Arnold the vicar said, "We all come into the world alone and go out of it alone." I don't know why he bothers going to church just to depress people.

9:46 p.m.

For once he is right, though. I am on my owney. All aloney.

9:48 p.m.

Now I really really am depressed. I am just looking out on to the dark void of life. The long, dark street of life, reaching into the distance of nothingosity.

Then I almost had a nervy spaz because Angus and Gordy suddenly appeared on the windowsill. They were doing pathetic meowing, looking straight into my eyes through the window. Well, Angus was. They were opening their mouths and really wailing.

It was a sign. They had sensed my pain and been drawn towards the front-room window of agony to give me comfort. They were wailing along with my inward wailing.

Except the funny thing was, I couldn't hear anything. I opened the window. And they went on doing the pathetic meowing and looking straight into my eyes. And I realised why I hadn't been able to hear them. They couldn't even be bothered making a noise. They were just doing pretendy silent wailing.

Well, they can stay outside. Why should I be nice to

them? No one is nice to me. Anyway, they just use me for kitty snacks and molesting, and then they go off to play without a second's thought.

I hope it snows.

Four minutes later

That would be quite unusual in midsummer, but it would fit in with my mood.

And serve the furry freak twins right.

In my bedroom
10:00 p.m.

Oh marvellous, the Mads are back. I can hear them singing, "We're all off to Dublin in the green, in the green" in crap Irish accents. I must pretend I'm asleep.

I leaped into bed fully clothed and turned the light off.

I snuggled down in the bed and my feet touched something furry. Which started to purr. The kittykats! How had they snuck into my bed? The tiny top window in my bedroom is open, but how would they get up there? They probably have cat abseiling equipment stashed among Dad's fishing rods in the shed. Too late to drag them out

 109

because I could hear an awful noise coming up the stairs. Please, please let it not be Vati coming in to sing Irish songs to me and do sad dancing with his trousers rolled up.

It was Mutti, because I heard her call to Dad, "Bob, make a cup of tea. I'll put Bibbs to bed and just look in at Georgia."

Then I realised what the awful noise was. It was my darling little sister snoring like a stuck pig. The snoring got quieter as Mum went into Libb's bedroom, and I heard her shut the door. Perhaps she would just go away. But no. My door opened and Mum came over to my bed. I could sort of sense her presence with my eyes tight shut. She whispered, "Gee, are you awake?"

I did a pretendy snore. And that's when I felt the kittykats stir. Something wet and rough touched my feet. Oh God, it was their tongues. They were licking me with their horrible cat tongues! Urgh urgh. It was soo disgusting, I couldn't stand it. But I must keep still, I must.

It was like in Latin when we learned about Sparta. Two boys from Sparta went out to steal chickens, and they saw the farmer coming so they put the chickens down the front of their trousers (or whatever Sparta people wore). The farmer said, "Oy, you two lads-us, have-us you seen-us any of my chickens-us?" (That's just a rough Latin translation.)

Anyway, the two boys said, "Your chickens-us? Not us, mate-us."

And the farmer said, "Me think-us you have us..."

And all the time the chickens were pecking and scratching the boys' trouser-snake addenda. Eventually the farmer went off and the boys staggered home, handed over the chickens to their mum and then died of their wounds. And the whole of Sparta honoured them because they hadn't cracked under pressure. As I have said many many times, Latin is crap.

Where was I? Oh yes, anyway, that's what it was like for me. I was being submitted to tongue torture. And I couldn't cry out or anything. Mum touched my hair. As she did, the tongues reached the back of my knees. Oh dear God, if they went beyond the knees, I don't think I could stand it.

10:10 p.m.
At last Mum packed it in and left the room. I turned the light on and ripped back the covers to expose the furry leg-munchers. I said, "Get out of my bed, NOW!!"

 III

They were blinking in the light. Angus put one big paw on my leg and let his claws come out. He was looking at me and I was looking at him with my sternest look. I know very well that he understands me. I am, after all, his mistress. I am his huge baldy mistress and he knows it is his duty to do what I say. Otherwise its goodbye kittykat snacks. He looked and looked and then he let the tip of his tongue pop out of his mouth. He was doing the tongue-lolling idiot-cat thing! Gordy was looking at me with one of his eyes, and then he just nodded off and keeled over.

What is the point?

Angus settled down and nodded off as well. I didn't have the energy to do anything about them, so I pulled the covers up over us all again. I felt like weeping. And I did. Tears started welling up in my eyes. How could this happen to me? I'm not a really bad person. OK, I was a bit snappy with Jas, but that was understandable. I can't bear to go to school again. Lindsay will know what's happened and she will make my life a misery.

I am sooo miserable and lonely.

Two minutes later

The cats started doing violent sneezing under the covers and then started wiggling their way up the bed.

Two minutes later

I have Gordy's head on one side of me and Angus's on the other. I believe they sense my pain.

Five minutes later

Angus put his tongue in my ear!!! How disgusting is that? I might not have a boyfriend, but I have got to number six on the snogging scale with my cat.

Saturday June 25th
8:30 a.m.

Woke up and thought I had gone blind. Actually it was because I hadn't taken my mascara off and my eyes had stuck together.

I trailed down to the loo. No one was up, of course. I could hear snoring from practically every room.

In the bathroom

I looked in the mirror. My hair was completely stuck on end, and eye shadow and mascara had dribbled round my eyes like a panda. Also, I must have fallen asleep on my face because my nose was flattened out. Who cares though? My nose could spread itself all over my head for all I cared.

I could become just a nose with arms and legs. A walking nose like Vati. No one likes me. I will never have a boyfriend.

Kitchen

I let the cats out because they couldn't be arsed going through the cat flap. They were just sitting in front of the door, looking at the cat flap and yowling. As soon as I opened the door they dashed straight over the wall and into Mr Next Door's fish pond. They always do this. Every morning they go straight to the fish pond and stare into it. They know very well that there are no goldfish in there. They know because it was them who ate them. Do they think that somehow miraculously during the night the Big Pussycat in the Sky made goldfish rain down?

Huh, I'd like to tell them there is no Big Pussycat in the Sky.

In my bedroom
Back in my bed of pain
10:00 a.m.

I have still got my panda make-up on. I like it. I may never wash again. Sounds of life downstairs. Mum called up: "Georgie, we're off swimming. Want to come?"

I didn't even bother replying. Panda Woman does not go swimming. She stays in her room like Lady Havisham in that Dickens book. What is it called? *Crap Expectations*, I think. Anyway, Lady Havisham is getting married but her fiancé doesn't turn up on her wedding day, so she just sits in her wedding dress gathering cobwebs for years and years. Until she accidentally sets fire to herself with a candle. He's a laugh, Charlie Dickens. Not. He should get together with Call-me-Arnold.

Thirty minutes later

They've all gone out. On my own, all aloney. AGAIN.

I know what will happen. The Ace Gang will be ringing all morning and asking me what happened.

Two minutes later

I wonder if he was with Wet Lindsay last night? I can imagine her face on Monday. All full of herself. Swishing her extensions around like a fool. Uurgh. Oh, I can't stand it. I must run away.

One minute later

I could catch the boat train to Paris and live in a garret.

I could cash in all my savings and just go.

Au revoir tout le monde.

Five minutes later

I haven't got any savings. I forgot I bought those cripply shoes that I had to have surgically removed by the doctor.

In Libby's room
Ten minutes later

I hate to do this, but I am desperate. I will have to raid Libby's piggybank. She will forgive me in years to come and know that her big sis had just had enough.

Two minutes later

What sort of mind thinks you put baked beans in a piggybank?

Unless she thinks it's a real piggy. Which she probably does.

Libby's room is like something in a horror film. There are bits of dolls' arms everywhere and hideous piles of pants with lumps in them.

11:00 a.m.

Heard the doorbell ring.

I'm not answering it. It will probably be Mr Next Door saying the cats have got his wife trapped in the greenhouse. Or they have eaten the Prat Poodles.

Or it will be the police because Grandvati has alarmed his neighbours with his surfing outfit.

Anyway, I am not answering it.

11:05 a.m.

Doorbell rang again. Go away.

11:07 a.m.

Doorbell rang again. I'm not answering it.

11:10 a.m.

The phone rang. Oh God, now what?

11:11 a.m.

I suppose it might be one of the Ace Gang. Maybe I should talk to someone about my inner pain. I feel so bored and depressed anyway.

"Hello, Heartbreak Headquarters."

"*Ciao*, Georgia."

It was Masimo! His voice was absolutely gorgey and groovy and mmmmmmmmmmmm.

Mine of course was like a Mousetwitgirl. "Er... *ciao*."

"Georgia, I am... how you say... *mi dispiace*... sorry I didn't call, but last night it got too late... I was... anyway, you are in now."

I tried to sound jolly and full of casualosity. Not like Panda Woman.

"Oh yeah, yeah I'm in now, in as two in things on... holiday in... In land. Hahahahahaha."

Did I just laugh out loud or was I doing brain laughing?

There was a pause and Masimo said, "So, you will let me in, then?"

I said, "Yeah, just ring the bell when you turn up and—"

The doorbell rang.

Oh giddygodspyjamas, he was at the door!!!

I said into the phone, "But I'm not, er... decent."

He laughed. He wasn't laughing on the phone, he was laughing through the door. I could see his outline through the frosted-glass bit.

I would have to speak back to him through the door! But if I could see his shape through the frosted glass, that meant he might be able to see my shape as well. I stepped behind the phone table. I don't know why. I could see my reflection through the hall mirror. *Gott* in *Himmel*, I looked like a Koch – you know, one of the Koch family from my German textbook. In fact, I looked like a Koch who had been adopted by wolves.

I couldn't answer the door like this. I said, "Erm, I'll just have to get dressed."

He laughed again, "OK, but for me you don't have to." And he laughed. "I will wait for you outside. Oh, here are your cats."

I said, "Don't let them near your trousers."

He said, "Er *che?*" But I had bounded upstairs.

Hysteria Headquarters
Two minutes later

Quickly, quickly put something on. Something sexy yet casually morningy. Jeans? Fringey skirt? Jeans or skirt? Skirt or jeans? OH NOOO, I'M NOT GOING THERE AGAIN.

Jeans on and top with "Groove on, groovster" on it? Yes, yes, good, get on with it.

Two minutes later

I didn't have time to cleanse and tone, so I just cleaned up the panda bits and reapplied mascara and lippy. My hand was shaking, so I didn't attempt eyeliner; I would have ended up with noughts and crosses all over my face.

And for the *pièce de résistance* my brain was having a little conversation with itself. Oh good: "Masimo sounded quite relaxed and cheerful, don't you think? Not in a dumping mood." "Yes. And he said that thing when I said I had to get dressed – 'OK, but for me you don't have to.' That was like a display of red-bottomosity, wasn't it?" "Deffo."

Two minutes later

Dashed down to the bathroom. I had the original bombhead. Oh noooo!!! I slicked it down with gel as much as I could. Then I swallowed about half a tube of toothpaste. My nose seemed a bit flat, so I rolled it around in my fingers to give it a bit more shape.

One minute later

Now then just a practice spontaneous smile. Tongue behind teeth and smile. Good good.

Get manic laughing out of system. Hahahahahahahahadiha hahaha!!!

And a quick burst of Viking disco inferno to stop the urge to show it to him. Kick kick, stab stab and huddly duddly... HOOORRRNNN!

One minute later

Ready.

Sunglasses?

Good plan.

Sunglasses on.

And open door.

And breathe.

There he was by the gate. His scooter was parked in the street and he was sitting on the seat with his back to me, looking at the kittykats. Mr Across the Road must have been cleaning his car, because there was a bucket of soapy water that Gordy was drinking out of. He had got foam all over his chin. Angus was actually *in* the car lying across the steering wheel. Oh yes, and there was Naomi, her head popping up from the front seat. Mr Across the Road would go ballistic when he found them. But who cares?

I didn't say anything. Partly because I was so nervy, but also because my smile meant I couldn't actually form any words. Masimo must have sensed me being there because he looked round. I nearly fainted. He was wearing a really cool ice blue zip-up top and shades. He took his shades off and in the sunlight his eyes were almost yellow. They were amazing, with really thick curly eyelashes that made him look like he was half asleep. He got off his scooter and walked slowly over to me. He even walks in an Italian way, sort of like slow dancing. He is tall and his hair is a bit longer than the lads here have been wearing it, and it's dark and slightly curly. I had forgotten how fabby-looking he is.

I couldn't move because I had lost all gross motor control.

He kept coming towards me. Maybe he would whip my shades off and say, "Why, Georgia, you are beautiful!" like they do in crap films. Or maybe he would whip my shades off, see my squashy nose properly, and shove the shades back on quickly. Shutup, brain, you are not in this!

After what seemed a zillion years, he was right in front of me. He still didn't say anything. He leaned down to me and I thought, *Sound out the bells of England! He's going to kiss me! Everything is going to be all right!*

He did the taking off of my shades thing, and then he gave me a kiss on one cheek and then the other. What did that mean? It was like a stereo lezzie-auntie kiss!

He said, "Let us go and have a little ride somewhere, *cara.*"

I managed to nod. And amazingly my head didn't fall off.

It was a lovely sunny morning and he handed me his spare helmet. I got on the back of the scooter. As he started the engine I was too nervous to touch him, but on the other hand I didn't want to shoot off the back of the scooter when he accelerated away. I put my hands on the back of my seat to hold on, but he said, "Hold on to me." I put my hands on his waist. Just a bit. But he took my hands and put them right round his waist and then accelerated off.

I was so happy to be with him again. He accelerated up the High Street, which was rammed with people. Sadly I didn't see anyone I knew. I wished old Octopussy had seen us. Then we tore down the street and off out of town. I hoped the helmet wouldn't give me the famous Richard III haircut look that is so popular with the criminally insane. I'd worry about that later.

We didn't talk. Well, he said, "Are you all right?" and I did confident nodding until I realised he wouldn't be able to see that unless he was part owl and could turn his head 360 degrees. So I yelled, "Yes, fine!"

Unfortunately, as I spoke, a flying bug flew into my mouth. A really big one, part bug part bat. I nearly choked to death and was trying to spit it out.

Thank God Masimo couldn't see me.

I was coughing and gagging and Masimo said, "What did you say?"

Erlack, erlack, I'd had a bug's bottom in my mouth! But I couldn't say that to a Luuurve God. I finally managed to spit it out and shouted, "I was just singing a song."

He laughed and squeezed my hand. Blimey.

Fifteen minutes later

He pulled up by Downland Woods and helped me off the scooter. I hoped I didn't have bits of bug leg round my mouth, or stuck on to my lip gloss. We left our helmets on the seat and started to walk towards the woods. I walked behind him and did a bit of hair jusshing. Crikey, it was like concrete. My knees were knocking together.

He didn't say anything until we got into the woods, and then he sat down on a fallen tree and sort of patted the space beside him.

Oh, this was fabby and marvy and everything. He was going to snog me. Thank God I had gone easy on the lip gloss. But what if we did that thing where you don't know which side to put your head and you crash heads?

He turned my face towards him and looked right into my eyes and sort of sighed.

Or what if I got Jas disease and had a lip spasm halfway through the snog and had to do pucker release, pucker release? And darty tongue, darty tongue?

Then he kissed me. It was quite a hard kiss and I gripped

on to the log because I didn't want to do my world-famous prat falling off a log act.

Oh, it was so nice to be snogging him again. He put both of his hands on my back and pulled me into him. What were my arms doing just lying there like fools? I thought back to the snogging-lesson days with Whelk Boy. What had he said about arms? Ah, yes, put your hands on his waist. I tried that. Good. The arms were obeying me. Nice work, arms. I don't know how long we were snogging because I didn't have my watch, also my brain had fallen out. I could have easily done it for the rest of my life.

Oh, thank you, Baby Jesus, my prayers have not been in vain. You have not as I thought been too busy to be bothered. I promise I will rescue you from the transvestite world as soon as I get home. And make you new sandals. And a beard.

Eventually Masimo pulled away from me. He gave me a little kiss on the mouth so I had time to recover. He had his hand on the side of my face and he was looking into my eyes. My brain quite literally stopped working. He smiled a really soft, slow smile. Oh, I love him, I love him. He kissed me again softly on the mouth and stroked my hair. (I bet that felt nice with twenty-five pounds of gel on it.)

Then he cleared his throat and said, "Ah, the lovely Georgia, I have missed seeing you. I think you are... how you say... 'mad'. In fact, the Stiff Dylans, they all say, 'Yes, she is mad, that girl.' But they like you. And I like you, very much. Dom told me that you try to get off with his dad and fell through his drum."

Was I going to have to go through this all my life?

Also, that was when I was with Robbie, the boy whose name I will never mention in this life. Anyway, never mind about him, who's name I have forgotten again; this was all good goody good good. I felt like singing, "The hills are alive with the sound of pants." But I didn't.

Then Masimo squeezed my shoulder and stood up. He turned to face me and said, "You asked me – you said you wanted me for you, like how you say in England... to be going out? Is this it?"

Oh yes indeedy, my Pop Star Rock God Luuurve Machine, that is it. He hadn't finished though...

Back in the cake shop of agony

In my bedroom
4:00 p.m.
I'm no longer on the rack of love. I've got off the rack, been to the oven of luuurve, and popped by for a cake from the cake shop of aggers. I'm now lolling in the dustbin of despair. With half-eaten cake all over me.

Masimo said that he doesn't want me to be his girlfriend. He doesn't want anyone to be his girlfriend. He said that it's too soon for him to have a serious relationship with anyone. He would like to still see me, but just like we were before. He said he just wants to have "fun".

Fun.

He said I was "a lovely girl".

Not lovely enough, though, apparently.

I couldn't bear to be with him after he had told me. He put his arm around me and said, "Can we please still see each other? Can I call you?"

I managed to have enough dignitosity to say, "No, I don't think so."

And he said, "I am very sad."

Then for some reason I cheerfully said that I was just popping off to see some friends of mine who lived at the other side of the woods. And I walked off, leaving him there.

After a few minutes I heard his scooter roar off. And I was alone in the woods.

And I didn't have any friends that lived in the forest.

And it took me two hours to walk home. I was so in shock after he had said the bit about not wanting to go out with me that I didn't even notice the two-hour walk home.

There were loads of messages for me when I got in. All from the Ace Gang. Like:

"Phone."

"Double phone with knobs."

And one from Sven: "Oy, missus!!!"

But I couldn't bring myself to ring them back.

5:00 p.m.

Mum brought me a cup of tea. I tried to hide my face when she came in by reading a book, but tears were plopping on to the pages. And it wasn't because the book was *Cinderella*.

Mum said, "Don't worry, the prince comes along in the end, and the shoe..."

But then she realised I was really upset, and she came over and put her arms around me. That made me blub like billio. I told her everything. I said, "He, I (gulp snort), when he came he said... at first I thought he wasn't coming, but he... and then I... to the woods... snogged but I didn't fall off the log... then he said no and I went to visit my forest friends... which I don't have."

Mum told me I would feel better.

I said, "No, I won't."

And she said, "You will."

And I said, "When? In forty years' time, when I am dead? When will I feel better? Today?"

She said, "Well, no, not today."

"This week then?"

"Well, maybe not this week."

"Next week then?"

In the end she said I would feel better "sometime".

It's not much to look forward to, is it?

She asked me if I wanted chish and fipps, but I can't eat anything. My stomach feels as if it's been punched in by twelve very annoyed blokes. And then their mates have come along and jumped on me for a good laugh.

6:30 p.m.

Libby came in to show me her clown shoes. Uncle Eddie has been buying her things from the joke shop. Normally it would have made me laugh, especially as she also had those glasses with eyes that come out on springs. I said, "Not today, Bibbsy. I've got a headache. You have to be quiet."

Amazingly, she did go away, saying, "sssshhhhh" and trying to tiptoe on her enormous shoes. She got out into the hall, still creeping and saying "sssshhhhh", then she closed the door really quietly.

Then she yelled, "Mummmmmeeeeee!!!"

Mum yelled back, "What is it, Bibbs?"

"Ginger's got a headache. FOR CHRIST'S SAKE, SHUT UP!"

Where does she get all this appalling language from?

Fifteen minutes later

I got dressed and went outside into the night. No one would miss me.

8:30 p.m.

I am sitting up the tree in the front garden. Like a dumped owl. My eyes are all swollen up, but I can see into Mr and Mrs Next Door's kitchen window. I wish I couldn't. Mrs Next Door has got a pink flowery winceyette nightie on. Ummm attractive. Mind you, you can't blame her. She is married to the dullest, fattest bloke in the universe (no, not my vati, otherwise that would be bigamy). The Prat Poodles are seated up at the kitchen table, drinking from saucers. How disgusting. AND they have little pyjamas on. Honestly.

Now Mr Next Door has come lumbering in to complete the nightmare scenario. He's got a dressing gown on and you can see his very thin legs – straining to support his vast bottom. They are very very white legs.

More like bean sprouts than legs.

Erlack a pongoes, I nearly fell out of my tree! Mr Next Door isn't wearing ANY pyjamas! He is in the nuddy-pants under his dressing gown! I have been exposed to his nakednosity!! When he picked up one of the Prat Poodles, his dressing gown came apart. I have inadvertently witnessed a porn film.

I quickly changed my position so that I had my back to the Next Doors.

Naomi is on the Across the Roads' wall dragging her bottom along it and mewling. It doesn't seem very romantic, as such, but it is the only way she knows to communicate her love to Angus.

Two minutes later
Well, the mewling and bottom dragging has worked, because here comes the manky tom from up the road. Sniffing around Naomi. Quite literally. And she is not what you would call playing hard to get. Unless you consider lying on your back and sticking your bottom into someone's face playing hard to get.

But that is the harsh reality of life.

Ten minutes later
I wonder what Masimo is doing now. Enjoying himself and his freedom? I bet he's not thinking about me. He probably

says that all the girls are lovely. I wonder if he's taken other girls to that wood.

The only thing I can think of that is worse than what I can think of now is if he starts seeing Wet Lindsay. I bet she would agree to anything he said, like, "Will you wear a bag over your head when we go out anywhere?" Which, I must say, I don't think is an unreasonable request.

Five minutes later

I was getting a bit cold and stiff up in the tree, so I thought I would go back into my bed of pain. Just for a change of places to be miserable in. But then I heard voices and Mark Big Gob came by with his mates, otherwise known as the Blunder Boys, and they sat down on our wall under the tree. They were all smoking like ninnies. You know, in that really crap way that boys who are crap do – taking really deep drags and then nearly choking to death. But still talking while they are choking. And talking such rubbish.

Out of the clouds of smoke and over the sound of the coughing I heard Mark Big Gob say, "Yeah, Charlotte with the big knockers was touching her hair well regularly, so I reckon I'm in."

One of the other super-studs said, in between coughing and scratching his acne, "I reckon we could have a foursome with her mate with the spaggy eye."

Are they mad?

Then Junior Mad came along – Oscar. Fabulous news for his parents that he's tagging along with the chavvest blokes in town.

Mark Big Gob said to him, "Want a fag, mate?"

Oh, this should be good. I'd like to see Oscar choking to death.

But he said, "Na fanks, mate, just put one out."

Yeah, in your dreams, Junior Blunder Boy and twit.

Five minutes later

God, I thought listening to Jas rambling on was boring, but she's like Ms Sparkling Personality in Pants compared to this lot. I will never criticise her for talking about voles again.

The lads stopped flicking ash over our garden wall long enough to start talking about a "ruck" they were planning. Nothing like a spot of recreational violence to impress the ladeez.

Then they all did that hitting-hands thing. Why do they do that?

Eventually they larded off and I could get down from the tree.

If this is what boys are really like, then maybe spinsterhood is not such a bad thing.

9:30 p.m.

When I went back into the house it was strangely quiet. I opened the living-room door and saw a horrible, horrible sight. You know when you read about people walking into their homes and there's a cat smeared all over the walls and a bloke with an axe humming to himself in his undercrackers?

Well, it was worse than that.

Mutti and Vati were in the room together.

Alone.

On the sofa.

Near each other.

And Mutti was stroking Vati's beard!!!

Sunday June 26th
9:00 a.m.

I left a note for Mum:

> Dear Mum,
>   Gone to church. I am very upset still and do not want to talk to anyone about it. Would you answer any calls for me and tell them I am out at Grandad's? I will be back for lunch but I can't eat anything.
>   Love Georgia
>   p.s. Don't tell Dad anything.
>   p.p.s. If you got that cannelloni stuff from Waitrose that I like, I might be able to manage that because it's not very chewy.

Walking to church
9:45 a.m.

Well, God cannot say that I do not try. I have fished his only begotten son Baby Jesus out of Libby's toybox and removed the Barbie frock. I couldn't get all of his blusher off, but I have made a replacement foot out of Blu-Tack. He is on top of my dressing table, and even Libby couldn't get up there. And the kittykats would have to erect scaffolding and a pulley to get him down. Mind you, I wouldn't put that past them. Sometimes when they are behind the sofa supposedly purring, I think they are drilling.

The last time I went to God's house, Call-me-Arnold lost his rag with me. Which is a bit un-Christian. After all, there was no real damage done vis-à-vis the elderly pensioner's scarf inferno incident. And it was her fault. And she hurt my shoulder with her handbag and I didn't mention that.

However, as I could be accused of only really chatting to God when I want something, I had better practise humility before I get there. As I walked along, I tried silent inward prayer: "God, you are so big. And omnipotent, not impotent like I once said by mistake. I would just like to say how we're all really impressed down here by your many wonderous deeds. In particular that turning the wine into, oh no, I mean changing the water into the wine thing, and the walking on water. I know that was Baby Jesus, but deep down it is you that is behind it all. I know that. You just don't blow your own trumpet. Not that you couldn't if you wanted to. I bet you can blow anything you like. Forgive me my trespasses and also my dreadful toadying, but you are just so super."

Home again in my room
12:30 p.m.
What a complete waste of time.

And also weird.

The lady organist (who didn't look to me like an ordinary lady, unless you think being six feet tall, wearing a twinset and having four days' growth of beard is ordinary) played a selection of songs from the shows. I don't think the elderly insane who made up most of the congregation noticed, but personally I didn't go to God's house to hear "Chitty Chitty Bang Bang".

And we had to join in the chorus. With actions.

Call-me-Arnold did his sermon seated at our feet on a beanbag. I think it was mostly about ice cream.

Who knows?

Who cares?

I wasn't listening.

Evening

But maybe even the effort of me going to his pad has in some mysterious way made God think I'm not such a bad person, because I have sort of cheered up. Well, not cheered up, I am still miz, but I have decided to look on the positive side as much as I can. Masimo didn't actually say he didn't like me. In fact, he said he did like me. He just doesn't want a girlfriend. That's not my fault; it's just the way it is. Also, Dave likes me, and I have good mates, and I am not a starving African baby. (In fact, I think I have eaten a bit too much cannelloni.)

So I am girding my loins with a firm hand.

Girdey loins

Monday June 27th

Girdey loins. That is my motto for the day.

8:30 a.m.

Speaking of loin girderers, Jas was waiting for me. Her knickers truly in a twist.

She was going, "Well? Well???"

I said, "Well, what?"

"You know, what happened with Masimo? What did he say? I rang about a zillion times."

"I know."

"All the gang phoned you."

"I don't want to talk about it just now; it's all a bit personal."

"He dumped you, then? Well, actually, he couldn't really officially dump you because you weren't officially going out with him. So technically you are not a dumpee. Which is good, pridewise."

What?

Assembly

All the Ace Gang kept looking at me, but I just held myself with great dignitosity. Maybe I held myself a bit too firmly because Ro Ro whispered, "What's the matter with you? Why are you standing like that? Have you been to the poo-parlour division in your knick-knacks?"

No sign of Wet Lindsay, so I haven't had to do pretendy cheeriness yet.

Break

I told the Ace Gang what happened. Everyone was really nice to me. You know, telling me wise stuff and giving advice. Rosie said, "Eat as many of my cheesy snacks as you like." And undid my crisp packet for me and so on.

Everyone was really really good pals to me.

Apart from Elvis, who came whinging along, telling us to

pick up our wrappers and put them in the bins. I said to him, "Just think, Mr Attwood, when you go to that Big Caretaking Home in the Sky, you can collect rubbish all day long. You could build a little shed made entirely out of rubbish and knit clothes made of... "

He went off complaining and moaning.

As I said to Jools, "Even in the middle of my tragicosity, I can still spread a little sunshine into other people's lives."

Blodge

Is it really necessary to schlep all the way to school to learn that we are lugging about 400 different types of bacteria in our tummies?

And that farts are made up of five different gases?

That will be useful when someone lets fly a knee-trembler. We can all sniff deeply and say, "Yes, yes, I think I got distinct tones of sulphur there, with just a hint of baked bean."

Games
Swimming pool

What you have to remember in times of poonosity is that

there is always someone worse off than yourself. I mean, of course, Nauseating P. Green. I don't want to be mean about her, but it has to be said she is very unfortunate looking. And she really does nothing to help herself. In the swimming pool today she was wearing this swimming costume-type thing that was, well, not normal. It was all frilly and had a sort of skirt on it. She jumped in the deep end to ironic applause, and the voluminous skirty-type fiasco filled up with water and she sank without trace.

Whistles were blown, someone set off the fire alarm, and in the mayhem Elvis was hit by a rogue lifebelt. Don't ask me how. Well, you can ask me how. In the excitement of the rescue attempt, Rosie got carried away and started chucking the lifebelts about with gay abandon and *je ne sais quoi*. Elvis, as usual, was in the wrong place at the wrong time. Which incidentally he always is.

How come he is on lifeguard duty for swimming, anyway? I bet he volunteered and Slim was too stupid to understand his pervy tendencies. Serves him right that he got smacked in the face with a bit of rubber tubing. It was only a glancing blow to his hooter but what a fuss he made. And is it all right for a caretaker/pervguard to say

144

"buggering" in front of minors with impressionable minds?

Then the scariest thing in the universe happened. When the sports student had fished Nauseating P. Green up to the surface and was dragging her to the poolside, Miss Stamp ripped off her trackiebums and dived in, yelling, "Keep breathing, Pamela."

As we sat on the side watching them trying to hook Nauseating P. Green out, I said, kindly, "It will take more than four of them to get her out of the pool: the costume alone must weigh four tons."

Rosie said, "Why is Miss Stamp wearing mohair tights?"

She wasn't wearing mohair tights. The mohair tights WERE her legs. I have never seen the orang-utan gene so rampant. If there had been any first formers in the pool they would have been running into the changing rooms scarred for life and yelling, "Run away, run away. It's a manlady, the manlady is coming."

3:00 p.m.
Still no sign of Wet Lindsay.

I'm sort of relieved and worried at the same time.

Where is she?

♡ 145

Maybe she is even now doing ear nuzzling with the Luuurve God. Despite my loins being as girded as is humanly possible, I do feel a bit of a blubbing extravaganza coming on.

4:10 pm.
On my way to late rounders praccy I passed the sports cupboard, and in it were the two little first-form titches I had seen being given a severe ear-bashing by Wet Lindsay. They were sorting out hockey sticks. Astonishingly Dim Monica was there telling them how to do it. Sadly, I think she actually really cares how the hockey sticks are stacked. In a perfect life she would be married to Elvis. (Not the one who dared to rock, the one who should have been hit by a rock.)

As the littlies lugged things around I said to ADM in a casualosity at all times way, "On your own then, Monica? Lindsay got a touch of bubonic plague, I hope?"

ADM said, "Not that it's any business of yours but Lindsay has been to a conference today, so I am taking over her duties. If that's all right with you?"

"Perfectly all right, Monica. I'm sure you will shove

around little first formers as well as the next man."

Home
I've said it before and I will say it again – whacking things about does really calm your nerves down. At rounders practice it did cheer me up to whack the ball and see all the fielders scampering after it like mad bunnies in knickers. Once again, Nauseating P. Green hit the heights comedywise. She has definitely had a bumper bundle day entertainmentwise. I may make her some sort of award. When it was her turn at batting, she hit the ball enthusiastically, missed it, lost her balance, fell backwards, knocking over Katie Steadman the backstop, who then fell backwards into Miss Stamp. It was like watching elephant tenpin bowling (with an elephant as the bowl).

6:30 p.m.
The whole loon contingency is in for once.

Dad said, "This will cheer you up, Georgia."

I looked at Mum, Mum looked at him and gave him her worst look, and he said, "Not... that you have anything to be not... er... cheered up about. But... great news! Maisie has

 147

been knitting again! I believe you will find something lovely and thoughtful in your bedroom. For myself, I don't know how I have lived without this." And he stuck his feet in the air. At least they should have been feet, but they were sort of one big sock thing with both his feet in. An enormous footwarmersock in subtle shades of purple and yellow.

Mum had got off lightly with a knitted powder compact holder, or so I thought until she showed me her crochet vest. She said, "I think it's, er, quite... well, I might wear it later."

I said, "Please don't."

She went off laughing into the kitchen. Why is everyone so cheerful? They are probably drunk. Or it's early senility. Marvellous. I'll just be old enough to go and live in my groovy pad in Notting Hill Gate and Mutti and Vati will start being brought home by the police because they've been having a picnic on a traffic island. They will want all their food mashed up. Noooooooooo. Shutup brain.

Anyway I won't care about them when I'm older because I will have given myself to the Lord and will be in a lesbian monastery fiddling with my beards... er, I mean beads.

In my bedroom
Ten minutes later

Oh, lovely. Just what I have always wanted. And so suitable for a long hot summer. How did Grandad's girlfriend know the size of my head to knit me a balaclava?

Five minutes later

She didn't, is the answer.

Also, shouldn't balaclavas normally have a hole in the front where your face looms out? Otherwise, to be frank, what she has knit is not a balaclava, it's a head sock. Still, let no one say that I don't know how to enjoy life.

One minute later

I stumbled down the stairs with my head sock on to show my parents my lovely gift. Mum said, "It's the thought that counts."

And I said, "I know, which is why I'm ringing the authorities right now. Anyone who thinks like she does should be locked up out of harm's way."

When I took the comedy balaclava off, I saw that Mum had her crochet top on. With just her bra under it. The crochet holes were so big that the whole of one of her nungas stuck out through it. That is how big the holes were.

Dad said, "Cor, Connie, you sexpot," and then lurched to his "foot" and hopped like a fool over to Mum, before crashing on top of her.

How very disgusting.

I went out into the hall to find Libby in her new knitted ear warmers. She had them over her eyes and was saying, "Naaaice and warmy."

Doorbell rang.

Mum said, "Gee, get that, will you? Your dad thinks his back has gone again."

Typico.

I went to the door.

It was Uncle Eddie.

Oh, the fun times just go on and on. His baldy head was glinting in the moonlight and he was dressed from top to toe in leatherette – a lovely look for a boiled egg. He scruffled my hair and said, "Never eat anything bigger than your head." And lurched into the front room to join the other loons.

In the kitchen

Mutti has just been in to get some *vino tinto* for the elderly loons. She is still wearing her crochet top. I tutted at her and she gave me a kiss on the cheek.

Huh?

one minute later

Miracle of miracles, there is something to eat! Macaroni chiz. Yum yum. Bonkerosity gives me an appetite.

I was scarfing it down when I heard the "music" begin. They are all laughing and cackling in the front room. I know this mood, the next thing it will be... yes, I was right, "Dancing Queen" by Abba.

Why are they so cheerful? Give them a gaily-coloured plastic bag and they'd be beside themselves with happiness. I wonder if I'm adopted. I am so different from them. Vati yelled out, "Georgia, snacks!"

Of course I'm not adopted. Vati is far too lazy to bother with the paperwork.

I was just going to go up to my room when Vati said, "Gee, if you bring snacks I will consider giving you a couple of squids."

Three minutes later

When I came back into the front room with the crisps, I was not amazed to see the horrific sight of Mum sitting on Dad's lap, wearing her prostitute's crochet top – in front of Uncle Eddie. Uncle Eddie was resting his wineglass on his tummy and saying, "I was in the curry shop and the waitress came over to ask me how the biriani was. I was eating my curry and she was practically resting her boobs on my shoulder."

I said, "Oh God, you said 'boobs', that is soooo disgusting!"

Uncle Eddie said, "I only said 'boobs' out of respect for your mother. Normally I say 'tits'."

I went up to my room. I feel physically sick.

My bedroom
8:30 p.m.

What kind of people have an impromptu mid-week vicars-and-tarts party to celebrate the fact that Dad and his mates who play football lost by only ten goals at their last match? My parents, that's who.

Vati burst into my room like a red-faced loon in a dog collar and black tights. Sadly he does in fact look quite a lot like Call-me-Arnold. He was quickly followed by Uncle Eddie, also in black tights and T-shirt. He has drawn a fringe with eye pencil all round his bald head like a mad monk. Good grief.

Uncle Eddie said, "Here's a joke to cheer you up, Gee."

I said, "Father, Uncle Eddie, if you could just go away for ever and be mad somewhere else, that would be lovely. Thank you."

But he just went madly on. "Anyway, this bloke goes up to this house and he's dragging a box behind him. And he says... and he says..."

And then he started laughing and choking so much, I thought I might have to do the Heimlich Manoeuvre, which I am actually in the mood for. Grabbing and shaking someone from behind might get rid of a lot of nervy spasmodosity.

Sadly he recovered himself and went on: "Anyway, he says to the woman who answers the door, 'Are you Mrs Jones the widow?' and she says, 'Well, I'm Mrs Jones but I'm not a widow,' and he says, "Ah, well, you haven't seen what I've got in the box.'"

And then he had to sit down in his extremely snug tights,

he was laughing so much. He will never ever get up again. That is a fact.

10:30 p.m.
The tarts and vicars are in the garden. They've put the loudspeakers outside so that the whole world can enjoy the joy of Status Quo "Down Down, Viva I'm Down."

Five minutes later
Dad has brought out a cake with a huge Roman candle firework in the middle of it.

One minute later
Dad is making a crap speech, which fortunately I can't hear, but I can see his chins wiggling about, so he must think it's funny.

One minute later
Now he's bending over and lighting the Roman candle.

One minute later
Absolutely top!!! Dad has set fire to his own moustache. Blazing!

I think I can sleep easy now. Life does indeed have a bright side.

Tuesday June 28th
In the kitchen

I noticed Dad was clean shaven at breakfast. I said to him, "Vati, what has happened to the little beaver that used to live on the end of your chin?"

But he didn't even bother to reply – just grumped around and went off to "work".

11:00 a.m.

On my way to English I stopped off in the tarts' wardrobe because I had an unexpected piddly-diddly urge. When I came out I saw Lindsay. Octopus head is back. Will we never be free?

She was walking along on her twiglike legs, swishing her naff extensions around. I ignored her but she had something to say: "Georgia Nicolson, well, well, without your silly mates for once. I'm glad that you took my advice about Masimo. I'd like to say you were sadly missed at the club last night, but you weren't. Anyway, we stayed up till way past your bedtime; it was gone nine thirty."

She knows, she knows. Masimo must have told her what happened. Oh, this is sooooo horrible. I don't think I can stand it.

English
In the gym

I can't think of anything except the fact that Lindsay knows about what happened. Miss Wilson wants us to "get in the mood" for *MacUseless*, so we're having yet another workshop fiasco in the gym.

Miss Wilson was rambling on in her sad pinafore dress – yes, pinafore dress – saying, "Oh, this is so exciting. Only days to go till the big night. Come on! Let's get the energy really building. Let's feel that energy, girls!"

While she did that, we all lay down on the gym mats. Or in Rosie's case, hung upside down on the wall bars. Like a bat in frilly black knickers. Mr Attwood will be in in a minute with his perv antenna on high alert.

Miss Wilson was trying to get our attention by clapping. Good luck. She said, "Girls, can I... could I just get you to... er, Rosie, would you mind coming down from the wall bars, and the girls under the vaulting horse, would you just come out now? I want us to begin today's intensive workshop by getting into different characters physically."

I said to Jools, "Lord save us, we aren't going to have to be vegetables again, are we? I'm not in the mood for cabbage dancing, or whatever."

Eventually we all got up and Miss Wilson shouted stuff out and we had to do it. She said, "Macbeth is tortured by his actions. How does that feel? What does it look like? No, Rosie, I don't think that Macbeth would, erm, hang himself with a skipping rope. Can you just put it down now? Right, first of all imagine the weary walk of someone who is feeling very depressed."

Brilliant. Thank you, God. Not.

Ten minutes later

Actually, even though I didn't have to imagine the weary walk of someone who is very depressed, because I WAS someone who was feeling very depressed, I did begin to cheer up at the comedy opportunities of the class. The Ace Gang did marvellous group limping as the Hunchbacks of Notre Dame.

Miss Wilson said, "Very good, girls, but perhaps the person is not crippled, just very depressed. And perhaps depression doesn't always involve so much dribbling. Let your imaginations flow. When I clap my hands and shout out, the next person quickly change into character – and (clap) – now be a happy slender young girl hurrying to meet her boyfriend – and change!"

Oh, the cruelty of life. If God is omniwhatsit, surely he is having a laugh. At me. First a depressed person, now a young girl going off to meet her boyfriend. God pretended he didn't mind about me not rescuing Our Lord from Libby's toy box sooner than I did, but this is his revenge. Nauseating P. Green was skipping round like a fool. If I was her boyfriend that she was skipping to meet, I would have run off quickly to the boyfriend-asylum-seeker's home.

Rosie was doing her famous orang-utan impression. Actually it was very realistic, and it is how she goes off to meet Sven.

Jas had a field day fringe-flicking wise, and actually when she thought I wasn't looking she was puckering and relaxing. And doing a bit of darty tongue. She is still haunted by her lip-spasm fiasco. Ah well, how sad, never mind.

Ellen was still sitting down on a bench dithering about. The bell will have gone before she manages to even set off to meet her imaginary boyfriend. So no change there.

Miss Wilson was encouraging people and walking round showing us what she would look like going to meet her boyfriend (scary, sad and with an alarming smile on her face). Then she said to me, "Georgia, you're still limping. And your back is all hunched over."

Yeah and it's not just on the outside.

Walking home
4:30 p.m.

Talking about the Wet Lindsay nightmare scenario.

Rosie said, "What makes you think that she knows?"

I told them what she said about the club and everything.

Rosie said, "Ah, I see, say no more, say no more, wink wink, nod nod." And started doing the mad nodding-dog thing, and chewing. They were all joining in. I was in the nodding-dog parlour of life.

Jas for once came up with a sort of sensible plan. "Look, I'll ask Tom what's going on." She looked at me from underneath her fringe and did quite a nice smile. "I'll tell

 159

him to be, you know, well, not shouty or anything."

I almost kissed her. I said, "Thanks, Jas, you can be a real pally sometimes and I, well, I..."

Rosie noticed I was about to go off on a blubathon and said quickly, "Hey, do you know what book Tarzan wrote? Eh eh?"

We all shook our heads, expecting the worst. And we got it.

"*Lord of the Swings.*"

It was so crap, I must say it did make me laugh. A bit.

Jools said, "Oh, by the way, I meant to tell you Katie Steadman is having another party at the weekend and we are invited."

I don't really feel like parties, but I suppose I have to go on being me.

Friday July 1st
1:00 p.m.

Something unusually good has happened! I think. Maybe.

We normally get made to go out at lunch and freeze around in the grounds while the Hitler Youth (prefects) loll around in the warmey warm inside. So that is why we creep back inside and lurk around the science labs, usually the physics lab, so that if there is a sudden Hitler Youth investigation we can leap into the fume cupboards and pull down the blinds. And crouch there until they go out again. As an additional security measure we crouch down underneath the windows so that we can't be seen from outside. And we heap our science overalls on top of us in case someone comes in and we don't have time to do the leaping-into-the-fume-cupboard scenario, and we can pretend to be a pile of science overalls.

Actually, as it happens, it is absolutely boiling today. At least 180 degrees in the shade.

Ellen said, "Can't we just go outside? Instead of, you know, er, being nearly dying from heat underneath a pile of old overalls... or something."

The rest of the gang started nodding. I had to take a firm grip of the situation. I said, "Yes, yes, of course It would be nice sitting outside in the sunshine, maybe sunbathing and so on... But remember Good Queen Bess – a principal is a principal and we will never give in to the tyrannical ways of... Anyway, everyone under the science overalls. Look natural!"

one minute later

Where was I?

Oh yes, under the window. Which was open. We were just chatting about the wedding. Rosie said, "Sven is wondering what to wear."

I said, "Oh dear. And, anyway, why is he bothering to worry about it? It's never going to happen. Even in five and a half years' time."

Rosie said, "Ah, well, you have always been cynical, Georgia; that is because you have been in the oven of love too many times. But as it happens we are going to have a practice wedding quite soon."

"Don't talk absolute WUBBISH."

Rosie raised her eyebrows at me and said, "So what do you think about flares versus lederhosen?"

We were just about to start discussing flares versus lederhosen when we heard voices and had to shut up sharpish. Especially as we realised it was Wet Lindsay and ADM (Astonishingly Dim Monica). We could hear them clearly, talking outside the open window. We formed ourselves into a convincing pile of science overalls and earwigged.

ADM said, "Well, what did he actually say?"

Wet Lindsay said, "He said that he didn't want to be serious because he had had a relationship before and he was, you know, having a break from serious relationships."

ADM said, "What are you going to do?"

Wet Lindsay said, "Well, of course I'm going to get him to change his mind. The only slight worry is that he started saying that he'd had to upset someone he really liked already, and it sounded like he meant someone here, not in Italy. But he wouldn't say who it was."

ADM said, "Do you have any idea who it is?"

Then Wet Lindsay said the fateful words: "I don't think it can be possible, because she is the most snivelling idiot I have ever come across, but... well... no, it can't be possible. He's not stupid or desperate enough."

ADM went on, "You don't mean... not...?"

Wet Lindsay said, "I know, it would be unbelievable, wouldn't it? But I'm going to keep an eye out, and if I see it's her, well... I just wouldn't be her, that's all."

Then they went off.

Rosie stuck her head out of the overall pile and looked at me. I looked back at her and she gave me the thumbs-down:

"Ohmygiddygodspyjamas, you are dead meat! Deader than the deadest meat in a dead-meat shop!! Give me back your wedding invite. I'll give it to someone who's going to be alive for the wedding."

Emergency Ace Gang meeting
Afternoon break

I said, "Do you think she thinks it's me?"

Jas said, "Well, it's pretty conclusive, isn't it? She said, 'the most snivelling idiot I have ever come across'."

I said, "I didn't know that YOU had been seeing Masimo. Tom the Slug King is going to be very upset."

That shut her up. But it didn't shut me up. "If it is me, then that's quite good in one way because he said he really liked the maybe-it's-me person. Which is really good, isn't it?"

Jools said, "Yes, but what if it isn't you?"

Oh God. What if there are two snivelling idiots that he likes?

Physics

Is it me?

Is he sorry he upset me?

Oh buggeration, I am on the rack of luuurve again. Pass the agony cakes.

Physics is unusually boring today. We are doing statistics. Why?

Rosie wrote me a note: Guess what Slim's vital statistics are: 84, 76, 84 — and that's just the chin area.

I gave her my Klingon salute.

I can't help thinking and thinking about the Wet Lindsay scenario. On the one hand, I am sooooo happy that he might be upset that he upset me, because that would mean he was upset about upsetting me. Which is *bon*. On the negative side, if it is me, Wet Lindsay will kill me.

But even if it is me, it still means that he's not going out with me.

But he might secretly sort of want to.

Five minutes later

I need to make him see that it's me that he wants. I must take advice from the *How to Make Any Twit Fall in Love with You* book and increase my mysteriosity and glaciosity so that he can come pinging back like an elastic band. Maybe if I had a pretendy boyfriend he would get jealous and realise the error of his ways.

Five minutes later
I'll ask Dave the Laugh what he thinks I should do.

One minute later
No, I can't do that because of what he said about the liking business and about messing it up. Also he would start all that Pizza-a-gogo thing again and pretend that Masimo was a girl in disguise and only cared about his hair, etc.

Two minutes later
But in essence, Dave the Laugh likes me.

Two minutes later
And I like him. Dave the Laugh likes me, I like him. What could be more simple pimple?

One minute later
It's not like we're silly children. What's needed here is maturiositiness. Which I have in abundance. Dave and I

could go out together just liking each other. That would be OK. It would be fun.

One minute later
Lots of fun.

Lots and lots of fun.

What's wrong with a boy and a girl who like each other having fun? I like going out. Dave likes going out. We both like having fun.

I can think of all sorts of things we could do. All kinds of places we could go out to.

One minute later
We could go to, oh, I don't know, we could maybe, er... well, for instance, just off the top of my head, er... well, there's a Stiff Dylans gig on in a couple of weeks' time. We could go there for fun.

One minute later
And dance about having fun.

One minute later

Dancing about having fun in front of Masimo – and then see how he likes that!!!

Two minutes later

Oh God, I have once more, in my mind, made Dave the Laugh my decoy duck.

A nip-libbling decoy duck. Who is vair vair good at snogging.

But I would never use Dave like that. Not in a trillion years.

One minute later

He would sus me out, anyway.

One minute later

Unless I was full of subtletosity.

And snogged him to within an inch of his life.

Two minutes later

I have got an internal red bottom that must be struck down. Get thee behind me red bottom!!!

Mad Headquarters
Otherwise known as MacUseless rehearsals
4:30 p.m.

Miss Wilson gave us her "rousing" rehearsal speech, but Rosie spoiled the effect by burping really loudly. She told Miss Wilson it was "pre-performance gaseous interchange". Let no one say that we don't learn anything in blodge.

Funnily enough, there is no sign of Dave the Laugh. I hope he's not got the lurgy.

Five minutes later

I don't know if it's just me, but there's a mood of hysteria about the company today. Probably because it's only a week to the performance and no one apart from old swotty knickers Jas knows their words properly.

Just as we were having to brief Spotty Norman on taking over on lights for Dave, the door crashed open and he walked in with his tie knotted round his head like a fool.

Miss Wilson started giving him her idea of a bollocking, i.e., "Well, this is really... I mean, it's ten minutes since we started and really it would be nice if you could, erm, be on time."

Dave said, "Time waits for no pants. But I'm here now; let's get this show on the road."

He said hello to his mates and then came over to where I was standing at the side of the stage. I kept my eyes down because I thought he might be able to read my mind and see that I'd been planning to use him as my decoy duck. Actually, he said, "Oy, missus, stop looking at my manly parts."

I tried to have a strop, but he does make me laugh, so I ended up smiling at him.

We started the rehearsal on a high note with the witches scene, "Hubble bubble toil and pants." Rosie in a fit of inspiration stopped stirring the cauldron and segued into a bit of the Viking disco inferno dance. She still had the branch that she used for stirring, but she was free-forming with it. Stab, stab to the right, stab, stab to the left and HOOOORN!

Dave and I burst into spontaneous applause, but Miss Wilson said she was being silly. Rosie said, "I have just introduced a note of Vikingness into the play, Miss Wilson. I think Billy would have liked it."

Miss Wilson was madly doing her buttons up. "Rosie,

Vikings had nothing to do with Shakespeare's *Macbeth*."

Dave said, "Are you sure, Miss Wilson? perhaps Billy didn't tell you everything."

Eventually Miss Wilson managed to get us all back in our positions and on with the play. For a while things were going relatively smoothly. But then it all went downhill. Nauseating P. Green accidentally set off the starting pistol used for the battle scene, and Dave started yelling, "Save yourselves, save yourselves," and racing around. Elvis Attwood came panting up with his fire bucket ready to bury someone in sand should fire break out. He told Nauseating P. Green to mind where she put her bum in future, and stomped off to fiddle with his extinguishers. Miss Wilson managed to get us back onstage again, but then we got to the banquet scene. Now I have to say, in all fairness, none of us really thinks that the juggling and fire-eating improvised scene is a good idea. Melanie is absolutely hopeless at the juggling oranges bit. She more or less just chucks them in the air and they fall all over the place and then she picks them up. It's not as such my idea of juggling. It is actually just chucking oranges about. And as I said to Miss Wilson, "Wouldn't Billy Shakespeare have written it in if he thought it was a good idea?"

Miss Wilson said, "Now, er, that's an interesting point, Georgia, because you see, in Elizabethan times, the play would be, er... well, a sort of moveable feast. The players would take the text and use... well, their own ideas. Like, er... I've had an idea about the juggling and, er, fire and so on."

Rosie said, "Well, what did the Bird of Avon think about your idea?"

Miss Wilson started fiddling with her cardigan buttons. "Well, of course he isn't, well, he couldn't comment on my idea because as you know—"

Dave said, "Was he angry with you because you wouldn't go out with him, Miss?"

Walking home together

The usual suspects. Ellen is going to develop very very strong legs if she keeps on walking home with us. She must be doing an extra ten miles walking a day, such is her luuurve for Dave the Laugh.

Rosie said, "I saw the way Nauseating P. Green was looking at Spotty Norman and I think I could smell romance backstage."

Rollo said, "Sorry about that. I let off during the witches bit."

Jools laughed like a loon on loon tablets. Honestly. Girls can be such divs around boys. Ellen dribbling about Dave, Jools laughing at fart jokes, and Jas hand-in-hand with Tom. Thank goodness I have some pridenosity.

Dave said, "Mr Attwood's a plucky little woman, isn't he?"

Ellen said, "Oh, well, he's not... I mean, he's not a woman."

I looked at her. Dave looked at her. I see no romance made in heaven for her and Dave.

Fifteen minutes later

Just me and Dave. Ellen once again will be nearing home by midnight. She caught the bus at last, still looking moonily after Dave. He gave her a bit of a lazy peck on the cheek and she almost fell over. After she'd gone, he looked at me and went, "What? What?" But he knows what. The sunlight caught his eyes and he looked really, I don't know... maybe it's the time of year, but I think I have slightly got the General Horn. But no no no, mine is not the way of the Horn.

Dave said, "I wouldn't mind being a girl for a day."

I said, "Wow, you mean so you could really know what it feels like to have girly like stuff?"

He looked thoughtful. Dave can be really deep and nice and he is good-looking. Oh blimey, if he tries to snog me, I don't think I've got the power to resist. Then he said, "Yeah, exactly, if I was a girl for a day, I'd just stand in front of a mirror and look at my nungas all day. And feel them whenever I wanted to. S'later, Kittykat."

And he went off quite quickly. How weird. Usually he comes nearly to my house with me, but he didn't. Maybe he's got footie practice or something. Or maybe he's meeting someone. A girl, maybe. A date.

Nearly home
Good. That would be good for him to have a date. Nothing to do with me.

In my room
I wonder who will be at Katie Steadman's party?

Masimo probably won't be there.

Dave will be, though, I should think.

Maybe with his new mystery girlfriend.

I bet she is vair plain.

Mate of the century

Saturday July 2nd

Downtown

Lunchtime

Even though I was not in the mood, the Ace Gang had a spontaneous danceathon outside a record shop. It was playing a really loud song that you could hear in the street, so we thought we'd give the shoppers the benefit of our disco inferno. I think they were impressed, although there was the usual grumbling from the pensioners.

1:30 p.m.

Churchill Square was full of lads all marauding about slapping their hands and fingers and generally acting like prats. One of the prats was looking so hard at our nungas as

175

we passed that he crashed into a shop window.

The theme of Katie's party is "rock".

And no, I don't mean we're all going as striped things with "Blackpool" written down the middle of us. Or boulders.

We have to go as rock chicks and air guitarists and so on. I suppose it will be a laugh and, anyway, I'm not impressing anyone, so who cares what I look like?

Boots

I've got some really dark red lipstick and nail polish and I know Mum will have some ludicrous top I can borrow in lurex or lycra. And I'll wear my three-quarter suede boots.

Evening

In the bedroom of life, tarting myself up for another long evening of goosegogging and silly dancing. But ho hum pig's bum, I mustn't forget that I may well be the person that Masimo likes and doesn't want to upset. Yessss!!! Or possibly noooooo. At least my mates will be there and also Dave the Laugh. You know, in a friendy way that will be nice.

Clock tower
7:00 p.m.

Jools, Mabs, Ellen and Jas were there when I came up the hill. Blimey O'Reilly's trousers, they are all quite literally rock chicks. Everyone is wearing black with just a hint of black. Even Jas has backcombed her hair. Because I will not be snogging anyone tonight, I have been able to risk the boy entrancers. I got some in Boots with the sparkly bits in them. I think they look vair vair cool.

I said to the gang, "Where's Rosie?"

Jools said, "She rang just before I left to say that Sven was having trouble getting his trousers on, so they would meet us at Katie's."

Good grief.

Katie Steadman's house
7:40 p.m.

The house looks quite cool, actually. Katie's got disco lights everywhere, and a boy dressed all in leather (hmmm, that will be nice later on as it's about a million degrees tonight) is at the record decks.

7:45 p.m.

There are fairy lights hung in the trees in the garden! I'm almost beginning to cheer up.

Katie gave us some snacksies and said, "Everyone is going to come – all the lads from sixth-form college, the Foxwood crowd, the St John's boys, er, who else? Oh yeah, the Dame and his mates, and the girls from Moorgrange are bringing mates. I even saw Dom, you know from the Stiff Dylans, and he said they would try and pop by."

She went away and I just stood there. I turned to Jas, who was eating her sausage roll like she hadn't eaten anything for about a fortnight, AND we'd had cheesy snacks on the way here. "Did you hear that, Jas? Did you? Did you? Did you hear that?"

She was chewing and went, "Ummmnff."

"Jas, is that yes or no?"

"Nnfff."

I took it as a yes.

"The Stiff Dylans are coming and do you know what that means? That means that Masimo will be coming, because he's in the Stiff Dylans."

She didn't seem a bit interested, too busy eating her

178

sausage thing and beaking around, looking at who was there and who they were with and so on. She is very superficial.

I was going to tell the others about the Luuurve God and ask their gang advice when there was the sound of yodelling. Sven had arrived. Crikey, his trousers were the tightest I had ever seen. And he was wearing a fringed cowboy jacket and cowboy hat. Both silver. I don't know what sort of rock bands they have in Lapland, or wherever he comes from, and I don't want to. Rosie was not much better. She had on the tiniest dress and thigh-length boots with shades. (I don't mean the boots had shades; they were not that famous.)

Sven came over to us. "Hello, you wild and sexy chicks. Take me! Use me, you lady animals!!!" And then he picked us up one by one, bent us backwards and kissed us full on the mouth. It is absolutely no use appealing to either him or Rosie. The music started and he went off into one of his alarming dance routines. How he manages to do the splits in those trousers I will never know. It was a very good job that Katie had cleared everything from the room. The leather DJ person looked alarmed. I bet he was hoping he chose records that Sven liked.

♥ 179

8:45 p.m.

The party is really rocking now. Masses of people have arrived. No sign of Masimo or the Stiff Dylans, though. My nerves are shot to pieces. I have to go to the piddly-diddly department about every two seconds. Should I take the boy entrancers off to save any incidents?

Having a breather in the garden
9:30 p.m.

As usual the whole thing has turned into a snogathon.

The Dame arrived with his mates and he made a beeline for me. "Hello, gorgeous, remember me?"

Oh yes, I remembered the Dame. Since I had used my sticky-eyes technique on him at one of Rosie's parties, he was like my slavey boy. I wouldn't mind, but I had only been using him to make Dave the Laugh jealous.

Speaking of which, I wonder where Dave is. Not that I care.

The Dame was looking at my mouth and then let his eyes drift down to my nunga area. Did he really think that was sexy? Then he said, "Do you fancy, you know, coming outside with me?"

I said, "We are outside."

Any normal person would have seen the light then, but not the Dame. "Yeah, but do you want to come even more outside?"

Is he mad? I am never using the sticky-eye technique again. I was wondering whether I could just deck him and run when Dave the Laugh appeared at my elbow. He winked at me. "Good evening, sensation seekers."

I've never been so glad to see anyone in my life. I gave him my biggest smile, not even bothering to not let my nose spread out all over my face. I said, "Dave!!! Fabby to see you!"

He looked a bit surprised. "Steady there, soldier. I know I'm gorgeous, but..."

I got hold of his arm and said, "I love this one – let's dance." And I dragged him on to the dance floor.

Half an hour later

I must say I do have a lorra lorra larfs with Dave, and he is a cool dancer. He does this pretend-air-guitar leaping thing that really makes me laugh. We even did a bit of back-to-back air-guitar dancing and lowered ourselves to the floor and back up again. Everyone clapped.

10:40 p.m.

Rosie was holding two drinks in her hands, talking to me about her lovely imaginary wedding. "I think for snacks we'll have a reindeer theme."

Then her "fiancé" came up from behind her and pulled her pants down. Honestly. Her pants were round her ankles and she couldn't pull them up because of her hands being full. Sven went off doing his mad dancing, shouting, *"Oh jah, oh jah!"* his electric-coloured trousers shining on the dance floor.

Rosie said to me, "Take the drinks, ohmygod, ohmygod, quick quick."

But I was laughing too much. I wanted to help her, but it was just too funny.

In the end she had to shuffle over to a table with her undercrackers round her ankles to put the glasses down. Then she pulled her knickers up and went on the warpath to find her "fiancé". Vair funny, actually.

11:00 p.m.

I lost everyone for a moment, and I was so hot from the dancing that I went outside to get some air. I was leaning against the wall when Dave fell out of the French windows. He saw me and said, "It's our song, Kittykat! Let's ROCK!"

He tried to drag me back inside, but I said, "Oh, I can't, I'm too hot, I've got to have a breather."

He said, "Hang on, missus, I'll get us drinks."

He disappeared inside and I could see him grooving his way through the dance floor, stopping to dance with groups of girls as he did. He is such a flirt.

He danced his way back with the drinks and we went and stood against a tree at the bottom of the garden. It was a really lovely summer's evening and I didn't even resent the stars any more. In fact, they reminded me of my night with Masimo. I wondered if the Luuurve God would come. Then I thought that even if he did, it might be quite good for him to see me in the garden with Dave. It might hint at the right amount of glaciosity.

As I drank my drink I looked over the rim of the glass at Dave and he looked back at me. It seemed like ages that we just looked at each other. Then he took the glass out of my hand and put it down on a bench. He took my face in both his hands (I don't mean he ripped it off my neck) and he leaned down and kissed me. He did his nip-libbling thing.

Wow, no one could deny – however much they might luuurve a Luuurve God – that Dave is top at snogging. I was just beginning to get the old jelloid knees and liquid-brain scenario when Dave stopped. No no no not the stopping thing!!!

He said, "Oh no, miss, I am not going through this again." And he lightly smacked my bum and went off into the house.

What? What?

Why did he smack my bum? Why did he stop nip libbling? What does he mean "I'm not going through this again"?

I may be having a spaz attack.

I stayed in the garden for a bit and then went back into the house to find the gang. Sven had taken over the controls of the music station, and the DJ was saying, "Er, could you give me back my equipment, mate?"

Sven put his arm around him. Hmm. Then he kissed the DJ on the lips. I thought Leatherboy was going to throw up. But he has senseless courage, that has to be said, because he wrestled the controls back from Sven. Sven didn't mind, he just stood with his arm around Leatherboy and nodded along to the music.

Jools and Rollo were snogging and dancing at the same time, so they were no use. Jas had gone home early because she wanted to be "fresh" for her ramble with Tom tomorrow. I could see Ellen chatting to Dave the Laugh, so I wouldn't be joining them. I couldn't find Mabs anywhere. She was probably under a pile of coats somewhere snogging. She has very little pridenosity when it comes to having the General Horn.

I went into the kitchen and Ro Ro was in there collecting snacks for Sven. She said, "It's a laugh, isn't it?"

And I said, "Not many, benny."

As she went out, Katie came in and said, "I'm having a groovy time, loads of peeps, aren't there? Really groovy crowd. It's a shame the Dylans couldn't come, but Dom said they had an important meeting."

Oh, typico.

As I came out of the kitchen I saw Dave coming out of the living room with his jacket on. I must have really upset him if he was stropping home. I said to him, "Dave, are you going, maybe I'll..."

And as I said that, Emma Jacobs from St Mary's came out of the room with her coat on. Dave took her hand and said to me, "Yeah, we're quitting the scene, maaaan. Stay cool, mate." Emma looked all girly at him, and they went off out into the night.

I didn't want to talk to the others about it, so I thought I'd give Dave and Emma a few minutes and then I would sneak off myself. I felt really really weird.

11:30 p.m.
I am quite literally tossed about on the sea of life.

Up whatsit creek without a paddle.

Or even a canoe.

Why do I feel so weird about Dave going off with someone else? Serves me right because I was only going to use him as a decoy-duckie thing. Except that it wasn't just that, because I really like him, and when I was kissing him I forgot about everything else. Even the fact that I am madly in luuurve with Masimo.

Five minutes later
The streets are really quiet and I can see into lighted houses where people are having indoor fun. And I'm outside on the unfun road.

186

I am full of confusiosity. Sometimes I feel so desperate, I almost wish I was like Jas. Not in the undercracker-obsession department, but the way she just luuurves Hunky and doesn't think about anyone else. Maybe it's because he really likes her and doesn't like anyone else and that encourages her. Or maybe it's because her mutti and vati are like that. Maybe if she had a prostitute and a madman for parents she wouldn't be so bloody smug and happy. Besides which, she went off home without even coming to find me and see if I was all right. So I am obliged to hate her.

Five minutes later
Dom lives around here somewhere. In fact, I think this is his street. I wonder if he's still going out with that girl? I expect he is; everyone else seems to stay together with people. They are not slaves to the Horn.

One minute later
Ohmygiddygod, there's Dom with his girlfriend! They're sitting on a doorstep. It must be his house. I don't want to let him see me walking home alone. He'll tell Masimo he saw me sadly wandering about like a cloth-eared loon, and

 187

that really will be the end of any chance I have for glaciosity and verve. If I walk really slowly backwards they might not notice me, and then I can get round the corner and—

Dom looked up to see me walking backwards. He called out, "Hey, Georgia, what's happening?"

Oh goddygod.

I waved casually. "Hi, Dom... just, just, dropped my er... keys."

What???

Dom got up and said, "Oh no, bummer, hang on, I'll come and help you look. Oh, and Masimo is inside. I'll tell him you're here."

What???

Nooooooooo.

I almost screamed at him, "NO... er, I mean, like, don't bother him, I..."

But Dom had already gone inside, followed by his girlfriend, who looked at me in a funny way. I bet she has got girl radar: I bet she knows that I haven't dropped my keys and that I'm just wandering the streets lonely as a clud. Maybe I could hide before they come back? Yes, yes that is it; that's the sensible thing to do. I could just duck down behind a car and they would go away.

Ducked down behind a car
Thirty seconds later

Yes, yes this will work. If I just stay here until they go away, that will be good and fine. Yes yes. Still as a little mouse. I am a small invisible mousey girl.

As I was crouching down a man came by walking his dog. He looked down at me and said, "Are you all right, love?"

And his bloody dog was licking my face.

I said, "Yes, yes, I..."

"Have you lost something?"

"No, er, I mean yes, yes, it's my keys." (Goawaygoaway, stop the licking thing, be gone!)

I heard voices from the other side of the road, and Mr Mad Neighbourly shouted across, "Dominic, there's a young lady here who has lost her keys. Come and have a look, will you? My eyes aren't so good at night."

Good enough to come and spy on perfectly innocent people hiding behind cars, you nosey wally-type person. Why couldn't he be like our neighbours – mad and unhelpful? But, oh no, he had to come HELPING along. What was I going to do?

One minute later

From my position on the ground I could see a lot of legs. This was beyond the Valley of the Very Nearly Quite Tragic and entering the Arena of the It's All Gone Terribly Terribly Wrong.

Then I heard the words, "Georgia? *Ciao. Come stai?*"

Excellent, a Luuurve God has landed.

How does he think I am?

He has dumped me because I am not full of sophisticosity, and now he finds me crouching down behind a car in the middle of the night, with a dog licking my bum.

The only possible thing to do was to look up with a casualosity at all times sort of air about me.

I did. I looked up and smiled and said, "Blimey, Masimo, what a... surprise! Yes, yes, I am, er... fabbio, thanks."

I stood up quickly and said, "Ahahahah! Found them!"

I was deliberately not looking at Masimo. Dom said, "Oh brilliant, where were they?"

"Oh, they must have dropped out of my handbag when I... when I got... when I got my... torch out."

Why did I say that? What kind of person carries a torch with them in a fully-lit street? I'll tell you what kind of person. An imaginary kind of person who is telling enormous porkies. Thank goodness it was night – at least they couldn't see that my whole head was scarlet with just a hint of beetroot.

I risked a glance at Masimo and he was sort of smiling. Does he have to look so gorgey all the time? Then it occurred to me, maybe he thought that I was stalking him, that I'd been hiding behind cars, looking at him. Oh nooo.

I said, "I... er... was at Katie's party."

Dom said, "Oh yeah, shame we couldn't come. Mind you, tight leather jeans are not my best look. But your, er, top is cool."

I looked down at my outfit. Oh excellent, how much like a prostitute did I look lurking around the streets in thigh-length boots and lurex? Happy happy days. I said, "Oh, thanks. Yes, it was a hoot, but it was a bit of a young crowd – you know, silly dancing, that sort of thing – so I took a shortcut home and..."

Masimo still hadn't said anything. But then he said, "Maybe I should walk to your house with you, in case you... lose another thing... maybe your, how do you say in English?"

He said something to Dom in Italian and Dom laughed and said, "Compass."

Oh God, they were laughing at me.

I felt an enormous uncontrollable strop coming on. I was deffo heading for nervy b central, so the best thing I could do was to leave quickly.

I said, "I'll be fine, thank you. I'll just say good night to you both."

Oh brilliant, I was sounding like some twat from Dickens. I was amazed I hadn't said, "And devil take the hindmost."

Masimo touched me softly on the arm. "Come, Georgia, let us walk for a while. *Ciao*, Dom."

Dom said, "*Ciao*," and went off back inside his house.

Two minutes later

We walked along the street in silence. I couldn't remember if I had checked my lippy before I left Katie's. I had left in such a tizz, I hadn't thought to check. Maybe I could just take a little peek now? I could sneak my hand into my bag, feel around for the lippy, unscrew it single handedly in the bag and sneak it up to my mouth while I was looking down.

Or pretend to look behind me and apply it then underneath a pretend cough. No, I daren't risk any more bag movement. Maybe there would be a car mirror? No no, too low. What about a passing bus or lorry mirror? Shutup shutup.

Masimo said, "Did you have a good party?"

I said, "Oh yeah, it was fab and also possibly verging on marv."

Masimo went on (he's got the most amazing voice), "Dom, he say tonight after our meeting that maybe we go to a party for later, but he doesn't say you are there, and I think, maybe I am not in for the party. My mood is not for dancing."

What did "my mood is not for dancing" mean? Did it mean he didn't feel like dancing, or did it mean he wasn't in the MOOD for dancing, i.e., he was in a sad mood. And if he was in a sad mood, what did that mean? Also, he said he didn't know I was there – would he have come it he had known? Or did he mean, he... oh, shut up, brain, shut up. If only he would stop talking and just grab me, that would sort everything out.

Occasionally as we walked along we bumped arms and it was like an electric shock. I really couldn't think of one thing to say, other than, "Snog me, snog me, you gorgeous Italian Luuurve Stallion!"

As we reached my street, Masimo stopped and looked at me. "Georgia, when I last see you, I didn't... well, I want to tell to say, to *spiegare*... to explain about..."

I said quickly, "Oh, there's nothing to explain, you don't have to, I understand."

Masimo touched my arm again. "I think I have hurt you and I didn't... this is not what I wanted. I..."

I smiled my incredibly false smile and said, "Really, honestly, I am fine as two fine things enjoying a fine day out in Fine land."

He looked puzzled. "So, you are saying... you are fine? Everything is all right with you?"

"Yes indeedy."

He smiled at me. "That is good, *cara*. I am happy for that. Now maybe we could be friends and..." Oh no, he had said that word "friends". He got a pen and paper out of his pocket and started writing on it. "Here is my number. Will you ring me, and we can have good times – maybe eat and go for dancing? *Sì?*"

I didn't say anything. I thought I would burst into tears. I just kept the smile on my face. In fact I was smiling so much, I probably would always have to smile because my face was fixed. He put the piece of paper into my hand. I still smiled at him.

Then he bent down and kissed my cheek. "You are so nice. I like you very much, Georgia. Phone me. We can be... how you say here... very good mates. *Ciao.*"

And he walked off back up the road. He turned round and waved and blew me a kiss. I waved back, still smiling, singing that old crap song "Smile Though Your Heart is Breaking".

In my room

Just me and the night.

And Angus and Gordy and Libby and her toys.

I don't want to be his "mate".

I've got enough so-called "mates".

Even bloody Dave the Laugh said, "See you, mate."

How come I've gone from "Sex Kitty" to "mate" in less than a day?

I don't want to "have fun" with Masimo.

What does he expect me to do? Go back to his place for a cup of coffee and then say, "Right, I'm off now, see you, mate?"

Five minutes later

Or hang around being a goosegog "mate" while he gets off with other girls at Stiff Dylans gigs. Shouting after him as he goes off with someone, "You chancer! What are you like? See you later, mate. Don't do anything I wouldn't do! That leaves you a lot of scope! Rrrrrrr."

Mate?

I'm not going to be his bloody "mate".

I can hardly be bothered to be "mates" with the "mates" I've got.

I'm already having to be "just mates" with Dave the Laugh.

That's enough "being mates" in anybody's language.

Thirteen minutes later

Mate.

Sunday July 3rd
10:30 a.m.

Jas phoned. "Gee, are you up?"

"No."

"Well, can I come round?"

"Why? Has Tom gone slug hunting by himself? I thought you were going to RAMBLE with him today, and that's why you couldn't be bothered to say goodbye to your besty pal last night."

"Er... no, I just want to see you and chat and do make-up and stuff."

"He's gone slug hunting without you."

"No he hasn't."

"What, then?"

"Well, they've started a Sunday league footie thing and well, you know, it's good for him. And, anyway, he's on a mission because I told him to find out all he can about the Masimo-type scenario."

"Huh."

"What do you mean, huh?"

"I mean huh as in huh."

"Shall I come round?"

"If you like. We can practise being mates, seeing as that's going to be my lifetime achievement award. I'll probably be on TV as 'Mate of the Year'."

Me and Jas in my bed eating cornflakes
12:00 p.m.

Jas thinks it's "fun" at my house. She thinks it's charming that we have mostly biscuits to eat and that my dad sets fire to his beard every other day. And that the cats have been next door and dug up the bones that the Prat Poodles had carefully buried in the compost heap.

And are now chewing them at the bottom of the bed. I can hear the horrible crunching sounds, but I am too tired to care.

It isn't fun at my house.

It's sad.

12:15 p.m.

Jas has just almost made me laugh by getting out of bed and adding a bit to the Viking disco inferno dance. It's sort of sniffing the air. So it goes step to the right, step to the left and then sniff sniff. Like a Viking bison might do. If it was trying to find its prey. And if there was such a thing as a Viking bison.

Excellent.

198

12:30 p.m.

I am preparing myself to forgive Jas. She has been almost nice to me since she came round. She said that she thinks my nose is shrinking. She spoiled it a bit by adding, "Either that or your head is growing."

Still, it's the thought that counts. Ish.

Is my head really growing?

As we measured it I told her about what happened at Katie's party. I told her about Dave the Laugh going off with Emma and she said, "But you don't mind that because you love the Italian Stallion."

"Yeah, that is clearly a fact but, well, I've known Dave a long time, and he did say that thing about maybe we should sort of be together."

"Yeah, he said that, but what do you think?"

"What do you mean what do I think? How should I know?"

"Well, I know that Tom is my one and only one."

"Yeah, but that is because you are so boring, er, I mean too, er... you are too blind with luuurve to hear the call of the Cosmic Horn."

"I know."

She is sooooo annoying, but I suppose she is just being her.

Because we were being so cosy and back to the old days of besties, I bared my whatsits to her. I told her about walking home and bumping into Masimo as I was having my bum-oley licked by a dog.

She said, "Oh blimey, mate."

She had said the "mate" word, but I let her off.

She went on: "So, are you going to give up on him now then?"

I said, "Yep, I tried the girding of the loins scenario, however my loins came ungirded. Which can be quite painful, especially if you're wearing tight jeans."

We had a bit of a laughing attack for a bit because it has to be said, even if no one except me will say it, that I am despite being sheer desperadoes and in the cake shop of aggers, etc., quite a good laugh.

When we had built up our energy with another packet of Wotsits, I went on: "I'm going to have to think that he doesn't exist and *ignorez-vous* him."

"So when we go to the Stiff Dylans gig will you pretend he is a figment of a sham?"

"No, I will not pretend he is a figment of a sham. I won't have to, and do you know why? Because I won't be going to the next Stiff Dylans gig."

"Blimey."

I nodded while I crunched through my Wotsits.

"That is a fact that is written in stone. I will NEVER be going to a Stiff Dylans gig again."

"Blimey."

"He gave me his phone number and told me to call so that we could go out and do mates-type stuff."

"Blimey."

"Jas, will you think of something else to say besides blimey, please?"

"OK."

"But I will tell you what I'm going to do with his telephone number. I'm going to go into the woods and ceremoniously burn it so that I will never be tempted to call him even in my darkest moments of jelloidnosity."

Jas started to say, "Blim... er... crikey."

In the woods
3:00 p.m.

I have burned the paper with Masimo's number on it and buried it under an oak tree. (Well, Jas scraped away a bit of

201

soil with a twig she found and we covered it with that. And it took her long enough to do that because she found a mushroom that she thought might be a "special" mushroom.)

9:00 p.m.

I don't even feel tragicostnosity. I feel nothingnosity.

Which is not easy to say, believe me – tragicostnosity in particular.

However, I will never feel anything again.

Good.

I am done with love.

It's a mug's game.

I am just going to sit in my room for the rest of my life not doing stuff.

10:00 p.m.

How boring is this?

It's as boring as double maths followed by a lecture from Slim on how life was when she was a girl and used to go to Sad Girls High with Queen Elizabeth and Tom Thumb, or whoever was lurking about boring the arse off people in those days.

10:10 p.m.

Got out my letters from the ex Sex God. I don't know why I keep them. Or the photos of him. Just to torture myself. I should throw them away with the rest of my life.

I will put all the things I have of his together and do that thing you're supposed to do when you are moving on in life – burn them to ashes and smithereens and never look back. Out with the old and in with the new lesbian monastic life.

10:15 p.m.

Robbie wrote: *It would be really nice to hear from you. I often think about you.* Well, that's nice, isn't it? In a way. At least he hasn't mentioned the word "mate".

10:30 p.m.

Maybe I'll drop him a line. Perhaps he'd like to hear from a lesbian monk. Who wouldn't?

10:35 p.m.

What harm can it do, anyway? He is miles away – he's over the Trans-Siberian Ocean, or whatever it is. In the land of rogue bores and exploding whatsits.

10:45 p.m.

What shall I say? I must tread a fine line between glaciosity and friendlinosity. With just a hint of "you don't know what you are missing, my fine feathered friend".

Midnight

It was quite hard to write the letter. But in my new mood of baring my all – oo-er – I told him everything. I thought, *Oh sod it! Devil take the hindmost! Take me as I am, the real Georgia. The real true person, no longer afraid to stand tall and proud. Burned in the oven of love and fattened in the cake shop of agony and...* Anyway, what was I saying? Before I wandered off into the cake-shop thing again?

Ah, yes, honestosity.

12:03 a.m.

Obviously I left out the bits about me making a complete and utter pratty baboon of myself. I told him all about the bison horns and the Viking wedding. I even mentioned that Herr Kamyer might be matron of honour.

12:05 a.m.

Actually it has quite cheered me up writing it all down. It doesn't seem like such a bad life when you think of the hours of fun the Ace Gang have had despite the Hitler Youth, parents, the orang-utan gene, lurking lurkers and so on.

I couldn't help myself adding a few details about Wet Lindsay and her astonishing stick-like existence. I thought it was a mistress stroke of seemingly nicenosity to say about her: I expect you know that Lindsay is head girl and she is making a very good job of it; some of the first formers may never go out on their own again. Also, she has once again put herself at the forefront of fashion vis-à-vis her interesting hair extensions. That kind of courage is rarely seen outside the circus these days.

I sort of skated around the boy issue. I mentioned the Stiff Dylans in passing because it would have seemed odd not to. But I just said: I've been to a few gigs, which have been quite good. They have a new singer called, erm, I think it's Masingo or something. He seems quite nice, but may be a froggy-type person. I saw Dom's Vati and he seems to have forgotten about the time he thought I was trying to get off with him because I thought he was a

♡

famous music-agent-type person. Speaking of vatis, my own portly one set fire to his beard, so no change there.

I had sort of lost all inhibitions by then. It was quite a relief to tell a boy everything (more or less), and what had I to lose? I didn't have to impress him any more.

12:07 a.m.
I didn't know how to end it. Was "with love" all right?

I am certainly not going to put "from your mate".

Finally I decided on: Well, I'm away laughing on a fast camel now. It would be great to see you again. Take care. Love, Georgia.

And I put a kiss.

But I thought that might be construed as a bit on the matey side, so I added two more.

Three kisses.

That's OK.

It doesn't imply rampant red-bottomosity. It implies *je ne sais quoi* with a hint of longing.

206

12:10 a.m.

But he probably has a girlfriend called Gayleen.

Or Noelene or Joelene.

Who is a wombat.

Monday July 4th
On the way to Stalag 14
8:20 a.m.

I am wearing a black armband because this is the day that the Hamburgese chucked all our teabags into the sea and said they didn't want us to rule them any more.

That is when they started making up their own language, and see where that's got them.

It's got them into the restroom of life.

And had them wearing panties instead of proper knickers.

But let them have it their way.

Let them wrap themselves in aluuuuuminum as much as they want.

We in Billy Shakespeare land do not hold grudges and will love them always.

Until they get more sense and let us rule them again.

♡ 207

8:30 a.m.

Met Jas at her gate and she did immediate armsies-linksies, which is nice. But I didn't let on.

I said to Jas, "Mum's the word."

She looked at me. "Why are you talking about your mutti?"

"NO, Jas, I mean that you mustn't say anything about the party and the Dave the Laugh scenario or me being Masimo's 'mate'."

"I know when to keep my mouth shut."

"Wrong."

8:35 a.m.

When we got to the postbox at the bottom of the hill leading to "school" I wondered if I should post my letter to the Sex God? Hmmm. I asked Jas, which is a terrible mistake. She said, "I thought that you loved either Masimo or Dave the Laugh, and now you're writing to Robbie."

"I know that."

"You are sort of three-timing except that none of them are your boyfriend."

"Shut up, Jas, you are not Baby Jesus."

"I know, I'm just saying that Baby Jesus will be very disappointed with you."

"No, he won't. He will luuurve me no matter what I do, and by the way, whatever I do is bound to be more interesting to him than what you do, O Voley One. Hey, Jas, don't be volier than thou! Hahahaha, Jesus will like that one; it's a religious/wildlife joke! I think I might be hysterical. What shall I do? Help me, little Jazzy, shall I post it or not?"

She looked thoughtful, which is always alarming, and then she said, "Well, let's use logic. If we see a white van in a minute, you should post it. But if the white van has a bloke with a baseball cap on, you should wait until this afternoon to post it, and if..."

8:40 a.m.

Saved the trouble of whether I should post the letter or not by a fantastically insane and grumpy postman who came along to empty the postbox. He just tore the letter out of my hand and put it in his bag. I said, "Erm, I haven't quite decided whether I wanted to post that or not."

He just said, "Bog off to school."

That's nice, isn't it? As I have said to anyone who will listen (i.e., no one), the point about public servants is that they should serve the public, i.e., me. But they just don't get it.

2:00 p.m.
Forty-five years of being cooped up at Stalag 14, interrupted by only two Jammy Dodger breaks.

Should I have posted the letter?

2:30 p.m.
What does it matter, anyway? With my luck it will either not get there, or he will not bother to reply, and then I will have been rejected by practically every man on the planet.

2:35 p.m.
That's it, I'm going to concentrate on my career. I may as well become a multi-lingual lesbian monk.

In the corridor, lolloping along to French
2:55 p.m.
I am keeping mum as two short mums, even though the Ace

Gang has been asking me what is going on vis-à-vis romance. When I said to Rosie, "Nothing has happened. There is zero to report," she just looked at me like a looking-at-me thing. But I didn't snap.

I would have been extremely good at being in the French Resistance during the war if anyone had bothered to ask me.

Which they didn't.

And even if I had been alive, I wouldn't have said yes because of that business of the French saying the English were a bunch of cheese-eating surrender monkeys.

Or did we say that about them?

Oh, I don't know. Stop asking me trick questions.

3:00 p.m.

By mistake I have overdone things and actually handed my French homework in on time. I thought Madame Slack was going to have an f.t. but she didn't, more's the pity. She just said, "Who did you copy this from?"

Which I think does little for student-teacher relationships in these troubled times.

on the way home
4:30 p.m.

For once in my whole school life I'm walking home on my own. I told the Ace Gang that I had to dash for a doctor's appointment, but I haven't really. Although if Mum had her way I would spend every waking hour in Dr Clooney's surgery so she could moon around him. It's just that I couldn't handle the risk that Dave the Laugh would come along and I would have to walk along with him and his mates as if everything were in Norman Normal land. I don't know why I don't want to see him. I just feel funny about him and Emma Jacobs.

I'm not the only one, either; Ellen practically had a nervy b. about it. At break at Ace Gang Headquarters she started talking about him going home with Emma Jacobs and going, "How... and why... why???" She had a full-blown head-shaking ditherama.

I had to practise extreme glaciosity and also extravagant bursts of manic Viking disco dancing just to stop the Ace Gang asking me why I left early and if anything happened to upset me and how I am feeling, etc.

But it is my own painful little secret not to be shared. The only person who knows anything is Mrs Big Pantaloonies.

Five minutes later
And I have told Radio Jas that she is sworn to secrecy.

One minute later
So the Ace Gang will know everything that happened by now.

One minute later
And also possibly how many times I have been to the loo in the last day.

Five minutes later
As I went down the hill I saw the two little titches from the first form, who had been duffed up by Wet Lindsay, hopping along. And I do mean hopping. Did I used to hop when I was their age? Surely not. As I passed them they looked exhausted, hopping along on one leg with their big heavy satchels. I suppose I have on occasion pretended to be riding a horse home, but not carrying a big heavy bag.

Life is a mystery.

Lesbian Monastery Training Headquarters, aka, my bedroom

Evening

I will dedicate myself to the pursuit of knowledge...

zzzzzzzzzzz.

MacPants

Wednesday July 6th
Afternoon break

Fortunately the Ace Gang has gone on to more interesting subjects than me. They are concentrating on the Rosie-Sven Viking wedding with gusto. Rosie said, "I have an idea for a lovely outfit for Sven. I will gather the materials on Friday at the *MacUseless* dress rehearsal."

She wouldn't go any further, except to say that Sven will be "thrilled".

And none of us really want to see that.

4:30 p.m.

Walking home with just little Jazzy Spazzy, who is muttering her Lady MacUseless lines to herself. I hope she

 215

isn't turning into a spasmodic or whatever it is when a person is two people at the same time.

I feel a bit nervy about seeing Dave again on Friday. I'm going to have to practise this "mate" malarkey with gusto. And possibly vim. What would a mate do when they saw their mate? What do I do when I see my mates?

Three minutes later
In Jas's case I will tell you what I'll do in a minute if she doesn't stop rambling on about spots.

Five minutes later
Unfortunately I said what was in my head out loud. "Jas, if you don't stop rambling on about spots, I will have to kill you."

Jas stopped mumbling, "Out damned spot!" and said, "Don't pick on me because you have got the Cosmic Horn for any boy that comes along, but they just want to be mates with you."

Fifteen minutes later
Here is my recipe for a mood enhancer: take a friend, preferably one with a really annoying fringe and outsize pants, and when she's rambling on, swiftly push her into a

ditch and run away.

Hahahaha.

Very funny to see Jazzy Spazzy plunging down the grass verge.

Hahahaha.

Friday July 8th
MacUseless Headquarters
4:50 p.m.

Dress rehearsal in front of the whole school at 5:30 p.m.

Tension mounts. It's showtime, showtime...

zzzzzzzzzzzzzzzzzzzzzzzz.

Miss Wilson gave us her world-famous pep talk, but we still managed to stay awake. Apparently the honour of the school is on our shoulders. We have two nights of parading around in tights yelling "och aye" to persuade everyone that going to school is not a complete waste of everyone's time. And just an excuse for people who would have nothing else to do, i.e., Hawkeye, Slim, Madame Slack, Herr Kamyer and the terminally insane Elvis Attwood, to go somewhere and not bother people on the street.

217

Thankfully we have Miss Wilson steady at the helm, so everything should be, you know, a shambles.

Jas was watching me like that mad Red Indian bloke in the film about Mohicans – Chingachgook. He trailed around in a feather hat, following bison poo and watching people. Jas hasn't spoken to me for two days because of the accidental grass-verge scenario. But she was really looking at me in a horrible beaky way when Dave the Laugh came in with the other lads.

5:00 p.m.
I kept a safe distance from Dave, but not so much that he would notice and think I was avoiding him. I stuck around with Ro Ro and Jools and the Ace Gang. Nauseating P. Green kept coming up to me for reassurance and asking me if my sword was comfortable. She actually believes that I am her husband, which is possibly the most tragic thing that has happened to me. And that is saying A LOT.

Still, no one can say that I'm not a taking-it-on-the-chin sort of a person. And believe me, I have taken it on the chin A LOT. I hope that my brain will stop saying A LOT soon. And I mean that A LOT.

Only half an hour to go till curtain up. Although as Spotty Norman is in charge of curtains, I have hope that this production will quite literally never see the light of day.

I had been busy in "make-up" with Ro Ro until Miss Stamp (And what has this production got to do with her? Is there a lesbian sports bit? Possibly, actually, as I haven't been arsed to see the whole play through, only my bits.) came in and took charge of the fake fur. Rosie was forced to remove her moustache, which actually was a homage to Miss Stamp in the first place.

I was doing my limbering-up exercises with Rosie, i.e., horn to the right, horn to the left, when Dave the Laugh passed close by, winking and lumbering bits of castle wall and so on. Fortunately, I had three foot of foundation on, so he couldn't have seen my vair vair red face. As he went by, I burst into peals of laughter as Jools handed me her witch's branch. Dave looked at me. Jools looked at me. Which was fair enough, as all she had said was, "Will you hold this while I go to the piddly-diddly department?"

Not exactly a joke.

But I wanted to let Dave know that I was fine and not bothered about the snoggus interruptus that we had done at

Katie's party. And also that I didn't give two short flying pigs' bums about who or what he went out with.

Ellen was also giving him her version of the cold shoulder. Which was hilarious. She said to me, "I'm going to let Dave know exactly what I think of his behaviour. I mean, that is what I'm going to do. I should do that, shouldn't I? I mean, do you think I should? Because I think that's what you should do – you should... anyway, what do you think?"

Oh dear Lord.

She shouldn't have bothered because her cold shoulderosity only lasted two minutes. Dave came by covered in twigs, saying, "Do you think my acting is a bit wooden, girls?" Ellen went bright red and giggled like a loon. Not exactly in my book tip-top cold shoulderosity work.

Moi, on the other hand, did an excellent job. I slightly-smiled in a way that meant I was an amusing sort of person, but not the sort of girl who really bothered what Dave the Laugh got up to.

5:50 p.m.
Jas brushed past me in her frock to go poncing around as Mrs MacUseless. I smiled in an attractive way, but she

*ignorez-vous*ed me. She'll come round; what other fool will listen to her talking about voles? I'm not on for a bit, so Rosie and I went back into the props box for a rummage. Oo-er.

Rosie pulled out a false nose and said, "Do you think if I put it on as a sort of two-nose effect anyone would notice?"

I thought back to the good old days of last year. Days when life had been so simple. I had luuurved the Sex God and been his nearly girlfriend. We were doing a production of *Peter Pan*, and like now, many fools were stropping around in tights. (Apart from Nauseating P. Green, who was a dog.) Rosie and I had been banned from the production and put on props. We found some theatrical fur, and every time we handed a sword or something to Wet Lindsay onstage, we would add more fur to our bodies. By the end of the show we had huge, furry hands and Rosie had one massive eyebrow and sidies. How we laughed our way to triple detention. Happy happy pre-spinsterhood days.

That's when Ro Ro said from upside down in the props box, "I am going to secrete this fur about my person and take it home for the Viking wedding."

It's pointless under those sort of circumstances (i.e., Rosie being utterly barking mad) to ask questions.

8:30 p.m.
Some fools actually applauded at the end as we took our bows. I only had one unfortunate incident doing my part, but I don't think anyone noticed.

Walking home with the gang
9:10 p.m.
Jas is keeping up her humpiness by walking as far away from me as possible. And she gave everyone except me one of her secret Midget Gem selection. I don't care because I think she keeps them hidden in her enormous pantaloonies.

Then in the distance we saw Dave the Laugh and his posse following behind us. Donner *und* Blitzen. I was going to *ignorez-vous* them with a firm hand.

I said, "My false beard fell off when I was doing the swordfight and I had to carry on one-handed while casually holding my beard on with the other one. Did you notice?"

And Ro Ro said, "Yes, who didn't? It made you look like

Mincing Macduff, the campest bloke in Och Aye land."

Excellent.

Not.

9:15 p.m.

Dave and his posse are doing comedy fast walking to keep up with us. They'll catch us up in a minute. Oh, I can't handle any more of this "mate" business. I said to the gang, "I fancy a bit of a run, actually, so I think I'll just go on ahead. See you for the final fiasco performance tomorrow."

They looked at me in amazement as I jogged off. After a minute of jogging I looked back and Dave the Laugh was also now jogging. Oh nooooo. I put on a bit of speed, but he caught up with me and just jogged along beside me, looking at me. He was looking basooma-wards and I didn't have my double strength over-the-shoulder-boulder-holder on. Drat and double dratty drat.

Still jogging
Two minutes later

This was ridiculous. As we jogged on side by side Dave put his arm through mine, so we were doing tandem jogging.

Eventually the weight of my basoomas got the better of me and I slowed down.

Dave said, "Have you got the hump with me, Kittykat?"

I turned to him, and in between panting smiled a really really beaming smile. "Dave, why on earth would I have the hump with you?"

He looked at me. "You have got the hump then."

Damn.

He went on, "You know that you don't want to go out with me and so I'm going out with someone else. That is OK, isn't it? Or would you just like me to sort of hang around on my own for ever just in case you feel like a quick snog?"

Actually, when he put it like that, I thought, *Yep, that is exactly what I would like.* But it didn't seem a very normal thing to say.

I was trying to think of what was a normal thing to say, which quite honestly I have never really had a proper education in – nothing my parents have ever said would pass for normal conversation. Anyway, as I was just flicking through my brain for something normalish to say, my brain went off for a little holiday to Hornland. I started thinking about the way Dave's eyelashes curl up and his mouth goes sort of down at the corners and how... And that's when he gave me a quick kiss on the cheek and went off back to his mates.

Bugger.

Midnight

So this is my fabulous night: my beard fell off and Dave the Laugh saw my basoomas unleashed.

And he is definitely going out with Emma.

Which I don't care about.

Much.

Ten minutes past midnight

I have decided to use art to express myself. Tomorrow night I will give the performance of my life. My part is mostly blubbing and fighting, and God knows I've had enough practice at that.

I will let Dave see that I can be as full of maturiosity and sophisticosity as the next fool.

Saturday July 9th

Even though I tried to give them the wrong date, my mutti and vati, grandvati and Maisie are all coming to the performance tonight.

7:00 p.m.

I've got about four tons of glue on my beard. With my luck, it won't come off at the end of the show and I will have to go immediately to the lesbian monastery.

7:05 p.m.

Backstage is a nightmare of tights. Jas is wandering around with her bloody dagger, muttering her lines to herself. It is very unnerving. She was saying, "Unsex me here and fill me from the crown to the toe top-full of direst cruelty... Is this a dagger which I see before me...?"

And then doing manic stabbing.

Like a loon.

Which she is.

I must remember never to fall out with her if she's cutting up sandwiches.

It's not likely I'll have the opportunity of falling out

with her as she is still *ignorez-vous*ing me.

7:30 p.m.
Curtain up, amazingly. I can see through a crack in the screens at the side of the stage and the hall is packed. Oh brilliant. My "family" are on the front row.

The banquet scene
8:30 p.m.
Everything not going too badly.

Apart from Dave messing up the sound effects. The banquet scene, which should have started off with bagpipe music, had seagulls instead. Which must have puzzled the audience a bit.

But then, after Jas and her "husband" Honour Stevens (also known as MacUseless the Thane of Cawdor) ponced around with their soon-to-be-dead guests, the improvised entertainment scene began. God knows we had all tried to advise Miss Wilson against the juggling and fire stuff, but would she listen? No. Melanie was doing her best with the oranges, flinging them around and dropping them and so on. She was being put off even more by ogling oglers (the

Foxwood lads) all crowded on the side of the stage, desperate for a bit of nunga-nunga jiggling. So oranges were crashing around, left, right and akimbo. And I distinctly heard my grandad say, "She's a big girl."

But the *pièce de* whatsit was Ellen on fire-conjuring duties. Anyone who thinks it is sensible to give fire to someone as divvy as Ellen has to go to a home, frankly. Anyway, Ellen had some special paper that you light and it whooshes up and it looks like you've set fire to your hands. But you haven't really. You just whoosh the fire about (or your flaming hands, as the audience thinks) and eventually the paper burns up and disappears into the air with no harm done. That is the whooshing-fire theory. And last night the whooshing had been without incident.

Credit where credit is due, Ellen lit the paper and did the initial whooshing of the hand with no lack a day or incident. But then she whooshed too near to Spotty Norman and his false beard, and the rest is history. Actually, Spotty Norman was almost history. As his beard flared up, Norm came offstage, shuffling sideways quite quickly. It was Elvis's moment of triumph. He appeared like Mr Mad the fireman with his fire extinguisher, and gave Spotty Norman and Nauseating P. Green, who happened to be standing nearby, a good dousing with foam. The beard was extinguished, but Norman and P. Green blundered around like blind blundering things for about five minutes.

Vair funny.

9:30 p.m.
We were at the big fight scene when Great Birnam wood comes to High Dunsinane. Everyone was dressed up as trees, etc., and as I said to Rosie, "Oh, it's a triumph, darling, a triumph lovie."

And it was, until Dave the Laugh, master technician and fool, struck.

I really thought Miss Wilson had lost her grip and would have to be airlifted to a secure unit. She had a complete and utter nervy tiz when Dave (on lights) plunged everything, not only the stage, but backstage, frontstage, sidestage, into complete darkness.

Most of the forest fell off the stage. I was at the side of the stage when he did it, and in the pitch black I felt a hand pinch my bum. OY!!!

I am convinced it was Dave, but when the lights went on

♡ 229

again he was just looking really surprised and going "What? What?" to everyone. He said that he had "fallen" against the light switch accidentally.

The audience applauded the Forest Folk plunging into the audience! They thought it was part of the modern interpretation, which just goes to show what fools parents are on the whole.

9:45 p.m.

Even if I say it myself, I was magnifico as Macduff. I actually blubbed real tears, and that wasn't very hard, given my life. As I came off the stage I sneaked a look at the audience, and even Hawkeye looked a bit wet round the eyes. Dave the Laugh gave me a hug as I went by and said, "Well done, Kittykat. You are a thespian of the first water and also your nungas look particularly perky in that tunic."

Oooh, he is soooooo aggravating.

9:55 p.m.

We got a standing ovation. Well, from those of the audience who could stand. I noticed Grandvati only managed to get to his feet at the same time as everyone else was sitting back down.

10:20 p.m.

Hoooray!!! Slim declared an armistice because of our vair vair marvy performance. She gave me and the Ace Gang our horns back!!!

We did a little celebration Viking disco inferno dance, but I don't think she got it. She just jelloided off to chat to the elderly insane.

Mr Attwood looked like he thought he was going to get a medal for his firefighting skills. He was going on and on to anyone who would listen, "Yes, luckily I've been practising for just such an emergency as this. I have a stuffed figure in my allotment which I regularly set fire to, and I've got my extinguishing time down to ten seconds."

Good grief, what a fabulous life he leads.

I say we all did a little Viking disco inferno dance, but Jas didn't. She is still sulking. I heard her say to Jools that she was exhausted from all of the emotion she'd put into her part. I don't see why – she only stabbed someone and then went on about a spot. Anyway, she left before us, snuggled up to her boyfriend. She was leaning against him as if she was a paralysed elf. It's pathetic. She said goodbye to everyone except me.

She won't be able to ignore me for ever.

Walking home with the rest of the gang
10:45 p.m.

I refused to get in the batmobile with my parents. Vati said, "Don't you want to accelerate through the night in my Lovemobile?"

Urgh, good Lord. And he said it in front of everyone. And he is wearing a T-shirt and tight jeans. Is there a book called, *How to Be Really Crap*, because if there is, he has got it.

Grandvati insisted on showing the gang his false teeth before we could bundle him on to the bus with his almost completely knitted girlfriend. Even her handbag was knitted. And her purse.

Midnight

When I got in, Mutti had made me a special supper and Libby had decorated my bed. Well, what I mean is she had her dressing-up fairy clothes on and had put tinsel on all her "fwends". And I do mean all her fwends – scuba-diving Barbie, Charlie Horse, Pantalitzer doll's head (which is all there is left of her since Gordy had a spaz attack and ripped her arms off), plus various bits of vegetables. They were all crowded in my bed, waiting for me in a really scary way.

Especially as the light was off, and when I turned it on there they all were in the bed. Libby shouted, "Heggo, Gingey, SURPRISE!!!"

You're not kidding. Even Gordy and Angus and Naomi were in there, tied in a shopping bag so that they couldn't escape.

You try getting your jimjams on with a toddler in wings clinging to your leg.

It's not easy.

But what is?

Sunday July 10th
1:30 p.m.

Let me just say this – never go to the park with a toddler round your waist.

Libby will not leave me alone.

2:00 p.m.

In the end I got up my private tree again just to escape from her. I have got post-performance exhaustosity. If I could just wedge my bum into the bit between two branches I could have a little zizz.

Fat chance. The kittykats are messing about in Mr Next Door's pine tree doing that all-legs-at-the-same-time climbing thing up the trunk. I shouted to them, "Oy, you two, get down. Don't you dare go up that tree!" And I threw stuff at them.

It worked, actually. They both stopped and lay on a branch and looked down at me, yawning. They did a bit of light bum-oley grooming, and then went back to the all-legs-at-the-same-time climbing.

Then I heard a scooter engine in the distance getting nearer and nearer. And it was him – Masimo on his scooter! On the bottom road coming towards my street! Wow!! I wonder if he'd heard about my outstanding Macduff performance? Shutupshutup.

Oh God, how am I going to get out of the tree without him seeing me? Actually, I think my bum is stuck. Oh brilliant. And I don't have my lippy on. Oh *merde, merde, merde, merde*! What should I do?

Maybe it's just a "mate's" visit?

At which point Masimo rode right by the bottom of my street without stopping.

Of course he did.

That is my life.

2:30 p.m.

Oh, excellent day. Really, really excellent in every way. I am on the rack of love again eating aggy cakes – with my bum wedged into a tree.

Four minutes later

I've unwedged myself, but I think I've bruised my bum-oley.

Walking up the garden path in a very odd way

I think my bottom's swelling up.

Five minutes later

For the *pièce de résistance* the kittykats really *are* stuck up the pine tree next door. At the top of it. They are on the top branches swaying about dangerously, crying and shivering.

I rushed into the house and begged my vati to do something. I said, "They might fall off and die."

And he said, "Good."

6:00 p.m.

Eventually the fire brigade were called. You have never seen anything as embarrassing as my mother. She was practically

♡ 235

dribbling as the "boys", as she called the firemen, got their ladders out. She was giggling and saying really stupid things like, "Oh, you must have quite strong arms to hold those big hoses." I was looking at her, but she ignored me.

In the end she accidentally phoned up her aerobics mates and they all came round to watch the "boys" as well, giggling like a bunch of giggling Gerties. It is soooo shaming.

6:25 p.m.
"Ben", Mum's new fireman friend, got to the top of the ladder to try to grab the kittykats to safety. He was reaching out from his big ladder with a net thing, and as he reached out to them Angus and Gordy stopped shivering and yowling and just scampered merrily down the tree and off into the undergrowth.

Unbelievable.

They are the devil incarnate in furry trousers.

They had been toying with the firemen.

Monday July 11th
Jas had already gone to Stalag 14 when I arrived at her gate.

Assembly

And she stood at the other end of the Ace Gang, not in her usual place next to me.

How long can she keep this up?

This is marathon *ignorez-vous*ing.

French

I snuggled up really close to her, but she shifted her chair further and further away from me until she was practically sitting on Ellen's knee.

P.E.

I said to her, "I like your pants today, Jas."

She still had her Huffy Pants on though.

Ace Gang Headquarters

The Ace Gang have been on at me all day to sing and the world sings with you. They want to go to the Stiff Dylans gig on Saturday, and they say they can't go unless I go because it will not be one for all and all for one. Also, Rosie is having a practice of her Viking wedding at the gig. She wants to dress up and try out the Viking bison dance.

237

She's got the confetti but fortunately not the vats.

They tried to bribe me with cheesy snacks, which is pathetic.

When I say "they", I don't mean Jas, who is still giving me the cold shoulder. This is a world record for her. Four days. I said to her, "Jas, are you going to eschew me with a firm hand for ever?"

She didn't say anything.

Rosie was going, "Come on, Gee, please come to the gig, pleasey please and double please with knobs. Please don't spoil my big day. You only get married to a Viking and madman once in your life. And anyway, what else will you be doing? Crying, that's what."

Jools said, "There might be some really cool boys there."

I said, "Look, Masimo will be there wanting to be my 'mate' and Dave the Laugh will be with stupid old Emma thingy and..."

Uh-oh. Ellen started: "What do you mean Dave the Laugh will be with Emma? Why are you, like, er, bothered by that? I mean has, er..."

Jas said, "Yeah, what do you mean about Dave the Laugh?"

I fell to my knees. "She speaks, it's a miracle, she can speak!!! The good Lord has given her back the power of speech."

Hahahahah. She couldn't go back on it; she had asked me a question. She had broken her vow of cold shoulderosity. I won, I won!!! (And distracted Ellen from the Dave the Laugh fandango.)

But I was magnaniwhatsit in victory. "I love you, Jazzy, and I'm sorry about the ditch incident. But you were being vair vair annoying, my little pally."

She humped around, but she was sick of not talking to me.

1:30 p.m.
I've said I might go to the Stiff Dylans gig. But if I do the Ace Gang has got to look after me like little guardey dogs. I said that, "If you leave me on my own while you all go off snogging, I will resign from the Ace Gang."

Rosie said, "This will be a magnificent evening. We will wear our newly liberated horns and show the world that romance lives."

I said, "Er, I don't think we need to bother with the

horns. I mean, why don't we just keep them for private moments that—"

Rosie said, "Aren't you proud to wear your horns?"

"Yes, of course, but—"

Rosie put her face very close to mine. "HOOOORRRRN NN!!"

Oh dear God.

We made a solemn Ace Gang vow, and did a quick rendition of the Viking disco inferno dance – with horns. We have also officially added in Jas's sniffing bit. Jas looked all thrilled.

As we huddly-duddlyed down to the floor for the final cry of "Hooorrrrn!!!" Wet Lindsay came by on rounding-up duty. Her extensions are growing out. Hmm, that's attractive. Not. She looked at us; we looked up. Her legs are getting thinner, I swear. Perhaps she is on a leg-thinning diet.

She said, "Get up, you idiots. You're a bloody disgrace, the whole lot of you."

That's charming language, isn't it?

She watched us as we went past her. I was last and she said to me quite quietly, "Don't think I don't know all about you. You're a pathetic, snivelling idiot."

Oh Blimey O'Reilly's trousers she does mean me!!!

German

Wrote a note to Ro Ro: What if Wet Lindsay is still seeing Masimo? And she might be because she has no pridenosity. What if she is with him at the Stiff Dylans gig? I couldn't handle that.

Ro Ro wrote back: One for all and all for one. We will think of a tactic if she is with him, but she won't be. He said that he didn't want to get serious with anyone. And besides – Hooooorrrrrrnnnn!!!

What is she talking about?

Should I go or not?

On the way home

Jas and me are besties again. Jas was still rambling on about the hidden depths she had found out about herself as Lady MacUseless, and Rosie was practising burping, when we saw the titchey first formers hopping along in front of us.

When we caught up with them, I said to one of the titches, "What are you doing?"

She was wheezing and red but managed to say, "Er, we're hopping, miss."

Miss?

I said, "I can see that, but why?"

And she said, "I don't know."

How mad is that?

Rosie was looking at them. "I wonder if they are related to Sven?"

Wednesday July 13th

Still can't decide whether to go to the gig or not.

I'm glad that Jas and I are pals again. She gave me two Midget Gems and a Jammy Dodger, which I have to say is nice. Even though she is vair vair annoying, I love her really, but not, you know, in a lezzie way.

4:10 p.m.

Walking home on my own. Which is unusual. Jas has gone off with Tom on a foraging expedition and the rest have gone into town on a make-up shopping spree. I wasn't in the mood somehow. No sign of Dave and his mates, either.

I am indeed Georgia Nomates.

Ah, well, that is the harsh truth of life in a cake shop of ag... Is that the littlies hopping again?

Surely not?

One minute later
It is, though. They are hopping like loons into the park.

One minute later
And there's Mark Big Gob and the Blunder Boys. What are the hoppers doing hanging around them? I sincerely hope they're not going for snogging lessons. Erlack apongo. If Mark Big Gob kisses one of them, they will be eaten alive. I know he likes tee-tiny girls, but this is ridiculous.

What is going on?

The girls are handing something over to Mark, still hopping.

One minute later
The Blunder Boys are all laughing and smoking as the titches hop off.

Three minutes later
I caught up with the hoppers, who were lying down on the

grass behind a bush. I said, "Oy, what are you doing?"

One of them said, "Nothing. Just having a lie down."

And the other titch said, "Because we're tired from hopping."

I said, "I can see that. But WHY? Are you a bit half-witted? And what were you doing with Mark and his mates?"

They were redder than red things at a red convention.

Half an hour later

It turns out that they're being tormented by Mark and his mates. They make the little titches hand over their lunch money and any sweet money they have, and if they haven't got any spondulies, the gang make them hop home. And they keep making surprise appearances so that the titches never know when to stop hopping.

What is the matter with Mark and his mates? Haven't they got anything better to do? I thought the day would never come when I would say this, but they are worse than the Bummer twins in their heyday.

In bed

I keep thinking about the stupid little hoppers.

Midnight
What if it was Bibbsy being made to hop?

12:10 a.m.
Yeah, as if. I'd like to see the boy who could make her do anything.

12:15 a.m.
But the little titches are such weedy blubbers.

12:30 a.m.
Oh blimey, I'm going to have to save them.

Thursday July 14th
At break I found the titches and said, "Your hopping days are over."

In the park
4:30 p.m.
Mark Big Gob and the Blunder Boys were louting about, waiting for their hopping victims.

The little titches hid behind a bush while I went up to see the lard arses.

♡

5:00 p.m.

After they had stopped leering at my nungas, I said to Oscar, "OK, Perv Boy, I'm going to tell your mum you smoke, and then you'll be a dead Perv Boy."

The other Blunder Boys started sniggering, and I said to them, "If you don't back off, I'm going to spread the word at school that you've all got infectious warts. No girl will ever snog you again. That is a fact."

5:30 p.m.

The titches followed me all the way to my gate. They were saying, "Thanks, Georgia. Would you like some Midget Gems, Georgia? What's your favourite colour? Which band do you like best, Georgia?"

Good grief.

I don't want any tiny hopping pals.

7:00 p.m.

Still don't know whether to go to the gig or not.

I feel like I haven't snogged anyone for years.

Do you know why that is? Because I haven't snogged anyone for years.

The last time was when I saw Dave, and that was snoggus interruptus at Katie's. Two weeks ago.

Who do I think is the best snogger between Masimo and Dave?

Well, Masimo, obviously, as he is the Luuurve God. And he did that neck-nuzzling thing that was mega-groovy and even thinking about it makes my legs go jelloid.

Not to mention my brain.

7:40 p.m.
On the other hand, Dave is the king of nip libbling.

I wonder if boys mark girls out of ten for snogging like we do?

I must ask Dave.

No, I'd better not. He has a way of knowing what I'm thinking about and he would know that I was thinking about him.

♡

Friday July 15th

10:00 a.m.

When I walked past Slim's headquarters today, I noticed the school photo had been put up. I stopped to look at it because I wanted to know if you could see the beauty spots the Ace Gang had all pencilled in on our top lips, especially for the photo.

One minute later

Ahaha. Yep, you had to look really closely, but there they were. The revolution starts here!!! Since the piggy-nose scenario last year, when our clearly hilarious joke of making little pig noses out of egg carton bits had resulted in mass bad-conduct marks and *ordure*, we had aimed for subtlenosity. And the photo was up and no one had noticed!

One minute later

God, what a bunch of losers the sixth form are. Look at the state of ADM's sad cardigan. And she's next to Miss Slimebum Octopussyhead, Wet Lindsay. And that is when I noticed – Wet Lindsay had a small Hitler moustache pencilled in on her upper lip!!! This was the hand of God at his most amusing.

I was so so excited and happy.

It was a sign – a cosmic sign!

Lunchtime

I told the Ace Gang about the photo and we did a triumphant Viking disco dance. Rosie said, "Let's go and have a look."

And I said, "No, we must display casualosity. If we all troop up and look at the photo, someone will see us and then they'll look and the finger of shame will point our way. Even though, sadly, we are not guilty."

Ellen said, "I wonder who did do it?"

Jools said, "Who really dislikes her?"

And I said, "No, Jools, the question is, who DOESN'T dislike her?"

Walking home

The whole Ace Gang has verified that in fact Wet Lindsay is now officially a member of the Hitler Youth.

I said, "If Miss Stamp sees her moustache, it will be love at first sight."

5:00 p.m.

As I went round the corner from the bottom road into my street, I caught sight of two little heads bobbing along behind me. It was the hopping titches. Oh good grief, now I was even a "mate" of first formers. Still, I stopped and they caught up with me. Ginger Titch said, "Did you think Wet Lindsay's moustache was funny?"

I looked at them and they looked all proud of themselves.

I said, "Yeah, it was brillopads, but how do you know about it?"

They giggled and said, "We did it for you, miss."

Hells bells. They love me and think I have saved them. I have turned into a combination of Superman and Jesus – not that Jesus would wear tights.

Saturday July 16th

11:00 a.m.

Jas on the phone in a pants frenzy. "Gee. Oooooooohhhhh."

"What? What?"

"Oh, this is so exciting!!!"

"Have you discovered a new kind of slug?"

"No."

"New panties that go right up to your neck?"

"No... oooh, I wish I could tell you."

"Let me get this right, Jas, you have rung me up to tell me something that you can't tell me, is that it?"

"Yeah!!!"

"Goodbye, then. Thanks."

I put the phone down.

Jas on the phone
Thirty seconds later

"I'll tell you a bit then."

I waited. Oh, the tensionosity. Not. It will be something so boring about Jas's life. If she tells me that she and Hunky are going to have a double wedding with Rosie and Sven, I may lose what little mind I have got left. She's bound to want to have a woodland wedding. We'll all have to dress as elves and huddle on twigs and...

Jas was rambling on: "Tom says if you come to the gig tonight, you're in for a big surprise."

I said, "Why? Has it been cancelled?"

"Noooo... oooh, I wish I could tell you, but I promised. Oh, it's so... oh, well, anyway, you've got to come now, please, will you? Please come."

"Say, 'Please will you come, I love you, you are my besty.'"

There was a pause. I said, "Don't you want me to come?"

She said, "Er, well... Please will you come, I love you, you are my besty."

I said, "I will think about it. Goodbye."

Yesssssssss!!! I win hahahaha. Jazzy Spazzy had to say she luuurved me. Teehee.

I'm definitely not going now.

3:00 p.m.

I've decided again to go to the gig. Partly to get out of the house because Grandvati is coming round tonight. And I am a bit interested in what Tom has to say. I mean, if it was just Jas that was saying I should go, I would be a bit suspicious because her idea of "exciting" and "good" are different to mine. But Tom is, on the whole, not entirely mad for a boy.

4:00 p.m.

I wonder what it could be? I wonder if he's spoken to Masimo? He did say that he'd try to find out stuff for me. Maybe Masimo has told him that the "mates" thing was a mistake.

5:00 p.m.

What on earth shall I wear?

6:30 p.m.

Grandvati turned up in his "leisure" wear. Is it normal for octogenarians to wear tartan zoot suits? With matching cap? And blusher?

I went downstairs to say hello, even though I am vair vair busy trying to find something to wear for the gig. He was in the front room giving Libby the bumps. I waved to him and he waved back and smiled. He hasn't got his teeth in. I said to Mum, "Mum, my venerated grandfather is wearing make-up."

She just turned her eyes skyward and said, "Don't start me off. They say women go through a funny patch as they get older, but they're practically saints compared to men. He says he's taking up waterskiing."

I said, "Will he be wearing a wet suit?"

She said, "I'm afraid so."

Good grief.

After Grandvati had given me the usual ten pence to "get something nice for yourself". (Like what? Half a stamp?) I went back to my boudoir.

There must be something perfect for me to wear that will have Masimo desperate not to be my mate.

7:00 p.m.
Ready at last. I finally decided on my pleated kilt, boots and cross-over top. I went downstairs hoping to nip out of the door without a Nazi interrogation from Vati, but sadly he was just emerging from collecting extra pie rations from the kitchen. He looked me up and down. "Er, I think you'll find that you've forgotten to put a skirt on, Georgia."

Oh, vair vair *amusant*.

Mum came out of the kitchen with a struggling Gordy and chucked him outside and banged the door. He was howling and then started hurling himself against the door. Mum went into the front room and said, "Libby, you must not put him in the fridge any more."

"He laaaikes it."

"I know he likes it. He was lying in the butter. It's disgusting."

Vati was still raving on about my skirt. "Have you seen this, Connie? Look at the state she thinks she's going out in. You can practically see what she had for her tea."

254

What is he talking about? And also, that's a laugh, what I had for tea. I didn't have anything for "tea". We don't have stuff for tea.

Mum said, "Oh, for goodness' sake, Bob, it's fashion. They all look stupid; it's not just her."

Oh, very supportive coming from someone who's wearing a top so tight that her nungas are practically extra arms. But I didn't say that because I saw a window of opportunity for an escape while they argued the toss about fashion and so on.

Vati was still going on: "Oh, so it's all right that she looks like a prostitute because it's fashion? I suppose if leather bikinis were fashion you wouldn't mind your teenage daughter going out in one?"

Mum said, "You're being stupid, Bob. Leather bikinis will never be the fashion."

Grandad said, "Leather bikinis not fashionable? You tell Maisie and the rest of the lasses at the Housing Association that!"

I can't begin to let that image into my brain. On the plus side, it did stun Dad so much that I was able to get through the door and escape.

Clock tower

I had forgotten for a minute how nervy I am. I am sure I'm having a heart attack; my heart is plip-plopping and racing. I must get a grip. This is going to be the ultimate glaciosity test.

Jas, Ellen, Mabs and Jools were all at the clock tower. We did our special Klingon salute. Jas was being very annoying coming up to me and hugging me and going, "Oooohhhhhhh, I am soooooo excited."

If it's anything to do with any form of livestock, this "exciting" thing that she is so excited about, I will have to simply and quietly put her out of her misery. A glancing blow to the head should do it.

We started walking to the gig. I said, "Where are Ro Ro and Sven?"

Mabs said, "The bride and bridegroom phoned and said they'd see us there."

Fifteen minutes later

I feel like every footstep is bringing me closer to my fate. I don't know what I expect, anyway. He has said he wants to be my mate; that's the end of the story. Maybe there will be someone else there that I like. Yeah, whatever.

In the tarts' wardrobe

Ironically, for once my hair is not buggering about and there are no lurking lurker incidents. I decided against wearing the boy entrancers. At first I thought I'd do a double bluff on Our Lord. I thought I wouldn't wear them because I might end up in a snogging scenario and they might come adrift with tragic consequences. But then I thought I SHOULD wear them because that would imply I didn't think that there'd be snogging action and God would think that was sad, and then He would give me a surprise by giving me snogging action. But then I thought that He knows our every thought, even when we are on the lavatory, so He would know I was doing double bluffsies. So in the end what it comes down to is what sort of mood Our Lord is in. I should tell Call-me-Arnold to put that in his sermon if he wants to depress people. If God is in a smiting mood He will smite away to His heart's content, and if He is in a peachy mood, it also didn't matter what I was wearing.

In the end, I couldn't get the entrancers on straight, and after I had stabbed myself in the eye with my mascara, I called it a day entrancerwise.

Still, I had done a good job on the old layering of the

♡ 257

mascara, and my lippy was good. It looked all poutey pout and so on. I was just inspecting myself from the side, smiling and looking confident, when Jas came out of the loo.

"Why are you doing an impression of a goldfish? Are you fishing for compliments? Or are you trying to look NETural?!" And she went cackling off. She really does imagine that she's funny. Also, she did that weird hugging thing again and also said, "Wrrrrrrrr."

Why?

8:30 p.m.
The Stiff Dylans are on in a minute. I am on piddly-diddly duty about every two minutes.

8:35 p.m.
It's rammed in the club. I couldn't see Dave the Laugh and his mates. Perhaps they weren't coming. No sign of the happy couple. Or Wet Lindsay.

I said to Jas, "Oh dear, no sign of Wet Lindsay. I hope she hasn't fallen down some grating on the way here. That would be tragic. Not."

8:40 p.m.

Then Ellen said, "Oh, look, there's Dave. He looks cool, doesn't he? He, I think, he's like on his own. Can you see Emma? I can't see Emma, can you? Can you see her?"

Ellen might be on my killing list as well as Jas at this rate.

Two minutes later

Tom arrived. He walked in and saw Jas. He did a thumbsie-up to her and she did one back. How sad and uncool is that? They only saw each other about an hour ago. It's pathetico. But quite touching when you're a spinster of the parish. I suppose I should be happy for them. I am, really. But if she hugs me one more time, I will definitely deck her.

Stiff Dylans onstage

My tummy turned over when Masimo walked out onstage. He is just so gorgey. Actually, I don't know why I thought he would like me – he is clearly a ten and as Jas so kindly reminded me, I once got nothing out of ten for my nose. In fact, my average for features was six and a half. Six and a halfs do not go out with tens – that is the law of the snogging jungle.

Half an hour later

The Stiff Dylans rule. They are groove personified.

I know I am wound up on the rack of luuurve and so on but the music is so good everyone has gone mental. The Ace Gang is giving our world-renowned disco inferno exhibition. Everyone except Rosie and Sven, that is. I wonder where they are? Probably snogging in the chip shop. I wish they were here.

Half an hour later

Still dancing. I am showing *joie de vivre* and *savoir faire* to Masimo.

I'm boiling but I don't care. I think a bit of a healthy glow is nice in a girl.

Jas said, "Blimey, you're red. You look like you've plunged your head into a vat of boiling oil."

Oh good. I dashed off to the tarts' wardrobe for a bit of a dampening-down and titivating session.

Back in the club
Five minutes later

Dave and Rollo and Tom came over and joined us in a sort of

semi Viking disco inferno dance. But without the horns; Rosie is in charge of horns. Dave added some moves of his own, although it was a bit of a surprise when he leaped up into my arms. I managed to take his weight for a minute before he leaped down. He does make me laugh. We even did linksie-up disco dancing. Then he went off and he shouted to me, "Off to the piddly-diddly department, and I won't spare the horses!"

As we were doing our dance routines in front of the stage, I like to think that Masimo was looking at me in an admiring way. Either that or that he was thinking, *My new mate has gone mad.*

But I refuse to be sad.

Actually, Masimo did smile at me quite a lot when he caught my eye. But I am not so stupid that I think it means anything. I said to Jas, "Did you see Masimo looking at me?"

She said, "Forget about him; he is yesterday's news."

Thanks.

10:45 p.m.

I was dancing backwards when someone kicked my ankle really viciously. Buggering bums bugger. And also ouch. I looked round and there was Wet Lindsay and Astonishingly

♥ 261

Dim Monica. They must have slimed in while I wasn't looking. They were doing exceptionally crap dancing with their other crap mates from Crap City.

I said to Lindsay, "Oy."

And she came up to me, still smiling in a really scary way, and said, "Oh dear, you danced into my foot."

And then she waved at Masimo, who annoyingly nodded back and smiled.

Jas said, "Boy, does she hate you. You are dead meat. You live in Dead Meat City."

Cheers, thanks a lot. Hurrah another two happy years of Stalag 14 with a sadistic stick insect who hates me. I'll be lucky to come out of school fully limbed.

Five minutes later
The Stiff Dylans are on a break.

I am in a complete ditherspaz as to how to handle the situation. I can't just be hanging around, looking like goosegog of the century, when Masimo comes offstage. I know what I'll do: I'll go and talk to Dave the Laugh, that'll be cool. Also it will get me away from Jas and Tom, who seem to have lost their marbles. They keep looking at me and going into huddles and laughing like excited newts. Still no sign of Ro Ro and Sven.

I went over to the bar where I had last seen Dave. There he was, leaning against it, talking to his mates. Perfect. I was just about to go up to him when Emma appeared. Dave had his back to me, so he couldn't see me, and Emma came up to him and kissed him on the cheek. And then in front of everyone he put his arms round her and gave her a proper snog. No mistaking it. Not just a cheeksie, but proper lip-on-lip action. I felt really sick to my stomach. When he eventually stopped kissing her, he put his arm around her waist and bought her a drink. It was like they were proper boyfriend and girlfriend. I was so shocked.

I turned to go to the tarts' wardrobe, and as I did Masimo came out of the dressing room. He saw me and smiled and started to walk over to me. Oh God, what should I do? What would a mate do? Smack him on the shoulder when he came over and do the Klingon salute? I don't know, I don't know. I've never done mates with boys before.

There was only one thing for it. I looked at my watch and then looked surprised, slapped my head in the manner of someone who has forgotten an appointment, and then quickly walked to the tarts' wardrobe.

In the tarts' wardrobe
I'll tell you why I looked surprised when I looked at my watch, shall I? I haven't got a watch, that's why.

one minute later
Also, what sort of person has an appointment in the tarts' wardrobe? An idiot, that's what kind of person.

A sad twat.

Me.

one minute later
I sat down on the loo with my head in my hands. What could be worse than this?

Jas and Mabs and Ellen came to find me. I told them what had happened. Jas said, "Oh, well, maybe something really NICE will happen."

I said, "Yeah and maybe Hitler was really lovable, just misunderstood."

Mabs said, "Er, I think there's something else you should know."

Oh yeah, like what? I've been going round all night with my skirt stuck in my knickers?

I said, "Go on, then, what else could be worse than what is already happening? Oh, I know, Wet Lindsay is with Masimo."

At that point, Lindsay stormed into the tarts' wardrobe with Monica trailing behind her. Lindsay was all red-faced and flustered and looked like she was going to cry. So there is a silver lining to every cloud.

Not. Because she was saying to Monners, "How could Masimo just turn up with some Italian bint? How could he?"

They went down the other end of the loos when they saw us.

I looked at Mabs. She said, "Ah, well, yes, the other thing you should know."

In the club

I had to see the full fiasco with my own peepers. Masimo was sitting at a table by the side of the stage and leaning in very close to one of the most lovely girls I have ever seen. I don't say that because I want to, but she was – she was just lovely. She might even be a ten and a half.

Word must have spread on the Radio Jas airwaves because Ellen came scuttling over and Jools and all of the gang. I must not cry.

Ellen said, "I just, you know, like, casually walked by and they are speaking in Pizza-a-gogo language."

I was frozen to the spot and couldn't help looking at them. Masimo put his hand up to the Italian girl's face and pushed back her hair.

I must go home.

I glanced across the room because I felt like everyone must know what a fool I was. I could see Dave the Laugh sitting at the bar with Emma. She was talking to Rollo and Dave had his arm round her. I don't know why, but he suddenly looked round and straight at me. Then he looked at where Masimo was sitting with the Italian girl. He said something to Emma and kissed her cheek. Oh good, more and more agony.

I must get out of here. I said that to Jas, "I'm going to go home now, Jas. I can't stand this."

She said, "No, no, please don't go. Er... maybe something good will sort of happen."

I looked at her. "Like what, Jas? The sprinkler system might go off?"

As I said that, I saw Wet Lindsay grabbing her coat and storming off into the night. She stropped past the table Masimo was sitting at, but he didn't even notice; he was still talking earnestly to his girlfriend. What a top night this was turning out to be.

I said to the gang, "Well, I can't remember the last time I had so much fun. I think it was when I had to be rushed to hospital with scarlet fever. I'm going to have to go."

As I went off for my coat, Dave the Laugh appeared. "Oh dear, Kittykat, what am I going to do with you?"

I just looked at him, and my eyes filled with tears. He put his arm around me and I so wanted to just have him look after me.

But he had Emma, so I pulled myself together(ish). I must gird my loins with a firm hand. Remember my proud nautical heritage and the Bird of Avon's example. As Sir Billy Shakespeare said in times of stress, "She'll be coming round the mountain when she comes."

I stepped back from Dave and then I heard a voice behind me say, "HOOOORRRN! Oh *jah*, HOOOORRRRRRN!!!"

Tarts' wardrobe

I was sitting on the loo AGAIN with my head in my hands (I practically live in here) when Rosie's horns appeared under the door. Ro Ro said, "Why did you just run off like that?"

I replied, "Well, you're used to Sven."

Ro Ro said, "Good point, but what does that have to do with anything?"

"Well, I was startled by his furry shorts."

Back in the club

Dave and his mates were gathered around Sven, admiring his shorts. The shorts were made out of bits of theatrical fur and a pair of old Y-fronts. Sven had completed his outfit with the bison horns and furry Doc Marten's. And, uh... that was it!

Rosie was wearing a leather skirt and a sort of metallic-looking nunga-nunga holder made out of pan lids.

I said to her, "Why have you got one huge eyebrow?"

And she said, "This is a well known Viking bridal outfit. Get your horns on!"

As Rosie shoved the horns on my head, Masimo appeared in front of me!!!

He looked at the horns and, after a few moments of gazing at them, he said a bit nervously, "*Scusi*, Georgia, may I speak with you?"

Oh great, now I was wearing horns and I was going to have to be mates with Masimo while he told me about his new girlfriend.

Dave looked at me a bit weirdly (who wouldn't?) and then he said, "I'll be around if you need me." And he went back to the bar.

Oh noooo, I was on my own. I only had my own brain to help me. God help us one and all. Oh noooo, Masimo was so lovely. His eyes were golden and soft and melty. Booo, no melty eyes, no melty eyes.

And then I remembered I was still wearing the horns. I took them off and looked at them as if I'd never seen them before. I said, "Good heavens, how did they get there?" and flung them on the floor.

He said, "Will you come outside with me, for a little chat?"

No. No. No chatting. No mates just chatting. No.

Perhaps he meant him and his girlfriend. Perhaps he wanted me to be mates with her as well. I couldn't see her anywhere, but she might come popping up any minute wanting to be mates. I am not putting myself through any more humiliation. I am just going to say, "No, I will not go outside with you, mate."

But of course I followed him outside like a suckling pig. Oh no, I mean a sacrificial lamb. There was no sign of the Italian bint. She was probably at home cooking up some pasta for when he got back from being with his horn-wearing "mates". The Ace Gang were all watching me trail after the Luuurve God. Other girls were looking daggers at me; they needn't bother.

Outside, it was a lovely night. Oh good, and all the stars were out hanging about waiting to see the next exciting instalment in the Georgia is a Prat saga.

Masimo leaned against the wall and looked at me. Please don't look at me like that, it's heartbreaking. Then he said, "Can I to explain things? Gina has come from Italy. She is... er, was my girlfriend, I tell you about. The one I have serious love with, and then we break up, and I... well, I say to you that I want nothing serious."

Yes, yes, I have been to this particular cake shop of aggers before. I didn't know what to say, so I thought I might as well practise my mate skills. Big breath, relax, casualosity and matiness at all times and, "Did you see the footie scores this arvie?"

He looked at me as if I was bonkers.

I am.

Then he laughed. "The footie scores?"

I nodded in an interested way.

He said, "Georgia, Gina has come to see me to tell me she has a new boyfriend."

Pardon?

He was still looking at me. "She was very, you know, had her heart breaking after us, so I felt well... hard for her, hard for me to have a girlfriend. Now she tell me she is better. So all is good."

Is it? What's going on now?

He was still looking at me.

"So, Signorína Georgia, what do you think? Now I am free man for you. If you still want for us to go out."

I was doing my very interesting and world-renowned impression of a goldfish with learning disorders when Jas and Tom appeared at the doorway, beside themselves with excitement.

What is the matter with them? And why are they bothering me now when I practically have a Luuurve God in my hand.

A car pulled up behind me and I heard the car door open and then slam. I was too paralysed to do anything, and besides, I felt like I was in a slow-motion movie.

Masimo was staring over my shoulder. He looked really surprised and said, "*Ciao*. But when did you get back?"

I turned round, and getting out of the car was Robbie.

Robbie.

Robbie whose name I wasn't going to mention this side of the grave.

Robbie who was in Kiwi-a-gogo land.

Playing guitars in streams.

And snogging marsupials.

Except he wasn't.

He was here.

I was quite literally speechless.

The Sex God had re-landed.

Georgia's Glossary

aggers · Agony. Like I said, no one has the time to say whole words, so aggers is short for agony. The unusually irritating among you might point out that aggers is actually longer than agony. My answer to that is – haven't you got something else to do besides count letters?

Alsatian · This is a big wolfy-type guard doggie, so called because it is from Alsatia, that well known place in, erm... Lederhosen land. Possibly. Oh, I don't know. Why am I being bothered with this? I am vair vair tired, and it's only a dog when all is said and done.

arvie · Afternoon. From the Latin "arvo". Possibly. As in the famous Latin invitation: "Lettus meetus this arvo."

balaclava · This is from the Crimean War when our great-great-grannies spent all their time knitting hats to keep the English soldiers warm in the very, very cold Baltic. A balaclava covers everything apart from your eyes. It's like a big sock with a hole in it. Which just goes to show what really crap knitters our great-great-grannies were.

bhaji · A bhaji is an Indian food. An onion bhaji is brown and round and full of fat, hence my hilarious joke about Slim looking like one. I exhaust myself with my good humour, I really do.

billio · From the Australian outback. A billycan was something Aborigines boiled their goolies up in, or whatever it is they eat. Anyway, billio means boiling things up. Therefore, "my cheeks ached like billio" means, er... very achy. I don't know why we say it. It's a mystery, like many things. But that's the beauty of life.

Blimey O'Reilly · (as in "Blimey O'Reilly's trousers") This is an Irish expression of disbelief and shock. Maybe Blimey O'Reilly was a famous Irish bloke who had extravagantly big trousers. We may never know the truth. The fact is, whoever he is, what you need to know is that a) it's Irish and b) it is Irish. I rest my case.

Boboland · As I have explained many, many times, English is a lovely and exciting language full of sophisticosity. To go to sleep is "to go to bobos", so if you go to bed you are going to Boboland. It is an Elizabethan expression. (Oh, OK then, Libby made it up and she can be unreasonably violent if you don't join in with her.)

boy entrancers · Ah, yes, the re-emergence of the boy entrancers. Hmmm... well... boy entrancers are false eyelashes. They are known as boy entrancers because they entrance boys. Normally. However, I've had some non-entrancing moments with them. For instance, the time I used too much glue to stick them on with. It was when I was at a Stiff Dylans gig trying to entrance Masimo. I was intending to do that looking up at him and then looking down and then looking up again thing, and possibly a bit of flicky hair (as suggested in *How to Make Any Twit Fall in Love with You*). I did the looking at him and looking down thing, but when I tried to look up again I couldn't because my BEs had stuck to my bottom lashes. So my eyes stayed shut. I tried raising my eyebrows (that must have looked good) and humming, but in the end, out of sheer desperadoes, I said,

"Oooh, I love this one..." and went off doing blind disco-dancing to Rolf Harris's "Two Little Boys". So, in conclusion, boy entrancers are good, but be alert for glue extravaganzas.

bugger · A swear word. It doesn't really mean anything but neither do a lot of swear words. Or parents.

bum-oley · Quite literally bottom hole. I'm sorry but you did ask. Say it proudly (with a cheery smile and a Spanish accent).

chav · A chav is a common rude rough person. They wear naff clothes. A chav joke would be, "What are the first words a chav baby says to its single parent?" Answer: "What are YOU looking at?" Or: "If there are two chavs in a car and no loud music playing, what kind of a car is it?" Answer: "A police car."

Chingachgook · He was the last of the Mohicans. He hung around with Davy Crockett and they both wore hats made out of old beavers. (They were dead, the beavers, not just old and having a little doze on Davy and Chingachgook's heads.)

chuddie · Chewing gum. This is an "i" word thing. We have a lot of them in English due to our very busy lives explaining stuff to other people not so fortunate as ourselves.

clud · This is short for cloud. Lots of really long boring poems and so on can be made much snappier by abbreviating words. So Wordsworth's poem called "Daffodils" (or "Daffs") has the immortal line "I wandered lonely as a clud". Ditto *Rom and Jul* or *Ham* or *Merc of Ven*.

conk · Nose. This is very interesting historically. A very long time ago (1066) – even before my grandad was born – a bloke called William the Conqueror (French) came to England and shot our King Harold in the eye. Typical. And people wonder why we don't like the French much. Anyway, William had a big nose and so to get our own back we called him William the Big Conk-erer. If you see what I mean. I hope you do because I am exhausting myself with my hilariosity and historiosity.

div · Short for "dithering prat", i.e., Jas.

double cool with knobs · "Double" and "with knobs" are instead of saying very or very, very, very, very. You'd feel silly saying, "He was very, very, very, very, very cool". Also everyone would have fallen asleep before you had finished your sentence. So "double cool with knobs" is altogether snappier.

duffing up · Duffing up is the female equivalent of beating up. It is not so violent and usually involves a lot of pushing with the occasional pinch.

fandango · A fandango is a complicated Spanish dance. So a fandango is a complicated thing. Yes, I know there is no dancing involved. Or Spanish.

fives court · This is a typical Stalag 14 idea. It's minus forty-five degrees outside so what should we do to entertain the schoolgirls? Let them stay inside in the cosy warmth and read? No, let's build a concrete wall outside with a red line at waist height and let's make them go and hit a hard ball at the red line with their little freezing hands. What larks!

froggie and geoggers · Froggie is short for French,

geoggers is short for geography. Ditto blodge (biology) and lunck (lunch).

f.t. · I refer you to the famous "losing it" scale:

minor tizz

complete tizz and to do

strop

a visit to Strop Central

f.t. (funny turn)

spaz attack

complete ditherspaz

nervy b. (nervous breakdown)

complete nervy b.

ballisticisimus

goosegog · Gooseberry. I know you are looking all quizzical now. OK. If there are two people and they want to snog and you keep hanging about saying, "Do you fancy some chewing gum?" or "Have you seen my interesting new socks?" you are a gooseberry. Or for short a goosegog, i.e., someone who nobody wants around.

gorgey · Gorgeous. Like fabby (fabulous) and marvy (marvellous).

havvies · Haversacks. Life is too shor to fini wor...

Horn · When you "have the Horn" it's the same as "having the big red bottom".

Jammy Dodger · Biscuit with jam in it. Very nutritious(ish).

jimjams · Pyjamas. Also pygmies or jammies.

joggerbums · Trousers that you jog in. Jogging trousers.

Kiwi-a-gogo land · New Zealand. "a-gogo land" can be used to liven up the otherwise really boring names of other countries. America, for instance, is Hamburger-a-gogo land, Mexico is Mariachi-a-gogo land and France is Frogs'-legs-a-gogo land. Masimo comes from Pizza-a-gogo land – land of wine, sun, olives and vair vair groovy Luuurve Gods. Otherwise known as Italy. (The only bad point about Pizza-a-gogo land is their football players are so vain that if it rains, they all run off the pitch so that their hair doesn't get ruined. See also Chelsea players.)

Late and Live · A late-night gig which has live bands on.

Manchester United · An English football team from the north of England, otherwise known as "The Scum". The most hated team apart from "The Blue Scum" (Chelsea). There is an important difference between them – one wears a red strip and the other wears blue. That is all you need to know.

Midget Gem · Little sweets made out of hard jelly stuff in different fruit flavours. Jas loves them A LOT. She secretes them about her person, I suspect, often in her knickers, so I never like to accept one from her on hygiene and lesbian grounds.

mug's game · As in "love is a mug's game". The beauty of Billy Shakespeare language is that it is multi whatsit. For instance "mug" can mean a cup. However, even the very dim amongst you (and I mean that in a caring way) can see that saying "love is a cup's game" is just silly. A mug can also mean a face. However "love is a face's game" doesn't have *je ne sais quoi* and verve. And this is where we come to my nub – mug can also mean a "fool", like for instance my vati. So there you have it. "Love is a fool's game." Which is *le* fact.

nippy noodles · Instead of saying, "Good heavens, it's quite cold this morning," you say "Cor – nippy noodles!!" English is an exciting and growing language. It is. Believe me. Just leave it at that. Accept it.

nuddy-pants · Quite literally nude-coloured pants, and you know what nude-coloured pants are? They are no pants. So if you are in your nuddy-pants, you are in your no pants, i.e., you are naked.

nunga-nungas · Basoomas. Girls' breasty business. Ellen's brother calls them nunga-nungas because he says that if you get hold of a girl's breast and pull it out and then let it go, it goes nunga-nunga-nunga. As I have said many, many times with great wisdomosity, there is something really wrong with boys.

Pacamac · A rainproof coat that folds up into a tiny packet that you can pop in your handbag. It keeps you dry but you look like a fool.

Pantalitzer · A terrifying Czech-made doll that sadistic parents (my vati) buy for their children, presumably to teach them early on about the horror of life. Essentially the Pantalitzer doll has a weird plastic face with a horrible fixed smile. The rest of Pantalitzer is a sort of cloth bag with hard plastic hands on each side like steel forks. I don't know if I have mentioned this before, but I am not reassured that Eastern Europeans really know how to have a laugh.

Pavlov's dogs · Pavlov was some Russian bloke who had some dogs. He trained them to dribble when he rang a bell. Don't ask me why. The Russians are, as we all know, a bit on the strange side. Cossack dancing for instance. I rest my case.

red-bottomosity · Having the big red bottom. This is vair vair interesting vis-à-vis nature. When a lady baboon is "in the mood" for luuuurve, she displays her big red bottom to the male baboon. (Apparently he wouldn't have a clue otherwise, but that is boys for you!!) Anyway, if you hear the call of the Horn you are said to be displaying red-bottomosity.

sailor's hornpipe · As I have pointed out many, many times, England is a proud seafaring nation and our sailors on the whole are jolly good chaps etc. However, when they were first invented in the olden days, they had a few too many rums and made up this odd dance called a "hornpipe", which largely consists of hopping from foot to foot with your arms crossed. Well, you did ask.

spangleferkel · A kind of German sausage. I know, you couldn't make it up, could you? The German language is full of this kind of thing, like lederhosen and so on. And *Goosegot.*

squid · Squid is the plural of quid, and I do know why that is: a bloke owed another bloke six pounds, or six quid, and he goes up to him with an octopus with one of its tentacles bandaged up, and he says, "Hello, mate. Here is the sick squid I owe you." Do you see?? Do you see? Sick squid – six quid??? The marvellous juxtaposition of... Look, we just call pounds squids. Leave it at that. Try and get on with it, people.

titches · A titch is a small person. Titches is the plural of titch.

toadying · This is when a person is all slimy and sucky and tries to get stuff by pretending to be nice.

tushy pegs · Tush rhymes with mush, which means face (keep up), so the pegs in your mush are your teeth. Now do you see? Well, just accept it.

vicars and tarts party · A traditional fancy-dress party that "grown-ups" think is hilarious. Everyone goes to the party either dressed up as a vicar or a prostitute. It is sad. What is even sadder though is that I was coming home once and accidentally bumped into Call-me-Arnold the vicar wheeling his sad bike home. I was trying to get away from him when a group of lads came by and said, "Oy, where's the party?" because they thought we were dressed up as a vicar and a tart. Good grief. It's quite bad for someone to think you're dressed up as a tart, but much much worse that they may have thought Call-me-Arnold was my boyfriend.

Wally · See prat. A wally additionally has no clothes sense.

Welligogs · Wellington boots. Because it more or less rains all the time in England we have special rubber boots that we wear to keep us above the mud. This is true.

Whelks · A horrible shellfish thing that only the truly mad (like my grandad, for instance) eat. They are unbelievably slimy and mucuslike.

Winceyette · Is like fluffy nylon material, usually pink. If you wear it, it makes your hair stand on end because it's so full of static electricity. The elderly insane LOVE it.

Woad · The Ancient Britons used to dye themselves blue with a plant called woad. I don't know why they didn't like pink as a skin colour. They just preferred to be blue. But that is the Ancient Britons for you.

Womble · Yes. Now, *The Wombles of Wimbledon* was a crap TV show about these creatures who lived in Wimbledon. The wombles were supposed to be giant hamsters but were quite clearly tubby blokes in hairy costumes. They mostly wandered about Wimbledon Common collecting litter. Oh, and they had a number one hit with "Remember You're a Womble". The lyrics were, "Remember you're a womble, remember you're a womble. Remember, member, member, what a womble, womble, womble you are." That is how great the whole thing was.

Woopsie · *Ordure* and *merde*. Ok, have it your way, poo.

'Luuurve is a ♪♫ ♩ many trousered thing...' ♡

A Note from Georgia

Dearest international and marvy chummly wummlies,

Yes, once again I have given you my all (oo-er), so here is 'Luuurve is a many trousered thing...' And it is, believe me.

I wanted it to be called 'Trouser Snakes-a-gogo!' but the grown-ups said that was too rude. I had the same trouble with '...and that's when it fell off in my hand.' The Hamburger-a-gogo "grown-ups" said that was too rude.

I said, "How do you mean? Do you mean that you think it might be something about a boy's trouser-snake addenda?"

And they said, "Yes."

And I said, "But if that came off in your hand, that would not be a comedy diary, that would be a medical book." But you can't tell people.

So you see how vair vair tiring the whole thing can be. But I struggle out of my bed of pain again only because I luuurve you all so much.

Lots of kisses, but not in a lezzie way,

Georgia

xxx

p.s. You will also notice that Jas has introduced the idea of virtual upper-body fondling to the snogging scale. This is typical of what I have to put up with.

p.p.s. If you have a Jas in your life, EAT HER - it's the only sensible thing to do.

p.p.p.s. Even though I'm vair vair tired, it's come to my attention that there are some people who haven't read my diaries before and keep asking me stuff about the Ace Gang, and the snogging scale, and disco inferno dancing. So for those vair vair lazy people, I've added some lists of things at the back of the book.

With deep luuurve to all the usuals. I'm not saying I'm bored with you, or that you are all usual because, believe me, you're not. Anyway, can we get on?

p.s. Thank you and blimey to Mr Urrrrr.

Hoooooorrrrn!!

Saturday July 16th

11:45 p.m.

Run away, run away!!!

Pant, pant, pant.

And double pants.

How in the name of God's novelty undercrackers and matching toga have I ended up running along the streets at midnight?

I'll tell you how. You wait ages for a Sex God to come along and then two come along at the same time. Where is the sense in that? If it is all part of Big G's divine plan, all I can say is this, "Keep it simple, Big G, just give me one Sex God to eat at a time. And then if I am not full up I'll have another one. Thank you. Regards to Baby Jesus."

That is all I am saying. Inwardly, obviously, as I am nearly dead with trying to run in my high-heeled boots. I may have to lie down in a ditch in a minute.

11:50 p.m.

I had to stop and sit in the hedge by the park. I'm so out of breath. Hurrah, I am sitting in the dark like a panting vole in a skirt.

Three minutes later

Pant, pant. So this is a brief résumé of Vole Girl's evening:

Scene 1

A top night at the Stiff Dylans gig, including an excellent Viking disco inferno dance* in honour of Rosie and Sven's forthcoming (well, in eighteen years time) wedding and Sven arriving in furry shorts.

*Note to the dim – and I mean this in a loving way – the Viking disco inferno dance goes stamp, stamp to the left, left leg kick, kick, arm up, stab, stab to the left... and HOOOOOOORN!

As the *pièce de* whatsit, Masimo, lead singer and Luuurve God that I have been dreaming of and longing for, asked me to go outside, and said, "So, Signorína Georgia, I am free man for you. If you still want for us to go out?"

Keep in mind that he said it in his gorgey porgey Pizza-a-gogo land accent. Looking at me like I was a Sex Kitty.

Scene 2
Just as I was experiencing Swoon City and melty pantaloonies a car pulled up and Robbie the original Sex God got out.

The one who had left me and gone to Kiwi-a-gogo land. To snog marsupials and so on for the rest of his life.

Not.

Scene 3
After a moment of silence I said in a quick-thinking and casual way, "Oh, hello, Robbie, do excuse me, I have a train to catch and time and tide wait for no

man." And walked quickly off before breaking into a slight trot. Then a light gallop. Then I ended up in the hedge and that is where all this started.

In conclusion I would say that after queuing up at the cake shop of luuurve for ages I have accidentally bought two cakes. And I am sitting in a bush.

11:56 p.m.
Oh, yet more marvellous, marvellous news, the Blunder Boys are lurking around in the park. Probably setting fire to themselves and practising being crap. Which they needn't bother doing as they are top at it anyway.

They'll sense I'm here in a minute and come looming out at me. The Blunder Boys have got radar for girls within half a mile.

Thirty seconds later
Mark Big Gob (who lives in my street and who I accidentally snogged once, and who has the largest lips known to humanity) larged out of the gloom and saw me panting in the hedge. He was looking at my nungas, which were heaving up and down.

Stop heaving and retreat into your over-the-shoulder-boulder-holder, you stupid nungas!

Mark said, "I see you are all pleased to see me, girls."

How repellant is he? I ignored him and got up with a dignity-at-all-times sort of attitude. As I was brushing past him, he said, "Steady darlin', you nearly knocked me over."

The rest of the trainee idiots had sidled up by then and they sniggered and choked on their fags. Still, on the bright side cigarettes stunt your growth, so with a bit of luck most of them will remain about three foot eight.

Mark Big Gob said, "I see you've got the Horn. Is it for me?"

Is he mad? Is he implying that I have got the Horn for him? I would rather plunge my head into a bucket of whelks than let him anywhere near me. I can't believe that his hand once rested on my basooma. And that his enormous gob had squelched around my face. Erlack. If anything, he gave me the Anti-Horn.

Sadly, it was then I realised that in fact he was right, I did have the horn. Horns actually. I was still carrying my Viking bison horns that I had worn to rehearse Rosie's wedding dance.

Still, what is so very unusual about that?

Five minutes later

Quite a lot, actually, when you think about it.

Which I won't.

Oh double *merde* and *ordure* and poo.

12:15 a.m.

Got to my street. My tootsies are killing me. The light is still on in the front room. Oh noooo. That means the terminally insane (Mutti and Vati) are still up. I must avoid them at all costs. I can't speak to them. Not now. Not any time if I have my way.

I snuck really really quietly through the front door and stashed my horns in a secret place where they will never be found (the ironing basket).

Aaahh. Safely in. Now quietly, quietly up the stairs to my room. Quietly, quietly like a little mousie. Mousie girl opening little doorsies. Shhhhh. Shhhh. Nearly safe. Quietly into the room like a quiet thing on quiet tablets. No sign of the Furry Freak brothers, a.k.a. my cats Angus and his cross-eyed son Gordon, thank the Lord.

As I opened my bedroom door Gordy's face appeared upside down an inch away from my fringe. I looked into his mad cross-eyes. Why does he do that – lurk on top of the door like a bat? He did a little croaky noise and licked my face with his horrid rough tongue. I managed not to cry out or be sick.

12:25 a.m.
There is a half-eaten mouse on my pillow.

12:30 a.m.
Oh God, that means that Gordy licked my face after he had crunched up the mousey head. I am almost bound to get the Black Death. Nothing nicer than a few pustulating boils when you have boyfriend trouble.

One minute later
Crept downstairs to get rid of the mousey. I had it on a piece of cardboard. When I say mousey what I mean is two ears and a bit of tail. Too crunchy for Gordy's delicate little murderer's gob, I suppose.

As I was going back upstairs Mutti called out from the front room, "Is that you, Gee?"

I said, "No," and went up to get into my snuggly bed of pain.

In bed under the sheets of life

One minute later

Can't be bothered getting undressed as I'm so full of confusiosity.

Five minutes later

I'd better make an effort though and at least take my boots off. My feet are probably all swollen from my mad running and I don't want to have them surgically removed again.

The boots, I mean, not my feet.

Anyway, the nub and gist is that I have accidentally acquired two Luuurve Gods.

I may never sleep again.

One minute later

I won't have time to sleep if I've got two boyfriends, tee hee…

zzzzzzzzzzzzzzzz.

Sunday July 17th

7:00 a.m.

Woke up from a dream where Dr Clooney was looking at my head and saying, "I have never seen anything like it! Her head is one enormous boil!" and for a minute forgot that I have two boyfriends.

I checked in the mirror and there has been no pustulating boil extravaganza, so I seem to have escaped catching the Black Death from Gordy's little mousey snack, thank the Lord. Although my head has exploded, hairwise. I may have to iron it.

7:35 a.m.
Crept downstairs and made some toast and tea. I must keep my strength up.

There is snoring coming from every room. Mum made Dad sleep in the spare room because of his snoring and she is louder than him! I must be kind, though: she probably has difficulty breathing because of the weight of her enormous nungas. If mine grow as big as hers I will definitely donate them to some charity.

It is a nice day. The birds are humming and the bees a-singing and I can see Angus the furry Luuurve Machine lolling around in the morning sun with Naomi. They are very much in love if the amount of bum-oley licking is anything to go by.

Back in my bed with snacksies
Five minutes later
I must consult with a book of wisdomosity.

Five minutes later
This double boyfriend fandango is not mentioned in Mutti's book *How to Make Any Twit Fall in Love with You.*

Three minutes later
Maybe Robbie and Masimo will have to have fisticuffs at dawn to decide who gets me. Who knows what the right etiquette is in this scenario?

One minute later
One thing is for sure. I will not be asking Dave the Laugh, my Horn Adviser and occasional snoggee, to the fight. He will only think it is a laugh and start shouting out stuff like, "Hit him with your handbag, Masimo!" or "Mind the hair, love!" Anyway, Dave is too busy to give me advice these days. He will be with his "girlfriend". I wonder what number they have got up to on the snogging scale?

Shut up, brain! I don't want to think about Dave – he is an ex-snoggee. And just a mate. I have enough to worry about without Dave popping up all the time (oo-er).

7:55 a.m.
This does mean that I am going to have to be on high beauty and glamorosity alert at all times. One of my multi boyfriends may be so driven by snognosity that he rushes round here first thing in the morning. I must be prepared. But no one must know. I must exude glamour but in a natural just-tumbled-out-of-bed way.

Soooo just a hint of foundation, touch of bronzer, lippy, mascara and tiny bit of eyeliner. Which I like to think looks like I have a touch of the Egyptian in my genes.

That is what I like to think.

8:00 a.m.
Now what to wear? Nightwear or daywear?

What would you wear if you had unexpectedly woken up to the doorbell ringing and you didn't know who it was but you suspected it might be a Luuurve or a Sex God?

8:01 a.m.

Not Teletubbies pyjamas, that is *le* fact.

8:06 a.m.

Denim skirt and a T-shirt?

   Yep.

8:12 a.m.

I took a peek out of the front window. No sign of any Sex or Luuurve Gods. The reverse, in fact, because I was alarmed to see Mr Across the Road in his garden in a shortie dressing gown. I hope he is not going to become a homosexualist in his twilight years. Then Mrs Across the Road came out in a massive pair of pyjamas. Was there the suggestion of a small moustache on her upper lip? Maybe that's what happens in the end when people are married: they change sex. My dad is certainly on the turn, but on the other hand no man alive has developed nunga-nungas like Mum.

8:30 a.m.

Why hasn't Jas phoned?

You would think that Radio Jas would have been on the airwaves of life wanting to know what happened to me, and also wanting to report what had happened after I left the gig. I suppose I will just have to wait until she wakes up, or the rest of the Ace Gang wakes up to let me know what is going on. I must use the steely discipline for which I am world renowned.

8:35 a.m.
That's it, I can't stand it any more.

Crept out of the house. I won't leave a note because no one will notice I am missing for hours. The last thing I want is a cross-examination from Herr Vati. Or Mum being "interested".

Outside on the drive
Angus is still lying on his back on the wall while Naomi licks his face, and now she has started on his bum-oley. How disgusting. Kittyporn first thing in the morning.

Also, they are both covered in what looks like snot.

Oh, Blimey O'Reilly's trousers, it isn't snot; it's frogspawn.

They have been marauding about in Mr and Mrs Next Door's new marine conservation area – known to other normal people as a bucket with disgusting tadpoles and slime in it. The Prat brothers, also known as Mr Next Door's annoying and useless toy poodles, were on marine conservation lifeguard duty. So all Angus had to do was duff them up a bit, round them up into their kennel, and then it was a night of splashing around in the bucket to his heart's content.

The Next Doors will go absolutely ballistic; they always do about the least thing. Mr Next Door has been hovering on the edge of a nervy spaz for the last year and this might drive him over the edge and into the rest home. His shorts will probably explode with the tension. Which is no bad thing, unless I happen to be around at the time and am exposed to the sight of his huge bottom looming about.

I said to Angus, "You are soooo bad, Angus, and in for big trub. That is a fact. *Au revoir*, dead kitty pal."

I'm sure he understands every word I say because he got idly to his feet, stretched, and nudged Naomi off the wall. He treats his girls rough.

Naomi leaped back on the wall and arched her back and raised her hackles, making that really mad screechy noise that

Burmese cats do. She was spitting at Angus and teetering backwards and forwards. Really, really mad.

Angus was frightened. Not. When she got near enough he biffed her with his paw and she disappeared over the wall again. You had to laugh.

Not for long, though, because after he had rolled about on the lawn to get rid of the frogspawn he began stalking me.

Oh no, not today, my furry friend. I am not having him tagging along with me all day causing mayhem and eating anything that moves. I said, "Clear off, Angus, stay there. Sit. Sit."

I even threw him a stick to distract him and he ran bounding off after it, but then came back to trail along behind me.

I started running.

He started running.

I hid behind a wall.

His head loomed over the wall at me.

In the end, to give him the hint, I threw stones at him – some of them quite big.

Five minutes later

This is hopeless. He doesn't care about having stones thrown at him at all. He is senselessly brave.

One minute later

He is trying to catch the stones in his mouth.

One minute later

He's just slightly dazed himself by heading one of them.

In Jas's garden
9:00 a.m.

No sign of Jas being up and her curtains are drawn. Damny damn damn. She is so lazy, snoozing in Pantsland. I don't want to arouse any interest in the elderly mad by ringing the bell. Even though Jas's M and D are on the whole more acceptable than most, in that they provide snacks and Jas's dad doesn't speak, they are still technically in the elderly-loon category.

Three minutes later

How can I get Jas to get up without ringing the doorbell?

One minute later

Oh, here we are! There is a ladder in the shed. I can use my initiative and Girl Guide training (which I haven't got and never will have) and use the ladder to make a small fire to send smoke signals past her bedroom window. Shut up, brain.

Five minutes later

It must be a child's ladder as it only reaches to just above the lounge window. I would have to have orang-utan arms on stilts to reach Jas's window. Poo and *merde*.

Two minutes later

As I was looking up wondering how to make my arms grow, something bit my ankle really viciously. Angus was on the ladder with me, looking at me and playfully biting my legs. Ouch, bloody ouch.

I reached down to strangle him and I was just saying, "You bloody furry freak, I'll kill you when I get down from here..." when I saw Jas's dad standing on the garden path with his paper, smoking his unlit pipe. He was looking at me, like I was Norma Normal.

I said, "Ah yes, I was just... thinking I'd see what your

garden looked like from up here. And yep, yep, it looks very, very nice indeed. Full of stuff. Growing and so on."

What was I talking about?

Five minutes later

Jas's dad is sensationally nice, or insane, it's hard to tell. He let Angus carry his newspaper into the house, and didn't even seem to mind when he ate it.

In Jas's bedroom

I managed to dig Jas out from underneath her owls. How many stuffed owls can one person collect? A LOT is the answer in her case. What is the matter with her? Also, she was vair vair grumpy when I woke her up with a kiss. It was only on her cheek but you would think she had been attacked by hordes of lesbians in cowboy outfits.

Blimey. She looks very odd in the mornings and her fringe was akimbo to the max. She looked like a startled earwig in jimmy-jams.

I said, "So, so? What happened?"

She looked at me and started early-morning fiddling with her fringe. Vair annoying.

She said, "You just ran off like a fool."

I said, "Yes, I know, I was there."

"Yes, you say that, but you weren't there, that is the whole point. And everyone was going, 'What's Georgia doing? Has she gone mad?' and so on."

"Jas, if I get you a little cup of tea and a snacklet will you try to be normal and tell me everything that happened? It is a matter of life and death. YOUR life and YOUR death."

Ten minutes later

It's quite nice and cosy tucked up in bed with Jas and snacksies. Except that I think I have an owl's beak up my bum-oley.

Jas was munching and rambling. "Well, first of all, after you had run off like a ninny – by the way, you run in a really weird way in those high heels. You looked like Nauseating P. Green when she's playing hockey. Her legs go all spazzy and—"

I hit her with Snowy Owl. She almost choked on her toast.

I said, "Jas, get on with it, I have only got about fifty more years to live."

"Well, first of all, the boys did that boy thing with Robbie."

"What boy thing?"

"You know, slapping each other on the shoulders, shaking hands, and so on."

"Yeah."

Jas went on, "Robbie was saying hello to a lot of people and Masimo got his jacket on. You were just approaching the park by then; we could still see you. Masimo said to Tom, 'She asked me about footie results. Then she ran away. Is she normal?'"

Ohmygiddygod. I said to Jas, "What did Tom say?"

"Well, he stood up for you, of course."

"I love Hunky very much, as you know, Jazzy Spazzy."

"Yes, he said you were quite often normal. He had seen you being normal once or twice himself. Usually when you were asleep."

Marvellous.

Apparently after I had run off to "catch my train", Masimo had gone home with the band, and just after he'd gone Wet Lindsay had come stropping back looking for him. Jas said her no-forehead was all crinkly and mad and her hair extensions were swishing around in a Nervy B. Central way. Then she had seen Robbie and was all over him like a rash and they had gone off together.

What, what???

I said, "Wet Lindsay went off with the Sex God?"

"Well, they did go out together once, didn't they?"

"Yes, Jas, I know, I was heartbroken. Do you remember?"

"I mean, maybe he still likes her. I don't know, maybe he has had a secret thing for her. Some people like lanky girls."

"Jas, shut up now."

"Well, I am just saying that absence makes the heart grow fonder, and so on. It's an ill wind that—"

"Jas, that is not shutting up, that is rambling on and on about rubbish."

She was chomping away on her Jammy Dodger like Wise Mabel of the Forest. I really, really wanted to shove it down her throat, but I knew it would take another million years to get the end of the story if I did, so I just said, "Jas, you know when you were going on and on about 'maybe something good will happen', and I didn't want to go to the gig in the first place but you persuaded me? Well, did you know that Robbie was going to be there?"

"Well, I sort of thought he might. I knew he was coming home because he rang Tom and said that he had booked his ticket. And that he would be back in time for the gig."

"But did he say why he was coming home?"

"Erm, no, not exactly, no."

Oh noooooo. I have left the cake shop of luuurve thinking I have accidentally bought two cakes and found out that I may have only got one cake. And I might have already eaten that. I may in fact be cakeless.

I said to Jas, "We must call an emergency Ace Gang meeting."

"Well, I thought I might go to the river with Tom and—"

"No, Jas, you thought wrong."

Park
Midday
Angus is still trailing me around like Inspector Morse in a furry coat (and on all fours).

On the swings
Rosie said, "I hope this is worth it. Sven and me were going to practise artificial respiration on each other in case anyone chokes on the vats of mead at our wedding."

Even the Ace Gang has no sense of community these days. Jas bleating on about missing Tom, Jools wanting to go hang around Rollo while he played footie, Rosie banging on about Sven – half-reindeer, half-fool – and Ellen... well, Ellen just being Ellen.

Five minutes later

Ellen, Rosie, Jools, Mabs, Jas and me are all swinging on the swings. Not backwards and forwards like normal people enjoying a day in the park, but sideways so that the Blunder Boys can't see anything. Life is not easy. The Blunder Boys are in the bushes watching us on the swings. They think we don't know they are there; it's pathetic. They are so noisy and keep falling over things and fighting with each other.

Five minutes later

Now the Blunder Boys are lying down on the ground, hoping they might see up our skirts. I can see their beaky eyes blinking under the branches. If they do happen to see our knickers they will think we are doing it on purpose to attract them. Dear God.

One minute later

Just then a Pekingese dog came hurtling by dragging its lead behind it, followed by Angus. Oh no. He loves Pekingese. A LOT. I hope it is a fast runner.

Anyway, I haven't got the time to worry about everything. If careless people will let their small dogs loll around in parks they are asking for trouble. It's a cat-eat-dog world.

Twenty minutes later

The general mood of the gang is that I should play it cool until I know what is really going on. Although what Ellen knows about cool I really don't know. She had a massive ditherspaz trying to describe how Dave the Laugh had said good night to her at the Stiff Dylans gig. Apparently, and I know this because I heard it about a zillion times, "Er, well... then he, well... and I didn't know what he meant, but then, well, he just said... he just said to me... he said..."

I shouted, "WHAT? What in the name of heaven, Ellen? WHAT, WHAT did he say?"

And I didn't even want to know; I just wanted to get to the bits about what happened after I left and what did people say about me and so on. But you know what people are like, it's just me, me, me with them.

Ellen went even more divvyish. Good grief. "He said, 'Well, good night then, Ellen, never eat anything bigger than your head.'"

I didn't know what to say.

No one did.

Fifteen minutes later

Anyway, the nub and the gist is that the Ace Gang are useless and don't know anything more than I do. It seems they all watched me run off like a loon (to catch my train) and then lolloped home. Useless.

However, I decided to forgive them. They are, after all, my besties.

And if I don't forgive them I will never find out anything. And also never go out again and stay in my house with my parents. So, grasping the bull by its whatsits, I said to the gang, "In order to make a full and frank decision boyfriendwise, I have to know the intentions of the prospective snoggees."

Ellen said, "Er, what are they? I mean who, what is, like, a snoggee?"

"Ellen, keep up, the prospeccy snoggees are Masimo and Robbie. Masimo said that he was single and free for me, but on the other hand did not come running after me and stop me getting on my train. And Robbie only had time to say hello and then not long after went off with Wet Lindsay. Soooo, did Robbie come to the gig to see me, or does he just want to be friends with me? Why has he come home?"

Rosie said, "Someone must go underground and subtly

find out what Robbie's intentions are. Shall I ask Sven? He could wear his camouflage flares."

I said, "No."

Jools said, "What about asking Dave the Laugh to find out?"

Ellen nearly fell over with pleasure. "Oh, yes, well, I mean, I could, well, maybe I could, like, go with him or something. Be, like, his assistant? But maybe that would be, like, too forward or something. What do you think... or something?"

I said, "No, Ellen, it has to be this year, really."

Jas had gone off into Jasland. She was fiddling with her fringe and I could tell she had Tom and voles on her mind.

I said, "There is someone here, isn't there, who knows Robbie's brother quite well, shall we say, and who could use subtlety and casualosity to find out stuff? Isn't there, Jas?"

Jas looked up like a dog when she heard her own name. "What do you mean? What do you want me to do?"

"I want you to find out about Robbie by asking Tom a few casual questions."

Jas said, "Oh, OK. Can we go now?"

"The key word here, Jas, is 'casualosity'. Casualosity. Can you say that, Jas?"

Jas got into her huffmobile. "I know how to be casual, Georgia."

"Wrong."

I am absolutely full of exhaustosity. How difficult can it be to be casual? We coached Jas for four hours. It was like talking to a lemming in a skirt.

First of all, we tried it her way. Always a mistake in my humble (but right) opinion. Her idea of casualosity essentially means that she says: "Does Robbie fancy Georgia? Or is he normal?"

I had to use clevernosity to get Jas to do what I wanted in the end. I said, "I've got an idea. You know how good you were as Lady MacUseless and everything, Jas?"

Jas said, "Yes, it took quite a lot out of me, actually. Do you remember the bit when I had the dagger and..."

Oh no, three million years were going to go by while she relived her big moments in the school play.

I interrupted her by hugging her so hard that her head was

buried in my armpit and said, "Yes, yes, now this is my idea."

I asked her to act out what she was going to do in an improvised scene, like in drama. She loves that sort of thing as she is such a teacher's bum-oley kisser.

Rosie volunteered to be Tom. She said, "I've got the legs for it."

Incidentally I'm a bit worried that she was able to whip out a false beard from her rucky. I said that to her, I said, "Rosie, do you carry a beard around with you at all times?"

And she said, "Well, you never know."

The Viking bride-to-be gets madder and madder. We are definitely entering the Valley of the Unwell.

Anyway, Jas was mincing around like a mincing thing, warming up, flicking her fringe at Tom (or Rosie in a beard, as we know him). It was incredibly irritating. I was on the edge of a mega nervy b. and supertizz as it was. I said, "Jas what in the name of arse are you doing?"

And she said huffily, "I am getting into character."

I said, "But you are being you."

She looked at me like I had fallen out of her nose. "I am finding the inner me."

Good grief. Her "inner me" is bound to be an owl.

Eventually she was ready and came pratting girlishly up to Rosie and twittered, "Oh, Tom, I found some vole spore down by the woods."

Tom/Rosie said (in a French accent, for no apparent reason – it must be the beard), "Ah, did you, my liddle pussycat? Would you like to, how you say... kiss my beard?"

Jas actually blushed and said, "Well, you know I would, Tom... but maybe, you know, in private, not in front of everyone."

I had to put a stop to this. It was like watching some pervy film, like *Two Go Mad in Bearded Lezzie Land*. I said, "Will you get on with it?"

Jas predictably lost her rag immediately over the slightest thing and said, "I was just getting in the mood, actually, and anyway this is stupid, practising to be casual. I know how to be casual."

I said, "Well, why don't you BE casual then?"

She gave me her worst look, but eventually after Mabs gave her a Midget Gem they started again. Jas said to Rosie, who now had a pipe, "Tommy-wommy?"

"*Oui.*"

"Well, I was just, you know, thinking about Robbie. It's nice he's back, isn't it?"

"*Mais oui – très très magnifique.*"

It was pointless objecting about the Froggyland language, especially as Ro Ro was now plaiting her beard.

Jazzy said, "Did he come back, you know, because he missed England and his mates? Do you think he will join the Stiff Dylans again?"

I looked at Jas in amazement. She had asked an almost good question in a quite subtle way and not mentioned me. Blimey.

And it only took four-and-a-half hours of torture. We had to leave it there because Sven came along yodelling through the trees (no, I am not kidding).

5:30 p.m.

When would be a good time to call Radio Jas? Surely she must have had time to talk to Tom by now? I should exercise discipline and patience, of course.

5:31 p.m.

Phoned Jas.

"Jas."

"What?"

"It's me."

"Oh, well, this is me, too."

"Jas, don't start."

"I'm not."

"Well, don't."

"Well, I won't."

"Good."

And I put the phone down. That will teach her.

Two minutes later

"Jas, what have you found out?"

"I've found out that I am having scrambly eggs for tea. Byeeee."

And she put the phone down.

Damn.

I have my pride, thank goodness. No one can take that away from me. I won't be bothering Jas again, not while she is so busy stuffing her gob with eggy.

6:00 p.m.

This is torture but I will never give in. Never, never. The Eggy One will never get the better of me.

6:10 p.m.

Phoned Rosie. I'll get her to phone Eggy and casually ask her, but not on my behalf.

6:20 p.m.

Rosie is out with Sven at the "pictures", her mum says. Oh yeah, as if. And the film they are watching is, *Number Seven on the Snogging Scale*.

I daren't ask Ellen, Jools or Mabs to phone Jas as they are bound to spill the beans to Eggy. The tragedy is that all three of them are such crap liars; it's a curse, really.

7:30 p.m.

She is soooooo annoying. She will never phone me if she has got the hump.

7:35 p.m.

Masimo hasn't called or anything. Maybe he really does think

I am insane. Or maybe he thinks I caught the train from the shopping centre and have gone away for a few days. In which case *he* is insane.

If I have an early night I can do skincare – cleanse and tone, and get everything ready for tomorrow just in case I have a chance encounter with one of my many maybe boyfriends on the way to Stalag 14.

8:15 p.m.

Blimey, I look about two and a half, I am so shiny faced and clean. Also, I am nice and baldy everywhere, except on my head, of course. I do not want to have an Uncle Eddie hairstyle.

Actually, my hair is a bit of a boring colour. It hasn't got *je ne sais quoi* and umph.

Bathroom

Five minutes later

Ahaha, Mum has got some hair dye. Warm chocolate. That would be nice and groovy. I could just put a couple of streaks in the front, like highlights, or is it lowlights? Hi, lo – it's lights anyway, which is all that counts.

Got the dye and went into the front room. Oh, how I wish I hadn't. Mum and Dad were all over each other on the sofa watching some old film with crying in it and blokes in tights and an Uncle Eddie bloke in a frock. Mum said, "Come and watch *Robin Hood*. It's good."

I said, "Mum, I'm just going to use your hair dye for a bit."

"No."

"Er, Mum, I think you are being a bit negative."

"No."

"But I—"

"No."

"Look at the colour of my hair! It's crap. I might as well be the Invisible Mouse."

"No."

"But I..."

Then Vati joined in. "Georgia, no, no, no, and thrice no. And also no."

"Vati, I am not asking you, actually, I am asking my dear dear mum about her hair dye."

"It's not her hair dye, it's mine."

What??? What fresh hell? HIS hair dye? My vati, not content with growing small badgers on his chin and wearing leather trousers and having a clown car, was now trying to be Lady Cliff Richard. Or Lady Paul McCartney.

"Please say you are not serious."

Vati said, "I am very serious. I am a man in his prime, as your mother knows." And he did that disgusting thing of grabbing one of her nungas, squeezing it, and going, "Honk honk!!!"

Mum didn't even hit him, she just went all girlie and said, "Stop it, you big boy."

Vati was still in Madland, however, and said, "Yes, I thought I'd get down with the youth, you know, dye my hair, get the old leathers on and maybe check out a few clubs. Which one would you recommend?"

I nearly fainted. Imagine bumping into my dad and his sad mates down at the Buddha Lounge!!! Any chance I had of having a Sex God or a Luuurve God or even Spotty Norman would be well and truly up the pictures without a paddle. My dad's impression of Mick Jagger dancing could reduce people to tears – and not of admiration.

In the kitchen
9:00 p.m.
I must have toast to calm down.

I was buttering it when my mad little sister Libby popped her head out of the airing cupboard. "Heggo, Ginger. Come in my nest. Now."

I looked up at her. "Libbs, I'm too big for it."

"No."

"Yes, I am."

Her face went all frowny and she started snorting and tutting like she has heard Mum do. I wasn't liking this. The frowny face is not one I like to see because usually I am in agonising pain seconds later.

However, this time it wasn't my turn to suffer. Libby disappeared into her "nest" and then scuba-diving Barbie came flying out, quickly followed by Mr Potato, Pantalitzer doll (well, the head) and finally, after a lot of panting and heaving and squealing, Gordy came hurtling through the air. He came to a skidding halt on the dish rack and then did that shivering thing before he hurled himself through the cat flap.

Libby popped her head out again and smiled in a terrifying way. "Come on, Gingey... it's naaaaaice."

Oh dear God. Still, what else was I doing this fine evening that I couldn't squeeze into an airing cupboard with my clearly insane sister? She looked me straight in the eye and said, "I lobe you velly times twice."

Aahhh. At least she "lobes" me, unlike my so-called bestie Jas, who is dead girl to me now that she can't even perform the slightest task.

Five minutes later
Sitting in the dark little cupboard, I had to bend double with my knees practically up my nose. Libby had snacks in there, which was nice if you like bits of banana covered in fluff.

11:00 p.m.
Libby was only persuaded out of her "nest" by Mum saying she could sleep in my bed. Thanks, Mum.

For a little girl Bibbs is very full of gas. Her farts are like gunshots and sooo smelly. If anyone lit a match we would all be blown to kingdom come. And back. And there would still be some fart left over to cook on for the rest of the year.

11:20 p.m.
And the snoring. It's like comedy snoring except that I'm not laughing.

329

11:25 p.m.

Tried to shove Libby over on to her side to stop her snoring and got a smack around the head for my trouble. She is even violent when she is unconscious.

11:30 p.m.

I wonder what Robbie really came home for? I can't believe it was to see Wet Lindsay. Surely Tom would have told me if he knew that Robbie fancied her. I bet she has been writing to him, pretending to be a nice person. How could he fancy her? Still, facts have to be faced, he did actually go out with her once before he started seeing me. And they must have been doing something in those months. They weren't talking about her ludicrous forehead.

He must have snogged her. If he went out with her for three months that is a lot of snogging opportunities. And she is bound to have been puckering up pretty much nonstop because she has no pridenosity. I wonder what number on the snogging scale they got to?

Five minutes later

Not number seven (upper-body fondling), clearly, otherwise

her false nungas would have made a surprise appearance.
Maybe that is what happened!!!

I wish.

Anyway, I don't want her nungas in my head. Get out.

Two minutes later
Does he like me or not?

One minute later
Do I like him or not?

11:40 p.m.
Hang on a minute, I've just realised something. I am on the
rack of love again. How did this happen?

Well, I'm not dangling about up here any more. I say no,
no, no, and thrice no to the rack. I am a free woman. That
woman Emily Plankton chained herself to a policeman and
chucked herself under a horse and so on so that I could vote.
I must not let her down.

11:50 p.m.
Although it does seem a bit over the top to chuck yourself in

front of a horse so that you get to vote.

One minute later
Especially as in fact she was dead, so she couldn't vote anyway.

Two minutes later
And neither can I.

Like I have always said, history is crap.

Midnight
On the other foot, Masimo said, "Now I is a free man." And that means he wants to go out with me. So that is that. I have been to the bakery of love and I have got an Italian cakey.

Five minutes later
But I might also have an éclair called Robbie, in case I'm peckish and the Italian cakey isn't filling enough.

Five minutes later
Some people, naming no names (but Jas) will probably say I'm greedy. But I'm not. I am just having a choice. I am not sad like

Jas, who only stays with one boyfriend because she has no special talents. Other than an unerring eye for a crap owl, or being able to spot a vole at a hundred yards. Or having the largest knicker collection in the northern hemisphere. And being the biggest and most annoying twit on the planet.

Two minutes later
Yes, the Good Lord has been kind enough to give me a couple of special gifts.

One minute later
Oh, that was a bit freaky-deaky, I had Dave the Laugh's voice in my head when I said "a couple of special gifts". And his voice said, "Ah, yes... the nunga-nungas." He is even rude when I make him up in my head. That is very rude indeed. It is rudey-dudey in absentia, as we say in Latin.

Every time I think about Dave the Laugh it makes me laugh. I've just remembered him (accidentally) switching all the lights off during *MacUseless* and the entire Forest of Dunsinane falling off the stage. God, it was funny.

One minute later

And his vair amusing "pants" thing – as in the famous song "The Hills are Alive with the Sound of PANTS".

Two minutes later

And when he put a FOR SALE sign on his school's roof – tee hee hee.

One minute later

Oy, shut up, brain! This is a Dave-the-Laugh-free zone!

Five minutes later

If I do decide on the Luuurve God, it will serve Robbie right. He will just have to check into Heartbreak Hotel, like I had to when he dumped me. He should ask for the sobbing suite.

12:30 a.m.

I have never had to check into Heartbreak Hotel because of the Luuurve God. Except, I suppose, I thought I might have to make a booking when he said he would tell me in a week's time if he was going to be my one and only one.

12:40 a.m.

But that was then, and now he has said, "I am for you if you want?" Which is vair vair good.

12:45 a.m.

Good night, Luuurve God.

12:50 a.m.

I hope he doesn't think it's odd that I had to catch a train from near the shopping centre.

At midnight.

When there isn't a train station there.

1:00 a.m.

To be fair, I haven't really given Robbie much of a chance. Maybe I should at least talk to him before I, you know, choose my cake.

1:10 a.m.

I don't suppose they would both consider a time-share girlfriend...

zzzzzzzzzzzzzzzzz.

Snot disco dancing

Monday July 18th

8:00 a.m.

This is the first day of the rest of my life. So why is my hair sticking up like a cockerel?

8:10 a.m.

Mum caught me ironing my hair. God, she made a big deal out of it. It's probably the first time she has seen an iron. Bloody hell, ramble on, why don't you?

She was all red-faced. "By the time you are twenty-five your hair will be like nylon."

I said, "Mum, who cares what I look like at twenty-five?

I will be in the twilight zone of life by then, like you."

If I hadn't used my athletic responses I could have been quite badly injured by Mum's hairbrush. She is very unstable.

8:20 a.m.
Scavenging around in the kitchen for something to eat. Luckily a piece of toast popped out of the toaster. Ah, good. I buttered it and ate it. Blimey, being a Luuurve Goddess can make you peckish.

Vati came dadding in. He didn't even say good morning, he said, "Is that my toast you are eating?"

I said, "To be honest, Dad, I don't think you need any more toast; you seem to have plenty stored away around the trouser area."

As usual in this house when anyone (me) tries to be light and amusing Dad goes ballisticisimus.

Mum came in trying to force Libby into her dungies while she still had a cup of milky pops in her hand which she would not let go of.

Dad was still moaning on about me. "Where does she get all this rudeness from, Connie? You are too easy-going on her."

Mum said, "I know. She's been ironing her hair."

Dad forgot about the toast fiasco and started on beauty. Something which, quite frankly, he is not an expert on. "How bloody ridiculous is that? You'll end up like Uncle Eddie."

I said, "Oh right, I'm going to turn into a mad bloke on a motorbike because I straighten my hair. I think women everywhere should be told."

8:30 a.m.

I hate my parents. They are so unreasonably mad.

8:35 a.m.

And so self-obsessed. They don't seem to understand that their lives are over, and I am covered in cake.

8:36 a.m.

I am nearly at Jas's house. I must exude calmnosity and friendlinosity. I must put the egg incident behind me and be nice to Jas – so she will tell me all she knows.

8:40 a.m.

When I got to Jas's gate it was to see her bottom waggling off in the distance. Of course Eggy had set off. She will still be having the huff with me. I must be at my most charming.

I did my fast walking until I caught up with her, and gave her a lovely smile as I linked up with her. "Hello, Jas, my little chummly-wummly."

She shook me off. "Don't hang on to my arm, Georgia, I'm not dragging you up the hill to school just because you are tired."

"I'm not tired, I am just so glad to see you, you lovely big-pantied loon."

I chucked her under the chin but she still wasn't having it. So I stopped and stood in front of her and looked into her eyes. "Jazzy Spazzy, you know I love you."

She went all red. Some Foxwood lads who had been trailing us uselessly as usual shouted, "Oy, you lezzies, won't she give you a kiss?"

And another one said, "Can we see your breasts, please?" Good grief.

Jas started flicking her fringe like a mad thing. "Now look what you've started."

We set off at a spanking pace for Stalag 14. As we went along I was doing my special pleading – it's very touching. "Jas, please forgive me. Did you find out anything? I know you will have done because you are so vair vair clever. And top girl at blodge and, er... everything."

As we took our coats to the cloakroom she relented a bit. "Well, I did talk to Tom in a casual way, even though you said I couldn't."

"Jas, Jas, I knew you could do casualosity big time. Don't forget I have seen you in your night-time panties, relaxing and at play."

As the bell rang for assembly I could see the Hitler Youth (prefects) approaching, keen to do a bit of poncing around like prats. I said, "Please, pleasey please tell me what Tom said."

"Well, he said..."

"Yes, yes?"

"Well, he said... he didn't know anything."

"Pardon?"

"Robbie is having a break from farming in Kiwi-a-gogo, but he doesn't know how long he is staying."

Is that it? Is that Detective Inspector Jas of Scotland Yard's idea of finding out stuff? I wanted to kick her shins, but just in the knickers of time remembered that she is my best pally and I gave her my "interested" smile.

Jas was starting to say, "Yes, so I don't really know if he likes you or not..." when Wet Lindsay slimed up alongside me with Astonishingly Dim Monica as sidekick slug and weed. Wet Lindsay's hair extensions have been redone. How vair vair chav and naff she is. Having longer hair only draws attention to her lack of forehead and general octopus tendencies.

I forced myself to laugh merrily and look at Wet Lindsay's forehead as if Jas had told me a good joke about it. Wet Lindsay said to me, "What have you got to laugh about, Nicolson? Have you caught sight of yourself in a mirror?"

Oh, my aching sides! How I laughed. Not. Astonishingly Dim Monica did, though, sniggering and snorting like a fool on fool tablets. I just said, "How very natural your hair looks, Lindsay. It really suits you and brings out all your best features, especially your knees."

She went a bit red round the earlobes and said, "Prat."

Charming. Absolutely charming. I said to Jas as we went into the hall, "Charming. Utterly, utterly charming. Who wouldn't want to go out with her?"

Ace Gang Headquarters
Break
Rosie blew a bubble-gum bubble that exploded all over her

nose. Very amusing. She had a big blob hanging off her nose like a huge bogey. She said, "Look how it dangles about. I bet I can swing it round and round in time to some music. Like a snot disco. You lot sing something jolly and I'll improvise on bogey work."

Five minutes later

I think despite being slightly singed in the oven of luuurve I may be going to die of laughing. The snot disco dance is officially born. Danced to the tune of *Eastenders*, it is: Swing your snot to the left, swing to the right. Full turn, shoulder shrugging, now nod to the front, dangle, dangle, hands on shoulders and kick, kick to the right, dangle, dangle, kick, kick to the left, dangle, dangle, and then full snot around and shimmy to the ground.

Excellent in every way.

As we strolled back for an action-packed morning of being bored and depressed I said to the gang, "I bet we could have the snot coming out of our nostrils all through German and Herr Kamyer wouldn't notice. Or if he does, we could pretend we have really bad colds. Hand over the bubble gum, girls, and get chewing!"

German

It was a triumph, darling, a triumph! We were all translating from our textbooks – what larks! The Koch family were off on another camping trip, taking an enormous amount of food with them, as usual. In our books there are hilariously bad illustrations of the Koch family, drawn by a blind person. Mrs Koch looks vair like Herr Kamyer in a frock. I never get tired of the Kochs. In fact, I am thinking of writing to the author of the textbook (A. Schmidt, no, I'm not joking) and asking where the Kochs live. I want to write a letter to them, thanking them for the endless hours of fun they have given us all.

I put up my hand to ask a pressing Koch question. When Herr Kamyer noticed my hand blowing in the wind he said, "*Jah*, Georgia?"

"Herr Kamyer, there is a strange-looking thing in one of the pictures of the Kochs. It looks like a very tiny poo on a plate. But that doesn't seem right."

Herr Kamyer blinked through his moley glasses. "Ah, bring up ze picture, Georgia, *und* we will see."

I quicky attached my bubble-gum bogey as I pretended to sneeze into my hanky, and went up to his desk with the snot rag still covering my nose.

Herr Kamyer didn't notice. He is so *interested* in things; it's tragic, really. He actually seems to believe that we want to learn things. I put the textbook down in front of him at the picture of the Kochs and pointed to the poo on a plate.

"Ach so, Georgia, *der spangleferkel...* oh *jah*, I remember ven as a youngen ve vent into the voods camping, we would cook up the *spangleferkel* and sing our songs around ze campfire. The fun ve had camping. You vould have loved it, girls."

I still had my hankie out to disguise the bogey when he started humming, "Gif me ze campfire light *und komt mit* me to *der liebe liebe Rhein*" and took his glasses off to clean them. Or perhaps he was crying. Who knows? Who cares? Anyway, when he did that I took the opportunity to let the bogey run free and wild. I even did a bit of the bogey dance slightly behind him and managed to get the hanky back in place before he finished. When I walked back to my desk the whole class spontaneously clapped. Herr Kamyer thought it was for his crap camping song and bowed. Quite sensationally German.

Five minutes later
Sadly, Herr Kamyer really thinks we love his camping stories.

He's going on and on about what they did. How they sang songs and cooked over the campfire.

Twenty minutes later
Swapping notes. Rosie wrote:

Dear fellow loons,
    Let us have a scoring system for bogey work. Gee gets 5 points for her excellent letting the bogey run free and wild over Herr Kamyer's head. Similar acts earn 5 points and the first to get to 20 gets free Jammy Dodgers for life. Well, for a bit, anyway.
    Ro Ro, advisor to the stars
    xxxxx

Of course there is always a dog in the manger of life. Jas wrote back and said it was silly and childish. Hilarious, really, coming from someone who practically snogs owls.

Ellen was dithering about. Even in her notes. She wrote:

Hi everyone, it's me,

  Erm, about the snot disco, well, you know, I don't know. Like, er, what if we, er, get into, er, like, trouble? What do you think... or something?

  Er... Ellen

  xxx

on our way to French

Jas and Ellen have formed their own little breakaway gang and they are living in a snot-free zone. They should grow up.

French

Drat and dratty drat drat! Rosie is catching up pointswise by letting her bogey dangle over Madame Slack's head as she was checking her homework. We were all trying not to laugh and Madame Slack must have sussed something because she unexpectedly looked up and nearly got the pretend bogey in her eye. As she was looking at Rosie, Rosie casually popped the "snot" into her mouth and started chewing. Madame Slack went ballisticisimus and Rosie has got detention.

4:10 p.m.

Home time for some. As we went by the hall we saw Rosie's face at the window. She pressed her nose against the pane of glass so that it spread out like a trapped piglet. Vair funny. She mouthed "I love you all" and then disappeared from view.

In my bedroom
6:00 p.m.

Lying on my bed. No phone calls or anything from any of my so-called maybe perhaps boyfriends. I'm all aloney on my owney. Even Dave never rings me these days, not even as a matey-type mate, which he is. And the Swiss Family Mad are out at some sad tea party, wrecking people's lives with their weird ideas and Dad's huge bottom.

6:30 p.m.

I may as well go to bed early and get as much beauty sleep as I can. Just in case all my boyfriends come home to roost at once.

I wonder what they are all doing?

Maybe I've imagined it all. Maybe Masimo didn't mean he wanted to be my one and only one. Maybe he just wanted a snog. Or maybe he thinks I still like Robbie and that's put him off. Maybe he's right – maybe I do still like Robbie. Maybe... I should just call him.

6:40 p.m.
Boom crash bang. Yowl yowl. Now what?

Then I heard the lovely tones of my father: "Bloody hell, that furry bastard has stuck its claws into my arse."

How delightful my home life is. It's practically like living in *Pride and Prejudice* it's so elegant. I will pretend to be asleep. Not that anyone cares. I have asked them to respect my privacy, but I bet they—

Ah, yes. My door crashed open.

I said, "Mum, I am asleep, actually."

Mum said, "Don't you want your letter then?"

I sat up in bed. "What letter?"

She held out an envelope. "This one. It was on the doormat before you got home from school. I put it in my bag and forgot about it. It must have been hand delivered, because it's only got your name on it."

I said, "Quick, give it to me, it is a criminal offence to tamper with Her Maj's mail."

"Who do you think it's from?"

"Er, Father Christmas. Possibly someone from beyond the grave. Mum, I don't know because you have got it and I therefore have not opened it."

Ten minutes later

At last she has gone. She hung about a bit hoping I would let her know who it was from, looking at my things and saying meaningless stuff like, "What is my black leather jacket doing in your wardrobe? And my Chanel bag?" Utterly pointless things. Tutting and carrying on like a tutting thing in a tut shop. But I just looked at her until she left.

Five minutes later

I am so nervy that I can't open the letter. My name is written in capitals so I can't even recognise the handwriting.

What if it is from Masimo to say that having seen me scamper off at high speed like a prat he has decided he is not a free man for me?

Or what if it is from Robbie, saying that he has always loved me and will I be his?

Or what if it is from Oscar, trainee Blunder Boy, asking

me on "a date" to go skateboarding? Or what if it is... Oh, shut up, shut up.

Two minutes later
When you are having a tizz in Nervy B. Central, Call-me-Arnold the vicar says you should always ask the question, "What would Baby Jesus do?"

One minute later
I don't know why, though, because clearly Jesus's dad is like a huge owly-type person, beaking about looking at everyone and everything, even when they are on the loo. As Big G is omniPANTSient and set the whole thing up in the first place, he would know who had written the letter and what was in it already, without having to open it. Or send it, even. So what is the point of asking what Baby Jesus would do?

Actually, when you think about it on the whole, life is a charade and a sham. It's a bit like mime, isn't it? Why do we have to guess what is going on? Why can't Big G just tell us and get it over with?

Five minutes later

What if the note is from Masimo and it just says, *"Arrivederci"*?

Or from Robbie and it says, "Oy, Georgia, stop looning about after me, you are only embarrassing yourself. I am deeply in love with a wombat that I met in Kiwi-a-gogo land and will play my guitar in rivers only for her. In fact I have written a song for Gayleen (the wombat), which I enclose. It is called 'You are my marsupial, my only marsupial, you make me happy when skies are grey, you'll never know dear, how much I love you, please don't take your furry face away'."

Ten minutes later

I have never had what is known as great letters from Robbie when you come to think about it. The first one he wrote me was to dump me and suggest I go out with Dave the Laugh.

Two minutes later

I wish I could phone the Hornmeister up now. This is when his Horn advice would be really good. Things have been a bit weird between us since he started seeing Emma. She's so nice, it's depressing.

Maybe that's why he's going out with her – because she's so nice he doesn't know how to dump her.

Or maybe he likes nice people. Even her hair is nice. And her nose. How annoying is that?

And she's nice to me.

I hate that.

Ten minutes later

Perhaps I can sort of sense what the words say by looking at the envelope and using my psychedelic powers. I saw some geezer in a frilly shirt on TV who said that we could all tap into our clairvoyant side if we just concentrated.

I am looking at the envelope and concentrating.

Five minutes later

My eyes have gone all blurry. Oh excellent, I am going blind. That's perfect, isn't it? Now even if I open the letter I won't know what it says or who it's from.

One minute later

I can see a bit now. However, I think this is a lesson for us all. Never trust blokes who wear frilly shirts and they are not doing it for a laugh.

one minute later

OK, this is it. I am opening the letter.

Five minutes later

The letter said:

> Hi Georgia,
>
> Since you had to, er, catch your train last Saturday I haven't been able to get to see you. Do you fancy going for a coffee tomorrow night? I'll meet you at the bottom of East Street at 7:30 p.m. and we can catch up. I promise not to bring any photos of sheep. Jas tells me that you are allergic to wildlife.   Robbie

Blimey. I am still as full of confusiosity. Is this good or bad? Am I glad it is from Robbie? Why hasn't Masimo got in touch? What does Robbie mean by "going for a coffee"? That is as bad as "see you later" in boyspeak.

One minute later

Does "going for a coffee" mean, you know, "going for a coffee"? Or does it mean, "let us start with coffee and end up at number seven"?

I must phone Jas.

Jas's dad answered. Blimey. I'd never heard him speak on the phone before. I'd only seen him sucking on his pipe, reading his paper or going out in sensible welligogs. Which is what you want in a dad – pipe sucking, silence and going away – but can you tell my vati that? No, you can't.

Jas eventually came to the phone. She said, "What?"

"Why did you say 'what' like that?"

"Like what?"

"Don't start, Jas, I have just had a letter from Robbie."

"Oh, did he dump you?"

"No."

"Really? Blimey. I thought he might have been put off by your running. It's really weird, you know."

"Well, he wasn't, and he wants me to go for a coffee."

"Blimey."

"Jas, can you say something else besides 'blimey'?"

"Yes."

"Well, what is it?"

"I have to go now because Tom's leaving and I won't see him again for seventeen and a half hours."

Oh dear *Gott* in *Himmel*.

Four minutes later

Back in bed trying to keep my mind on higher things.

I wonder what number Jas'n'Tom have got up to on the snogging scale. I have been very lax about finding out.

For the sake of science I think I had better do a survey of the Ace Gang and see if anything needs to be added since ear snogging.

Ten minutes later

I don't know why I am bothered, though. There might as well not be a snogging scale as far as I am concerned. I am well and truly a snog-free zone, which is unusual when you are supposed to be a boy magnet and have two or more Luuuurve Gods in your handy pandies.

In fact, when was the last time I snogged anyone, man or beast? (Not counting accidental tonguesies with my sister.) I may have forgotten all my skills, which I had better polish up on in case I have to pucker up for the Sex God.

What is that ludicrous thing that Jazzy Spazzy does? Oh yes, pucker, relax, pucker, relax.

Five minutes later
I am full of snogging practice exhaustosity.

Two minutes later
I hope doing this puckering malarkey is not going to mean I end up looking like Mark Big Gob. I had better not overdo it; no one wants to go out with a whale.

When was the last time I snogged the Sex God? Also, where is the last letter he wrote to me from Kiwi-a-gogo land?

One minute later
Oh, I know, I hid it on the top of my wardrobe in the only snooper-free zone in my so-called room.

One minute later
Why would a cat eat a letter? Why? It can't be hunger. But if you start asking questions about cats you'll end up with the rest of the loons in the twilight home. Why do they eat

spiders? That would be another one. There is not much nutrition in a spider, is there? And also, Angus doesn't really eat them, he just lets them loll out of the corner of his mouth in a disgusting way.

Two minutes later

I've managed to read bits of the chewed-up letter. And found my missing fountain pen. Also heavily chewed. Don't tell me Angus and Gordy are co-writing a book: *Cat Tips on How to Really Annoy Your Baldy Owners.*

1. Hide their things and chew them.
2. If you are soaking wet from the rain, here is a top tip: leap on to your owner's lap and get nice and dry there.
3. Sit on walls and just look at them.

Five minutes later

The only sense I can make from Robbie's chewed-up letter is: *Tom told me about your excellent dancing to "Three Little Boys"... and you are in the nicest possible way quite possibly clinically insane.*

This does not give the impression of sophisticosity that I want.

8:20 p.m.

I think I will just play the special CD he recorded for me before he went to Kiwi-a-gogo, to get me back in the mood.

8:45 p.m.

I tell you what I will not be doing: I will not be lying with my head in his lap while he sings "I'm Not There" to me. I have just remembered doing that in the park the summer before he went away. And I could see right up his nose. If I had been looking. Which I wasn't because I had my eyes closed and was nodding my head along in time to the music.

Two minutes later

I've just remembered something else. I had a lurking lurker. Oh brilliant, now I have thought about lurkers, I am almost bound to get one.

One minute later

I must not get stressed out; that is the kind of thing that lurkers love. I must be calm. Ohm.

Three minutes later

Ah, my little furry letter-eating pals Angus and his adolescent son Gordy have come to keep me company in bed. That will be nice and soothing having them purring beside me. They seem in a nice sleepy mood for once.

So night night, world. Sex Kitty signing off.

Ten minutes later

Fat chance. Other people have pets, and I've got the Furry Freak brothers. They've done flattening the bed down, pacing round and round, and now they are doing that really really irritating prodding-with-their-paws thing, kneading me like a dough person.

I will be a hollow-eyed wraith at this rate if I don't get some beauty sleep. I must do some inner calming exercises. Ohmmmmmm ohmmmmm.

Ohmygod. Mum has slammed into my inner sanctum carrying the spawn of the devil in her night-time nappy and deelyboppers.

I said, "What? What is it you people want of me???"

Oh brilliant, Bibbs is being bunged into my bed with me because she won't go to sleep without me. I said to Mum,

"Mum, I am sure there is some European law against this kind of overcrowding. Even in poor people's land I bet they don't have as many people and stuff in bed with them as I do."

She just said, "Don't be silly, Gee, read Bibbsy a little Boboland story."

Libby had a big book with her that she smashed me in the nose with in a loving way as she snuggled in, pushing Gordy out of bed. He had just nodded off and crashed to the floor. He went ballisticisimus, yowling and shivering and attacking the bedside light before leaping back on to the bed and burrowing up from the bottom. His head popped up in between the book and me and he spat at me. Good grief.

Libby said, "Aaaah naaaaice and comfy. Ready book, Ginger. About Sindyfellow. Now."

I am a slavey girl in this family of loons, furry or otherwise.

Ten minutes later

Blimey O'Reilly, I thought that *Heidi* was boring – cheese and goats and old grumpy blokes for as far as the eye can see – but *Cinderella* takes the bloody bee's pyjamas on the boring and depressing front. This is the story: Cinderella lives with her ugly stepsisters. They hate her because she is pretty, although I can't say I blame the uglies. Looking at the drawing of Cinders I would be inclined to give her a bit of a duffing-up. She has a very irritating sticky-up nose.

I read the story as fast as I could to get it over with: "Cinders is doing cleaning. Some poncy bloke in a wig invites the sisters to a ball. Cinderella can't go because she is in rags, and then some bint turns up in wings and changes her frock into a ballgown and some cats and mice and a pumpkin into a coach and horses. Moaning Minnie (Cinders) dances with some other poncy bloke in a wig (not the first one), leaves at midnight, tries on a shoe, and marries Prince Wiggy. The end."

Libby laughed like a loon the whole way through. I don't know why. I don't want to know why. You see, this is the sort of story that irresponsible fools (my mutti) make their children read. No wonder they are all mad and covered in cat food like my sister is.

And, of course, the whole facsimile of a sham turned to violence because Libby wanted to change Angus into a horse like in the story and banged him with her "wand" (my tennis racket), and the rest is history. Well, the vase in the knitted coverlet that Grandad's girlfriend Maisie gave me is history. Angus leaped up (not exactly changed into a horse as such) on to the windowsill and careered about, scattering my CDs, photos and the vase all over the place.

How can I be expected to have a decent snogging relationship with anyone while my home life is so bonkers?

Tuesday July 19th
Stalag 14

I had to practically iron my face this morning. I had slept face down because I was so exhausted from the night-time shenanigans and *ordure*. My nose was flat like a plate, all across my head. I had to use hot flannels to smooth it into a reasonable(ish) state. The only positive thing is that we have German today so at least I will be able to do my pre-make-up make-up in peace.

In the cloakroom

Talking to Jassy about my letter from Robbie. I said, "How come you told Robbie that I hate wildlife?"

"You do."

"That is not the point. You should tell him something about my finer points, not ramble on about rubbish."

"What are your finer points?"

I may have to kill her, but I won't be able to do it in assembly because Hawkeye is on seeing-eye dog duty this morning. She never seems to tire of hating us. I reckon she limbers up every morning at home, shouting, "I hate all girls, I hate them. What do I do? I HATE THEM!!!"

Fifteen minutes later

Oh for heavens sake, why does Slim bother going on and on? What is she talking about now? Isn't it bad enough that we have to get up at the crack of eight o'clock, get dressed, turn up, hang around all day being bored and depressed and usually get detention for our trouble? But she wants to talk as well. Why? What can she possibly say that would...

Then I heard the dreaded words, "Form Ten A are going on an exciting field trip in the last week of term."

What? What???

I looked at the Ace Gang and they looked at me.

Slim went on in tip-top jelloid mode. Her nungas were practically doing the Charleston. Separately. She said, "I think it's marvellous, and just shows the kind of spirit that we foster in this school. Herr Kamyer came up with the idea after form Ten A expressed interest in the camping trips that he used to go on in the German forests. I am sure that this is a lovely surprise for all of Ten A. Instead of normal lessons next Friday you will go by school bus to the lovely Cow and Calf Valley and camp there overnight. There are printed details for you to take home to your parents. Round and about the site there is an absolute cornucopia of wildlife; riverlife abounds. And in the evenings Miss Wilson, who has volunteered to accompany Herr Kamyer, will be teaching you some of the games and songs that she was taught herself as a young lady. The whole thing sounds like a real treat. I only wish that I were able to come myself."

We were all absolutely speechless. Rosie pretended to faint, which I thought was very funny. Wet Lindsay came bustling over and said, "Get up, you twit."

Rosie said, "Oh, where am I? Am I in heaven? Are you Gabriel?"

Lindsay said, "Think how excited you will be if you get to help with gardening duties after school."

Rosie did actually make quite a startling recovery. She said, "Oh, I feel much much better now after my little rest." And Lindsay slimed off. How I hate her. It gives me energy, the amount that I hate her.

Ace Gang Headquarters
Break

I am definitely beyond a shadow of a doubt not going on the camping trip. Not. Never. And also NO.

I said that to the gang. Jas said, "I think it will be really good fun."

I looked at her.

Rosie said, "I told Herr Kamyer that I will be having my period, because usually if you mention anything like that he has the ditherspaz to end all ditherspazzes and his head drops off with redness. But he just said, '*Ach*, hmmm, vell pop along to see Mizz Vilson. She is in charge of the ladies' area of things.' And I couldn't discuss it with Miss Wilson as she would probably tell me about what she does when she has a period and then I would die."

I said, "We must make a plan. Perhaps we could all have a sort of accident."

Mabs said, "Like what?"

"Erm, we could fall in a hole."

Jools said, "What hole?"

I said, "Er, we could dig one."

Jools said, "We could dig a hole and then fall in it?"

"Yes."

Rosie said, "Excellent idea, Georgia, quite startlingly insane, even for you."

Ellen said, "It might, you know, it might like be, well, you know... like, well..."

I said, "Crap?"

Ellen dithered on, "No, it might be, like, quite a good laugh."

Alarmingly all of the Ace Gang don't seem to mind the trip. They seem to think it might be "a laugh".

Five minutes later

We discussed the "coffee with Robbie" scenario. Rosie said, "So he says he wants to 'catch up with you', but he sent you a letter, so that means it's not like a casualosity sort of fandango because he would have just phoned you if it was, wouldn't he?"

I nodded and went, "Uh-huh, uh-huh..."

Jools said, "When you meet him, let him say stuff. Don't you start talking rubbish first."

I nodded and went, "Uh-huh, uh-huh..."

And Jas said, "Georgia, why are you doing an impression of one of those nodding dogs in a car?"

Five minutes later
It's surprising how much relief from tensionosity you can get merely by giving Jas a Chinese burn.

3:00 p.m.
I have managed to take my mind off my "coffee" with Robbie by applying two coats of nail varnish and colouring in all the O's in my Charlie Dickens book *Crap Expectations*. There are many more than you think; it may well be a lifetime's work.

4:20 p.m.
As I skedaddled home, all the Ace Gang gave me the Klingon salute for luck. Jools said, "So is it Robbie you like, then?"

I said with great dignitosity, "He is on my list."

I thought I heard Jas say "tart", which is unnecessary. And also at some time will cost her a quick plunge into the nearest ditch. Maybe if I am forced to go on the ridiculous camping fiasco I can think of an amusing revenge involving twigs and her pants.

Home
Anyway, I am going to get this camping thing out of the way so that I can just concentrate on my love life.

I wonder why I still haven't heard anything from Masimo. It's been three whole days now. And no one seems to have seen him.

Two minutes later
What does it say in the *How to Make any Twit Fall in Love with You* book? I'm just going to open it randomly and see what it says.

One minute later
"Boys live mostly in their heads." What is that supposed to mean? I wouldn't live in my head, I can tell you that. It's full of rubbish.

One minute later
Oh well, I can only think of one cake at a time. My hands are full (oo-er).

6:00 p.m.
What is the matter with my parents? They will not do the least thing for me. I simply asked my vati to send a letter saying that I could not go on the school trip to a field

because we had planned to do something as a family.

Vati said, "We haven't planned anything."

I said patiently, "I know that, Vati, it is merely a cunning ploy."

"You mean a lie."

"Yes, exactly... er, I mean, well, not really. You see, what it is is that I am allergic to the countryside."

Vati, as usual when he is intellectually challenged, resorted to coarse and unnecessary language. "You do talk absolute bollocks, Georgia."

That is a nice way to talk to a sensitive growing teenager, isn't it? No wonder my hair won't go right and I am almost constantly in detention.

Then he walked out of the room. I followed him. Was he wearing hipster jeans or was it just that his bottom was growing? I decided not to ask. "Dad..."

"Georgia, you are going on the field trip. We can take Libby to Grandad's and then your mum and me can have some time to ourselves for once."

"Mum doesn't want time with you, you will only talk about rubbish and set fire to your farts and so on. Please, please don't make me go. I may die in the forest eaten by voles."

"Good."

6:30 p.m.

God I am so tense. I've spent precious sex-minxy make-up time trying to talk some sense into my father and now I have only an hour to get ready for the Sex God. I must concentrate.

6:32 p.m.

How do I feel about meeting Robbie? I had eschewed him with a firm hand. And now he wants to shake my hand, and put my hand... Shut up about hands! Stop going on and on about hands!! Be a hands-free zone!!!

Oh, brilliant news, my brain has popped off on an away day to Loonchester!

6:35 p.m.

I've put really loud music on to drown out my brain while I do my make-up. I wonder whether he will have a Kiwi-a-gogo accent? He will probably say "gidday cobbler" or whatever it is they say.

I've got this stuff that you paint on your lipstick and it makes it stay on, even through snogging. I tried snogging my arm in a very passionate way and it remained lippy-free. So resultio!!!

one minute later

But I don't know why I'm bothered about snogging because I might just be drinking coffee.

I wonder if I put the stuff on my eyeliner it will stop it coming off as well. Sometimes when I go to the loo after dancing like a loon I look like Polly the Panda.

7:10 p.m.

Ow buggery bugger. It's like putting paint stripper on your eyelid.

Ow.

My eyes will probably all swell up now. I must keep them very wide open.

7:15 p.m.

I've got my blue leather skirt and black top on and my ankle boots. I might take a jacket just in case he wants to, er... wander about in the woods or something. My hands are shaking so much I can't do the buttons up.

I must be cool and calmy calm. I must not under any circumstances turn into ditherqueen and remind Robbie how

♡ 371

much younger than him I am. I must exude sophisticosity at all times.

Nearly fell down the stairs because I was trying to keep my eyes open.

Mum came out of the kitchen. "Where are you going?"

"Just round to Jas's."

"What, with half a ton of make-up and your shortest skirt on?"

"Mum, just leave it for once. Remember when you were young? There must be some papyrus scroll somewhere that will remind you of what it was like."

She looked at me. "Georgia, that is not the way to get a favour out of me."

I would have to risk it. I said, "Mum, the letter was from Robbie. You know, from before? Well, he has come back unexpectedly and I don't know why but he asked me to meet him tonight. Please don't ruin my life."

To my amazement she said, "All right, but you must be back at a reasonable time, otherwise your dad will have one of his turns, and no one wants that."

What? No argument?

As she went off she said, "You look lovely. Why wouldn't

he want to go out with you? Just try not to do that thing that you do when you are nervous and your brain drops out. And why are you staring at everything?"

I gave her a quick kiss and leaped out of the door.

Ten minutes to get to East Street

Pant, pant.

Five minutes later

Nearly there. I must stop my starey eyes now and prepare for sticky-eye work like what it says in *How to Make Any Twit Fall in Love with You*. Yes and it was also time for hip work. And... hip swing, hip swing, flicky hair, flicky hair, licky lips, hip swing, hip sw—

There he was! Robbie the Sex God. How many hours had I spent longing for this moment? How many times had I cried myself to sleep just dreaming of him coming to meet me?

He looked vair cool and tanned. Not in an English way, which is a bit like crispy bacon bits with a touch of tomato sauce, but in a groovy gravy sort of way. He was wearing all black. A suit with a collarless black shirt. My heart went all melty. And my legs. And my brain. Hurrah, jelloid girl was back!

He turned round and saw me and smiled and shook his hair back out of his eyes. They were incredibly blue-black against his tan and he looked like he really liked me; they were all softy looking. I held my hand out for him to shake. Why? Had I turned into the Duke of Edinburgh? He smiled in a puzzled sort of way but took my hand and shook it.

"Er, how do you do? You're not dashing off for a train, are you?"

I went beetroot. "No, I... well, that was a bit of a misunderstanding, trainwise."

"What, you mean as there is no train station in town?"

"Yes, that will be the one."

He laughed then. "I'd almost forgotten how interesting life can be around you, Georgia."

But he said it in a sort of nice way.

And I said, "Hgnnfff." Which is a quite brilliant thing to reply if you want someone to run away.

Robbie looked at me. "Look, let's just try and relax and have a nice time, it's OK. We haven't seen each other for ages."

Two minutes later
He really is vair groovy looking. I had slight jelloid knickers.

Then I heard Jas's voice in my head saying "tart". I don't see why, though, because I am still a free woman. I haven't plighted my troth with Masimo. I haven't had a chance to plight anything as he hasn't bothered to get in touch with me. I am officially an untrothed person.

Robbie suggested we go to La Strada, which is a cool Italian bar-coffeehouse sort of place with sofas and stuff. All the groovy types go there; it's perfect for showing off in.

Three quarters of an hour later

Robbie has been telling me about his time in Kiwi-a-gogo land. He's made me laugh quite a lot but I must say there is a high level of tensionosity. He hasn't actually said anything that would make you think he was not just a mate, talking about wombats and sheep to another mate. He hasn't said, "You're the one for me, Sex Kitty." Actually, from my point of view, it's a bit tricky thinking of safe things to talk about. I don't feel I can talk about the Stiff Dylans because then Masimo would come up (oo-er) and what would I say then? I don't know if anyone has snitched to Robbie about Masimo being my maybe boyfriend. I can tell you this for free, though, if anyone has said anything bitchy it will be Wet Lindsay.

Using my world-famed subtlenosity, I must subtly find out, in a subtle way, what she has told him. I said, "Erm, I heard that Wet... I mean Lindsay... turned up on the night you arrived back. Did she have any... er... news?"

He looked at me. "I didn't think you got on all that well with Lindsay."

I said, "Who does? I'm only human."

He laughed, thank goodness.

At which point, and this is unbelievable, Miss Octopus Head herself walked into the bar with her indescribably dull and sad mate Astonishingly Dim Monica. She was flinging her hair about and doing that hippy walk thing which is vair vair common. (Unless I am doing it.) She went over to the bar and turned round to say something to ADM and that is when she saw us. She looked like someone had just stuck a burning poker up her bum-oley.

She turned back to the bar to order her drink and when she got it she walked over to our table. Oh brilliant, I was going to get a Coca-Cola over my head. But she ignored me completely and just spoke to Robbie. "Hi, Robbie, great night on Saturday, I'll see you at the after-gig party next week. I'm looking forward to it."

Then she looked at me like she had just spotted a bit of gob having a cup of coffee and said, "Georgia, out a bit late, aren't you? Looking forward to going off camping with your little mates? It sounds ever so exciting and you will probably get to stay up late playing games and so on. I remember I used to love camping when I was your age. See you." And she slimed off.

Oh, I hate her.

Robbie looked at me. "She doesn't seem to really like you that much. Er, camping?"

I said, "We are being made to go and thrash around in the undergrowth for German. I should have never mentioned the Kochs."

Oh, well done, brain, talking complete gibberish and mentioning the Kochs. Super. Thanks a lot. Good night.

Lindsay was talking in a really mad way to ADM, shaking her extensions and looking over at us. I was definitely a dead person when I got to Stalag 14. Lindsay was going to make it her life's work to kill me. At the very least I was going to be Stumpy the girl from Stumpland.

As my brain was prattling merrily along by itself Robbie looked over my shoulder towards the door. He said, "This is a popular place."

I looked round. Oh excellent, just when you think things can't get any worse, they get worserer. There at the door was Masimo with Dom from the Stiff Dylans. It was awful. Robbie and Masimo looked at each other and did that nodding thing that boys do. Masimo looked at me in a sort of odd way; I couldn't tell what he was thinking. Phwoar, I could tell what I was thinking, though: he is, it has to be said, gorgey porgey plus nine. And that is, as any fool can tell you, a lot of gorgey porgey.

He and Dom came over to our table and did a lot more of that boy stuff:

"How's it going, mate?"

"Cool."

"Are you cool?"

"Yeah, I'm cool. How are you?"

"Cool."

Total WUBBISH. I don't know why girls get told off so much for being superficial and only caring about make-up. Boys are worse! They never say anything that lets you know what is going on. Even if they have the fight to end all fights with someone and their head gets pulled off they'll say (with difficulty, because of the missing-head scenario), "No, it's fine, all cool. We're cool with it."

Masimo said to me, "*Ciao*, Georgia, how are you?"

I said, "Oh, me, well I'm alrighty, as alrighty as... er... anything."

Shut up, shut up, shut up now.

The lads chatted for a bit about the band while I sat there like the goosegog fiasco of the year. Dom said, "Do you fancy coming and jamming with us at the gig?"

Then they started the cool thing again! Robbie said, "Yeah, that would be great if it's all cool with Masimo."

Masimo said, "For me, it would be OK. This would be a cool thing *per* me, and you come and sing maybe a few of your songs. Yes?"

He was talking to Robbie but looking at me. I was just sitting there like a fool in a skirt (which I was). I could not think of anything except the last words I had said to Masimo, before I had run off for my imaginary train, which were, as I recall, "Did you see the footie scores this arvie?"

Perfect. What could be more sane than that? "Anything" is the answer you are looking for.

Through the mists of horror and *ordure* I heard Dom saying, "See you then, mate. Bye, Georgia." And they all went off to another table.

As they sat down, some girls from St Mary's Sixth-form College came skittering in and joined them at their table, doing that ridiculous kissing-on-both-cheeks thing. Why were they sitting with them? One of the girls was whispering in Masimo's ear and flicking her hair about. What was going on?

Robbie said, "Shall we quit the scene? Do you fancy a bit of a stroll?"

I managed to nod without my head falling off and we left the cafe.

Lindsay looked absolute daggers at me as I went past her. I don't know what Masimo did as we left; I couldn't bear to look at him. I have never been so full of confusiosity in my life, and that is truly saying something.

Robbie was a bit quiet as we walked along. He had his hands in his pockets so at least I didn't have the lurking arms scenario to worry about.

As we got to North Street he stopped and turned to face me. "Georgia, I know that when I left you were really upset and I am sorry that I hurt you so much. I just felt that you were so much younger than me and that..." He stopped and looked into the distance.

What, what? And that what? *And that I was wrong. You are so full of maturiosity, Georgia, that I would like to snog you within an inch of your life?* Is that what?

And that's when I felt a sort of dithery strange energy. Like there was a mad person behind me. There was.

"Oh, er, hiiiiiiiiiiiiiiiiiii... I was just out in the street, like I am now and I, well... Hi, Gee... hi, Robbie..."

Ellen. What was she doing? Lurking about like Lurkio in the streets. On her own. But not in casual gear. She was all tarted up. Was she following us? Hoping for a threesome? How weird and French.

But no, she wasn't following us – because that is when I saw Dave the Laugh with his posse. Oh noooooooooo! I must hide, hide. I wished I could turn my skin to bark like those iguana things and then I could just blend in with the trees... What was I talking about? There were no trees, there were just shops. Well, I wished I could have skin like a shop then, and then... SHUT UP!!!

Dave clocked us and came swanning up all full of casualosity and *joie de* whatsit and winked at me. "Oy, Robbie, Georgia... and, oooh, it's Ellen. What are you hip cats up to then?"

Ellen went absolutely purple, and was just opening and

closing her mouth like a purple trout. She managed to say, "Oh, Dave... wow... er... hi. Fancy, fancy seeing you here... er... here in... with your..."

Dave said, "Trousers on?"

Ellen went on and on, "Er no, no, not the trousers... well, yes, because, well, you have got them on but... but... well, anyway I must be going." And she went off.

She must have been secretly trailing Dave around. Blimey. I have eventually met someone who is even more full of bonkerosity than me.

Dave shouted after her, "Missing you already, Ellen."

That's done it; now we will spend the next month discussing with Ellen whether he really was missing her "already", and when was already and what did he mean by "missing". I felt sorry for Ellen, in an irritated way, because she really does luuurve Dave the Laugh. She has never forgotten the eight and a half minutes they went out together.

Dave was looking very cool indeed; there is something about him that reeks of naughtinosity. My lips started that puckering-up business all by themselves. And I did a bit of ad-hoc hair swishing. I'd missed seeing him.

He seemed completely at ease with me and Robbie.

Didn't he mind that we might be going out together? He seemed to have forgotten about his "What if you really liked someone and then you lost them" fandango.

Which is of course a good thing. Really good. I'm glad. That means we can just be mates. Which I like. As everyone knows. Mateyness is my besty thing.

He said to me, "Nice skirt, Georgia. Has your grandad's girlfriend knitted you anything unusual lately? I saw her on the back of your grandad's bike the other day in a sort of one-piece thing – it may have been a knitted swimsuit. She's a goer, isn't she?"

I said, "That is one way of putting it."

Robbie said, "I didn't know your grandad had got a girlfriend. The last thing I heard from Tom was that he was arrested for being drunk in charge of a bike."

The boys laughed together. No, no, no, stop laughing about my stupid grandad. This was not the way things were supposed to be between love rivals.

Two minutes later
When we reached the Buddha Lounge Dave's posse said "s'laters" and went off inside.

Dave said, "We're having a pool match, Robbie, if you fancy it? Or are you otherwise engaged?"

I went completely red and had to pretend to look for something in my bag.

Robbie said, "Maybe catch you later."

The gate to Bonkers Hall (i.e. my house)
10:00 p.m.

When we got to my gate Robbie looked me straight in the eyes. Oh goddy god he was going to snog me. He took his hands out of his pockets and I did my famous looking down and then looking up thing. At which point Mr and Mrs Next Door came along walking the Prat brothers. What is it with this town? Did someone on the radio say, "Snogging alert, snogging alert. There is a chance that Georgia might actually have a snogathon with one of her many maybe boyfriends. Why not go out and annoy her by popping up unexpectedly?"

Mr Next Door went all puffed up and insane when he saw me. He said, "Just the person I wanted to see."

Mrs Next Door was saying, "Don't upset yourself, dear."

"Upset myself, upset myself!!! Do you know what that furry ruffian you call a pet has done now, do you? Do you?"

Actually, I did have a bit of a clue, but I didn't say.

Mr Next Door was going on and on. "He has absolutely DECIMATED our aquarium. DECIMATED it. There were tadpoles all over the rockery. It's a bloody disgrace. In fact I have got a good mind to get on to the authorities and get it removed to a place where it won't be a danger to the public any more."

I said, "Yes, I agree, aquariums can be very dangerous."

I really thought that he was going to implode, so I said soothingly, "He's just high spirited. He thinks the tadpoles are egging him on, waggling about like that. It's his nature, he's a hunter, he likes killing things."

Mr Next Door said, "You don't have to tell me that."

Eventually he went off grumbling and moaning on and on, the Prat brothers yapping away. They had completely spoiled the snogging mood.

Robbie said, "I'm going to get off now, Georgia. Nice to see you." He looked like he was going to say something else and then he just went, "See you at the gig."

And that was it. He did give me a little peck on the cheek, but what does that mean?

Two minutes later

I watched him walk off down the street. He walks in a really cool way. I watched him right down to the end of the street and he didn't even look back when he went around the corner.

10:15 p.m.

I have accidentally got home at a decent time. When I came in, Mutti just looked at me in amazement. She said, "You're in."

Then she went to the kitchen and came back with a bowl of cornflakes, which she gave me. I said, "Blimey, you never usually cook, Mum."

Five minutes later

In bed lying down just thinking.

One minute later

How weird is this?

Five minutes later

So this is my wonderful life. I start off not knowing what "going for coffee" means and now I'm wondering what "see you at the gig" means. Does it mean "see you at the gig, my new girlfriend" or "see you at the gig, my old mate"?

I may or may not have two boyfriends and none of us seem to know. And even if I did have two, maybe I only have one now because Masimo will think that I am going out with Robbie. But I'm not. Am I?

Goodie, now I am queuing up at the bakery of love, strapped to the rack of love, which makes it very difficult to even get inside the door in the first place.

Just then I heard baldy types sniggering in the hall outside my door. Oh dear God, now what? Dad and Uncle Eddie have obviously been at the jungle juice because Uncle Eddie said in a really crap Chinese accent, "Special deliverly." And underneath the door came a sort of postcard thing. I heard a piggy type snort, from Vati.

It's unbelievable at their age. I suppose I will have to look, otherwise they will be crouching outside my door all night.

One minute later

Oh how vair vair amusant. The postcard said: TEENAGERS, FED UP WITH BEING HARASSED BY YOUR STUPID PARENTS? TAKE ACTION, LEAVE HOME, GET A JOB, PAY YOUR OWN BILLS. WHILE YOU STILL KNOW EVERYTHING.

I said, "Yeah, good one. Good night, you pranksters."

They went snorting off. Good grief.

Two minutes later

Where was I? Oh yes, strapped to the rack of love, not being able to get through into the bakery. Well, how about if I undo the straps, chuck the rack away, and enter boldly, shouting, "Give me a dozen mixed cakes, please!"

No, no, no, no, no! No to red-bottomosity!!!

One minute later

What if I said, "Yes, I have made my selection. I would like the Italian cakey, please."

One minute later

"No, no, no, make that the creamy Robbie éclair."

One minute later

"On second thoughts, could I have the... Oh *sacré* bloody *bleu*, I will be up all night worrying about..."

zzzzzzzzzzzzzzzz.

Return of the Hornmeister, quickly followed by the Luuurve God

Wednesday July 20th
On the way to Stalag 14

I have decided to gird my loins and "tak' the high road", etc. or whatever it is that our Och Aye friends drone on about. Anyway I am going to be positive. And actually the day did start in tip-top form. First of all Angus set fire to his own tail by sitting near the oven. Which I have to say was very funny. Libby laughed so much I thought I would have to do the Heimlich manoeuvre on her. Which I think is an omen for everything going my way boywise.

Ran up to Jas at her gate and gave her a firm handshake and said, "This is the first day of the rest of our lives."

She said, "What does that mean?"

I said, "I don't know, but let's disco dance."

We burst into a quick bout of the Viking disco inferno dance. Well, the stabbing and leg kicking. Jas wouldn't do the all-over body shake because she didn't want to mess up her fringe.

I told her a bit about my night but I let there be an air of mysteriosity about things.

Mostly I lied.

Assembly

Slim was moaning on as usual. "Why is it necessary for me to remind you that the science block skeleton is not a toy? Whoever thought it was funny to dress it up in Mr Attwood's spare overalls and sit it in his hut with a flask is very childish. Mr Attwood got quite a start." etc. etc. blah, blah, rave on, rave on.

But then the music started (or Miss Wilson playing the crap piano, as some people call it) and we realised it was the *pièce de résistance* comedy hymnwise. Not "Jerusalem".

Obviously it would have been top if it had been "Jerusalem" with its famous refrain "And was Jerusalem builded here amongst England's dark satanic PANTS". But it was even better than that because yesssssss it was "Gladly My Cross I Bear", or as we know and love it, "Gladly My Cross-eyed Bear". Oh, yes! Klingon salutes all round for the Ace Gang.

Hawkeye was giving us the hairy eyeball because normally we do not bother singing, we just mouth the words. But touché Hawkeye, girl torturer and centre of poonosity, today the Ace Gang has triumphed comedywise.

Then, to put the icing on the pyjamas, as we trooped out along the corridor Elvis Attwood tripped over his mop and had a magnificent spaz attack and started hitting the mop. I think he is tipping over the edge into insanity and mentaldom.

Blodge

Miss Finnigan is absent, probably exhausted by hauling her nungas around all day – they are quite literally giganticibus. Nearly as obscene as my mum's. As a special treat Miss Wilson has been sent on as sub. Joy unbounded.

As we lolled into our seats Miss Wilson was fiddling around with a TV. Rosie said, "Ooh good, is it *Gladiator*, Miss?"

Miss Wilson had a complete ditherama and practically lassoed herself with the leccy cable. She was all flushed. "No, no, it's not *Gladiator* because it's—"

Rosie hadn't finished. "We are always allowed to watch *Gladiator* on Wednesdays. And as it is set in olden times we are also allowed to practise our Viking bison horn dance. Do you want to see it?"

Smoothing her bob in between plugging stuff in, Miss Wilson said, "Now, Rosie, you know that it's biology and so I will be showing a relevant film. So settle down, girls, and... Julia, please do not set fire to the plants with the Bunsen burner; that is not what they are for."

Jools started then: "What are Bunsen burners for then, Miss? I thought that was what the huge flame thing was for."

I didn't give Miss Wilson much chance of making it through to the end of the lesson.

Five minutes later

Miss Wilson is sensationally red. Rosie offered to help plug stuff in and accidentally turned the fan full on, which nearly blew Miss Wilson's bob off. She has outdone herself fashionwise today. And I am not saying that just to be nice.

She must have found the only corduroy shop in the world and today she is wearing a pinafore dress made out of it, with ankle socks. They are not made out of corduroy, actually, but it would be good if they were.

I said to Mabs, "If this so-called film is anything to do with reproduction by any creature on the planet I am definitely putting chewed-up paper in my earlugs."

Two minutes later
The film turns out to be about bees. It is a film about a bee centre. How crap is this going to be?

An hour later
That was the best thing I have seen for ages. We made Miss Wilson rewind the bit where the two queens were having a bitch fight. I didn't know how fab bees were, and so sensible they could teach us a thing or two. For instance, the queen bee kills her sexual partners by tearing off their reproductive equipment (or bee trouser-snake addenda) once she has had her wicked way with them.

As I said to Jas, "That would solve my multi-boyfriend *problemo*."

She said, "Georgia, excuse me if I am right but one of your so-called boyfriends took you out for a coffee and didn't snog you, and the other one hasn't even got on the blower. That is not what I would call a multi-boyfriend *problemo*."

I kicked her shin. "I hate you, Jas."

"Well, I am only telling you the truth. That is what friends are for."

"Is it? Well, I don't tell you how stupid your fringe looks, do I?"

"Yes."

She is so unreasonable and mad. And so full of herself just because she has a boring old boyfriend. However, for once I don't mind because I feel that I have learned quite a lot today. I may become a beekeeper/model/backing singer.

Did you know that baby bees are fed bee bread? That is *le* fact.

Also, when they sting you they lose their bottoms.

On the way to English

Miss Wilson is beside herself at the prospect of going camping. As we left blodge she said, "Girls, it's going to be such fun."

I said to the gang, "I tell you this for free, I am not doing anything to do with mime or clowning, and that is final."

394

English

Blimey O'Reilly, how many plays did Billy Shakespeare write? He can't have got out much. Apparently most of the rude words we know are from him and his mates – so I don't know why we get told off for using them. And also, violence and binge-drinking are not a new invention – Billy and his fellow twits in tights were not exactly kind to each other. For a laugh they used to put people in stocks and so on. In fact that was their entertainment – that and baiting bears.

For instance, here is a real conversation between Elizabethan mates, Tight-us Tight-us and Mind-us my Cod-us Piece:

M.C.P: "Prithee Tight-us Tight-us, what do you fancy doing tonight-us?"

T.T: "Sirre, what-us about drinking a pint or two of gin and annoying-us the bears?"

M.C.P: "Nah. Let-us just bugger off down to the stocks and throw tomatoes at the weirdo."

French

I am going to have to kill Rosie because unfortunately she has got pre-pre-weekend bonkerosity. Or a touch of the Svens, as some might say. She has just sent me a French joke.

Her notelet said:

Bonjour, mon petit pain,
   What do you call a French man in sandals?
   Au revoir.
   Roz.eeeeeeeeeeee

I wrote back: I don't care.

But she gave me her raised eyebrows and nodding head thing until I had to mouth to her, "Oh go on then."

And she wrote back: Philippe Philoppe.

On the way home
4:15 p.m.

The Blunder Boys are trailing along behind us doing what they think is gay repartee. Saying things like, "Hey love, lie down, will you? I need somewhere to park my bike."

What are they talking about? I'll tell you this, they will be the last to know.

After about ten minutes of this, I turned round to them and said, "Er, why don't you go away? A LOT!"

And amazingly that baffled them. I think it was having a clear instruction that they couldn't cope with. Apparently boys and dogs have stuff in common. That is what the Hornmeister told me once.

At that moment, as if he had been earwigging in my brain, the Hornmeister appeared over the horizon with two of his mates. When he saw us he did this mad running-towards-us-with-his-arms-outstretched thing. Sort of skipping like from *The Sound of Music*.

"Hello, ladeeeeeeez, the vati is back! Sound out the PANTS of England!!! Let the Cosmic and General Horns be heard! Hooooorrnnnnnnn!!! Who are my bitches???"

Ellen said, "Er, we are... er, are we your, erm, bitches?"

We looked at her.

I said in a dignified at all times way, "Oh hello, Dave, you're not going to do your rapping thing and then fall over a wall again, are you?"

He looked at me and licked his lips. Honestly. "Georgia, I know that is just your little way of saying, 'Hey, big boy, hold me back because you give me the Horn big time.'"

I just looked at him. I wasn't going to smile at him, if that is what he thought. He was too full of himself and his red-bottomosity. But he would not get me to... Oh blimey, I have accidentally given him my full nostril-flaring smile! Damn.

He linked up with us all and then his two mates did the same so that we looked like we were doing the Hokey-Kokey. I hope we didn't have to negotiate any lampposts or the elderly insane.

He said, "Trot on, girls. Do you like my new trainers? I feel like Jack the Biscuit in them."

They were quite cool, as it happens.

One of his mates, Declan, was linked up to Ellen, and he said, "We had a laugh today. There was a minor rumble in the corridor because Phil the Nerd and his mates tried to be top dog in the lunch queue. So clearly he had to be binned. Excellent."

I knew I shouldn't ask, but somehow I did. "What do you mean he had to be binned?"

In my bedroom
I know that I have said this many, many times but boys are a bloody mystery. Apparently when they get bored boys go on a "binning" session. They got Phil the Nerd and put him botty-first into a litter bin. As soon as he managed to heave

himself out his "mates" put him back in. Then when he got out again Dave and Dec and company turned up and put him back in again. And so on until the end of break. Why?

5:30 p.m.

I hate to admit this because of my position as mate to Dave the Laugh, but there is something that goes on in the jelloid-knicker department when I see him. He's sort of familiar somehow, and he does make me laugh. But shut up, brain, because mates do not snog or even think about snogging. That is *le* fact. I have too many maybe boyfriends to worry about without thinking about Dave the Laugh and his snogging abilities. Which I'm not even thinking about, by the way.

Two minutes later

I was just thinking about when I first snogged him at the fish party. That really was the beginning of my red-bottom phase. I blame him. He started me on the slippery slope with his lip-nibbling techniques and so on. But I will just LET IT GO because he is not on the snoggees list; he is just a boymatetypefandango. Which is good.

One minute later

I wonder what number he has got up to with his "girlfriend". He never mentions her. Mind you, *I* never mention her.

I wonder if she mentions herself?

I wonder if she has ever asked him about me.

She isn't with him much; perhaps he has dumped her.

Ten minutes later

A lot of thumping on the stairs. "Come on, dollyboy, Josh boy, bring pussycat in here lalalalalalalala. Pussycat, pussycat, where have you beeeeeen, I've been to London to see a sardine!!! Hahahahahahaha."

My door crashed open and a very red-faced sister loomed round. She had Gordon by the neck and he was struggling like billio. Yeah, good luck, furry chum. She had her other chubby little arm around the neck of her "boyfwend" the unfortunate Josh. Libby lobes Josh. She treats him just like the rest of her toys – Pantalitzer doll, Angus and Gordy, scuba-diving Barbie, Jesus/Sandra, me – really, really badly. The only difference is that as yet she hasn't been able to remove bits of his body. Pantalitzer doll is quite literally just a head now.

"Heggo, Gingie, my Gingie, I LOBE my Gingie. Kiss Joshie the dollyboy."

"No, Libbs, I don't think that Josh wants a kiss, and you are holding him too tightly round his little neck – his head is going red, isn't it, Joshie?"

Libby smiled her alarming smile. Lately she has taken to opening her eyes really wide when she does it and sticking her teeth out, like a bonkers hamster who has just seen a really big carrot. "He laaaikes it."

And she dragged them off into her room. If I hear sawing noises I will go in. Although why I have to take responsibility I don't know. What are my "parents" doing? If they aren't interested in their children they shouldn't have them. I might say that to them. I might say... no, hang on a minute, I know what will happen then – they *will* start taking an interest in me, just to annoy me.

Went down to run myself a bath and as I passed Libby's door I could hear her talking. "Now then, a bitty lit of lipstick. Mmmmmm."

Josh is going to look like a toddler drag queen by the time his mum picks him up. Still, if she bans him from coming round it might save him from something far, far worse.

As I came out of the bathroom Vati was coming out of the kitchen, wearing what he likes to think is "leisure wear". Essentially jeans and a T-shirt that says, "I'm a grown up. So nanananana." How pathetico. But I didn't say.

He started rambling and moaning, though. He only has to see my head to start complaining. "Georgia, you had better not be in that bathroom for the rest of the night. There are other people in this house, you know."

I said, "I know, that is what I complain about as well."

"Don't be so bloody cheeky. The day you start paying the water bill is the day you can start being cheeky."

Oh, drone on. Just because as yet I am not the girlfriend of a pop star and a squillionnaire beekeeper/backing singer etc. I am picked on by old Huge Botty. Still, live and let die is what I say.

If Mum and Dad were bees, he would be a dead bee by now. And that is not easy to say.

He hadn't finished, though: "And feed your bloody cat; it's attacking my trousers."

Who wouldn't? I thought, but I didn't say.

I turned the bath on and went into the kitchen. When he saw me, Angus shot through the cat flap into the garden.

Then he came back in doing his comedy coming-through-the-cat-flap-backwards thing and yowling like he hadn't eaten anything for days.

I know that is not true because of the complaints from the neighbours. Mr Up the Road said that Angus even ate some lard he had put out for the birds. The Prat brothers have to be fed inside now because Angus is so sneaky he can dart out within seconds and gobble down their food. He is like the James Bond of Catland – they seek him here, they seek him there, they seek that puddy-tat everywhere.

I have seen him leap down from the bedroom windowsill unexpectedly, right into the Prat poodles' food bowl. Or from the roof. Or out of the dustbin. You have to admire him, really.

Owwwwwwwww. Bloody hell, I think he may have eaten my ankle.

I put Angus's food in his bowl and he was purring and pushing himself against my legs. Aahhh. Then he sat on the table and just looked.

I said, "Don't you want your kitty-kat food?"

He shut his eyes.

I went and checked the bath and put in some of Mum's

strictly-banned expensive bath oil that she hides in her wardrobe. Honestly, it is so tiring trying to have a bath around this place.

When I went back into the kitchen Angus was sitting in his food in the food bowl.

I didn't know what to say.

As I was just looking at him and he was looking at me Gordy came into the kitchen. Fully made up. Honestly. If I didn't know better I would say that he had false eyelashes on. He was covered in foundation and rouge, and around his eyes were big black rings and some sort of blue stuff. I noticed he had some clip-on earrings on as well. And a bow on his tail.

I went off into the bathroom.

The odd thing was, Gordy looked strangely happy.

Maybe he is a homosexualist cat.

Angus will disown him.

In the bathroom

Aah, at last I can relax and think about myself properly.

It is amazing how floaty nungas are. I wonder why? Perhaps it is in case of flooding and then girls, who of course are the most important sex, would float to safety. It may be a genetic floaty survival thingy.

Two minutes later
I don't like to criticise Big G unnecessarily but it does on the whole seem like a useless genetic floaty survival thingy. Much the same as the body-hair fiasco. What is the point of having rogue hairs shooting out of the back of your knee, for instance? Or the big curly one I found in my eyebrow. How could that help the human race survive? Unless there was a time when wild animals were really really frightened of eyebrows.

Back to the nungas though... (I can hear Dave the Laugh saying, "Yes, let us get back to the nungas, Kittykat!" Shut up, shut up, Dave the Laugh's imaginary voice! Get out of my bath!!!!) Where was I? Oh yes, if it is down to floatiness clearly Wet Lindsay would sink without a trace as she has got pretendy nungas, which is a GOOD thing, but Melanie Griffiths would be floating around with me for sure. I mean she's all right and everything, but not exactly tip-top brainwise. I wouldn't want her and me to be responsible for repopulating the earth after a flood.

Fifteen minutes later

I heard the doorbell ring. Please let it not be Grandad in his bicycling shorts, with Maisie his knitted girlfriend. Thank goodness I have the door safely bolted.

I could hear muffled voices as I put my face mask on. Aaahh, this was the first time I had been relaxed for ages, well, since I had my little zizz in maths this arvie. I find trigonometry vair vair soothing.

Two minutes later

Dad said through the door, "Georgia, are you still in the bath?"

Uuuurgh, my dad was talking to me while I was in the nuddy-pants! How disgusting. I put a flannel over my nungas. "Dad, go away."

"There is someone to see you."

What? The Ace Gang usually ring before they come round. I bet it was Mr Next Door come to complain about his stupid aquarium fiasco. But I hadn't heard any shouting. I said, "Who is it?"

Then I heard his voice. "Georgia... *ciao*, it is Masimo. I came for to see you. How are you?"

I couldn't believe it. I couldn't believe that I was talking to

Masimo in the nuddy-pants. Me, not him, I mean, unless it was an Italian tradition to call round at a girl's house with no clothes on. You never know, of course, but... shut up, shut up!!!

This called for hidden depths of sophisticosity. Maybe I could pretend I wasn't in the bath, that I was just, like, in the bathroom. No, no, that was much worse because if I wasn't having a bath what was I doing in the bathroom? He might think there was a loo in here. There *is* a loo in here. Oh no, nononoooo. Why had my stupid, stupid father let him come near the bathroom door?

I could hear my dad say, "I know she is in there because I spoke to her just before you came round. Who knows what girls do in there, eh? Where did you say you come from in Italy?"

Masimo said in his gorgey Pizza-a-gogo way, "It is a small place near Roma."

I stepped very, very quietly out of the bath. Don't make a ripply water noise, just shushhyshush.

I needn't have bothered, though, because Dad was still pratting on for England. "Oh yes, very nice, I went on a footie excursion with the lads to Rome, had a lot of your *vino tinto*!!! *Muchos* nice."

Masimo laughed. "Ah yes, I like to play footie. When I go

home I with my mates, we play in a how you say, in a league."

"Yes, I like to keep in top condition myself. Would you like a drink?"

"Ah well, thank you, that would be nice, Mr Nicolson."

"Call me Bob."

And I heard them go off into the kitchen.

Call me Bob??? No, I tell you what, why don't we call you, "You big fat prat!!!"

How could this be happening? I could have drowned in the bath for all they knew. I dried myself and washed off the face mask.

But I was still trapped in the bathroom with no make-up on, with a Luuurve God just two inches of wood away.
Oh, what should I do? There was nothing to improvise with, make-upwise. Mum told me that Maisie used to use shoe polish as eyeliner because they were so poor in the olden days. And bite her lips to make them go red. Come to think of it, she looks like the bride of Dracula now, so years of lip biting have paid off. Grandad likes that living dead look.

I put my ear to the door and I could just make out my dad pratting on and on about his football "career" i.e. being generally a large lazy lardy lump on legs. Then I heard Mum come out of the lounge and shout up the stairs, "Libby, you and Josh are very quiet. What are you doing?"

I heard a bit of scuffling and then Libby saying, "Nothing, Mummy."

And I thought I heard Josh shout, "Help!" but I had no time for toddler trouble just now. I had my own emergency.

I whispered as loudly as I could, "Mum! Mum!!!"

She came over to the door. "What? Why are you still in there? Masimo is here. God, he's gorgeous, isn't he?"

"Mum, I am stuck in here in my crappy T-shirt and joggy bums and no make-up. What are you going to do about it? Because if you don't help me I will be in here for the rest of my life."

She said, "Say please."

"PLEASE help me, Mum. Otherwise I will kill you."

Eventually, after she had made me plead properly, Mum went off and sneaked me in my make-up bag and jeans.

My hand was all trembly and my face had that attractive red quality that you long for when you have a Luuurve God in the house. Anyway, I did my best. I thought I would go for that, "ooooh, you caught me washing my hair" scenario. So mascara, eyeliner, lippy and lip gloss, and a towel around my hair (to disguise the fact that it looked like an elephant had had a poo on it).

Big deep breath and open the door.

In the Kitchen

Oh, it was sooooo embarrassing. Vati was trying to talk to us like we were all mates. Why couldn't he just go away? For ever.

He had one leg up on a chair drinking his beer and saying to Masimo, "So have you got a motor, then, Mas?" (Mas... ohmygod he was calling him Mas!!!)

Masimo was looking at me but he said, "Er, oh no, I have a scooter."

I said, "Do you want to, erm, go and sit outside for a bit? And chat?"

Mum came in dragging Josh and Libby with her. My worst fears were realised – Josh was dressed as a drag queen. A drag queen with half a Mohican haircut.

Mum was livid. "What is Josh's mummy going to say? You naughty girl! I told you not to play with scissors."

Libby was very cross as well. "He's been to London to see the sardine."

Dad said, "Don't be cheeky, young lady."

Libby put her hands on her hips and shouted at him, "Don't YOU be cheeky, bad mummy!!!"

As Dad was momentarily distracted by being called mummy, I said to Masimo, "Quickly, let's get out of here!" and we went and sat on the wall. I made sure we were hidden by the tree so that M and D couldn't spy on us from the house.

I still had my hair up in a towel, but I like to think it made me look a bit like a Thai bride or something. That is what I like to think.

At first we just sat there in silence. I didn't know what to do. Eventually I said, "I'm sorry about the train fandango, Robbie turning up like that, and you saying, you're free for me, and then I was carrying the horns... I just went a bit mad."

Masimo didn't say anything. Oh no. Then I felt his hand on my face, and he turned my face towards him and looked me straight in the eye. I was melting, I was melting!!!

"Georgia, for me, it is the same. For you, I don't know. I see you with Robbie in the cafe and he is nice guy, you for him was liking before. So I don't know."

You and me both, pally. You for me don't know. But fortunately I didn't say that. I didn't know what to say. I was just looking in his eyes, his lovely yellow cat eyes, and then he kissed me on the mouth. Really gently. Then he did it again. And my naughty lips started going on snogging alert. He put his other hand on the back of my neck and pulled me nearer to him. I hoped my towel didn't fall off and reveal mad elephant-poo hair. This time he kissed me long and hard. It was so groovy and warm and I couldn't tell where his mouth finished and mine started and then... some absolute arse shouted, "Oy, does his boyfriend know you are snogging him?"

We both looked up and couldn't see anyone, then I noticed a bit of a rustling behind the hedge of Mr Across the Road's garden. I leaped across and looked over the hedge and there, in his ridiculous sports cap, was Oscar, otherwise known as junior Blunder Boy and tosser.

I leaped over the hedge, gave him a swift kick in the kidneys and then hopped back to Masimo.

Masimo was laughing. "Georgia, everyone is here. It is how you say, very busy."

He smiled at me and got up and sat on his scooter.

I looked at him.

He looked at me.

He said, "So, Miss Georgia, now what shall we do? I am free for you. Are you free for me also?"

Good point. Well made. But what was the answer?

I started thinking about mentioning my untrothness, but then thought about trying to describe that to anyone normal, and also Italian. Instead I took a deep breath and said, "I really like you, and think you are the bee's knees, etc."

Masimo said, "I am the knees of a bee?"

I said, "Well, forget about the bee thing, it's just that... well, I think I have to talk to Robbie first, properly."

Masimo smiled a little smile. "Yes, I think so, too. It is fair."

I watched him go down to the bottom of our road on his scooter. Oh no, now what had I done? I had practically refused to go out with a Luuurve God. I am clearly mentally deranged.

I watched him get to the end of our street and indicate left... and then he did a big u-ey and came hurtling back, screeching to a halt in front of me.

He said, "Georgia, I forgot for what I came to tell you. I am going home to Italy after the gig for a month to see my family. Can you, would you, if you decide you are free for me, come and stay with me, with my family for a little?"

Wow. We were practically married!!! And me in my towel!!!

I didn't really know what to say, so he said, "Think about this, *caro*, it would be beautiful."

And he rode off.

I floated past King Buffoon (Dad), cleaning his car, and I didn't even laugh when he said, "Fancy giving me a hand polishing the old Lovemobile?"

In the Kitchen

Mum has tried to make Josh look like a human being, but the hair is scary. His mother will definitely inform the authorities. But ho hum, pig's bum. I said as I went to my bedroom, "Don't bother booking me up to go to Ireland with you, Mum, as I will be holidaying just near Rome this summer."

She didn't even bother to reply, which is a bit rude, but typical of her self-obsessed attitude.

Thursday July 21st

8:30 a.m.

Walking to Stalag 14 with Jas. I told her about Masimo coming round and snogging me. She said, "So what number did you get to?"

"Well, I suppose officially it was only a number four but his mental vibe was more like eight."

"Are you saying that mentally he was doing upper-body fondling indoors?"

"Yep, I certainly am."

"But you were sitting on your wall outside."

"Well, officially, but..."

"And he had his hand on the back of your neck, which is not your upper body."

"Yes it is."

Jas was chewing on her chuddie and had that annoying look on her face, like she was thinking. I hate that. She was droning on and on like Mrs Droning-on Knickers, which she is. "OK, in that case, if upper-body fondling doesn't mean your nungas it just means anything on the top of your waist, then number seven and eight could be, like, nose fondling or chin fondling."

God, she is soooooo annoying. And fringey. "Jas, I am just trying to tell you what happened; this is not the Spanish Inquisition. You are not El Quasimodo."

She got into her Huffmobile then. "I didn't make these snogging rules up, Georgia. You did."

We were just passing a litter bin and for a minute of ecstasy I thought about shoving her in botty-first like Dave and his mates did. But actually if I did shove her in there she might get stuck because of her enormous pantaloonies and I would have to call the fire brigade to cut her out. Besides which, I must remember I want to stay at her house on Saturday night after the gig in case there are any ad-hoc snogging opportunities. So instead of hitting her or anything I just smiled my loveliest smile and said, "Jas, you know that you are my besty pal, and like the Wise Woman of the Forest to me. Can I just tell you what happened?"

She flicked her fringe about but said, "Go on, then."

I told her all about the Italian holiday idea. Even she was quite impressed by that. "Wow, well, that is like almost being an official girlfriend, isn't it? You are really going to have to decide soon. But you don't really know if Robbie likes you, do you? I mean you know he likes you like matewise, but does he think you are girlfriend material? I couldn't stand being you, not knowing who my boyfriend was and everything. I was with Tom last night and we were just, you know, rearranging my owl collection into sizes together... it was really, oh, I don't know, and then he got hold of my hand and put my fingers in his mouth and sucked them."

I said, "Blimey! Hand snogging! What number is that on the scale?"

Jas said, "I dunno, four and a half, do you think? It was

416

only the fingers, not the whole hand."

I didn't ask her who she knew that could fit a whole hand in their mouth because it was all making me feel a bit queasy.

Stalag 14
9:30 a.m.

Wet Lindsay is on my case big time. As I was passing her to go to games, she said, "Walk properly."

What does that mean?

Tennis courts

I was playing singles against Melanie Griffiths. Honestly, it shouldn't really be allowed. Her nungas are definitely a health hazard. I don't think she can really see over them to hit the ball. I was winning, by about eight-five million – nil. The most dangerous times were when she had to bend over to pick up the balls. Quite often I thought she was just going to topple over.

Then Wet Lindsay and Astonishingly Dim Monica came sliming along and actually came into the court and sat down on the chairs by the net. Wet Lindsay was just looking at me, and if looks could kill I would be deader than a dead person on dead tablets. In Deadland.

She looked at me but went on talking to ADM really loudly. "If I had a big nose I think I would find it very difficult to disguise. It is just something you really can't get away from, isn't it? I mean people say Barbra Streisand is a good singer, but mostly they say, 'What an enormous nose'."

I didn't mean to but I found myself sucking in my nostrils as I was serving. Maybe I could just "accidentally" hit Lindsay and knock her off her chair. I didn't dare, though, because she would probably snitch to Miss Wilson or Hawkeye and I would be made to polish Mr Attwood's spade collection for the rest of my life.

Octopus Head hadn't finished, though. "I don't know what to do about Masimo and Robbie. I mean, they are both gorgeous, aren't they? And you don't want to upset anyone's feelings, but..."

I could see as I was dashing around the court, or waiting for Melanie to regain her balance, that ADM was nodding away like a nodding-dog person. Lindsay was rambling on, flicking her stupid extensions and crossing her nobbly knees. God, I hate her. On and on she went. "I feel in a way, though, that Robbie has sort of blown it with me. He went away and so on when we had been quite serious. So if his work comes first you would never be really sure that he was totally there for you. But he is so keen, you know? And of course Masimo has that Latin charm, and..." She raised her voice. "...absolutely fantastic in the snogging area. I mean they do know how to do it, don't they, the Italians?"

The bell rang just as Melanie actually really did reach down for the ball and fall over forwards into the net. I went to help her get to her feet and as Wet Lindsay and ADM left the court, Lindsay said, "Your backhand is pretty weak, Nicolson. Maybe when you grow up a bit you can take on proper players."

She seemed like she was talking about tennis but I know very well what she was talking about.

Ace Gang Headquarters
Lunchtime

I am absolutely livid about Lindsay and what she said. Is any of it true? Is she really snogging Masimo when I am practically his child bride?

I told the Ace Gang all the news. Ro Ro said, "So Masimo came round and snogged you and asked you to go to Pizza-a-gogo land but you think that he might be double-timing you with Wet Lindsay?"

419

Jools said, "Who do you like best – Robbie or Masimo?"

I said, "I don't know what to think."

Ro Ro said, "This is when you need your mates around you to give you the benefit of their wisdomosity. Hand me my beard."

We all sat around and watched her as she put on her beard and then launched herself into a solo version of the Viking disco inferno dance. It was, even if you live in Confusiosity house, Confusion Lane, East Confusion (which I did), vair vair *amusant*.

Then she sat down again, panting, and said, "If only I had a pipe, but Sven took it to college with him today, he wanted to repaint it for Saturday. Did I tell you that he has got a job dj-ing now?"

Dear God.

Then she said, "What we must remember is that boys are quite literally a mystery and, as it says in the book, we have to keep them on an elastic band. Let them go wild and free and then they will come pinging back. I know that Sven comes pinging back with a vengeance. I have the love bites to prove it."

Jools said, "This is the plan: we have to be on high alert on Saturday at the Dylans gig and see what we think. You know, see if Masimo gives any signals that he likes Lindsay or if Robbie likes you as a girlfriend-type person."

Jas said, "Why would he do that? He's not mad."

I gave her my worst look. But actually the whole thing is giving me the megadroop. I said, "Even I don't know which one I really like. I mean, I did like the Sex God first. He was the one I first snogged."

Jas, or Mental the Memory Man, as she should be known, said, "Well, that is not true, is it? Because you snogged Whelk Boy first, and then you let Mark Big Gob snog you and put his hand on your basoomas, almost on the first date. Perhaps Masimo has heard your reputation. A woman has to be very careful about her honour."

Right, that was it, I was going to turn her big fat knickers inside out and ram her into a sports locker at the very first opportunity I had.

Rosie said, "What has been happening snogwise to everyone? Anything to report? I have. I'll just say this: hello, number eight."

Half an hour later
The result of the snogging survey is that Ro Ro and Sven are in

the lead with an eight – upper-body fondling indoors. Ellen lags behind on four "or something, I mean, is it? Well, I don't know if I..." Most of the others are on five.

Jas, after a lot of red-faced looning about, admitted that she and Nature Boy had also "sort of" got to number seven. I said that officially I was on seven but mentally I thought really it was eight. Jas meanly said, "You mean you are on virtual eight."

I gave her my worst look but she pretended she was sunbathing. After a bit I said to Jools, "So Jools, where are you at with Rollo?"

Jools astonished us all by saying that she had got to number nine.

I went, "What, bwa? Below-waist activity???"

She said, "Well, sort of."

"Sort of???"

We were all looking at her. This was amazing.

It turned out that she had shown Rollo her panties as a dare in the street.

I said, "Is that it?"

And she said, "Well, I shook my hips about a bit. He seemed to like it."

I don't know if I can stand much more of this. I may have to go and be a lesbian beekeeper.

In bed

I have got my hair in rollers for extra bounceability. I bet boys don't go through this. I can't imagine a bloke lying in bed with big prickly things in his head.

Two minutes later

I know boys do stuff that they think will make them more attractive to girlies, like having a long fringe and so on. Walking along with their hips thrust forward and their hands in their pockets. Wearing pongy stuff that some fool in advertising says is irresistible to women, and that as soon as they smell it they want to get to number six with you.

I passed Oscar the trainee tosser this evening and practically passed out. I have *never* smelled stronger Brut or Impulse or whatever it is. I was choking. I tell you what, if he lights up a fag as well, that will be the end of him.

One minute later

I could offer him a fag and retreat to a safe distance.

Friday July 22nd

Got up at the crack of 8:00 a.m. Looked at myself in the mirror. Is that the beginning of a lurker on my chin? Nooooo. I quickly squirted the lurking lurker with my perfume. No boy alive likes a girl with two chins and that is *le* fact. Well, unless Slim has got a boyfriend, in which case there is someone on the planet who likes a woman who has eighteen or nineteen chins. And not all of them on her head. Hahahahahahaha. Oh dear God, I have got pre-boyfriend-choosing hysteria.

8:20 a.m.

My charming but insane sister is on the telephone. The fact that she has the receiver upside down and that there is no one on the other end of it doesn't seem to spoil her little chat. She was saying, "I know, yes, yes, Mr Bum Bum is coming to school today in his poo pants! Hehehehehahahahaha lalalalalala." Then she started snorting and shouted, "Bye-bye arsey!!!" and slammed down the receiver.

When she saw me she came over and wanted to be picked up. She's not small and quite hefty. I had to lean against the door to use it as a support. Once I had managed to pick her up, she started kissing me. "I lobe you, I lobe you my hairy sister, I looooooooobe you."

Hairy sister? Has she seen something I haven't? Has the orang-utan gene leaped out to be friends with the lurker? I put her down and distracted her by saying, "Look, Bibbs, Angus is doing a big poo in Vati's tie drawer." Which actually he was.

I went into the bathroom.

One minute later
No, all seems in order rogue-hairwise. I am quite literally smoothy smooth as a baby's bottom but without the bulging nappy scenario.

My bedroom
6:00 p.m.
For once in my life I have already decided what to wear on Saturday. My new leather skirt, ankle boots and crossover top. That's it. Thank goodness I have decided. I can just concentrate on make-up and hair now.

Five minutes later
Ankle boots or my pink shoes?

425

Two minutes later
I hate my leather skirt, it's really naff.

Three minutes later
Blue dress, then. That's the one.

Five minutes later
Do I really want to look like a chav?

6:30 p.m.
I went downstairs and outside to sit on the wall. It was still really warm. I could see Mr and Mrs Next Door out in their garden having what they fondly imagine is a Mediterranean supper. But I don't know many Italians who have egg on toast for din-dins. With chipolatas.

Also they are glaring at me. Italians don't glare, they sing and caress their guitars.

Still, if Mr and Mrs Next Door want to eat chipolatas and glare, that is their choice. They are having a nice time; that is what counts. My new philosophy is I am going to enjoy my life and just see what happens. As Jas says, when I let her, "*Que sera sera*, whatever will be will be."

Because "I have no time for fussing and fighting, my friends" as some pop legends said once. Because, and I think it was the same pop legends that said, "Love is all you need. Nananananaaaaaaa." Love is what really matters. Not what mad neighbours with massive arses eat for their supps. Or what clothes a girl who may or may not be loved by so many Luuurve Gods wears.

It's not the dress that counts, it's the heart pumping underneath the dress.

Five minutes later
Phoned Jas.

"Jas, what shall I wear tomorrow?"

"What?"

"Tomorrow, for the gig of my life, what shall I wear?"

"I'll tell you what not to wear, don't wear any high heels in case you have to run off and catch a train like last time!" And then she started laughing and honking like an annoying goose. I could hear someone else laughing as well.

I said, "Jas, that is a really crap thing to say for a besty sort of person, and who is that laughing in the background?"

"It's Tom. He's helping me pack for the camping trip."

I so wanted to hit her. But I had to stay calm because of wanting to stay at her place on Saturday night. What is more, I had to listen to her listing the really, really boring things that she is looking forward to doing when we are camping. Who could possibly be interested in building a night-time "hide" that you can crouch in and watch ferrets and badgers and so on do all the indescribably boring stuff that they do at night-time? Digging and pooing mostly.

Well, Jas is riveted by that sort of tosh. She said, "If we are really lucky, Tom says we might see some foxes."

I said, "Yippppeee!" in a sarcastic way, but then I remembered staying over at her house and had to change it to a sort of "Yipppeeee, I do hope we do see some foxes and maybe even some, erm, goats."

Jas said, "Why would we see any goats? They are not wandering about in the woods, are they? They would be on farms."

I said, "Perhaps they are bored with farm life and fancy getting out a bit, making new woodland friends."

"You are being silly now."

"Jas, I am just remarking that it doesn't seem fair that all the foxes and badgers, who do not as far as I know lift a paw to help others, should be allowed to wander willy-nilly in the woods, and the poor old goats, who give milk and so on, should have to stay in. That is all I am saying."

"I am going now."

And she put the phone down.

One minute later

She is soooo annoying, but I must remember that I need to stay at her place after the gig. I phoned her back. "Jas?"

"What?"

"Please don't get upset about the goats."

"You were being silly."

"I know, but it's only because I'm all nervous and excited. Please be my pal. Pleasey please please?"

"Well..."

"I promise to be excited if we see some foxes."

After about ten minutes of nicenosity, Jas forgave me. Phew. Thank goodness. Having a best pally is the most v important thing in the world. Your pals will be with you, even though Luuurve Gods may come and go.

Also, she has said I can stay at her place. Hurray!

In the Kitchen

Mum was making some snacks. She said, "So tell me what is happening tomorrow?"

Oh God. Still, I had better tell her something as it looks like I might have to borrow her Chanel bag again. Even though I am banned for life after spilling hot chocolate in it. I said, "Well, you remember there is a gig on and that I am going to stay over at Jas's because it is nearer."

"It's not nearer if Dad picks you up in the car."

"Yes, but that is not going to happen."

"Why, have you asked him?"

"No, it is not going to happen because it is not going to happen."

"And besides that, I don't remember saying you could stay at Jas's."

"You said I could go to the gig last week."

"I know, but what has that to do with staying at Jas's?"

"I ALWAYS stay at Jas's after gigs."

"No, you don't."

"Well, if I don't it's only because you want to spoil my life."

"What?"

"You know how important tomorrow is. I told you about

Robbie, and then Masimo came round when I was in the bath and so on, and I STILL am not allowed to dye my hair so I look like a boring person, and I have to traipse along to the gig with my ordinary hair while EVERYONE else is allowed to dye their hair. And now you are telling me that even though you said I could stay at Jas's now you don't even know about it. I give up. I tell you what, I will just stay in my room for the rest of my life. Are you HAPPY now?"

Ten minutes later

Mum was so frazzled by me that she has let me stay at Jas's! Yessssss! And borrow her bag!!!

So even though I will be naked tomorrow because I can't decide what to wear, I will at least have a nice bag.

In bed snuggled down

If I go to sleep early then time will pass quickly and it will be tomorrow today, if you see what I mean.

I do.

Night-night.

9:00 p.m.

I am going to make a pro and con list of all the good and bad qualities of the Sex God and the Luuurve God. Now let me see, I'll start with the most important things: looks.

Twenty minutes later
This is it.

Masimo

* Looks: 10 deffo.
* Special attributes: cat's eyes, Pizza-a-gogo charisma.
* Snogging skills: *muchos buenos.*
* Sense of humour: probably. Hard to tell. I haven't heard any Italian-type jokes yet. Or maybe I have but just don't understand them.
* Personality: yes.
* Caring: yes, because when he was finishing with his ex he was quite nice and everything. Also, even though I didn't like it, he was straight with me when he said he would think about going out with me.
* Minus points: hmmmmmm... there might be a touch of the "oooohhh, mind my hair, do you like my handbag?" about him. Although, thinking about it, I don't know that

I have actually noticed the "handbag, mind my hair" business. Dave the Laugh has mentioned it. A LOT. And Junior Blunder Boy did shout out, "Does his boyfriend know you are snogging him?" Does that mean that there is the suggestion of the homosexualist about him?

* **Wet Lindsay Factor**: does not seem to entirely realise what a complete arse above all arses she is. On the plus side, he has not spent more than one or two evenings in her company. As far as I know. Ergo, may not have snogged her. Even though she has implied that he has.

Now then, over to

Robbie

* **Looks**: yummy scrumboes. Maybe, though, just for scrupulous accuracy and fairness I should mark him down half a point because I do prefer yellow eyes to blue ones. So let's say nine and a half.

* **Special attributes**: ability to get on with me even when my brain has slipped off for a little holiday. Is nice about Angus even when Angus once ripped his trouser bottoms to shreds. Also, he laughed rather than rang for the police when I ran my hand through my hair and the bleached bit of it snapped off in my hand.

* **Snogging skills:** you're telling me. Well, you *are* telling me because it is so long since I snogged him that I have almost forgotten. I remember his ear-nibbling technique being surprisingly good. Or was that Dave the Laugh?

Oy get off this list, Dave the Laugh, you are not on it. This is not a "just good mates" list.

* **Sense of humour:** generally good, although I don't think it extends to his songwriting skills. As I have said before, "Oh No, It's Me Again" about Van Gogh cutting his ear off is one of the most depressing songs ever written. And believe me, I know; Dad has played me "Agadoo" too often for me not to know what a depressing song is like.

* **Personality:** yes, I think so. Yes. Again, though, as Dave the Laugh says, you can't entirely trust someone who wears rubber shoes because they don't believe in leather.

* **Caring:** he is nice to Angus and Libby, which are tough darts. So I think he probably scores about an eight.

* **Minus points:** hmmmmm... well, there *is* the aforementioned obsession with the planet, wombats etc.

There is definitely a touch of the Jas about him. And to be frank, he did once choose wombats over me, so once bitten twice whatsit.

* Wet Lindsay factor: it cannot be ignored that his lips have made contact with bits of Old Slimey's anatomy. He did officially go out with her. I really have no excuse for that. And even now he has not given her the severe mental thrashing that she so richly deserves. But the major minus point is that I don't know if he just wants me for a matey-mate or as a prospective girlfriend.

What I really need is someone to discuss this with. If it was all alrighty with Dave the Laugh I would deffo ask for his Hornmeister opinion.

One minute later
Actually, why isn't it alrighty with Dave the Laugh? He didn't seem at all bothered when he saw me with Robbie. He even asked him to go play pool with him. In anybody's language that is a matey-mate type person and not a prospective snoggee, so I could ask him. I think that is what I will do.

one minute later

Although I don't feel I can just call him and ask him ad hoc and willy-nilly because of his girlfriend situation, so maybe I can get him on his own at the gig tomorrow night and ask him then.

Good plan.

Now I have got all excited in my brain box. I will never sleep I...

zzzzzzzzzzzzzzzzzzz.

The piddly-diddly department of life

Saturday July 23rd

9:00 a.m.

Is it too soon to start getting ready yet?

Phoned Jas.

She is not even up yet.

9:30 a.m.

None of the Ace Gang are up. How lazy can you be?

Maybe I will take a quick morning jog over the back fields to get the old corpuscles flinging themselves around in my body.

10:15 a.m.

This is quite pleasant out here in the elements. My little stripy chums the bees are buzzing about in the flowers. Even now at home in the hive the queen bee might be ripping some drone's trouser-snake addendas off. It's a lovely thought. Or two queen bees might be having a bitch fight. Or perhaps all of them are just humming a merry song together, knitting stripy jumpers.

Jog, jog, jog, not too bouncy, keep the nungas flexed so that they don't hit me in the eye and jog, jog, jog.

Oh look, there are Mr Next Door and Mrs Next Door walking the Prat Poodles. They throw them the stick and off they go yapping after it. They are a ludicrous waste of space really... and the poodles are no better! Hahahahaha I have made an inner joke. I'd better get as many inner jokes out of the way as possible before tonight, because if there is one thing I have learned it is not to let my brain run free and wild. All sorts of rubbish will come out of my mouth.

I jogged past the Next Doors and waved cheerily to them. They looked a bit alarmed. What is the matter with them? What possible harm can I do them in my running shorts?

11:00 a.m.

I'm just going to go to the edge of the woods and then back home. It's about 11:00 a.m. now, so I could start my steam and cleanse routine. Deep-condition hair at the same time. Then a spot of lunch lovingly prepared by my mother (oh, I've just accidentally made another inner joke). After lunch, a lie-down with cucumber slices and face mask till my lunch has been munched up by the billions of germs and enzymes lurking around my body. They'd better do something to repay me for lugging them about all the time.

That would bring the time to about two thirty, long luxurious bath with Mum's special unguents and a very thorough going-over in the mirror for any orang-utan genes. I plucked my eyebrows the day before yesterday so I should just about be all right, although those dangly squiggly ones seem to sprout in minutes.

Spring out of the bath about five and then have a bit of a dash to get make-up done by six thirty.

One minute later

Jog, jog. I might have to cut short my bath just to be on the safe side, because if something goes wrong make-upwise –

you know, dodgy eyeliner or stab in the eye with the mascara brush – I need extra time to cope.

In the bath
4:00 p.m.
Oh, how relaxing is this? Not, is the answer. Dad is driving me insane with his, "Can I possibly get into the bathroom this side of the grave!!" shouting through the keyhole type stuff.

I am sure he just lounges around waiting for me to have a bath so that he can come and annoy me. He's been doing DIY this arvie so he's bound to be off to casualty in a minute, and then at least I will get some peace.

Why is he so daddish about doing stuff that he is hopeless at? Mum wanted the kitchen painted and he has insisted that he and Uncle Eddie can do it. It was only a minute and a half before he accidentally painted over the chopping board.

In the Kitchen
4:15 p.m.
Dad and Uncle Eddie are almost entirely buttercup yellow. They look like they have had a paint fight.

Two minutes later

The kitchen looks like it has had a paint fight.

Mum just looked at me.

I looked at her.

I said, "You chose him." And I went off to my boudoir.

It just shows you how vair vair careful you must be when you are choosing your partner. She should have made Dad fill out a questionnaire with questions like: Are you sane? How are your DIY skills? For instance, can you mend a bike wheel without getting your hand stuck and having to go to casualty? And if the person (Dad) said no to both questions then you run like the wind.

Mind you, as I said to Mum, I wouldn't even have had to bother with the questionnaire as a quick glance at his enormous conk would have been a deciding factor for me.

In my bedroom

I had almost forgotten about my nose until Ms Octopus Head mentioned it again. Let me see.

Looking in the mirror

Well, it's not small, that is a fact. But providing I don't do any ad-hoc smiley smiley without reining my nostrils in, I think it could pass for almost normal. I don't know why, perhaps my face has grown around it a bit.

7:10 p.m.
I am ready. Well, as ready as I will ever be.

My make-up went well and I have applied anti-snogging sealant to my lips, although not to my eyes this time. I decided on my short blue dress in the end, with ankle boots. My hair is not bad for once, it has bounceability and umph.

7:15 p.m.
Phoned Jas.

"Jas, are you ready?"

"Yeah, are you? Tom is walking there with Robbie so I'll meet you and the gang at the clock tower if you like."

"Okey diddly dokey. I'm a bit nervy. I hope I don't have a spaz attack on the way there."

"Please don't. The last time you did my tights got laddered when we crashed into the postbox."

Clock tower

7:40 p.m.

The Ace Gang rides again!!!

Rosie was all in black, as was Sven. Also Sven was wearing a cowboy hat. He said, "*Ciao* baby, *hasta la vista*."

What fresh hell?

Rosie said, "He's gorgeous, isn't he, my fiancé?"

I said, "Er... yeah."

Ellen, Jools, Mabs, Honor and Soph (trainee Ace Gang members), Jas and me walked along chatting together while Sven and Rosie brought up the rear (oo-er). There was a big queue outside the Old Market but Sven swanned up to the front and chatted to the bloke on the door. Oh brilliant, we would probably be banned before we even got in.

But to my amazement the bloke said, "Come straight through, girls," and ushered us in. Right past Wet Lindsay and her pals. Yessssssss!!! She was as livid as a livid thing.

Stiff Dylans gig

Inside it was already rammed. The Dylans have built up a massive following. It is going to be vair tiring constantly going out as I will have to when I am Masimo's girlfriend. I

♡ 443

still can't believe it, actually. You know when you dream about something for so long and then it happens.

one minute later

Well, maybe going to happen if I choose him over Robbie. Unless Masimo really is two-timing me with Lindsay and Robbie is only my mate. In which case I am a fool and a loser.

9:30 p.m.

I am sooooo hot and full of tensionosity. Masimo has smiled at me from the stage but I haven't actually spoken to him. And also, he has smiled at quite a few girls. I have been having a laugh but also don't quite know what is going on.

Ro Ro came up. "OK gang, this is a fast one. We could practise the Viking bison dance. Have you all got your horns?"

I said, "Oh drat, I forgot mine, never mind, you lot carry on."

Ro Ro looked at me. "Don't you luuurve the Viking bison dance? Don't you want me to have a happy wedding?"

I said, "Yes, I do, but as I have another eighteen years to practise the dance before you get married I am not too bothered."

444

Rosie said, "Have it your own way. I can't stand chatting to you all night, I have my fiancé to snog." And she went and hurled herself on Sven and snogged him right in front of everyone. And he was eating a packet of peanuts at the time.

Forty-fifth visit to the tarts' emporium

Lippy still nice and pink and glossy. Which isn't surprising as I haven't exactly been living in Snog City.

I was just doing a bit of nunga-nunga adjusting and pouting practice when I noticed a little head bobbling about behind me. Then it was joined by another little redhead. Two little heads bobbling about behind me. The little titches from school. What were they doing here? Also they were covered in make-up. They looked like Martha and Minnie the daft vampire twits (whoever they are).

I turned round and said, "What are you two doing here?"

Titch Number One said, "We like a bop on a Saturday night."

Are they insane? They are only about twelve.

Then I noticed their skirts. Or not, as it happens. They were wearing what looked like belts. I said that to them, I said, "You seem to have come out without your skirts on. It's not PE, you know."

They both started shuffling their legs. "It's fashion, Miss."
Fashion? Miss? Hang on a minute, I have become my vati!!!

Ten minutes later

I gave them a stiff talking-to about the birds and the bees. Well, the bees anyway. I told them about the bee-arse thing etc. But I also said that Wet Lindsay was here and that if she saw them they were definitely for an ear-bashing and possibly another visit to the elephant house, or Slim's study, as some fools call it.

They looked a bit frightened, and one said, "We just wanted some fun. We are never allowed to do anything; it's like being in prison. My dad shouts at me when I am on the phone, or in the bathroom, or using his razor and everything."

I was nodding along. "I know, I know, I know. Yep I know."

They are very young to know the tragicosity of life, but there you are. Anyway, I told them that if they stood in the dark near the bar they could watch the band for another half an hour but then they must go home.

Strangely they seem to think I know what I am talking about and do what I say. It's a bit like having a couple of ginger retrievers in make-up.

Back in the gig

I took the titches to a space behind the bar where it was really dark, and left them there all giggly. Wet Lindsay and her tragic mates were "grooving about" (or pratting about, as some might call it) at the far end of the club by the stage. Masimo didn't seem to be paying any attention to her. But then he hadn't paid any attention to me either, other than smiling at me.

Fifteen minutes later

The band had done one cracking set. No sign of Robbie yet. Masimo is a fabby singer and his dancing is grooviness personified. All the twittish girls at the front were going mental. I wouldn't be surprised if they started throwing their knickers at him. Very very shaming; they have no pridenosity.

I turned to Jas and said, "You wouldn't fling your knickers on stage, would you, Jazzy?"

She said, "Well, not the inner ones."

Is she completely insane? Does she actually wear two pairs of knickers? Outer ones and inner ones? I was just about to make her let me have a look when a sort of scuffle type thing took place by the bar. Oh great, I might have

known, the Blunder Boys had turned up and Mark Big Gob
was having a go at someone.

Ellen and the rest of the gang wanted to go and see what
was happening so we went over.

One minute later

Wow and wow and wowzee wow! It was like the shoot out at
the OK Corral. Dave the Laugh and his mates were sizing up
to the Blunder Boys. Apparently one of the Blunderers had
been hitting on the titches, twanging their bra straps and
trying to snog them, and Dave had noticed and stepped up.

Mark Big Gob said, "Pick a window, you're leaving." And
the next thing I knew, Dave the Laugh was sitting on Mark
Big Gob's head.

Two minutes later

The bouncers chucked the Blunders out. They are so
pathetico, they were yelling, "Watch your back, mate, we
know where you live."

Dave said, "Yeah, but do you know where *you* live, that is
the point, you twit."

As they left Mark did that putting two fingers to his eyes

and then pointing them at Dave and then doing a pretend cutting-his-throat thing. Amazingly naff.

The titches went up to Dave all mooney, and he said, "Home, girls, now, quick as you like."

And they said, "OK, Dave," and left all girly.

Blimey.

I said to Dave, "They luuurve you."

Dave looked at me. "I am, it has to be said, Jack the Biscuit." Then he puckered up and did a really mad fast twisting dance. He was shouting, "Just call me Big Dave!!!"

I was laughing when Emma came over with a drink for him. She said "hi" to me and then gave him a kiss and a hug. Weird. Well, the kiss and the hug weren't weird, but it made me feel sort of weird.

I sloped off to the Ace Gang.

Break

Robbie arrived. Wet Lindsay must have been on high alert because he had only just got through the door before she flung herself on him and took him to the bar. God, I hate her. I must say he didn't look too thrilled to see her and he was looking around. Maybe he was looking for me. I had a sudden spaz attack and said to Jas, "Jas, I am going to hide behind you, don't move, I want to see what is going on."

Jas was useless as camouflage. She kept forgetting her role and every time she said anything to me she turned round to talk to me and revealed me crouching down behind her. What is the point in that?

Lindsay was being all animated, if an octopus can be animated. Robbie was being polite but he looked a bit distracted. Then he saw the Dylans coming from backstage to the bar and said something to Lindsay and went over to speak to them. As he turned his back on her Lindsay reached down the front of her top and did a bit of adjusting. Ah-hah, her false basoomas must have come free from their lashings. Good.

The Dylans sat down at a table and were immediately surrounded by girls all fluffing and farting about. Jas said, "I'm going to the bar with Tom. You'll have to fend for yourself."

I said, "Jas, Jazzy, don't leave me, just walk slowly across to the bar and I will lurk behind you." So I shuffled over to the bar behind her.

But just as we got almost opposite the Dylans table she bumped into Sven. Oh no. Sven could see me sort of lurking behind Jas and he said, "Aha!!! Let us groove, baby, Sven likes to groove." And he picked me up and started doing this sort of jive-type dance, only my feet were not touching the ground. It was horrific, and I am pretty sure you could see my knickers and therefore my tights. Which must have looked really erm... crap.

I said, "Put me down, Sven, please."

Eventually he lost interest in me because Rosie came up in her bison horns and said, "I feel the Horn coming on." And Sven put me down on a table.

The Dylans table.

The table that both Masimo and Robbie were sitting at.

Oh marvellous.

My bottom was inches away from a Sex God and a Luuurve God.

What would a person full of sophisticosity and maturiosity say?

I said, "Anyone know the footie results?"

Oh no, I had déjà whatsit. I slipped off the table and everyone looked at me.

Masimo half-smiled and said, "Miss Georgia, I hope you have not a train to catch tonight." And he and all the lads laughed. I, of course, went beetroot. Thank God it was so dark. I shambled off to the tarts' wardrobe.

As I went past her Wet Lindsay put her face really near mine and said quietly, "Did the little girl make a fool of herself in front of the big boys? Diddums."

Tarts' wardrobe

All the Ace Gang assembled.

Mabs said, "You sat on their table?"

Jools said, "You asked about the footie? Again?"

Rosie said, "Did you say you had to catch a train?"

Ellen said, "I mean, you could see, erm, your... knickers."

Jas said, "I bet you wish you had my big knickers on now."

Back in the club of life

On the way back from the loo I bumped into Dave. He smiled at me in his groovy way and said, "Ah, Sex Kitty, have you just been to the piddly-diddly department?"

I said in a dignitosity-at-all-times way, "Er, no, I certainly haven't."

He said, "Ah... so it was the poo-parlour division, then?"

Oh, it was sooo nice to see him. We both laughed. He

looked at me from underneath his eyelashes for a bit. He has got really nice eyes, smiley and sexy at the same time. I wondered if I should...

And then he said, "I'm just off for a wazz."

I said really quickly, "Dave, can I ask you a question in your capacity as official Hornmeister? What do you think Robbie thinks about me? I mean, do you know anything? You know, any boy-type signs that I might not know about?"

He looked at me again, and then he looked over to where his girlfriend was talking to her mates. She waved at him and he waved back. He said, "Well, I think that Robbie does like you, but he is not sure where he stands and he doesn't know what is going on with Masimo so he is playing it near to his chest and cool bananas."

I love Dave the Laugh.

But only in a, you know, matey way.

Then we saw Masimo coming our way. He was being stopped by girls as he pushed his way through the crowds. Dave said, "Oy, hold up, here comes the Italian Stallion. I hope he is not going to hit me with his handbag because I am talking to you."

I said, "Dave, he hasn't got a handbag."

But Dave still wouldn't leave it alone. He said, "Well, I hope he doesn't hit me with his sports bra then."

He really is vair vair annoying.

Masimo came up to us then, and Dave said, "Cracking set. I'm just off to the wazzarium." And he went off.

Masimo said, "He is going to the wazzarium? What is this?"

Oh dear God. I said, "Well, it's, you know, like the boys... erm... piddly-diddly... no, no, forget that. Er, he's gone to the loo."

Masimo smiled. "My English is still, how you say...?"

And I said, "Crapio?"

Fifteen minutes later

I am on cloud ninety-five, I think. Masimo is catching his plane to Italy early in the morning and he said he has to pack up after the gig, but can he meet me and I can go round to his place and see him off. I said yes, but this is going to take some planning. Jas will have a spaz attack if I don't report back to Jas Headquarters like I am supposed to do. So my cunning plan is this: I go home with Jazzy, do pretendy going to bed, slip out of her house when everyone has gone to bed (using Jas's key, which she will lend me) and meet Masimo for a few hours. Then he drops me back at Jas's in time for me to do pretendy getting up after a good night's sleep.

All I have to do now is explain to Jas what an excellent plan it is.

Perhaps I could just hit her over the head with a particularly heavy owl and sneak out.

11:45 p.m.

How cool!! Robbie joined in with the last two songs of the gig. We were all dancing like loons. But loons that have sophisticosity and whatsit. It was fabby having two singers. They sounded really groovy together. I don't know why we can't have a *ménage à trois* actually... Everyone does in *la belle* France.

Midnight

Getting our coats. Robbie strolled over and said, "All right, girls?" Then he smiled at me. "I haven't had much chance to talk to you, Georgia, do you need a lift home?"

Oh Blimey O'Reillys trousers, he really did have dreamy blue eyes, really dark blue like a dark blue sea or like a... hang on a minute, my lips were puckering up without my permission!! Stop it, stop it!!!

I said, "Well, I'm staying at Jas's, but..."

At which point, in unusually crap timing even for her, the creature from the lagoon, Wet Lindsay, came sliming up. She totally *ignorez-vous*ed me and linked up with Robbie and said to him, "How about that drink you promised me?"

Robbie looked at me and I looked at him. Now was the time for me to say, "I need to talk to you." Yeah, that was the thing to do now. But if anyone knows what to do it won't be me.

Lindsay said to me, "Bye-bye, don't be late home," and started leading Robbie off. And I just stood there not saying anything.

He turned back and said, "Maybe another time, Georgia?"

Wet Lindsay turned back as well and gave me the evils. What a prizewinning cow she is.

Five minutes later

I was still spluttering about her. "What a slimy octopussy cow she is! She made Robbie have a drink with her. He said, 'Do you want a lift home, Georgia?' and there she was like the bride of a jellyfish, lurking and sliming about."

Rosie said, "We must eat her; it's the only solution."

As we left the club Masimo was packing up on the stage and

he shouted to me, "*Ciao*, Georgia, see you soon." And all the girls who had been hovering around looked over at me and *they* gave me the evils. If I was a voodoo doll I'd be covered in pins from head to foot.

I waved back in a casualosity-at-all-times way. Ooooh, I didn't know what to think.

Ellen started dithering for England, "Er, what, why did he... I mean, what does he mean 'see you soon'?"

I said, "Well, I am going round to his house later."

Rosie said, "I thought you were staying at Jas's?"

I said, "Well, I am in principle, but then I am going to sneak out and he will pick me up at the end of Jas's road."

Jools said, "Blimey."

I said, "I know. Pizza-a-gogo-type snogging for me. I'll let you know if he does any unexpected tongue work."

Mabs said, "How has Jas explained it to her mum and dad? There's no way I could get out of my house without the flying squad being called."

I said, "Oh, well, they are cool with it."

They all looked at me.

Rosie said, "You haven't told Jas, have you?"

"Well, not as such."

Rosie said, "She will have a nervy b. and probably pop off to Strop Central."

God, life is complicated. As I said to Rosie, "This is what comes of being too likeable."

She said, "Who?"

I said, "Me."

She did that slapping me on both cheeks thing she does and said, "Don't be mad."

Walking home with the gang

I made them shut up about my night visit to Luuurve land when Jas and Tom came and joined us to walk home.

Four minutes later

I think I might be in a good mood. Because a Luuurve God in the hand is worth two on the bus, and I am meeting up with a Luuurve God later, even if a Sex God has gone off on the bus... anyway, you get my drift.

I am even in the mood to join in with the mad ramblings of Radio Jas. She was all snuggled up with Tom as we ambled along, and every now and again they would stop and have a little kiss. Not full-on snogging but just a pecky affair. Sweet, really. If you like that sort of thing.

Just then there was a mad ringing-of-a-bell fiasco and Sven came riding up on a child's bike. "Hi, girls, rock and roll!!!" And he did a wheelie before crashing into a tree. Then he just left the bike on the ground and got hold of Rosie and put her over his shoulder. You could see her knickers. Sven said, "I am a wild and crazy guy!!!"

He's not wrong there. Rosie said from upside down, "Tatty bye! Sven and I are going to snog for a bit."

Then Sven peeled off into the park, with his hump/girlfriend.

Ellen and Jools and Mabs and Honor were all being taken home by Mab's dad. She had made him park two streets away from the market in case anyone saw him. And also, as a double precaution, he had to pretend to be reading a newspaper so that none of her friends could see his head. You see, they say that teenagers show no initiative and so on but we are constantly having to think about this sort of thing. It is vair vair tiring.

After we'd said s'laters to everybody, Jas and Tom and I continued on to her place. Tom said, "Good gig, wasn't it? He's a cool guy, Masimo. Don't you think so, Gee?"

It is a bit awkward for me being completely honest

around Tom, him being Robbie's brother and so on. I sort of mumbled something.

Jas said, "Yeah, do you think he is cool, Georgia?" and looked at me in a meaningful way. I didn't say anything, so she opened her eyes really wide and raised her eyebrows. I raised my eyebrows back at her.

We could have gone on doing that all night but then Tom said, "So have you had 'the talk' with my bro?"

I said, "Well, erm, not really. He went off with Lindsay."

Tom said, "Yeah, well, I wouldn't exactly call it that. She sort of made him take her for a drink – that isn't the same as him asking her for a drink."

I decided to take the bull by the legs and hurl it about a bit and strap a little hat on its head and... shut up, brain. I decided to ask Tom what he thought was going on. I said, "Has Robbie said anything about what he thinks about me?"

Tom shuffled about a bit and said, "Well, he's always said how much he liked you, and that he was really sorry that it didn't work out between you... and that it was, like, more or less just to do with the fact that he thought you were a bit... well, young for him."

Jas said, "She is too young for him. She's too young for anyone, actually."

I looked at her and said, "Oh thanks, besty pal."

She was in Wise Mavis of the Woods mood though; she should get a stick and grow a beard. Ramble ramble. "I am just being realistic, Gee. You are not a serious sort of person. You are giddy, you like snot dancing and so on, you are not ready for a proper relationship, you just want to blow your Horn. That is just *le* fact."

I didn't know what to say to that. Perhaps she is right. Perhaps I am a hollow sham of a person who will end up on my own in a cellar. Or as the co-owner of a corduroy shop with Miss Wilson.

It made me feel a bit miz.

Not as miz as I felt ten minutes later when I had to hang around the garage like a goosegog while Jas and Tom kissed good night. I wasn't allowed to go into the house because Jas said we had to go in together. I would have ignored her but I still hadn't broken the news about my early-morning Snog Fest. I tried not to notice them but I could sort of hear them snogging. Squelchy noises and breathing and rustling. It was like being a pervy. In fact I had become the female equivalent of Elvis Attwood. Bloody hell.

Four years later

Eventually Jas dragged herself away from Tom and after about ninety-five years of her saying, "Bye, then," and then rushing after him for one last kiss, I managed to get her through the door.

Jas's house

Jas's mum came into the kitchen in her (sensible) nightie. No suggestion of nungas akimbo like there would have been round at my house. She said, "Did you have a good time, girls? I have left some snacks out for you, you must be ravenous. I'm off to bed. I made the bed all snuggly for you. Night, God bless." And she went off. Amazing.

No third degree. No "And who did you dance with, was there any snogging?" from Mum, or "What bloody time do you call this? You treat this house like a bloody hotel!" from Dad. Just some snacks and good night. Quite, quite amazing.

Upstairs

Jas has been ages in the bathroom. What is she doing in there? I said through the door, "Jas, what are you doing in there?"

She said, "I am applying night-time moisturiser."

Good Lord. She must have used a bucket of it by now.

In bed

I am fully dressed.

Jas said, "Georgia, you are fully dressed."

"I know, I am going out in a minute."

She said, "What???"

I said, "Yes I told you, I am being picked up by Masimo at one a.m. He is setting off to the airport at three a.m. so I should be back about then."

She said, "You did not tell me you were meeting Masimo, but it doesn't matter because you are not meeting him. That is a fact."

"Jazzy."

"And anyway, what about Robbie? What have you told him? What will he think about it? Anyway, he won't think anything about it because you're not meeting Masimo."

"Jazzy."

"No, if you get caught I will be grounded for years."

"Yes, but Jazzy I will not be caught. I will just do creepy creep out of the back door using your key, creepy creep down to the bottom of the street, be picked up by my gorgey fabby Luuurve God, snog, chat, snog, chat, maybe do a bit of quiet crying as he says *arrivederci*. But not enough crying to spoil my eye make-up – and also I will be seeing him quite soon when I go on my holiday to Rome..."

Jas was having a massive tizz and hump, even for her. "This is so typical of you. If anyone gets into trouble it will be me, and you probably won't do creepy creep, you'll probably fall over something and wake everyone up, and even if you do get back into the house you will go into the wrong bedroom or something."

I gave her a big hug. "Don't you want me to be happy, Jazzy?"

"No."

That's nice, isn't it?

I said, "Look, I'll do a practice creep now. I'll creep into the kitchen and see if you can hear me."

12:40 a.m.

I can't believe this. Jas made such a fuss about me making a noise but by the time I got back from creeping around she had fallen asleep!!!

There is a similarity between Jas's house and mine – her vati and mutti both snore. Which is good because it means they are asleep.

12:50 a.m.

I wonder what it will be like being with Masimo? For two hours? All aloney with the Luuurve God. Or maybe Dom, his flatmate, will be there and we won't get time to snog. *Sacré bleu!*

In the bathroom

I look OK. I don't know whether to do just lip gloss because of the maybe snognosity of the situation, or to rely on the lip-sealant stuff and do full lippy.

Ohhhh, I don't know.

12:55 a.m.

Time to girdey the loins and pucker up.

Crept downstairs and into the kitchen. I had already opened the back door so that I wouldn't make any noise at all. Stepped out into the back garden. Stars all twinkling about in the sky, looking down on me like twinkly, erm... twinkly things.

I know that I had said they were useless, like sort of dim blinky torches, but now I could see that they were jolly. Like tiny jolly lights, lighting my way to a snogathon. That's how good a mood I was in. Vair vair good.

1:05 a.m.

Sitting on a garden wall at the end of Jas's street. Brr, it's a bit nippy noodles even though it is the middle of summer. And a bit quiet and creepy.

Maybe he won't come? Maybe he was talking to the rest of the Stiff Dylans about me and they said, "Are you mad, mate?" Or maybe his ex-girlfriend phoned up and they have decided to get back together, or...

And that's when I heard his scooter approaching.

I stood up. Then I sat down again. What would a cool person do? Would they stand up or sit down in a casualosity-at-all-times sort of way? I wish I smoked – at least I would have something in my hand. Although with my luck I would probably set fire to my head. I know what, I could be looking through my bag and just look up when he got to me.

I started rustling about in my bag as the scooter got nearer.

Then he was there. I looked up and he was sitting on his scooter. He took his helmet off and shook his hair loose. Good grief and jelloid leggies akimbo. He was quite literally gorgeous. And he had actually come to see me. For once I just felt sooooo happy to be me. And lucky. I was in love with the world. Yes, even Jazzy. The whole wide world. Apart from Wet Lindsay.

Masimo smiled and said, "*Ciao, caro*," and blew me a kiss. Then he got the spare helmet and patted the seat behind him. "Come, let us ride."

It was like being in a film. He even put the helmet on for me, and as he fastened the chin strap he kissed me on the lips. I really did nearly fall over. Then he said to me, "Are you OK, safe? Hold on to me."

I put my hands on his waist. Blimey, touching him was like getting an electric shock. Beam me up, Scotty, as they say in one of those TV things that boys like so much, full of people from other planets with weird heads like cauliflowers. Why do boys like things that look so weird – hobbits and elves and mekons and so on?

I don't know and I don't care because I had a Luuurve God in my hands who didn't have a cauliflower for a head. And who LIKED me!!! Yessssssss!!! I had a song in my heart, and it was not "Funky Moped" by Jasper Carrott.

We drove through the dark streets, it was absolutely fabby. There were still a few people around coming home from clubs, singing and dancing about. We pulled up at the traffic lights and Masimo said, "I thought we would go to my place and I can give you Italian coffee... and other Italian things."

Blimey O'Reilly's trousers! At this rate I wouldn't be able to get off the bike for jelloidness.

1:30 a.m.

Masimo's flat is cool. He shares it with Dom and a mate of Dom's. It's quite tidy and there is no undercrackers pile like in Mum and Dad's room. I wonder what sort of undercrackers Masimo wears? Italian-type ones. Maybe musical ones that play "Arrivederci Roma" or "Nessun Dorma". No, no Masimo would never wear novelty undercrackers... Why have I wandered into the underwear department?

Masimo has made me proper coffee in a machine-type thing, with some little biscuits that taste of almond. I feel *très* European.

As I sipped my coffee he finished his packing. He has some cool shirts. When he finished he shut his case and looked at me. "So, Miss Georgia, does Robbie know about us?"

I looked at him. "Well, he... I..."

Masimo put his arms around me. "Perhaps I can help you, *caro*..."

2:30 a.m.

Crikey, I feel like a dozy bumble bee. Masimo has to be the best snogger ever. He kissed me really slowly for ages without a break. It wasn't even number four (kiss lasting three minutes without a break), it was more like number four times three (a kiss lasting at least a quarter of an hour).

And he talks and stuff. Not while we are snogging because clearly you wouldn't be able to know what he was saying, other than "nnuummppphhhmmmernuummmpphh". But what I mean is the in-betweeny bits, when he'd stop kissing me and then look in my eyes and stroke my hair, saying stuff like "*bellissima*" and so on.

And for a bit he was running his hands up from the bottom of my throat to my lips and then putting his fingers just slightly in my mouth. Gadzooks! It was fabby. Apparently girls are supposed to have about two hundred thousand million more sensory nerves than boys. We are pleasure machines!!! Masimo seemed to like it just as much as me.

2:50 a.m.

Masimo looked up at the clock. "Oh my God, my plane. I so do not want to leave you, Georgia, I wish I could stay here

469

all night with you. I really like you. Please will you come and visit with me? I don't want to wait for a month to see you. Will you try?"

I tried to get my lips under control. They felt like they had swollen to about fourteen times their normal size. Masimo was speaking in Pizza-a-gogo land talk as he made sure he had his passport and tickets. Ummmm, how groovy did *that* sound? The fact that he was probably saying, "Buggeration, where's my sodding pants?" didn't matter because he was speaking the language of luuurve.

Not just some crap foreign language, like German. It wouldn't have sounded at all the same in Lederhosen talk. "I zink *du bist ein gutten* looken *fraulein. Du bist wunderbar* like ze big *spangleferkel. Ich* vant to frontal *knutschen* you!!! Oh *ja*, oh *jah*!!!"

While my brain had been off to Loonland Masimo had got his stuff together. He grabbed his coat, and then as he was putting it on got hold of me and pulled me towards him. He smelled sooooo nice, sort of him and a perfume thing all mixed up. He kissed me very hard on the lips for a long time and then put both of his hands round my head and looked me in the eyes. "We like each other, it will be good, Miss Georgia."

The doorbell rang and it was the cab. We bundled in the cab and carried on snogging and within seconds it seemed like we were at Jas's corner and I had to get out and leave him. Noooooooooooooo. I think I am in luuuuurve.

Masimo kissed me again and looked really sad. "I will miss you."

I got out in a sort of daze and waved to him as the cab pulled away.

And then I realised that I actually *was* crying. Real tears. Not pretend tears. My heart felt really soft and full and sad. It all seemed like a dream. I could still feel his kisses on my mouth.

I will never ever be able to sleep tonight. I don't want to; I want to remember this for ever.

I walked around the back of the house. It was a beautiful night, with a deep black sky, and I could hear the soft hooting of an owl in the distance. Normally I would have been annoyed but tonight I thought, *Good night, Mr Owl, I hope you have a Mrs Owl at home to keep you company... unless you are in fact a Mrs Owl, and then I hope you have a Mr Owl at home, and if you don't you could always join Jas in her bed. If you like stuffed owls, that would be a HOOT!*

Yes, it is official, I am actually telling jokes to owls. I must be in love.

I let myself in the back door and crept up the stairs of the silent house and into Jas's room. There she was all curled up with her arm around Snowy Owl. Hmmmm. Well, live and let live, I say.

I got undressed and settled down among my friends the owls.

Blah, blah, rubbish, rubbish, dribble, dribble, arse!

Sunday July 24th

Woke up at the crack of 9:30 a.m. Jas was still snoozing on her side of the bed. I forgot where I was for a minute, but then I remembered everything that had happened.

Oooohhhhhh Masimo. I'm missing him already. He will be in Rome by now. I wonder if he is thinking about me.

Because I love the world so much I may go down and ask Jas's mum if I can have a cup of tea for me and my little fringey matey.

 473

Went downstairs. There was no one around. On the kitchen unit was a note that said:

Dear Jas,

    We are out on a bit of a ramble. We have our flasks so may be gone for the day. There are eggs and stuff for brekky, and I thought you and Georgia might like a pizza later so I have left you some money. Have a lovely day.

    Lots of love

    Mum

Wow. Now that is PROPER hands-off parenting. Just leaving food and buggering off. Top.

I made some tea and even boiled a little eggy for Jas because I know how much she loves eggs. I put it on a tray and went into her bedroom. I put the tray on the bedside table and leaned over Jas. I got one of the smaller owls and made it kiss her with its little beak. She shot up in bed and was all surly and her fringe was standing on end like an electrocuted hedgehog.

"What have you done? Did you get caught coming in?"

I told Jas that her M and D had gone out rambling and

then I said, "Do you want to know all that happened with me and my new boyfriend the Luuurve God?"

She said, "No."

But I knew she wanted to know, really.

In my bedroom
4:00 p.m.
So that is it. It is official news because I've told Radio Jas that Masimo is my new boyfriend. I've been into the the cake shop, I've dithered about for a bit, but I've finally chosen the Italian cakey.

How many hours is it since I last snogged him? I have already got snogging withdrawal and that is *le* fact.

Phoned Rosie.

"Ro Ro have you ever had your neck stroked by Sven?"

"Only when he is wearing his gardening gloves. Why?"

"Well, it's just that Masimo did it last night. It was fab. Also we did number four but it was times four."

At that point my vati came looming unexpectedly out of the front room and said, "What is number four?"

My dad had accidentally entered my snogging space. Erlack. I just looked at him and said, "This is a private conversation, actually, Dad."

5:30 p.m.

Uncle Eddie arrived. I scampered upstairs before he could tell me any "jokes".

I must try and distract myself from thinking about Masimo. I will do something that I can really get involved in.

6:30 p.m.

I must get some eyelash curlers. Everyone in *CosmoGirl* uses them.

7:00 p.m.

Doorbell rang.

Now it's some of Mum's aerobics mates coming round. I wonder why? They normally only come round if there are firemen here.

7:30 p.m.

Oh please let that not be Abba playing.

8:00 p.m.

Libby is singing along to "Dancing Bean".

8:30 p.m.

What are they doing down there? All I can hear is helpless laughing from Mum and Libby. And really crap loud music. With the occasional bang like someone has fallen over.

9:30 p.m.

Things are not getting any better, in fact they are getting worserer. I have never heard so much laughing and squealing. What are they doing down there?

9:40 p.m.

OK, I have had it. They are playing that song from *The Full Monty* – what is it called? When the blokes at the end take off their uniforms and dance about in their nuddy-pants. "You Can Leave Your Hat On", it's called. And all Mum's mates are cat-calling and yelling, "Get them off!" I am going to have to tell them to be quiet.

9:45 p.m.

When I opened the living room door, Uncle Eddie was waggling his bottom around to the music. In his undercrackers.

Midnight

I will definitely have to go into The Priory for counselling. Uncle Eddie is going to be a stripper. Honestly. You know when you can order a policeman or a fireman or a James Bond-o-gram for a hen night or a birthday? Well apparently, and I cannot imagine the kind of people this involves, there is a demand for a baldy-o-gram. And Uncle Eddie is going to be it.

Grown-ups are absolutely obsessed with sex. It's horrific.

12:35 a.m.

Libby has seen a baldy bloke in his undercrackers. She will certainly be scarred for life and end up with a phobia about boiled eggs.

It all adds up. Dad dying his hair, the leather trousers, the prancing around like a loon. He is having a midlife crisis, even though in my opinion his life is two-thirds over.

12:40 a.m.

If Vati cannot be relied upon to be a proper dad, I must take responsibility myself.

12:45 a.m.
This does not mean I will be growing a little beard.

Monday July 25th
Morning
I have written a "Dad's Book of Rules" and posted it under Mum and Dad's bedroom door. This is what it says:

DAD RULES
* DO NOT ASK ME WHO I AM MEETING.
* IF I ALLOW YOU TO DROP ME OFF SOMEWHERE
IN YOUR "CAR" DO NOT EVER ROLL DOWN THE
WINDOW AND SHOUT SOMETHING AFTER ME. EVEN
THOUGH I WILL PRETEND I CAN'T HEAR YOU,
SOME OF MY FRIENDS MIGHT HEAR YOU.
* DON'T GIVE ME MONEY IN FRONT OF EVERYONE.
* NEVER ENTER MY ROOM UNASKED (YOU WILL
NEVER BE ASKED).
* DO NOT SNOG IN FRONT OF ME AND LIBBY
OR MY FRIENDS OR ANYONE. OR BETTER STILL
DO NOT SNOG. THERE IS NO NEED FOR IT AT
YOUR AGE.

* WEAR PROPER DAD TROUSERS.

* BAN UNCLE EDDIE, OR THE BALDY-O-GRAM MAN FROM OUR HOUSE. THE VISION OF HIM IN HIS COMEDY UNDERCRACKERS WILL BE WITH ME TO THE GRAVE.

THANK YOU
GEORGIA

8:10 a.m.

I scampered out of the house before anyone was moving around. I heard a lot of moaning from the bedroom, which serves everyone right. As Romulus or Remus or Ethelred the Unready (anyway, one of the clever-dick philosopher types) said, "Ye cannot have your fun and eat it." Elderly men should learn to leave off the *vino tinto* and keep their pants on.

Careers talk

10:30 a.m.

Miss Wilson is in charge because Hawkeye is off girl-baiting (she says on a course but we know what she does really). So the career talk, usually a very dull time, offers many,

many comedy opportunities.

Rosie started by saying, "Miss Wilson, what openings might there be in casual work for Viking brides? I am particularly interested in reindeers and vats."

Miss Wilson said, "Rosie, please try and be serious."

Rosie looked puzzled. "I am."

And the sadnosity is that she is telling the truth.

Ellen says she is interested in nursing, which is the first I have heard about it. I tell you one thing: I will not be going into any emergency department that has Ellen in it. The last thing you need when your arm is hanging off is to have Ellen saying, "Erm, well, is it your left arm or, erm, do you or something, or is it the other one?"

Ten minutes later

To think she showed us the bee film, Miss Wilson is very ill informed on courses for beekeeping and backing singing.

4:20 p.m.

As I was ambling home with Jools and Rosie the two little titches came pelting up to me, all keen and red-faced.

"Er, Miss, wasn't it brillopads at the gig? Is it the singer one that you like? He's like..."

I said, "Brillopads?"

And they both went, "Yeah!!!" like twin mini loons.

Then Titch Number One said, "But, you know what, I think Dave is the grooviest of them all. I know he's not a pop star or anything, but I think he's lovely."

She went absolutely beetroot.

The second little titch said, "We love him." And then they ran off.

Blimey. Dave the Laugh has a growing fan club.

Teatime at Bonkers Headquarters

Grandad and Maisie are here. I wasn't allowed to go to my room but had to sit around listening to madnosity for hours.

Grandad said, "I have an announcement to make. Maisie has just made me the happiest man alive."

I nearly said, *Why, is she going on a knitting tour of the world*? But I didn't. Grandad reached over and took one of Maisie's hands. (Well, as much as he could as she was wearing multicoloured mittens. Keep in mind this is July.)

"She has agreed to marry me."

Kitchen

10:00 p.m.

Mum was making some coffee and the "swingers" Grandad and Maisie had staggered off home. Mum said, "It just shows you that you must never give up on love; it comes when you least expect it."

I said, "Mum, it is sad and weird."

She said, "I think it's lovely and romantic."

I said, "You won't when you have to wear a knitted jumpsuit for the wedding."

Mum was still in Elderly Loon land because she said, "Age isn't everything. Grandad says she's a fine body of a woman underneath all that wool."

Erlack a pongoes!

Anyway, who cares about the knitted folk? Is now a good time to get Mum to agree for me to go to Pizza-a-gogo land? I am having very bad withdrawal symptoms from the Luuurve God. I dreamt about him last night and it was a bit alarming. He had been doing the neck-stroking thing and my neck had started stretching like it was a piece of clay. You know when you see those programmes about potters making vases and they stretch the clay. Anyway that was happening and then my head fell off.

I think it is probably Freudian. I think it means I mustn't lose my head. Especially as in the dream my head rolled off into a corner and Angus came and started biffing it around like a ball.

Where was I? Oh yes. Asking Mum when I could go to Pizza-a-gogo land. "Mum, which do you think would be the best week for me to go to Rome? I finish term next week and then there is the ludicrous camping weekend, but I could go the weekend after that."

She said, "Why are you talking rubbish about going to Italy?"

I laughed in a lighthearted way. "Oooh, Mum, you prankster!!! You know what I mean. I mean about going to visit Masimo's family as we agreed."

"Agreed?"

"Yes."

"Where was I when we agreed?"

"You were, er, near me, agreeing."

"Georgia, a) I did not agree and b) nothing you say will make me agree. And c) the first two times a million."

Five minutes later

I HATE my family. Why do they want me to hang around all the time? Why can't they make their own fun? Well, this time I will show them. If they won't let me have the money to go to Italy to see my boyfriend, then I will get the money myself. I will sell something.

Ten minutes later

Looking through my cupboards.

How much would I get for my slightly worn leather boots? Where do you take stuff to sell it? I don't know. Oxfam? A selling shop?

I like them, and anyway, what would I wear in Italy for disco wear?

And also I am very, very tired. It's the end of term. I have been working like a dog. I haven't got the energy to go traipsing around earning my own money.

Midnight

I am going to not speak to my mum and dad until they let me go to see the Luuurve God.

Tuesday July 26th
Breakfast

Mum asked me if I wanted some toast and I *ignorez-vous*ed her. It won't be long before she snaps.

As I was silently leaving the house Mum said, "If you are planning to keep up the silent treatment I'll just have to guess what you would say. Which is quite handy, actually, as I want you to babysit tonight. I'm guessing that you want to. Yes, yes, I can see you do. That's good. Tatty bye."

Damn!!!

2:00 p.m.

I can't believe I'm being made to go on this camping fiasco. In German Herr Kamyer showed us a lot of things you can do with a Swiss army knife. All of them indescribably useless and naff.

I said to Ro Ro, "In my humble opinion if a horse gets a stone stuck in its hoof, that is just carelessnosity. Why should I have to lug a heavy knife around just so I can get it out?"

Ro Ro gave me the Klingon salute. "You are all heart, Georgia. Do you want to practise a sheepshank knot with me?"

I just looked at her.

Jas adores doing sheepshank knots. Please make this camping trip go away, God.

4:15 p.m.
Detention! I can't believe it!!! Hawkeye has only been back about five minutes from her girl-baiting course and she has given me detention.

I was three minutes late for her class because I had to go to the piddly-diddly department after German and noticed a lurker situation that I had to deal with by squeezing the living daylights out of it and then covering it with soap. I don't know why; it seemed a good idea at the time. Anyway, when I panted into class Hawkeye said, "You should have been here at three o'clock."

And I said, "Why? What happened?" in a tone of interest and curiosity. And the next thing you know I am in detention writing, "Rudeness masquerading as wittiness results in detention."

Unbelievable.

In my room
6:30 p.m.
Still thinking of ways to get to my beloved. I wonder if he will ring me from Pizza-a-gogo land? I would ring me if I were him. Well, you know what I mean. Mind you, I would have rung me on Monday.

Five minutes later
I wonder why he hasn't phoned me?

I'd phone Jas and ask her what she thinks but she is in Twig land. If I hear one more thing about this bloody camping trip I will go insane. Also, and this is annoying, Jas would not do sharesies in her tent. She is dossing down with Ellen and Mabs. She says they are more "reliable". What does that mean? I don't care. I am sharing with Rosie and Jools, which will be more fun anyway. Jas will have all these stupid "tent rules" like "Toothbrushes should be kept in the toothbrush jar" and "When you go to bed at night check that your sleeping bag is not crushing some unusual wildlife". Rubbish stuff.

What are you supposed to take clotheswise for a camping nightmare scenario? We got a list somewhere from Miss Wilson. Where is it?

Two minutes later

- Warm evening clothing
- An anorak
- Walking shoes
- Casual daywear

Good lord. Oh, and this is the terrifying bit:

Bring your bathing suits, girls, because there is a river nearby, and of course if you have any instruments that you play bring those along to make the evenings lots of fun!

It is going to be a cross between a Call-me-Arnold the Vicar guitar extravaganza and *Carry on Camping.* I can guarantee that the mountain-rescue people will be called out. It will possibly be something to do with Melanie Griffiths running and her basoomas sending her out of control and into the river. That or Herr Kamyer will be savaged by sheep (with a bit of luck).

7:00 p.m.
Rosie rang.

"Gee, I am taking the horns with us on the camping trip."

I said, "Why?"

She said, "So we can brush up on our Viking disco inferno dance and also we can don them if we are attacked by rampaging cows. Pip pip."

Good grief.

Ten minutes later

I suppose in some horrific way the camping fiasco will pass the time until I can figure out how to get to Masimo.

Two minutes later

I wonder how Robbie is? Every time I can't avoid going near Wet Lindsay she says something about him to one of her slimy mates, implying that they are an item. Maybe they are. Well, if they are, it is a good way of curing me of him. Anyone who could choose someone as nobbly as her can't be all good.

One minute later

But he did ask me if I wanted a lift home before she trapped him with her octopussy extensions.

490

one minute later

And Dave the Laugh said he thought Robbie liked me but he was playing cool bananas because of the Masimo fandango.

one minute later

Oh no, I've been thinking about Dave the Laugh again. He somehow still pops up (oo-er)! If I think of anything funny, I always want to tell him about it. I don't because, well, it seems a bit odd just being mates with him. It was cool on Saturday night when he saved the little titches.

I wonder if he laughs with his girlfriend Emma like he laughs with me?

I wonder what number on the snogging scale they have got up to? Shut up, brain!

Phone rang.

Maybe it's Masimo! I ran down the stairs. No one is in because Mum said she'd decided I couldn't be trusted to look after Libbs so she has taken her over to Grandad and his knitted live-in lover. Oh, much more trustworthy. Not. I nearly said that to Mum but it's difficult when you are not speaking to someone. Why can't I have normal parents who do stuff for you? Mum and Dad have gone to Uncle Eddie's first booking as a baldy-o-gram, and that in anybody's language is not normal behaviour.

I answered the phone.

It was Robbie.

Crikey.

Three minutes later

I have agreed to meet him on Thursday for a "talk".

Whatever that means.

Well, in my case it will mean me going, "Blah, blah, rubbish, rubbish, dribble, dribble, arse."

Thursday July 28th
Last day of term

Got the "whole school is looking to you for an example" speech from Slim about the camping trip. And she said, "We are all looking forward very much to the interesting stories and observations that Ten A will be coming back with."

Oh yes, the merry hours we will have talking about the night we saw a badger scratch its bum-oley. And how many sausages we ate.

As we lurched along to Latin I said to Rosie, "Why isn't Slim coming with us, actually? I personally would give quite a lot of money to see her in a tent."

Rosie said, "She was wearing one today."

Jas was hysterical with twig madness. "Have you packed yet, Gee?"

"No."

"I have."

"Really, how many pairs of knickers are you bringing?"

"Well, I thought just in case of nippy-noodles weather I would bring those thick long ones that—"

"Jas, I am not serious."

She huffed off.

She is so self-obsessed it's amazing. It's all just me, me, me, Tom, me, stuffed owls, knickers and, er... me with her. If you see what I mean and I think you do.

I told her on the way to Stalag 14 this morning that I was on the horns of a whatsit vis-á-vis the maybe-two-boyfriends situation. And I am. I am feeling quite weird about seeing Robbie this evening.

She gave me the usual Jas lecture. "Well, you have to choose and then stick with your decision. You can't just do what you like – tart around all your life, choosing new boyfriends at every wiff and woo."

At every wiff and woo? What was she talking about? And "tarting around". That's nice talk, isn't it?

I said, "Jas, I am not a tart, I am a teenager. Just because you have thrust aside your red bottom with a firm hand and are subscribing to *Vole Weekly* doesn't make you right, you know."

She said, "Yes it does."

"No, it doesn't."

"It does."

"Jas, it doesn't make it a debate when one person just keeps saying 'yes it does'."

That shut her up for a nanosecond, and then she said, "Yes it does."

She is so annnnoyyyyiiing.

In my room
Teatime

Robbie will be here in a minute. Blimey. I hope it doesn't rain; it's looking a bit overcast.

Oh God, that has just reminded me of when I first went round to Robbie's house. The very first time; I can't believe it's only a few months ago. I have become a woman since then. I have lived, loved, and suffered.

One minute later
Well, I've suffered and my nungas have grown quite a lot.

Two minutes later
When I first met him I didn't even wear a bra. How weird is that? And stupid as it turns out because it rained on my T-shirt and I got soaking wet when I was going round to his house. And when I looked down at my T-shirt there were two bobbles sticking out. And they were my nip-nips and I couldn't get them back in again. I had to keep my arms crossed over my nips for ages. Then he played me one of his songs and I sat there not knowing what to do, so I let an attractive (I like to think) half-smile play on my face. Unfortunately it was a long song and by the end of it my cheeks were aching quite a lot, and I was trying to keep my nose sucked in as well. I had to go to bed with face strain when I got home.

And then, after all that effort, the Sex God dumped me because I was too young for him and said that he knew someone that I might like called Dave the Laugh. And that is when Dave the Laugh entered stage right and I tried to use him as my decoy duck to make Robbie interested in me.

I still feel slightly bad about that bit, the decoy duck bit, especially as Dave spotted it. Actually it's quite amazing that we are mates.

Two minutes later
Because that is what we are. Tip-top mates. Which is good. And how it should be. We would have been no good as a boyfriend and girlfriend because... erm... Well, he's not a Sex God or a Luuurve God. He's just a sort of Dave God. And that is not on the God list. You don't have Thor and Woden and Dave, do you?

Two minutes later
He is funny, though.

Ten minutes and Robbie will be ringing the doorbell. I have tarted myself up to within an inch of my life. I don't think I can stand being in the house just waiting. Maybe I will go and sit on the wall and wait for him there. Does that seem a bit keen? Yes, it does. I'll just stay here and use disciplinosity and glaciosity.

Sitting on the wall

Right, what am I going to say to him? What about the snogging question? What if he wants to snog me? I can't really snog him when I am nearly officially the maybe girlfriend of a Luuurve God. Can I? We should have a snogging scale for exes. For the "once just for old time's sake" type snogging.

Mind you, I've snogged Dave the Laugh a number of times since he has been my ex. So the "just for old time's sake" rule seems to be "yes, yes, and three times yes".

Well, it used to be. Nothing has happened like that for ages. Maybe he has gone off me? I don't know why he should unless he really really likes his "girlfriend". Maybe he thinks she is nicer than I am. Maybe she *is* nicer than I am. But that is clearly not my fault; look at my parents.

Anyway shut up about Dave! How did he get in here???

Two minutes later

Then Robbie came round the corner and into my street. He looked very cool and sort of grown-up. I remembered all the months and months I had followed him around and dreamed of him, and gone to Stiff Dylans gigs hoping to bump into him. Or for him to talk to me. And then he had kissed me, and said we should see each other. And for a few days I had been soooooo happy. And an irresistible boy magnet. And then he dumped me again! To go to Kiwi-a-gogo land and play guitar with wombats. Or was it the maracas? I don't know.

I was about to get off the wall and say something normal(ish) to Robbie but then he completely surprised me by just bending down and kissing me on the mouth. And not just a soft friendy kiss. A proper kiss, quite hard that lasted for about thirty seconds. My brain was chatting on about, *Oooh I must get a watch because Jas is sure to ask me how long I think a proper kiss lasts, and how did I know it was thirty seconds, did I time it by the sun's shadows, etc...* Shut up, brain, shut up!

And then for a moment or two my brain did shut up and I just felt stuff.

Then he stopped kissing me and said, "Hi."

And I went, "Hi." Almost like a normal person.

He sat down on the wall next to me. I looked at him, and he smiled back at me.

He said, "Shall we amble down to the park, like we used to?"

In the park

It was lovely in the park, the sunlight was filtering through the trees and making leaf shapes on the ground and there were the sounds of children laughing. I mean proper children's laughing, not like the mad heggy heggy heg heg that my sister does. Just merry little friends playing together. And a few couples holding hands and wandering about or sitting on the grass.

We hadn't been talking much. I didn't mind because, to be frank, there wasn't much in my head that I wanted to let people know about. For instance, I found out today in history that Shackleton, so-called hero and explorer, got stuck in the ice on his ship and so he shot his cat Mr Chippy to make more room or make the boat lighter or something, and then they got rescued anyway! And Mr Chippy had been the ship's cat for years and years and years. Why didn't he shoot himself if he wanted to make more room? Historical people are vair vair selfish. I must tell Dave about Mr Chippy when I see him.

I came out of my little cat tragedy to hear Robbie saying, "Do you remember this tree? I think it was here that I sang you the song I wrote for you. Do you remember?"

Yes, I did, actually. And if I am honest it wasn't altogether a vair fond memory because Robbie had sort of encouraged me to put my head on his lap while he...

Robbie said, "Let's sit down for a bit. I think I can

remember the words more or less..."

Oh no. It was all happening again. Well, this time I was definitely not going to put my head on his lap.

One minute later
Oh dear God, I had my head on his lap and I was once again glancing up his nostrils while he sang me a song about a dolphin.

In bed
11:00 p.m.
Blubbing.

I thought I had plumbed the depths of tragicosity boywise but I was wrong. I don't even know why I am crying really, it's just so sad. Robbie was my very first one and only Sex God and he still is, but... oh, I don't know. He sang me the song and I did the avoiding the nostrils scenario and also I had to keep an eye on any undue nunga jiggling AND try not to let my brain run wild and free. So in the end I was all sort of tensoid and not really myself. Which of course Jas would say was a good thing.

Robbie and me snogged and did a bit of number six, and

he is very good at it. No one can deny he is good-looking in the top-twenty sort of way. His clothes are nice (apart, it has to be said, from the rubber shoes from the vegetarian shop) and he did say that he and Lindsay are absolutely not an item.

He walked me home, holding my hand, and when we got to my gate he kissed me really hard and long. I don't think there was any sign of virtual number seven but you never know.

Then he was looking at me in the moonlight (so were five other eyes until I threw my shoe at the wall and Angus, Naomi and Gordy took off). I looked at him and he had a lovely face, really lovely. And he is lovely. But... oh, I don't know. I felt my eyes suddenly fill with tears. I couldn't help it. Everything seemed so sad, and sort of not quite right. I looked down so that he wouldn't see my blubbing.

And he stroked my hair and said, "Gee, what are you thinking?"

Oh no, what *was* I thinking? I just blurted out, "Well, you left me and you have been gone so long, and the wombats and so on and then I, well, I started liking Masimo and he..."

Robbie looked really sad, and then he sat down next to me on the wall and was quiet. I didn't know what to say.

After a minute he said, "So you really like him, then?"

I couldn't make my voice work, I just nodded.

He still didn't say anything. I looked sideways at him. He was looking straight ahead, and as I looked a little tear came out of his eye and slipped slowly down his face. Ohhhhhhhh, this was unbearable.

I was going to say, *No, no, don't cry, I'll go out with you. Anything, but don't cry...* But I still couldn't make my voice work.

And then he sort of cleared his throat and said, "Georgia, don't feel bad. It's always tough to hurt someone and tell them the truth. I know that. You're a really lovely girl. Lovely... mad... but lovely. I'll always like you. Don't worry."

There was another little pause. And then he stood up and said, "Anyway, I suppose you'd better be off, you've probably got a train to catch."

At least he smiled when he said that. Which was good because I could feel the old waterworks coming on big-time.

Midnight

The long and the long of it is that he is going back to New Zealand. He says there is a girl that likes him there. I stopped myself from saying, "Is it Wilma the Wombat?" But it did make me feel a bit funny to think of him with someone else.

And also going away again. Oh, I don't know. Would I want to go out with him if he was staying?

It's all very well writing books about how to make any twit fall in love with you, but what do you do when you have got them? That should be book two, *What to Do with a Collection of Twits When You Have Accidentally Done What Some Fool in a Book Told You to Do and Now They Are All Hanging About with You.*

12:05 a.m.

Rosie and Sven seem happy together. And they are, as we know, planning to marry in eighteen years time. But will they? They quite clearly have nothing in common besides snogging, snogging, snacks, mad dancing and snogging. But perhaps that is a good relationship. Who knows?

And then there is Jas'n'Tom. They have far, far too much in common, but they seem happy.

One minute later

The only thing is, to be happy like Jas I would actually have to be Jas.

No, I just cannot go there. I have to be me.

♥ 503

And I have to face the fact that I have sounded my Cosmic Horn and therefore my red-bottomosity has led me into the oven of luuurve, on to the rack of pain and out again on to the horns of a whatsit.

Owwwww.

Well, I have made my decision. Now I will have to lie on it.

Tent head

Friday July 29th

Mum woke me at 8:30 a.m. "Gee, can I borrow your leather skirt? You won't be taking it on the camping trip, will you?"

I was blinking in the blinding light because she had ripped my curtains open and was scrabbling through my wardrobe. "Mum, why would you want to borrow my leather skirt and who are you lending it to? Which incidentally you can't."

Damn! I had broken my vow of silence!!!

Mum said, "I'm not lending it to anyone; the girls and I are going to another of Uncle Eddie's gigs on Saturday. It's a sort of showcase thing and there will be him as the baldy-o-gram, there's a Viking Thor-o-gram, a Postman Pat-o-gram and there is a —"

"Mum, please stop there, as you know I am very artistic and this could send me over the edge. Are you trying to tell me that you are intending to wear my leather skirt and go watch mad blokes ponce around in their undercrackers?"

She said, "Oh no… they take those off as well."

How disgusting!!!

Half an hour later

I've let Mum borrow my skirt and she's said that she'll talk to me about Pizza-a-gogo land when I get back from camping. Yessssss!!!

I accidentally told her about the Robbie thing. And for her, she was quite nice about it. I cried again when I told her. And I said I felt like a mean and wormy girl.

She said, "Well, it is true that you are a pain in the bum-oley most of the time. But I suppose as a teenager it's really your job. I think I was the same before I grew up."

I didn't say, *Are you mad?*

Then she went on, "Actually, I am quite proud of you. It's hard to tell the truth sometimes, especially if you don't want to hurt someone. And you did – you said what you feel. And you must do what is right for you, not what other people say is right."

She gave me a big hug and to my amazement I gave her a spontaneous kiss. Which surprised both of us.

11:00 a.m.
We have to be at Stalag 14 to meet the coach at 3:00 p.m. I wonder if I just didn't turn up they would bog off without me. I doubt it. I should think they would send out a hanging party led by Mr Attwood and Wet Lindsay. Ooooh, I cannot believe I have to go on this ludicrous camping thing.

It's pointless taking any beauty products because unless I suddenly go mad and start fancying Herr Kamyer there will be no other males around, apart from Miss Wilson. I am just going to bung some jumpers and jeans in a bag with some essential snacks and hope that I can sleep through the next two days. Maybe I could get one of the Ace Gang to hit me over the head with something and knock me out and I could wake up smiling on Sunday.

I wonder if Wet Lindsay knows that Robbie is going back to Kiwi-a-gogo? She will go ballisticisimus. So every cloud has a silver lining.

♥

2:00 p.m.

Lugging my bag up the hill to Stalag 14. Jas has scampered ahead because Tom is helping her carry her things to school. She's only phoned me four times to tell me how excited she is. I said to her in a moment of lighthearted repartee, "Jas, have you got a special toothbrush mug?"

And she said, "Of course. Who hasn't?"

Stalag 14

Things have gone horribly wrong already. Herr Kamyer is wearing shorts. That cannot be right. Or even allowed. I tried not to look at his legs. They are incredibly pale and have sort of ginger hair on them. Erlack!

We piled on to the coach and the Ace Gang secured the back seats. Rosie said, "We could moon the drivers behind us." She is a sophisticate and no mistake.

Tom waved us off and Jas cried and blew him kisses. What has she got to cry about? She hasn't been in the mangle of love like me.

Miss Wilson is delirious with excitement; her bob is practically dropping off. As we drove off she stood up and said to us all, "Now then, girls, just to get us in the mood shall we sing a few songs? What about 'Ten Green Bottles'?"

Is she mad?

But then we discovered that we had a bus-driving Mr Attwood at the wheel, because he said to her, "There is no singing on the bus, madam, without the full permission of the vehicle transportation facilitator."

Miss Wilson said, "Erm, well, when, er... who is the vehicle, erm, facilitator?"

Mr Grumpy Arse said, "Me."

And Miss Wilson said, "Well, can we, erm, would it be all right for us to sing a few songs to—"

He just said, "No," and accelerated so hard that Miss Wilson fell over and on to Herr Kamyer's knee.

We all went, "Whey hey!!!"

An hour later

I told the Ace Gang about the Robbie evening. They were all going "Oh, that is so sad" and so on. And it was. Even Jas put her arm round me. I gave her a little brave smile. It is quite tough being a boy magnet, actually. More tiring than you would think.

Then Jas said, "Well, I hope you have done the right thing. If Masimo decides you are too silly to go out with, you will be on the shelf of life again."

I didn't even bother replying to her, she is so annoying. I just pulled her stupid outdoors camping hat down over her eyes.

Half an hour later
In the middle of nowhere in the middle of a field. What is the point of that? Jas is practically skipping around with excitement. She went off to "explore" in the woods. Or Twig Heaven, as some people might call it. I went to look at the bathroom facilities.

Ten minutes later
I said to the Ace Gang, "I will not be going for a poo for the next two days and that is a fact."

The "bathroom facilities" are some chemical toilets and a sort of overhead tap that is supposed to be a "shower" in some crap hut thing. I wouldn't be surprised if a pig pops its head up the lavatory pan when you sit down. Not that I will be sitting down.

I said to Miss Wilson, "This is inhumane treatment of youth. I want to make a complaint to the European Court of Human Rights. Get them on the blower."

Miss Wilson said, "Well, of course, yes, things are rather basic. But that is half the fun of it. I remember when I was a girl we went camping and there were no toilet facilities at all. We had to take our little spades and dig a hole in the woods for our bowel movements."

Oh, oh, Miss Wilson had mentioned her poo in front of me!!! I felt abused and dirty.

An hour later
Rosie and Jools and me are still trying to put the sodding tent up. I said to Herr Kamyer (who is sitting on a deck chair outside his tent, which even has a sort of awning over the opening), "Herr Kamyer as you are so *gut* at putting stuff up, why don't you put ours up?"

And he said, "I zink it vill be more satisfactory for you if you achieve this thing yourself. It is *gut* for the personality."

Well, he is very, very wrong if he thinks that the fact that you can put a tent up is good for your personality. For instance, the people who have put their tents up are him, Miss Wilson and Jas. That speaks volumes in my book.

Jas is incredibly irritating even for her. And that is really saying something. She is scampering around like a fool, and doing her teacher botty-kissing thing. She said to Herr Kamyer, "Herr Kamyer, shall I go foraging for firewood for the fire?"

And he said, "Vat a *gut* idea, Jas. Do you know the right kind of wood to look for?"

Jas said, "Ooh yes, Herr Kamyer, Tom, well, he's my boyfriend, we often have fires when we go out rambling. In fact we went on a special fire-making course, so actually I can make a fire without matches."

I felt like shouting, *"WHO CARES??? JUST PUT OUR BLOODY TENT UP FOR US, YOU TWIGGY TWIT!!!"*

Half an hour later

At last we have got our tent up and are sitting in it. Is this it? Is this what people go on and on about? Sitting in a pokey thing looking at a field?

Ten minutes later

God, I'm bored. When's tea?

I went over to Jas's tent and knocked on the flap – which I thought was amusing. Jas popped her head through the gap. "What do you want? Your tent looks a bit of a funny shape."

I said, "Don't start me on things that look a bit of a funny shape, Jas. What are you doing in your tent? What are we supposed to do? Let me see."

She said, "Well, be careful where you put your big fat feet, it's all nice and organised in here."

Blimey. They really did have personal tooth mugs.

Jas said, "I've already found a great crested newt in one of the pools by the river."

I looked at her ironically, but she didn't get it. Babbling on and on like Lord Baden-Powell. "Miss Wilson took a microscope with us to the pools and there were some hydra around the edge and—"

I interrupted her, "Jas, I believe I may have mentioned that I am not interested in great crusted newts."

"Crested."

"Whatever. Crusted, toasted, fried, I am and will always remain a newt-free area. Have you got any snacks stashed around your person? I'm really peckish."

I made her give me one of her secret Jammy Dodgers, which she had hidden inside her owl pyjama case. Honestly.

Darkness starts to fall on the camping fiasco

As it got towards dusk Herr Kamyer and Miss Wilson started busily getting pans out and lit a fire. Miss Wilson said, "Girls, you will notice that Herr Kamyer has made a fire break between the fire and the meadow. One must always be aware of the danger of forest fires in high summer."

Oh yes indeedy, forest fires are high on my list of worries. Has she any idea what my luuurve life is like?

Half an hour later

Actually, I hate to say this, but it really is quite good fun sitting round the old campfire eating *spangleferkel* and beans from tin plates.

I don't know why but I felt a *Rawhide* moment coming on. I said that to Rosie and Jools. "I feel a touch of the cowboy coming on."

Rosie said, "Oo-er, shall we do a bit of cattle rustling after supps to fill in the long hours until we can get back to civilisation and snogging?"

I said, "Alrighty."

So we are going to skip off and find some cows to rustle after our fruit tarts. Leave it.

Fifteen minutes later

Us "campers" were all sitting around the fire as some of the eager beavers, i.e. twits and fools, went to wash the plates in the river. Jas was, of course, one of them – laughing and giggling and saying stuff like, "Why, isn't that a meadowlark?" and "I think I spotted a badger trail. It will be exciting to watch for them tonight." Absolute tosh. Why is she so happy in the outdoors? Perhaps she has a touch of the wild pig in her gene bank.

When everything was stashed away in Stashing land Herr Kamyer said, "Now then, girls, ve haf now the entertainment."

I said, "Yes, I was wondering where the TV would be plugged in."

Herr Kamyer said, "*Nein*, we have something *sehr* better, besides which, I haf not got any equipment."

Oh, we laughed. I must be giddy with crying and fresh air because I couldn't stop hooting with laughter for ages, while Herr Kamyer just looked at us in bewilderment.

"Vat is ze joke about? Why when I say I haf no equipment do you laugh? Anyway, for ze entertainment Miss Wilson has brought some cocoa tins and ve vill fill them with *der* rice like so."

He got a tin and filled it with rice and then Miss Wilson started filling other ones. Then the worst thing in the world happened. They started shaking them like maracas and singing "Tie Me Kangaroo Down Sport" by Rolf Harris.

It was awful. When they tried to get everyone to join in, shaking the tins and so on, I said, "Well, I am just going to see what the cows are doing on this fine evening."

Rosie and Jools leaped to their feet saying, "We'll come. We'll come."

Ten minutes later

We couldn't find any cows. Well, actually there were some but the field was about a hundred miles away. Anyway, I didn't want to see them, really, I just wanted to rustle them.

There were some dozy-looking sheep nearer, though, so we went into their field. Blimey, sheep poo a lot. Like little pellet things. Angus would love it here – things to chase and annoy, poo, sausages, tiny innocent voley things to massacre. Cat heaven.

Rosie has decided to "improvise" cattle rustling using the sheep and her wedding horns.

Eight minutes later

Rosie strapped the bison horns on to a sheep with some of her tights and she is attempting to ride it like a sort of mustang. The sheep stands there in its horns and when Rosie gets nearly on it, just shuffles away a bit. She came at it from its bottom end and managed to stay on it for a second before plunging into some sheep's poo. What hilarious country larks we are having.

9:30 p.m.

Surely it must be time for bed now? The sheep were no fun. In the end they just huddled together at the far end of the field. How dim can animals be? We headed back for the campfire because we had nothing else to do. The nearest village is about an hour away and that is probably full of the elderly insane.

9:42 p.m.

After the excitement of the singing fiasco the atmosphere really heated up, because for our further "entertainment" Herr Kamyer started doing shadow animals in his tent with a lamp. He said people couldn't get enough of it when he went camping in the Black Forest. Do we know any German comedians? No is the answer you are searching for.

Anyway, live and let live, I say. Herr Kamyer made the shape and then we had to guess what it was. Jas was keen as mustard – she got the rabbit, and the eagle, etc. On and on it went. I don't know how anyone knew what animals they were supposed to be when it was clearly just Herr Kamyer's hands.

9:50 p.m.

Then he said from inside his tent, "I zink that is enough, girls, I finish now." And he reached to get something from his haversack. You could see him all silhouetted in the tent.

I shouted out, "Erm, an elephant."

He said, "Ach no, I haf now finished, I am not making the animals any more." And he came out of his tent with his toothbrush.

Rosie said, "A llama on holiday."

Herr Kamyer started going over to the "bathroom facilities". "*Nein, nein,* I haf finished now."

As he went into the facilities I yelled, "A Koch!" But he didn't hear me.

Jas did, though. Jas, representative for the Wildlife of Great Britain Club, said, "You are being silly, Georgia. I'm off to the hide now to see if I can see any badgers. Anyone want to come with me?"

Is she insane?

Two minutes later

Actually, amazingly, some people did go with her.

Is it time for bed yet?

Rosie, Jools and me went into our tent and got into our sleeping bags. The tent is a bit droopy and saggy. I can't actually see Rosie in her sleeping bag because of the droopy bit in the middle. And she is next to me. Ah well.

I will never be able to sleep for all the hooting and scurrying going on. And that's just Jas...

zzzzzzzzzzzzzzzzz.

Midnight

The tent collapsed. I woke up struggling with what felt like a big duvet and couldn't see a thing. I could hear muffled voices and Rosie saying, "I've gone blind, I've gone blind!!!"

Eventually we managed to get free of the tent and stood shivering in our pyjamas. All the other tents were in darkness and I could hear snoring from Miss Wilson's tent. I wonder what she sleeps in? Can you get corduroy pyjamas? Well, if anyone can, she can.

I said, "I'm not going through all that putting-the-tent-up-again fiasco. We will have to crawl in with our best mateys."

Ten minutes later

Jas is sooooooo unreasonable. We crawled into her tent and I tried to squeeze into her sleeping bag with her but she wouldn't let me. Then Rosie trod on the special toothbrush mug and all hell broke loose.

12:30 a.m.

In the end Mrs Grumpy Knickers and her gang put our tent back up again just to get rid of us. It wasn't as droopy this time.

Jas said, "You had the main tent pole in the wrong place."

So? What is that supposed to mean?

1:00 a.m.

I am dying to go to the loo. I made Rosie come with me.

Poooooooo. How horrible is it sitting on a sort of box full of stinky stuff in a tent? Vair vair horrible. It makes Gordy's kitty litter box seem like luxury.

Saturday July 30th

Morning

What a racket: birds chirping, cows mooing, sheep bleating. People jogging. Oh yes. That is a sight for sore eyes first thing in the morning – Miss Wilson and Herr Kamyer in their running shorts. Good Lord.

I looked in my mirror. Yep, tent head.

I don't care, though, as this is deffo a Sex God-free zone.

Afternoon

An action-packed day full of getting up, eating more sausages, having to play a game of rounders.

Actually, I must say I did quite enjoy that – I socked the ball into a marshy bit and Jas had to go and get it. She said to me, "You did that on purpose."

And I said, "Don't be so silly, Jas."

And then next time I was in, I smacked the ball into exactly the same place. *Zut alors!!!*

Herr Kamyer showed us how to make a hammock and Miss Wilson told us how to identify poisonous fruits of the forest. Which she couldn't find and ended up having to show us pictures of in a book.

I said to Ellen and the gang, "The whole forest can be poisonous for all I care. I will never be coming into the wilderness again anyway."

Rosie and I managed to escape the forced march to the newt pond by slipping off and finding a tree that we could climb and hide in. We hoisted ourselves up and we could look down at the "merry campers" scampering around looking at stuff and drawing it. How anyone can be interested in drawing amoeba I will never know. Why would you bother coming miles and miles into Nowheresville when you could get much the same effect at home drawing some snot?

3:00 p.m.

It was nice and dreamy up in the tree, actually; the sun was lovely and warm and we could stretch out on a branch in our shorts. I could do tanning work, so at least I wasn't completely wasting my time. Rosie was plaiting her hair into tiny little plaits.

I said to her, "It makes you look like a halfwit."

And she said, "Really? It looks that nice?"

Then she started missing Sven. "Are my lips shrinking?"

I looked at them. "No."

"They feel like they are. I've been snogging Sven every day for months."

I said, "Don't you do anything else?"

Rosie looked at me. "Of course we do."

"What?"

"Pardon?"

"What do you do?"

"We make things – furry shorts, Viking drinking boots and so on. It's not an easy life being the bride-to-be of a Viking, you know." And she fished out her beard and put it on.

Just then we heard some voices and had to shut up so that no one would see us. We could see down through the leaves. It was Miss Wilson and Herr Kamyer. Both in shorts. Good grief. Herr Kamyer said, "It is ver varm, *nicht var?*"

Miss Wilson was dithering about with a towel, and said, "Yes indeed, I think I'll have a refreshing shower." And she bounded off to the "bathroom facilities".

Herr Kamyer busied himself with his magnifying glass. I think he was trying to start a fire with it. What is the point of that?

Rosie whispered, "I do hope he sets fire to his shorts."

Five minutes later

Some of the merry campers have come back from the newt pond and are having another game of rounders. Nauseating P. Green, who has been keeping a low profile this weekend, thank the Lord, is a fielder out by the bathroom facility.

I said to Rosie quietly, "I don't want to be mean or anything but Nauseating P. Green is unusually unusual-looking."

Rosie stopped plaiting for a minute to look. "Please let her fall over. There's nothing funnier than seeing her trying to get up again."

At which point Melanie Griffiths socked the rounders ball really hard over to where N. P. Green was on fielding duties. Melanie ran for first base, and even Herr Kamyer stopped setting fire to things to look up. As I may have mentioned before, Melanie's nunga-nungas have a life of their own when she's running.

I said to Rosie, "Any minute now she will come careering past us and into the woods."

Everyone was shouting at N. P. Green, "Catch the ball, four eyes, catch it!"

I said, "She can't even see the ball. The ball would have to be the size of her arse to see it through those glasses."

At which point the funniest thing known to humanity happened. Nauseating P. Green was running backwards, trying to catch where she thought the ball might be, and she crashed into the bathroom facility. Half of the bathroom facility (also known as a piece of old tent) collapsed around her, to reveal Miss Wilson blinking out from underneath the shower.

Rosie and I nearly fell out of the tree.

Three minutes later

My ribs hurt from laughing. Seeing Miss Wilson in the nuddy-pants, apart from a spotted shower cap, is possibly the sight of the century. She just stood there blinking in the sun with her soap on a rope.

Rosie said, "Cor!"

Ten minutes later

Miss Wilson managed to crawl under the rest of the bathroom facility and has just come out with her clothes on. As she came out, Herr Kamyer walked quickly into the woods.

Five minutes later

I said to Rosie, "Imagine if it had been Slim."

Rosie said, "No."

Ten minutes later

Miss Wilson is fiddling about near the cooking area, and Herr Kamyer has just come out of the woods whistling. Miss Wilson is pointing across to the bathroom facility. Herr Kamyer is taking off his glasses, pointing at it and shrugging his shoulders. It's like watching mime.

Then I got it. "Herr Kamyer is pretending that he did not see Miss Wilson in the rudey-dudeys!"

One minute later

Back to the important things of life. I said to Rosie, "I wonder if I did the right thing about the Sex God? I wonder if I do like Masimo more than him."

She said, "You've got to get your priorities right in life."

Blimey, she was getting a bit deep for someone who was sporting a head full of tiny plaits and a full beard.

I said, "How do you mean?"

"Well, to put it another way, who is the best snogger?"

Hmmmmmmmmmm.

Two minutes later

I gave Masimo nine out of ten for snogging, and Robbie eight.

Rosie said, "Well, there you are, then."

Yes, when you put it like that.

Then she said, "What is the best snog you have ever had? Don't think about it, just say what comes into your head."

"I think it was when Dave the Laugh nibbled my lips."

Blimey. I've just said something that has amazed even me.

Rosie looked at me and scratched her beard. "How did Dave the Laugh get in here?"

Good point, well made.

In our tent
9:00 p.m.

Well, nearly time to get back to civilisation. I can still hear the rest of the campers around the fire. Rosie, Jools and me are all in our sleeping bags. I have got some choccy and we are trying to suck it and see who can make it last the longest. That is how exciting life is.

As we were lying there sucking we heard a sort of scrabbling at the side of the tent and then a hand came looming into view at the bottom of the canvas. We were being plundered, probably by farmers.

I said, "Oy, why don't you bog off back to where you came from? I have a gun."

And a voice said, "Yes, but what colour pants have you got on?"

It couldn't be?

It was, though! Dave the Laugh, Tom, Sven, Rollo and Dec and another mate called Edward I didn't know had all come down in Tom's car to visit us. They were camped just down the road by the river.

Yes, yes, yes!!!

We were talking quietly to them through the tent wall. Dave said from the other side of the tent, "If you pretend to go to the loo, you can all come back in and say good night to the teachers like you are going to sleep for the night, and then burrow out the back of the tent and come with us. For a laugh. You know you want to!"

He is such a cheeky cat. How exciting, though!

Tom's voice said, "Get Jas to come out as well."

Dec said, "Yeah, and get two other ones."

I said, "Two other what?"

Dec said, "Girls."

Boys are really unbelievable. I'm sure Mabs and Ellen are not going to come out and just be with some blokes who call them "two other ones". Even Ellen has got a bit of pridenosity. Ish.

The lads told us how to get to their campsite and said they would wait for us there. We got into our clothes and then put our dressing gowns over the top of them. Jools, Rosie and I trooped over to now re-erected loos, passing by the fire where the rest of them were singing "Ging Gang Gooley Gooley Gooley".

Fortunately Rosie had thought to bring emergency make-up supplies and when we got in the "loos" (poo-ey) I had a quick look in the mirror. My tent hair had calmed down a bit during the day, and I did a mascara, lippy, lip gloss thing. Rosie was leaping about undoing her plaits and practising puckering up. Jools said, "So what is the plan?"

I said, "Here's the plan. We go back to the tent yawning, and pretend we are shattered from having so much camping fun that we are having an early night. Then we burrow under the bottom of the tent and sneak off down to the

529

boys' camp for fun and frolics and snacks."

Rosie said, "And snogging."

Jools said, "How shall we get the rest of them away from the ging-gang-goolie fiasco?"

I said, "We must use sophisticosity and *je ne sais quoi*."

When we got back to the campfire the "party" was still on. Herr Kamyer was showing the campers how to do some ludicrous knots. What is the point of that? When was the last time anyone used a knot? I think it might have been Admiral Nelson.

As we passed by yawning like the yawners of Yawnington I said in a casualosity-at-all-times way, "Oh, Jas, Ellen and Mabs, I forgot I... er... have something to show you in our tent."

Jas looked at me and didn't even bother to reply. Ellen said, "Oh right, shall we, erm... is it, can I... are we all..." and so on.

I gave Jas my most meaningful look but she didn't know what I meant.

I said, "We found it this afternoon. I think it might be quite good for your newt collection, Jas."

She said, "Is it a crusted one, or a toasted one?" And she didn't say it in a nice way.

I was about to do stormies off but then I thought I might

have to listen to her ramble and moan on for the rest of my life if she found out that Tom had been here and I hadn't told her. So I said, "Oh, I think you will find it quite HUNKY if you know what I mean, Jas."

That got her attention all right. She leaped to her feet like a surprised loon.

I said, looking at her with my eyes really wide, "Why don't you all pop round to our tent for a good night, er, look at it?"

We all trooped off to our tent. Miss Wilson said, "Don't be up all night chattering, girls, it's been quite a day and you're all very excited, I expect. I know I am."

Everyone looked at each other and tried not to laugh.

Miss Wilson was still burbling on, "Did you have an exciting day, Herr Kamyer?"

And Herr Kamyer looked at her and said, "*Yah*, it was ver exciting."

Oh my giddy god, please don't tell me Herr Kamyer has the Horn for Miss Wilson.

Life is too weird for me and I've only been on the planet for a bit.

Back in our tent

It was very crowded in the tent. I took off my dressing gown and Jas, Ellen and Mabs had a go on the emergency make-up supplies. When they were sufficiently tarted up we started our burrowing tactics. It was dark by now and we had to switch off our lights so that you couldn't see us burrowing. Actually when I say burrowing what I mean is pulling up the canvas so that we could scamper under it out into freedom!!!

We crept along the back of the campsite keeping to the treeline.

In the boys' tent

They have got a big green one (oo-er). It was quite groovy in it, even though it was a tent. When we put our heads through the flap the boys cheered and offered us some pizza they had got from the village. Yum yum. Sven immediately almost ate Rosie and then sat on her knee. Dec snuggled up to Ellen who went bright red (even in the dark) and Edward said hello to Mabs. She was pleased because her blind date was a) not blind and b) very fit looking. Tom and Jas went off to the river because Jas said, "Tom, come and see the badger hide; it's amazing." I laughed ironically, but she just looked at me and went off with Hunky.

Dave patted the ground next to him. "Come and sit down, Kittykat, you must be exhausted from all the fun you have been having."

Half an hour later

What a hoot and a half. Dave does make me laugh. I'd forgotten how groovy he can be. Ellen and Dec and Mabs and Edward seem to be grooving along together. Quite nice to see Ellen not watching Dave like a seeing-eye dog.

Dave played some music and we had a mini disco inferno in the tent. It was hysterically funny, actually. We had to dance really close to each other and sort of do it half bending over. If you see what I mean.

Twenty minutes later

Naturally Sven made the tent collapse with a reckless diving tackle on Dave at a fast bit. I could hardly stand for laughing.

The lads put the tent up again and I was resting with Dave by some bushes. Dave said to me, "Do you fancy a quick swim in the nuddy-pants?"

I said, "You're mad."

He looked at me. "You're mad."

"No, you're mad."

Then he just pushed me over into a bush. I said as I got up, "You can't do that – that is assault and battery."

He said, "No, wrong, Kittykat, this is assault and battery." And he pushed me into the bush again!!! Then he said, "I'll count to ten and then I am coming to get you."

"Dave, I'm not going anywhere."

He said, "I would if I were you. Anyway, if you don't go anywhere how can I come and get you?"

I don't know why but it seemed to make sense so I started jogging off. What was I doing? As usual I would be the last to know. I bet I could outrun Dave anyway.

Five minutes later
Wrong.

He caught up with me at the river. I stuck my feet in it, I was so hot. Dave came and sat down next to me and put his feet in as well. It was a beautiful dark night, and the air was soft and warm. I felt really happy and relaxed.

I know I shouldn't have, but you know when you shouldn't say anything but you still say it? Well I had that. I said, "How, erm... how is your girlfriend-situation type fandango going?"

He looked at me and half-smiled. "How is your maybe-two-boyfriends fandango going, missy?"

I didn't know what to say. Then I blurted out, "Well, Robbie said he liked me, but then I told him I liked Masimo, but Masimo wants me to go to Pizza-a-gogo land, and really it should be groovy and so on, but I don't really know."

Dave said, "You don't know what, Kittykat?"

Oh, I wished I could just put my head on his shoulder. I always want to tell him everything. But instead I said, "What's your advice, Hornmeister?"

And he started doing pretend beard-stroking and said, "Well, luuurve is a many trousered thing..."

What in the name of arse does that mean? I repeated, "Luuurve is a many trousered thing? That is your idea of advice?"

Dave said, "Well, put it another way – maybe you like more than one pair of trousers. Maybe you like Masimo, and maybe someone else..."

What exactly were we talking about now?

He went on, "Yes, for instance, I like Emma, but I like someone else, possibly better."

I couldn't help myself, even though I knew this was dangerous red-bottom territory. I said, "Who else might you like?"

After a pause he said, "The queen," and stood up.

I was looking up at him. I said, "You like the queen? The other person you like maybe more is the queen? The queen who's just celebrated her 80th birthday? The queen? The one who's had her hips replaced?"

He said, "That was her mother, actually. Please don't be rude about my girlfriend."

I stood up but I couldn't quite see in the dark, and I put my foot down some bloody badger hole or a twig trap that Miss Wilson had made or something, and I fell backwards into the edge of the river.

Dave was laughing, but he came to help me up out of the riverbank. "Oh, you are good value, Georgia. You are very nearly an honorary bloke. And that is why I love you."

Did he... did he just say what I thought he'd said?

He reached down and put his arms round my waist to lift me up. I hope he didn't feel my wet knickers and think I'd had an elderly loon moment.

He said, "Have you wet yourself, Gee? Your knickers are soaking."

I said, "No, but I think they're full of tadpoles, and actually my bum-oley really hurts."

As he pulled me up the bank I said, "I think I may have broken my bottom."

He looked at my face and he was really smiling. Then he said, "Are we never to be free, Kittykat?"

And I looked at him, and he said, "Oh bugger it, it has to be done."

And he snogged me.

Five minutes later

Oh no. I've just unexpectedly paid a visit to the cake shop of love. I haven't put back my Italian cakey but I've accidentally picked up a Dave the Tart...

The Ace Gang

Georgia – *Moi*. The *pièce de résistance*. Bee's knees etc.

Jas – Supposed best pally. Prone to rambling on. Wears enormous pantaloonies.

Rosie – A Viking bride-to-be. Known for her beards and eccentric dancing.

Jools – Good in an emergency, e.g. usually has secret lippy supply.

Ellen – Ditherqueen of the universe and beyond.

Mabs – Generally all-round good egg. Keen on snogging and snacking.

Honorary bloke members

Dave the Laugh – Famously said he would like to be a girl so he could look at his nunga-nungas all day. Also known as the Hornmeister.

Tom – Brother of the Sex God and Jas's boyfriend. Actually, as boys go, not entirely mad.

Sven – From Reindeer land (possibly). Spectacularly mad, e.g. wears flares that have flashing lights down the seams.

Trainee members

Honor and Soph – Coming on nicely. Already involved in the snot disco triumph and the hilarious putting a skeleton dressed as Mr Atwood in his hut.

The New and Improved Snogg

$^1/_2$. sticky eyes (*Be careful using this. I've still got s[...]
twit following me around like a seeing-eye dog.*)

1. holding hands
2. arm around
3. goodnight kiss

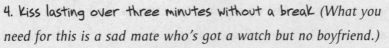

4. kiss lasting over three minutes without a break (*What you
need for this is a sad mate who's got a watch but no boyfriend.*)
4 $^1/_2$. hand snogging (*I really don't want to go into this. Ask Jas.*)
5. open mouth kissing
6. tongues
6 $^1/_2$. ear snogging

6 $^3/_4$. neck nuzzling
7. upper body fondling - outdoors
8. upper body fondling - indoors
Virtual number 8. (*When your upper body is not actually being
fondled in reality, but you know that it is in your snoggees head.*)
9. below waist activity (*or bwa. Apparently this can include
flashing your pants. Don't blame me. Ask Jools.*)
10. the full monty (*Jas and I were in the room when Dad was
watching the news and the newscaster said, "Tonight the Prime
Minister has reached Number 10." And Jas and I had a laughing
spaz to end all laughing spazzes.*)

Groove on groovsters!

In case you haven't noticed, me and the Ace Gang have created some of the grooviest dance moves ever invented. I always find that a quick burst of disco inferno dancing is a fab way of getting rid of tensionosity and frustrated snoggosity. So because I love you all so much, I have written down our fave steps so you can get grooving too.

The Viking bison disco inferno
We're still practising this for Rosie's forthcoming (i.e. in eighteen years time) Viking wedding. It is danced to the tune of *Jingle Bells* because even Rosie, world authority on Sven land, doesn't know any Viking songs. Apart from *Rudolph the Red-nosed Reindeer*. Which isn't one.

For this dance you need some bison horns. If you can't find any bison shops nearby, make your own horns from an old hairband and a couple of twigs or something. Oh, I don't know, stop hassling me, I'm tired.

Instructions:

Stamp, stamp to the left,
Left leg kick, kick,
Arm up,
Stab, stab to the left (that's the pillaging bit),
Stamp, stamp to the right,
Right leg kick, kick,
Arm up,
Stab, stab to the right,
Quick twirl round with both hands raised to Thor (whatever),
Raise your (pretend) drinking horn to the left,
Drinking horn to the right,
Horn to the sky,
All over body shake,
Huddly duddly,
And fall to knees with a triumphant shout of
"HORRRRNNNNN!!!!"

p.s. In a rare moment of comic genius, Jas, who is clearly in touch with her inner bison, added this bit too – it's a sort of sniffing-the-air type move. Like a Viking bison might do.

If it was trying to find its prey. And if there was such a thing as a Viking bison.

Stab, stab to the left,
And then sniff sniff.

Hahahahahaha!

The snot disco inferno

For this dance you will need a big blob of bubble gum hanging off your nose like a huge bogey. It needs to dangle about so you can swing it round and round in time to the music. Dance this to the tune of *Eastenders*, or your favourite TV show theme tune. It goes...

Swing your snot to the left,
Swing to the right,
Full turn,
Shoulder shrug,
Nod to the front,
Dangle dangle,
Hands on shoulders,

Kick, kick to the right,
Dangle dangle,
Kick, kick to the left,
Dangle dangle,
Full snot around,
And shimmy to the ground.

Excellent in every way!

Georgia's Glossary

airing cupboard · It's a cupboard full of air, you fools. If you haven't got enough air, you go into the airing cupboard in your house. Not really! It's a cupboard by the hot-water boiler and you put towels and sheets in and they get all warm and snuggly buggly. Don't start saying you don't know what snuggly buggly means...

arvie · Afternoon. From the Latin "arvo". Possibly. As in the famous Latin invitation: "Lettus meetus this arvo."

Black Death · Ah well... this is historosity at its best. In Merrie England everyone was having a fab time, dancing about with bells on (also known as Maurice dancing), then some ships arrived in London, full of new stuff – tobacco, sugar, chocolate, etc., yum yum. However, as in all tales in history, it ended badly, because also lurking about on the ships were rats from Europe – not human ones. And they had fleas on them that carried the plague. The fleas bit the people of Merrie England, and they got covered in pustulating boils and died. A LOT. As I have said many, many times, history is crap.

Blimey O'Reilly · (as in Blimey O'Reilly's trousers) This is an Irish expression of disbelief and shock. Maybe Blimey O'Reilly was a famous Irish bloke who had extravagantly big trousers. We may never know the truth. The fact is, whoever he is, what you need to know is that a) it's Irish and b) it is Irish. I rest my case.

blodge · Biology. Like geoggers – geography, or Froggie – French.

Boboland · As I have explained many, many times English is a lovely and exciting language full of sophisticosity. To go to sleep is "to go to bobos", so if you go to bed you are going to Boboland. It is an Elizabethan expression... Oh, OK then, Libby made it up and she can be unreasonably violent if you don't join in with her.

bum-oley · Quite literally "bottom hole". I'm sorry but you did ask. Say it proudly (with a cheery smile and a Spanish accent).

bunged · Shoved. Put firmly in place. For example, "Jas was going on an on about voles, so I bunged a Jammy Dodger in her gob."

chav · A chav is a common, rude, rough person. They wear naff clothes. A chav joke would be: "What are the first words a chav baby says to its single parent?" Answer: "What are YOU looking at?" Or: "If there are two chavs in a car and no loud music playing, what kind of a car is it?" Answer: "A police car."

clown car · Officially called a Reliant Robin three-wheeler, but clearly a car built for clowns, built by some absolute loser called Robin. The Reliant bit comes from being able to rely on Robin being a prat. I wouldn't be surprised if Robin also invented nostril-hair cutters.

conk · Nose. This is very interesting historically. A very long time ago (1066) – even before my grandad was born – a bloke called William the Conqueror (French) came to England and shot our King Harold in the eye. Typical. And people wonder why we don't like the French much. Anyway, William had a big nose and so to get our own back we call him William the Big Conk-erer. If you see what I mean. I hope you do because I am exhausting myself with my hilariosity and historiosity.

double cool with knobs · "Double" and "with knobs" are instead of saying very or very, very, very, very. You'd feel silly saying, "He was very, very, very, very, very cool." Also everyone would have fallen asleep before you had finished your sentence. So "double cool with knobs" is altogether snappier.

duffing up · Duffing up is the female equivalent of beating up. It is not so violent and usually involves a lot of pushing with the occasional pinch.

Emily Plankton · Hang on, now you mention it, I may be getting muddled up between the famous suffragette, Emily Whatsit and stuff that fish eat. Was it Emily Pancake then? No, wait a minute, Pankhurst – Emmeline Pankhurst. What is this, anyway, some kind of general knowledge quiz?

fandango · A fandango is a complicated Spanish dance. So a fandango is a complicated thing. Yes, I know there is no dancing involved. Or Spanish.

f.t. · I refer you to the famous "losing it" scale:
    minor tizz

complete tizz and to-do
strop
a visit to Stop Central
F.T. (Funny turn)
Spaz attack
complete ditherspaz
nervy b. (nervous breakdown)
complete nervy b.
ballisiticisimus

gadzooks · An expression of surprise. Like for instance, "Cor, love a duck!" Which doesn't mean you love ducks or want to marry one. For the swotty knickers amongst you, "gad" probably meant "God" in olde English and "zooks" of course means... Oh, look, just leave me alone, OK? I'm so vair tired.

goosegog · Gooseberry. I know you are looking all quizzical now. OK. If there are two people and they want to snog and you keep hanging about saying, "Do you fancy some chewing gum?" or "Have you seen my interesting new socks?" you are a gooseberry. Or for short a goosegog, i.e. someone who nobody wants around.

gorgey · Gorgeous. Like fabby (fabulous) and marvy (marvellous).

Hoooorn · The Particular Horn is when you fancy the arse off one boy. The General Horn is when you fancy all boys. And the Cosmic Horn is when you fancy everybody and everything in the universe – even doorknobs.

Kiwi-a-gogo land · New Zealand. "A-gogo land" can be used to liven up the otherwise really boring names of other countries. America, for instance, is Hamburger-a-gogo land and France is Frogs-legs-a-gogo land.

Lord Baden-Powell · You don't know who Lord Baden Powell is? Blimey, you are, it has to be said, v v dense. Lord B-P invented Scouts and camping, and knots, and going into the country for no reason. Ergo, Lord B-P was clearly mad as a hen.
   p.s. Not content with the camping fiasco, he also invented enormous shorts, which he wore proudly.

Midget Gem · Little sweets made out of hard jelly stuff in different flavours. Jas loves them A LOT. She secretes them about her person, I suspect, often in her panties, so I never like to accept one from her on hygiene and lesbian grounds.

nippy noodles · Instead of saying, "Good heavens, it's quite cold this morning," you say "Cor, nippy noodles!!" English is an exciting and growing language. It is. Believe me. Just leave it at that. Accept it.

nuddy-pants · Quite literally nude-coloured pants and you know what nude-coloured pants are? They are no pants. So if you are in your nuddy-pants you are in your no pants, i.e. you are naked.

nunga-nungas · Basoomas. Girls breasty business. Ellen's brother calls them nunga-nungas because he says that if you get hold of a girl's breast and pull it out and then let it go, it goes nunga-nunga-nunga. As I have said many, many times with great wisdomosity, there is something really wrong with boys.

Pantalitzer doll · A terrifying Czech-made doll that sadistic parents (my vati) buy for their children.

Pizza-a-gogo land · Masimoland. Land of wine, sun, olives and vair vair groovy Luuurve Gods. Italy.

plight my troth · Give your word luuurve-wise. Another way of saying, you are my one and only one. So if you are "untrothed" you can display red-bottomosity ad hoc and willy nilly.

red-bottomosity · Having the big red bottom. This is vair vair interesting vis-à-vis nature. When a lady baboon is "in the mood" for luuurve, she displays her big red bottom to the male baboon (Apparently he wouldn't have a clue otherwise, but that is boys for you!!) Anyway, if you hear the call of the Horn you are said to be displaying red-bottomosity.

Rolf Harris · An Australian "entertainer" (not). Rolf has a huge beard and glasses. He plays a didgeridoo, which says everything in my book. He sadly has had a number of hit records, which means he is never off TV and will not go back to Australia. (His "records" are called "Tie Me Kangaroo Down, Sport" etc.)

The Sound of Music · Oh, are we never to be free? *The Sound of Music* was a film about some bint, Julie Andrews, skipping around in the Alps and singing about goats. Many, many famous and annoying songs come from this film, including, "The Hills Are Alive With the Sound of PANTS", "You Are Sixteen Going on PANTS" and, of course, the one about the national flower of Austria, "IdlePANTS".

Spangleferkel · A kind of German sausage. I know. You couldn't make it up, could you? The German language is full of this kind of thing, like *lederhosen* and so on. And *Goosegot*.

tatty bye · Now this is interesting, so gather round and get your ears on, as Yogi Bear used to say. (Don't start asking me who Yogi Bear is, otherwise we'll be here all day and night.) "Tatty" is another word for potato in olde English. Mrs Billy Shakespeare would say, "Shall we have tatties and pheasant for tea, Billy?" So when you are saying goodbye, English people say "tatty bye", and it quite literally means – "goodbye potato".

vino tinto · Now this is your actual Pizza-a-gogo talk. It quite literally means "tinted wine". In this case the wine is tinted red.

waz · Another expression for piddly-diddly department. Possibly named after the sound the piddly diddly makes as it comes out of the trouser area. I don't know, to be frank. Only boys say it. And who knows why boys say anything? The whole thing is a mystery.

wazzarium · A place where you go to have a waz.
   p.s. You will not be finding me in there.

Whelk Boy · A whelk is a horrible shellfish thing that only the truly mad eat. Slimy and mucus-like. Whelk Boy is a boy who kisses like a whelk, i.e. a slimy mucus kisser. Lilack a pongoes.